THE
DRAGON
SHIP

THE FAE WAR CHRONICLES
BOOK SIX, VOLUME I

THE
DRAGON
SHIP

JOCELYN A. FOX

Book design by Maureen Cutajar
www.gopublished.com

ISBN 13: 978-1985669741
ISBN 10: 1985669749

Prologue

Queen Andraste, ruler of the Unseelie Court and all its lands, monarch of the Night and the Winter, sat on a plain chair in the healing ward of the great cathedral, determined not to let her weariness show. Sayre and Guinna, her two self-appointed shadows, stood behind her, though she'd told them to sit down as well. She could feel their tiredness as well.

Most thought that she had become the Unseelie Queen when Titania had placed the star diadem on her head beneath the icy dome of that cursed throne room. In reality, power had rushed into Andraste the moment that Rye's silver-haired twin had thrust his dagger through Mab's throat. Andraste had felt her sister's death with a peculiar thrill, as though at her very core she recognized that Mab's demise meant her own ascension to the throne.

Her new power, stinging her bones with its intensity, reached out immediately, seeking, trying to find vessels. Three vessels. Through the chaos of the battle and the force of the regal fire raging through her, Andraste tried to resist choosing her Three. For too long, her sister had ruled the Unseelie Court with such outdated notions of birthright and hierarchy, rigid social structure and cold courtesy – at least before her descent into madness.

Queen Andraste pulled her mind away from contemplating that dark morass of guilt. She would reexamine that at a later time, after she had staunched the dying of her people.

But try as she did, she had not been able to stop her new power from choosing two, from touching Sayre and Guinna, finding them sound of body and loyal in heart. The absence of the third she felt like an open wound, aching and pulsing every moment as though she were missing a limb. The presence of the other two of her Three soothed the pain. Guinna's steady presence and Sayre's youthful vigor buoyed Andraste, even as she watched the healers continue to move more and more Unseelie into the ward.

Guinna had told her that the healing ward in the cathedral had been empty save for a dozen or so of the badly wounded from the battle against Malravenar. Even thinking his name sent a shiver down her spine, which in turn kindled a spark of anger in her breast. She was Queen. She was free of him. She need not cower at his name.

Now the healers filled the once-empty pallets with her people. She had assented with formal courtesy to the offers of assistance from Queen Titania and the High Queen. Her chest ached as she remembered yet again that her once-thriving Court, the jewel of Winter, was now reduced to the wounded and the dead. Mab had killed so many for so little reason.

"My Queen?" Guinna said softly, holding out a steaming mug. "*Khal*, since you don't intend to rest anytime soon."

Andraste smiled slightly as she took the mug and sipped experimentally. "At least good *khal* has not much changed. Rye taught me how to make it."

"The Vyldgard especially enjoys it," Guinna replied with a nod.

"The Vyldgard," Andraste murmured thoughtfully. How ironic that the instrument of her ascension to the throne had been this new Wild Court. Sayre had told her the story of the Laedrek's daring foray into Unseelie territory during Mab's attack on the cathedral. His youth made her feel ancient, though a glimpse at herself in one of the polished silver discs in the High Queen's chamber had told her that she still looked as she had centuries ago…save for the scars.

She finished the mug of *khal* in silence and handed it back to Guinna. As they so often did in the days since her memories had been restored, her thoughts swirled up like a whirlwind engulfing her mind. She didn't yet understand this new world, this world without Mab and without the regal *ulfdrengr* in the North, this world in which she had fought against her own people in the service of Malravenar. This world in which Finnead did not love her. She gathered all these painful thoughts and set them aside. Now was not the time for grief and self-pity.

Now was the time to see what this new queenly power could do, except she intended to use it to save what was left of her Court, rather than destroy it. Gathering her dark skirt in her hands, she stood and looked down the healing ward. Whether she was ready or not, her people needed her.

Chapter 1

Quinn took the light saddle and flying straps from Selaph's back as soon as Niamh finished unbuckling it.

"I didn't ask for your help," Niamh said in mild reproach, her voice still husky from the burns she'd suffered to her throat and lungs during the battle for the White City.

"Well, you're still going to get it," he replied with a smile. Her blue eyes flashed but she grudgingly let him carry it over to the Valkyrie armory on the other side of the paddock. He couldn't resist glancing over his shoulder for another look at her, admiring the strength in her slender figure as she efficiently dried Selaph's gleaming coat with a soft cloth. Sometimes he couldn't forget how close he came to losing her, and that made every moment sweeter.

"When will we see you up on a winged mount?" asked Moira with an arched eyebrow as she joined him in the armory, hanging her own harness on a set of pegs.

Quinn chuckled. "I'll take that as a compliment, but I'm more of a ground fighter myself." He carefully hung Niamh's harness on its pegs, carefully checking that none of the straps were twisted. The saddle and harness looked even more complicated when it wasn't on Selaph. He could hang it up for Niamh, but he certainly didn't ever try to put it on her mount.

He glanced at Moira. "Plus all the Valkyrie are women. I wouldn't want to ruin the sorority."

"Sorority?" Moira repeated the unfamiliar word as she finished checking over her own harness. She seamlessly transitioned to readjusting the band of bright blue cloth that held back her riotous mane of curls.

"Name for a group of women who all join a kind of club," explained Quinn.

"This sounds interesting." Moira completed tying her hair back and looked contemplatively at Quinn.

"Well, to be fair, a lot of it is about partying and stuff," he added as they headed back toward the paddock.

"Partying. Like feasting?"

"Something like that," he answered slowly.

"Perhaps Vivian will know more about this *sorority*," Moira said with a nod. "She is our Paladin, after all."

"She's a what?" Quinn found it was his turn to squint at a strange word.

"Paladin," repeated Moira happily. "She is of the Bearer's blood, which helps, but that is not necessary for a Paladin – or at least, that is what Knight Niall told me."

"That did not explain anything at all," Quinn pointed out. "If anything, it just confused me more."

Moira sighed and shook her head.

"Look, I'm just a dumb mortal," he said with a grin. "I don't know all these fancy words you guys use for all these different mystical positions of power."

"I didn't know of the Paladins, either, until Knight Niall told me," Moira replied in a confessional tone. They reached the fence of the paddock. "But apparently the Paladins once lived in the White City, mortals who studied *taebramh* and the fighting arts, and swore to work alongside the Sidhe to keep the balance between the worlds." Her curls swayed as she finished her recitation with a nod.

"So you popped through the Gate with Tess and you came back with everyone plus a Paladin," Quinn said. "Interesting."

"It is quite interesting," Moira agreed seriously. Then she grinned. "Perhaps *you* could be a Paladin!"

"First you want me up on a flying horse, now you want me to be one of these Paladins?" Quinn grinned and shook his head.

"Well, you are particularly good at smashing stools into people's faces, so perhaps you should stick to that," replied Moira with a wicked gleam in her eye.

"It was totally warranted," Quinn said firmly.

Moira chuckled, nodded in greeting to Niamh, and walked past them to go find her mount.

"I would say it gladdens my heart to see you getting along so well with my Valkyrie sisters, but I do not think my heart is able to be glad anymore," Niamh said without looking away from Selaph.

Quinn took a deep, calming breath and ran one hand through his dark hair, combing its now-shaggy lengths back from his forehead. This wasn't the first time Niamh had said something like this, and he knew it wouldn't be the last. "I know it feels like that," he said, his voice just this side of gentle. Nothing got Niamh angry faster than when she thought someone was condescending or pitying. "But it'll get better. I promise."

"How can you promise?" she returned, narrowing her eyes and vigorously rubbing Selaph's coat as though working faster would somehow ease her emotions. The white *faehal* snorted and flicked her ears in enjoyment, half-spreading her magnificent wings. Niamh flashed a look at Quinn. "You have never lost a twin."

"Not a twin, no," he answered steadily. "But I've watched the guys I call my brothers die. I've watched other innocent people die in terrible ways. Bombs, mortars, collapsed buildings from bombs and mortars...different sizes of bullets...throats slit...drowned...you name it, I've probably seen it." He shrugged and met her eyes as she looked at him again.

"What about burned alive?" she said in a low voice, her beautiful face stretched tight with anger.

"I've seen that too," he said.

Niamh gracefully slid beneath one of Selaph's wings and worked in silence for a few moments. When she emerged, she said vengefully, "She should have been here with us. She should have been fighting alongside me against Mab."

"But she's not," Quinn replied. "And she never will be."

Niamh bared her teeth at him in a mute snarl.

"You don't wanna hear it," he pressed, even though his chest hurt at the raw fury etched into her features. She was a bit thinner now than before she'd been wounded, and a few threads of silver scars traced her jaw and spread across other parts of her body. But he thought she was even more breathtaking than when he'd first glimpsed her on Selaph's back, flying low over the forces of the three Queens trekking across the Deadlands. "I get it. You don't wanna hear it because every time you hear it, it hurts more or it hurts less, and you can't ever really tell which way it's gonna go. You're afraid that if it hurts more you'll just…break in half. And you're afraid that if it hurts less, you're somehow dishonoring the person you lost." He swallowed and pressed his lips together. "Trust me, I've been there."

"I don't think you have," Niamh replied in a low, bitter voice.

Quinn stepped closer. God, this would be so much easier if he could just sweep her into his arms and kiss her until she forgot her own name. He wanted to do just that, but he stopped himself, crossing his arms over his chest. "How do you know that? You don't know what I've seen back in my world."

Niamh made a quiet sound of dismissal that punched into his gut harder than a physical punch. They'd had versions of this conversation a few times before, but it had never progressed this far. He tried not to let his rising irritation spark into anger. That wouldn't help the situation.

"Your world," Niamh said derisively, twisting the words into an insult. "You should go back to your world."

"Why would you even say that?" Quinn asked, spreading his hands as he shook his head. The sun gleamed on his brown skin and picked out the red and blue of the tattoos wrapping his forearm.

"Because I'm tired of worrying about you!" the slender Valkyrie burst out. "I can't go into battle thinking about you! It's a *weakness*! I *hate* it!"

Quinn peripherally saw the other women in the paddock feigning deafness in the face of Niamh's explosion, all of them still industriously grooming their *faehal*, checking gear and taking off their armor. It had only been hours since the overthrow of Mab, but somehow it felt like days. He blew out a long breath as he let Niamh's words wash over him.

"I don't think you hate it," he said finally. "I think that you're afraid of it. You're afraid of losing someone else, and I hate to break it to you, but I'm actually a pretty good fighter and I'm really hard to kill. Still standing after all this time in your world, after all." He raised his eyebrows and tilted his head, trying to inject a little levity into the tense conversation.

"Maire was better than *pretty good*. Maire was one of the best. Maire was *hard to kill*," Niamh growled through clenched teeth.

"You were a lot less angry before you were able to get back on that horse," snapped Quinn. Some part of him instantly regretted the words; he'd had a temper when he was younger, but training and combat had mellowed him. He'd had to adapt or be burned up by his own anger. Sometimes it still flared.

"You were a lot less of a know-it-all before I was knocked *from* this horse," retorted Niamh, eyes blazing. "I liked you better when you were dazzled and dazed."

"Then you didn't like *me* at all," replied Quinn, hearing his voice harden. "*Dazzled and dazed*, my ass." He clenched his jaw. "I stood by you. I *stayed* with you. I almost started a *war* for you."

"And I did not ask you for any of that," said Niamh.

Each of her words tore a little piece of his self control away until tremors began to shake his hands. He clenched his fists and grasped at his last shred of dignity. "Then I'll just find something else to occupy my time."

Niamh didn't reply. He thought that maybe he saw hurt flash through her anger for an instant, like lightning through a thundercloud, but he wasn't sure. He never felt sure with her anymore, not in the weeks since she'd been able to leave her bed and start training again, start flying again. She didn't need him, and she'd just made it abundantly clear that she didn't *want* him either. Some logical part of his mind – a very, very small part – tried to make him see that this really wasn't what she wanted, this was anger and hurt all bundled together and snarling up the thoughts in her head.

But he'd learned the hard way that he could only help people who wanted to be helped, so he turned and walked away, telling himself that the sharp pain in his chest was the still-healing wound from when Mab had blown up the training yards only a few days ago. He took deep breaths as he walked alongside the cathedral, heading for the front entrance. He'd seen the other fighters begin to return to the Wild Court's stronghold a short time after the Valkyrie who had gone to fight in Unseelie territory had landed alongside the paddock.

The Seelie and Vyldgard fighters who'd made their way through the city on foot after the battle walked toward the cathedral in knots of three and four. For a moment, Quinn wondered if he should help with a few of the wounded, but as always, the Sidhe were efficient and capable. Most who weren't able to walk on their own looked Unseelie, and all the Unseelie, wounded or not, looked shell-shocked. He paused at the base of the great stone steps and watched for a few long moments, Niamh's words still ringing in his ears. *You should go back to your world…I liked you better when you were dazzled and dazed.*

"Dazzled and dazed," he growled under his breath again, crossing his arms over his chest. He hadn't gone to fight in with the Seelie and

Vyldgard in Mab's winter-cold stronghold because he'd agreed to stay here, to help guard the healing ward from any further attack while Niamh circled overhead, an airborne sentry. If she hadn't stayed here, would he have stayed? He clenched his jaw.

"Quinn!"

He turned at the call and found a blood-spattered Luca striding toward him. The *ulfdrengr* held out his hand and they grasped forearms firmly, the sign of friendship among the wolf-warriors.

"Well met," said Luca with a nod.

"Glad to see you," returned Quinn, eyeing the gore still staining the edges of the axes thrust into Luca's belt. "What's the good word?"

"The good word is that the Mad Queen is defeated," replied Luca with a solemn nod. Then he half-grinned. "The battle was glorious."

"You think most battles are glorious," pointed out Quinn.

"And you do not?" asked Luca, affronted and looking at him with mild surprise.

He chuckled humorlessly. "I mean, yeah, the rush is there, but it always wears off when you find out who's been hurt or killed."

"There were many less killed than we anticipated," said Luca, one hand stroking the flat of one of his axes in a seemingly unconscious gesture.

"Killed from our side, you mean."

"No," he replied simply. "We carried out the Queens' desire that killing those under the Mad Queen's spell be avoided as much as possible." He shrugged. "In some cases, it was unavoidable."

"And Mab?"

"Dead. Her sister Andraste is Queen now." Luca's pale blue eyes glittered in the deepening golden light. He glanced at Quinn. "You did not see her leave this place? The Vyldretning had left her in her own chambers to be kept safe during the battle."

"Didn't see anything," Quinn replied truthfully. "If she was heir to the Unseelie throne, I'd think she would have power of her own. She probably found another way out of the cathedral."

"True." Luca nodded.

"And the bone sorcerer, you guys get him too?"

Luca's face closed into that inscrutable expression that Quinn had always associated with the Sidhe, not the *ulfdrengr*. "Yes."

Quinn cleared his throat. Clearly, he'd have to get that story from someone else. "Good, I guess. Everyone come back through alright?"

"Our plan worked quite well," said Luca. "Better than I expected."

"Well that's...good," he said again lamely. His anger and hurt at Niamh's words still fogged his brain.

Luca clapped him on the shoulder. "I will go see where I can assist our healers."

"Sounds good," he replied, feeling distinctly out of place as Luca strode up the steps, taking them two and three at a time and pausing halfway to seamlessly assist one of the wounded Vyldgard fighters flagging in his attempt to walk unaided.

So much of his daily existence over the past weeks – *months*, he realized with mild shock – had been dedicated to Niamh that now he felt unmoored. She'd cast him off like a threadbare shirt, held close until the fabric thinned and the colors lost their vibrant edge. Had she used him? Had she just needed a pleasant diversion from her own woes? Barely watching the teeming scene of returning fighters, he stared into the distance and combed through his memories. Even before Maire's death and her injury, had Niamh viewed him as simply an amusement, something pretty to pass the time? It wasn't the first time the thought had occurred to him, but, he thought with rueful and savage self-loathing, that was before he'd gone and let himself fall for her.

"It never ends well," he said to himself, shaking his head. Harmless fun was all well and good, but when real emotions started getting involved...he should have known better. He'd tried to be gentle and she'd gotten angry. He'd tried to understand and she scorned him. He drew back his shoulders, ignoring the prickle of the still-healing cut across his chest. "Enough," he told himself firmly.

"Staring into the distance and talking to yourself is never a good sign," said Liam.

Quinn didn't even feel the irritation that his old team leader so often sparked these days. He mustered a smile. "Yeah, and what do they say about going stiff as a board and seeing visions of the future?"

"Either a symptom of insanity or a harbinger of destiny," replied Liam with exaggerated dramatic flare, widening his blue eyes and grinning so that Quinn knew he was joking.

"Harbinger of destiny," Quinn repeated with a snort. He looked his friend up and down.

"A few scratches, nothing too bad," Liam said lazily, resting one hand on the hilt of the sword at his hip.

"You're in a good mood."

"I didn't think the plan would work so well," replied Liam in a confessional tone.

"Not the first time I've heard that recently," said Quinn, raising his eyebrows. "Either it was a stupid plan or you guys are just really pessimistic."

"A bit of both, I think," Liam said easily. "I Saw a few things, so that helped."

"Oh, your symptoms of insanity were actually useful?"

"Believe it or not, yes. I can point everyone in the right direction sometimes."

"What did you See?" Quinn didn't know why he was trying to prolong the conversation. Part of him didn't want to talk to anyone, but another part of him thought that maybe if he just carried on like everything was normal, he'd either stop feeling this black-hole sensation in his chest or Niamh would come to her senses.

"I Saw Molly and Mab fighting," replied Liam, his irreverence gone.

"Molly…Tess's friend?"

"She used to be Tess's best friend. She was the one who first came through into this world with her."

"So what, she decided to be the hero? Heroine, sorry," Quinn corrected himself, holding up a hand.

"Not exactly," Liam said soberly. He pressed his lips together. "She went bad, Quinn. Crossed over to the other side. Made some sort of deal with the bone sorcerer, used his power. She forged some sort of Dark sword."

"She *forged* a sword?" Quinn repeated skeptically.

"Maybe that's not the right word. She took Ramel's blade – do you know Ramel, reddish hair and one of Mab's Three? – and used some powerful sorcery to turn it Dark. That's what she used to fight Mab."

Quinn gave a noncommittal grunt. "And she won?"

"Almost. One of the Exiled finished Mab off."

"Well that's…unexpected."

Liam shook his head. "Not when you take into account the fact that they've had centuries to think about revenge on Mab. She was the one who banished them to the mortal world."

"Weird, isn't it," said Quinn slowly, watching the arrival of two Seelie on horseback, each of them holding a wounded Unseelie in front of them, "that they've been in our world all that time and we never knew."

"There are a lot of things in our world that we don't know," Liam said.

They stood in silence for a moment.

"So, what happens next?" Quinn asked.

"Do you mean for us, or for the Courts, big-picture?" Liam replied. A coppery spark escaped his lips as he spoke, and he waved it away as casually as though he'd just sneezed.

"Either. Both."

"I've heard Vell talk about heading back North to the forests," said Liam. "She's been wanting to find the right Northwolves to help rebuild the *ulfdrengr* for a while now."

"And I guess the Seelie and Unseelie are gonna split off and do their own thing too."

"Some will probably stay to finish rebuilding the White City," replied Liam. "Though I don't think Vell is quite as invested as Titania, and I don't really know about Andraste. She's a bit of a wild card."

"A wild card, but better than Mab," said Quinn.

"True. She's young…young*er*, I suppose is the better word, than her sister, so she might be open to new ideas and collaborations with the other Courts."

"She's also not insane." Quinn paused. "I mean, that's been verified, right? She was held for centuries by Malravenar, controlled to do his bidding…she's all there?"

"Whether she is or not, she's their Queen now," said Liam.

"That maybe demonstrates a bit of the advantage of the democratic process," Quinn said, raising his eyebrows. "You know, rather than this whole power-by-birthright thing."

"It's hard to advocate a democratic process when you have ancient deities racing around shoving power into people," replied Liam.

That surprised a chuckle out of Quinn. "True. I mean, was it pretty instantaneous? Like when Mab kicked the bucket, the throne was automatically transferred to Andraste?"

"As I understand it." Liam nodded.

"Hell of a way to inherit," murmured Quinn, shaking his head.

"Not so different from how inheritances usually work," pointed out Liam.

"Also true." Quinn had to concede that point. He rubbed at his healing chest absentmindedly. "What's next for you?"

Liam tilted his head back and looked up at the magnificent structure of the ancient cathedral, its huge doors gleaming in the sun. Quinn thought that the carvings on those doors changed every now and then, but he hadn't ever mentioned it to anyone. He waited for his teammate to answer.

"I'm one of Vell's Three. I'm staying here. This is my life now."

"You're more than one of her Three," Quinn said quietly.

"You already knew that."

"Yeah, but sometimes I gotta remind you that I know. It's not a big secret."

Liam shrugged. "I never saw why it should be, but Vell didn't want anyone to be distracted from her first days as Vyldretning."

Quinn said nothing. He thought about Niamh's joyful abandon in the first days after they'd become lovers. She hadn't cared who had known, who had seen them kiss, what anyone said. How had that gone south so quickly? It felt like years and it felt like yesterday. He'd fought at the Dark Keep and she'd flown over the White City, and then there was that interminable stretch of time in the healing ward. Now she was able to fight again, but she let her grief become a river between them, one she wasn't willing to cross. And Quinn was a pretty good swimmer, all things said and done, but the strength of her fury gave him pause. He might drown in the currents of her rage and sorrow if he tried to reach her himself.

"Well," Liam said with a brotherly nod, "I'm going inside. Don't be a stranger."

Quinn dredged up a half smile even as the irony of Liam's words struck him. Weren't they all strangers now? He thought he knew people, and they showed a completely different side. "Sure."

Liam slapped Quinn's shoulder in their team's well-worn good-bye, stepping forward to take the steps leading up to the carved doors two at a time. Quinn folded his arms over his chest again. He could go make himself useful in the healing ward, but that reminded him of Niamh and there was a good chance he'd see Maeve. He knew after seeing the head healer he'd be unable to stop his mind from making the comparison to her daughter. They had the same almond curve to their eyes and the habit of biting their lower lip when concentrating…

He wrenched his mind away. No healing wards. Definitely not. "Then a shower at least," he muttered, brushing at the dirt and grime on his shirt.

Just as he'd made his decision, one of the Valkyrie swooped low, landing in front of the cathedral with delicate precision. The wind from the *faehal*'s magnificent wings swept dust into the air as a passenger slid down from behind the Valkyrie, grinning and not bothering to even try to keep her riotously curly red hair out of her eyes. She had a pack on her back but she also wore a sword at her hip, along with a kind of tool-belt filled with a variety of odd little implements. Even through the crash after the adrenaline of the argument with Niamh, Quinn felt a little nudge of curiosity.

"Thanks, Trillian," said the redhead to the Valkyrie rider, who wore a patch over one eye. "That was fantastic!"

Trillian bowed from the saddle as her *faehal* arched his neck and pranced. "It was my pleasure, Paladin." Her remaining eye sparkled as the girl – the Paladin? – surveyed the winged mount once more, sighing with a mix of pleasure and envy.

"You know, I always wanted a horse growing up," the Paladin said with a hint of nostalgia. "Now I'm hopelessly in love with these beautiful creatures."

Trillian laughed. "Perhaps one day, Paladin, you will find a creature worthy of you."

The redheaded girl turned a delicate shade of pink. "I…thanks."

Trillian gave another bow and then whistled to her mount. She sprang into the air, her massive wings sweeping down and missing the Paladin by a matter of inches, but she didn't flinch. She just grinned and watched them bank toward the paddocks at the back of the cathedral.

"I think they were trying to impress you," said Quinn, raising his eyebrows.

The girl jumped. Apparently she hadn't noticed him in her enraptured study of the Valkyrie. "What? Oh, I don't really think so. I think everyone's a little giddy after the battle." Her face turned pink again.

Quinn felt a strange surge of affection for her. She looked like she could be Liam and Tess's kid sister, or maybe a younger cousin from a different side of the family. Something about her eyes and the set of her chin.

"Vivian," she said, thrusting her hand out.

"Quinn," he returned, shaking the offered hand.

"You must be one of Duke's teammates," said Vivian before they'd even released hands.

"How do you figure that?"

"Well," Vivian said, "you're not Fae. For one, you don't *look* like you're Fae, though I suppose there could be more than just Seelie and Unseelie. And Vyldgard, of course. But you also have tattoos, which I think is a purely mortal phenomenon."

"Purely mortal phenomenon," Quinn repeated, half-impressed and half-amused. Even though she looked young, Vivian sure put the pieces together quickly.

"At least for now," she added. "I think there might be some merit with experimenting in different types of ink for Sidhe skin, because if there are going to be travelers through the Gate on a semi-regular basis, it could be easier to make the runes of protection permanent."

"You're the Paladin," said Quinn.

"Yep," she replied brightly, "that's me. First Paladin in centuries, apparently."

"And they let you come through the Gate to fight."

She looked mildly offended. "Do I not look like I can fight?"

Quinn realized he was treading on uncertain ground, but what else was new? He'd already ripped his most important relationship in this world apart at the seams, what was offending one fresh-faced kid? "Not really, to be honest."

Her face hardened and for an instant he saw something like the expression that Niamh had worn when he'd told her she wasn't strong enough to fight. She raised her chin.

"I'll have you know I killed one of the Exiled in single combat," she said frostily.

"Did you, now." He knew he was being an asshole. He knew it

was a defense mechanism, like an armadillo rolling into its armored ball, but he felt like he couldn't stop it. It was like he'd started sliding down a steep hillside, scree loose beneath his feet, and now he was just waiting to be thrown into the air by an unexpected obstacle.

Vivian studied him for a long moment. Then she adjusted the straps of her backpack on her shoulders. "Everyone reacts differently to stress. I learned that in one of my psych classes, so I'll give you a pass, since you're one of Duke's friends, but I'd appreciate it if you don't talk to me again until you pull your head out of your ass."

She tossed her mane of red hair over her shoulder and turned to the stairs, the annoyance fading from her face and replaced by a tinge of wonder as she took in the vast, beautiful architecture. Quinn waited until she was halfway up before he slowly followed, knowing that he'd regret his words and have to apologize later, but when he was mired in one of these moods, it was like being in the middle of a night out with the boys: He knew he was drinking a bit too much, and he knew he'd have a hangover in the morning, but it was just too satisfying to indulge his baser instincts at times.

Sometimes he just had to let his inner savage have a little time at the surface. He trudged up the stairs and wondered morosely how he'd make himself useful in this world of magic and mayhem now that Niamh had cast him aside.

Chapter 2

Vivian paused at the top of the stairs, contemplating the beautifully detailed carvings on the great doors. She blinked. The carving clearly depicted the battle in the icy throne room of Mab's stronghold: two women locked blades in the center of the scene, the resemblance to the mad queen and the bone sorcerer's apprentice clear. Vivian tilted her head and examined a few of the other vignettes, feeling a little spark in her chest each time she recognized another face in the almost life-sized figures: Tess at the edge of the battle, her sword in hand but her eyes fixed on Molly and Mab; Niall, beside Queen Titania once more, locked in a duel with a blank-eyed Unseelie fighter; Tyr, his panther-like grace somehow captured by the carving as he leapt toward an opponent, fighting his way toward Mab. And then, with a jolt, Vivian saw herself, her hair spread in a nimbus around her head as she whirled, sword in hand, her face fierce as she turned from one enemy to the next. She remembered that moment suddenly with a rush of clarity, and she hadn't felt graceful or composed as she looked in the carving. She'd grabbed a few deep breaths, her legs and arms burning with exertion and sweat sliding down her back as she looked for the next fight, determined not to die in her first battle as a Paladin, terrified in the back of her mind that she'd make a stupid mistake like slipping in a puddle of blood and impaling herself on her own sword.

She reached toward the door and traced two fingers down the graceful coils of her hair. It felt like looking at a stranger. Was she truly that beautiful and terrible in battle? Or was this magnificent frieze an artist's rendering, some magic that gave those who viewed it what they wanted to see?

The smooth cool surface of the door – maybe brass, she thought – suddenly warmed beneath her fingers. She snatched her hand away, though the warmth hadn't been unpleasant, and watched with wide eyes as two spots of light – her fingerprints – pulsed gently and then grew brighter and brighter until they burned so white-hot that Vivian shielded her eyes. She felt a tremor through her boots and thought in panic that maybe she'd set off some sort of defensive spell against mortals ingrained in the great doors. The pendant at her throat warmed as well. She grabbed at the cord, ready to rip it off.

"The White City is welcoming you," said Tyr from behind her, catching her shoulders as she stumbled backward.

"I…what?" she said.

The bright white light detached from the great door and hovered an arm's length in front of them. In the distance, or perhaps it was an echo, she couldn't be sure, Vivian heard bells ringing, a chorus of celebration, sweet and wild. The globe of light began to spin, first rotating slowly on its axis and then whirling faster and faster until it looked like a small tornado, though the air remained perfectly still around it. In the back of her mind, Vivian noted that Tyr stepped away from her, putting a few steps of distance between them.

She stood rooted to the spot, still clutching the cord of the pendant that Tess had placed around her neck. The part of her that wasn't completely focused on this tiny, contained maelstrom before her recognized that the pendant warmed beneath her fingers and pulsed with her heartbeat. The tornado stretched, expanded until it whirled as tall as Vivian. And then it slid forward and enveloped her.

Vivian felt a cool sensation caress her skin, as though she'd slid into a still pool of water. The light changed around her, blue and silver, creating patterns of reflection on her body. She turned her head slightly and saw that her hair coiled into the air as though she were truly underwater. The blue and silver light whirled around her, creating a different world meant only for her. She swallowed and lifted her chin. Tess's pendant gave a reassuring pulse of warmth.

Tiny points of light detached from the whirling walls, coalescing quickly into two figures, a man and a woman. A strong sense of familiarity stole over Vivian, even though she was sure she'd never seen the faces depicted in glowing relief by the points of light. The woman spoke, though Vivian couldn't be sure if she actually made a sound or if she just heard the woman's voice in her head, like she had Tyr.

"We bid you welcome to the White City, sister," said the woman, her beautiful face shifting beneath the grotto-like reflections.

"Much has changed since we walked these paths," said the man.

"You are young, but so were we," said the woman. Their voices twined together, as though they were one person speaking from two different mouths.

"And youth is no true barrier to wisdom," continued the man.

As Vivian listened, understanding dawned on her. These were other Paladins – maybe the last Paladins to walk the White City. A thrill of excitement coursed through her. She suddenly wanted to stay in this whirling circle of blue and silver for hours, asking them questions. She wanted to know why they had left. She wanted to know what had happened.

"We know you have questions," said the woman.

Vivian wondered, again with piercing familiarity, whether the two glowing figures could read her mind.

"But we do not have enough time to answer them," said the man.

"And you must find the answers yourself," continued the woman.

The longer they stood there, the more details that Vivian picked out in both their dress and their faces. They had fierce faces with pointed chins, too similar to be anything but brother and sister, maybe even twins; the man wore his hair as long as the woman, both of them with it braided back in a style that reminded Vivian of Luca. Both of them also bore scars: the woman, a line from the corner of her mouth down her jaw, and the man had lost part of one ear lobe. Vivian tried to speak, but her voice made no sound.

"We give you what we can," said the man.

"Restore the Paladins," said the woman.

"Restore our honor," said the man.

"Bend the knee to no one." The woman's voice became fierce.

"Blind loyalty benefits none." The man sounded fierce as well, but Vivian picked out a thread of sorrow in his words. She wished she could tell them to slow down – they were throwing so many weighty phrases at her, she felt bombarded and confused, afraid she wouldn't remember it all. What if they disappeared and she forgot? What kind of Paladin would that make her?

"Defend those who cannot defend themselves, in both worlds," the woman continued firmly.

"And when you journey afar, look to the sea," said the man. "They will return."

Vivian opened her mouth again, trying to ask them the questions burning in her mind: Who would return? What sea? Had their blind loyalty been their downfall? How had they lost their honor?

"Our time draws to a close," said the woman.

The man and woman stepped forward simultaneously. They each raised one arm and placed their hand on Vivian's shoulder, the woman grasping the right and the man her left. A roaring, rushing sensation overtook Vivian, and she felt like the whole spinning whirlwind was funneling into her, squeezing her lungs and pressing against the inside of her skull, muffling the beat of her heart and blurring her vision with silver light. It was more than the sensation, though. She felt knowledge filling her, sliding into her mind too fast for her to fully comprehend, though she grabbed at bits and pieces as they rushed by her consciousness: a flash of a circular tower, its walls lined with shelves and those shelves filled with books and scrolls and instruments to which Vivian couldn't put names; a room with two long tables, young Sidhe and a few mortal children sitting side by side as a younger version of the man with the braids in his hair stood at the front of the room; another room with a circular table, polished and gleaming, twelve seats around it filled with fierce and other-worldly faces, some bearing traces of a lineage Vivian hadn't ever seen, pale blue skin and scales glittering upon their brows, along with the Seelie and Unseelie, the *ulfdrengr* and the Paladin.

And then with a silent roar the silver maelstrom vanished. Vivian stumbled, feeling like a swimmer who had just been spat out of a whirlpool; Tyr caught her, holding her upright with little effort. The sensation of his strong hands sparked warmth that helped awaken her dazed mind.

"That was…unexpected," she managed, trying to get her feet back under her.

"You have a talent for understatement," said Tyr, a trace of amusement in his melodious voice.

She turned as he released his hold on her, grinning at him. He smiled. Neither of them had taken substantial wounds during the battle in Mab's icy throne room. The sight of him leaping toward Mab, dagger flashing silver in his hand, surfaced in her mind's eye. It surprised her a little that the image only evoked a feeling of satisfaction, because she knew it was Mab's downfall. What kind of person did that make her, if she felt *satisfaction* at another person's death?

"They left you something else," said Tyr, drawing her attention back to the present. He nodded to a point on the ground behind her. She turned and saw the silver key on the smooth floor. As she bent and picked it up, a little shiver passed through her. It sat in her palm, no heavier than a feather and the length of one of her fingers, not particularly ornate but drawing the eye all the same. She turned it over curiously: there were no teeth at the end of this key. What good was a key that wouldn't turn the tumblers in any lock? But she already knew better than to discount any object that had been given to her by those two silver figures. Had they been ghosts, or enchantments laid into the door, designed only to respond to another Paladin's touch? What if she hadn't touched the doors? How had they known that she would do that?

Tyr said nothing as she unclipped the clasp of the pendant and slid the key onto the length of leather, where it slipped behind the pendant bearing the image of the tree with the sword in its trunk. Her mind circled back to the image of the circular tower with books and instruments lining its walls, stretching up as far as the eye could see. Did this key open that tower? Or perhaps it opened the room with the desks where they'd been teaching, or maybe the room with the gleaming circular table. She sighed. She already had more questions than answers, and she'd only been in the Fae world for a few hours. Distractedly, she pressed one hand over her hair, trying to tame it, impossible after both her flight with the Valkyrie and the weightless underwater effect of the silver whirlwind.

Vivian took a deep breath, taking in the scene around her. If anyone else had seen the whirlwind of silver, no one gave any sign that it was anything unusual. Seelie and Unseelie and Vyldgard still strode past, some bearing stretchers and some helping the wounded to walk or carrying them between two able-bodied fighters. The great cathedral arched overhead, more massive and beautiful than any building she'd ever entered. In some places, what looked like a silvery gray tent created the ceiling – she could see through the smaller doors of the healing hall that the tent enclosed that section. But other passageways and doors branched off from the main entrance all with no tent overhead. Vivian wondered if they were restoring the great building in different sections. It seemed sensible to her. Glasidhe messengers streaked overhead like miniature shooting stars, leaving neon trails in their wake.

She took another breath and tried to untangle her emotions. On the one hand, she'd survived her first battle, so there was a relief tinged with excitement. On the other hand, fighting in her first battle had been nothing at all like she'd imagined, even with all the books she'd read and all the things that she thought she knew. Living through it was something else entirely. And now that the battle was over, what was she supposed to do? Tess was presumably here somewhere, doing Bearer things; Ramel had fought in the battle, but she didn't see him either. She felt very small and very alone for an instant, but then she pressed her lips together and drew back her shoulders.

She was the First Paladin. And besides, she had Tyr, who also had his voice back. She felt a sudden rush of gratitude that he'd stayed with her. After all, he knew what it was to be thrust into a different world, though admittedly the circumstances of his exile and her willing travel into Faeortalam were completely different. She hiked up the straps of her backpack, trying to decide which doorway seemed most likely to lead to a hot shower and food.

A Glasidhe messenger zoomed to a halt in front of Vivian, bowing to her with a flourish. He wore a blue feather tucked jauntily behind his ear, his puckish face somehow familiar to Vivian. He fluttered his incandescent wings as he tried to decide the proper manner of greeting to render to Tyr, settling on a second, shallower bow.

"Lady Paladin," he piped, "the Vyldretning sent me to bid you welcome and show you to your quarters, if you please."

"Thank you," said Vivian. She couldn't help but smile at the Glasidhe's bright voice and spirited delivery. He bowed to her again and whirled to guide her with a flick of his wings. She glanced at Tyr, but he was already following a step behind her. His silver hair and scars stood out among the other Sidhe; occasionally one of the passing healers or warriors paused to better look at him, but most of them recovered their courtesy and continued on their way. She didn't miss the fact that Tyr rested his right hand on the hilt of his sword, his face impassive and his eyes constantly roving their surroundings.

"This way, Lady Paladin!" said the Glasidhe messenger.

"You can just call me Vivian," she replied without thinking, smiling as she followed the diminutive Fae. He led her through one of the smaller doors, down a passageway built of white stone lit by orbs filled with softly glowing white light.

"Oh, Lady Tess tries to do that as well," he replied with an elfin grin, "but we do not forget our courtesy."

"I don't find it rude not to be called 'Lady Paladin,'" pointed out Vivian as they wended their way through the passages of the cathedral. She stopped trying to keep track of the twists and turns as the thought occurred to her that this structure was most likely enchanted to some degree anyway.

"But it would be rude of me not to call you that," said her small guide with an air of finality.

Vivian chuckled. "Can I ask your name?"

"Haze, Lady Paladin!" He spun in midair and bowed again as he flew backward. "I had the good fortune to travel to your world and meet many mortals! My cousin Wisp was jealous when I surpassed him, you know."

"Surpassed him in what?"

"The number of mortals I have met! And you count as one more," he added gleefully. "The First Paladin!"

Vivian pushed away the feeling of discomfort at being equated to an object in a collection, something to be coveted and bragged about. Instead she said lightly, "Well, I'm just the first Paladin in a few centuries." She cleared her throat. "I guess I can't expect everyone *not* to call me the First Paladin for a long while, huh?"

"I do not think there are any alive beside perhaps Queen Titania and her Vaelanseld who remember the last Paladins," continued Haze, as though he hadn't heard her.

"And how many remember the Exiles?"

Vivian looked sharply over her shoulder at Tyr as he spoke. His voice still sounded breathtakingly new each time she heard it, but that didn't completely negate her surprise at his direct question. She narrowly avoided knocking one of the glowing glass orbs from its place on the wall of the passageway.

Haze spiraled higher and gazed down at Tyr, his aura sparking and pulsing. "Now that is a question you cannot expect me to answer."

"Why not?"

They'd come to a halt. Vivian looked between Tyr and Haze, Tyr's beautiful, scarred face smooth and unreadable, the Glasidhe glowing with bronze and scarlet hues that made Vivian guessed meant he was unsettled or perhaps even angry.

"It is unfair," said Haze finally with a flick of his wings.

"How so?" asked Tyr with cool, unruffled courtesy.

"It was not our *choice* not to remember," the Glasidhe replied.

"Though things may have changed, I remember that your people did not submit to either of the Queens." Tyr tilted his head slightly, the light catching his scars. Vivian noticed that he had gone very still, like a cat watching a bird.

"And you are correct," replied Haze stiffly. "We have served as messengers when the other Queens have asked of ours. And when we have done so, we abide by the Seelie and Unseelie courtesies out of respect."

"So that means you did not talk of the Exiles?" Tyr lifted one silver eyebrow fractionally.

"I did not say that," said Haze, his aura flaring.

Vivian stepped forward, angling her body so that she interjected herself between the hovering Glasidhe and the intent Exile. As much as she wanted the conversation to continue so she could learn more about the dynamics between the Courts and the diminutive Fae, as well as where the Exiled fit into all of it, she thought that keeping the peace would be a better option for their first night. "I'm sorry," she said smoothly, "but I'm really tired, and I'd like to take a shower. Or a bath, whatever is available. I'm not picky."

Haze immediately turned his attention back to her. "Forgive me my discourtesy, Lady Paladin," he said. Vivian didn't miss the flick of his wings directed at Tyr, and she was sure Tyr didn't either, but to her relief the Glasidhe turned and continued down the passageway. She reached out to Tyr through their silent channel of communication, hoping it would still work in Faeortalam.

Are you going to be confrontational with everyone we meet? she asked.

He didn't answer her.

I know you can hear me, she pressed, hiking up the strap of her backpack on her shoulder. *Don't go giving me the silent treatment. You've got your voice back, after all.*

That garnered a flicker of something like amusement in Tyr's eyes as they rounded yet another bend in the passage.

"Nearly there, my lady!" piped Haze encouragingly, as though Vivian looked ready to give up on the trek any moment.

"I never doubted you, Haze," she replied with a smile.

"I would hope not, Lady Paladin," he said, shaking his head.

"Do you know Forin and Farin?" she asked curiously.

Haze whirled, his aura sparking excitedly. "Oh, yes, Lady Paladin, they are also my cousins!"

"It sounds as though you come from a very illustrious family, then."

Haze's aura glowed golden at the compliment, but he didn't reply.

You wasted no time in understanding how to handle the Small Folk, said Tyr silently.

Vivian raised an eyebrow at him. *Well, you certainly weren't being diplomatic.*

"Here we are!" said Haze, hovering in front of a mirror with an elaborate golden frame. Vivian brushed the intricate filigree with one finger and the mirror rippled, its opaque silver surface suddenly transforming into a window, and then into a doorway with no barrier between Vivian and the room beyond.

"That's fantastic," she murmured.

"Shall I show you to your quarters?" said Haze begrudgingly to Tyr.

"I'll see the Lady Paladin settled in, thank you," Tyr replied.

"My lady?" Haze looked to Vivian for clarification.

She felt a blush rise to her cheeks as she realized that this would be the first time she and Tyr would be *properly* alone – no one just on the other side of the door, no easy escape into the common area of the house. A little thrill coursed through her, excitement mixed with a bit of fear. Even though she trusted him, Tyr was still…wild. *Dangerous*, as Niall would say. She blinked. "Yes, that's fine, Haze, thank you. Would you be able to carry a message to someone for me?"

"Of course!" Haze bowed.

"Would you please tell Knight Niall of the Unseelie Court that I'm in my quarters, and he is welcome as a visitor at any time?"

"I most certainly shall tell the Vaelanseld so," said Haze approvingly. The Glasidhe glanced at Tyr, sniffed and then whizzed away.

"This is so clever, but I don't think I'm going to be able to find it again on my own," sighed Vivian as she stepped through the frame of the mirror into her quarters, careful to lift her feet high enough not to trip on the bottom edge. She took three steps into her room, marveling at the perfect riot of color: azure and emerald and ruby hangings on the stone walls created a mesmerizing mosaic of patterns and textures, contrasting the white and gray furs thrown across the floor. A fire blazed merrily in a hearth that was almost as tall as Vivian, though the room was comfortably cool, as though they were underground. Dark silken curtains draped around a low bed in one corner, and in the other corner of the room thicker curtains parted at the center to reveal a huge copper bathtub, already gently steaming. Vivian sighed in ecstatic anticipation and turned to see Tyr's reaction.

Except Tyr hadn't followed her into the room. She frowned, staring at her own reflection in the mirror. She reached out and touched the frame of the mirror. The surface rippled, transformed to glass and then disappeared as it had before. Tyr stepped through the doorway.

"You need to touch the frame of the entry for anyone to enter," he said, watching as she withdrew her hand and liquid silver poured into the frame, solidifying into the mirror once again.

"What would happen if someone was caught halfway?" she asked in morbid fascination.

"I imagine they'd be cut in two," he replied speculatively. "Or perhaps burned. It would depend on the structure of the enchantment."

"I'll make sure it doesn't happen," she said, swallowing hard.

"It could be a handy self-defense tool," Tyr countered.

"I don't need to cut someone in half with an enchanted mirror in self-defense," Vivian retorted indignantly, stepping farther into the room and stopping to unlace her shoes before she tracked grime all over the beautiful furs on the floor. She looked longingly at the steaming tub as she tried to keep her balance, one leg raised like a flamingo as she picked at the knot in one shoelace. Losing the battle, she sat down with an undignified thump and a sigh. Apparently being a Paladin didn't make a lick of difference with her clumsiness. Triumphantly, she pulled off her shoes and set them aside, wrinkling her nose at her damp, grimy socks.

"I don't remember getting wet," she muttered to herself.

"There was melting ice in the throne room," replied Tyr. "And there are many things you may not remember from the battle until you encounter something that reminds you of it."

"Yeah, well, I think we got off pretty light. Wet socks don't really figure high on the scale of bad things that can happen in a battle." Vivian peeled off her socks and wriggled her toes, examining them in the firelight. Tyr didn't reply. He padded over to one of the chairs by the fire and sat down, peering into the flames.

She eyed the curtains around the bathtub. They seemed opaque enough to provide enough privacy…and, she pointed out to herself, it wasn't as though she was a total innocent. She'd done much more than take a bath in the same room as a man, but somehow every sensation seemed new and raw with Tyr. "I'm going to take a bath, so don't, you know, be weird about it."

Tyr leaned forward and rested his elbows on his knees.

"Okay, good talk," she said brightly, picking up her backpack and walking over to the bathtub. A stack of soft cloths filled a shelf on the wall near the tub, and on a low table there were several little wooden bowls of various creams and what looked to Vivian like curls of soap. The steam from the tub wafted around her invitingly, already fragrant with a scent that reminded her of roses. "Nice," she breathed, setting her backpack down by the table.

As she drew the curtains closed, she glanced at Tyr, still silhouetted by the fire...but her desire for a hot bath eclipsed her concern for him. She wiggled her toes against the soft fur laid like a bath mat by the tub and then gleefully stripped out of the rest of her battle-soiled clothes. The amount of blood and grime on her skin surprised her. She remembered dropping and rolling on the stone floor a few times to avoid impalement on one blade or another during the battle, and she'd been so exhilarated not to be dead after the fact that she hadn't really paid much attention to how *dirty* they all were.

Wrestling with the elastic in her hair, she finally unleashed her curls and threw the elastic onto the pile of dirty clothes. After a moment of hesitation, she decided against taking off the Bearer's pendant and the silver key. She couldn't really say why, but she wanted to keep them against her skin and she somehow knew that water wouldn't harm them.

Sliding into the hot, fragrant water seemed to Vivian one of the purest pleasures she'd ever experienced in her entire life. She became aware of all the aches in her body just as the heat of the water began to soothe them. The tub was just the right size for her, deep enough that the water submerged her to her chin and long enough for her to stretch her legs out fully beneath the surface of the wonderful water.

She lay blissfully in the hot water with her eyes closed for a few moments, unmoving, just feeling the heat seep into her skin and uncoil the tightness in her muscles that she hadn't realized had been there. The only sounds in the room were the distant crackling of the fire in the hearth and the small ripples of water against the sides of the copper tub.

Finally, she pried one eye open and glanced down at the water, watching with detached interest as the layer of grime from her skin moved across the surface of the tub, drawn by some invisible current toward her feet. Then the dirty water seemed to slide up over the edge of the tub, like a reverse fountain. Vivian opened her eyes fully and sat up in alarm, peering over the side of the tub. The beautiful furs would be ruined!

But no water pooled onto the floor, and the level of water in the tub didn't recede. She let out the breath she'd been holding as she watched the steady migration of grayish water to the edge of the tub, replaced by some unseen spring. It would definitely take a while to get used to such casual magic, but she certainly appreciated its elegance and utility. Would the bath remain filled with hot water all the time, she wondered idly as she dipped a finger into a blue-tinted cream, or would it only fill if she asked it?

After experimentally using one of the creams on a section of her hair, Vivian washed her hair and scrubbed herself with the curls of soap. Bruises appeared from beneath the veneer of dirt, chronicling hard falls and near misses from the battle that she really didn't remember with any specificity. But nothing felt like it was broken. Her stomach rumbled as she finished rinsing her hair after washing it a second time. She reluctantly took it as her cue to finish bathing.

Pulling on a t-shirt and shorts from her packed clothes after toweling dry, she pulled back the curtain, still sponging her hair dry with one of the cloths. Tyr sat exactly as she'd last seen him. She reached for him with their invisible connection, but she couldn't feel him. Would it fade now that they were in the Fae world, or had he just shut her out? She resisted the urge to sigh as her stomach growled again.

Food had appeared on the small table by the fire, or maybe she just hadn't noticed it when she'd first entered the room. She made a quick sandwich out of pieces of rustic bread and chunks of cheese. For a moment, she contemplated trying to toast the bread and melt the cheese over the fire, but then she shook her head. Too much effort and time involved in that.

"So, do you still need blood, or will you just need regular food now?" she asked Tyr after swallowing her first mouthful of her sandwich. "This is good," she added in mild surprise.

"Did you expect the food to be inedible here?" he said without looking away from the fire.

"Well, no," she admitted. "I thought maybe it would be…different." She took another bite. "And you didn't answer my question."

"Because I do not know the answer," he said.

"Okay," she said slowly. She finished eating and brushed the crumbs from her hands. "You know, I thought you'd be more…I don't know. Excited?"

"Why?" He still didn't look at her.

"Because you killed Mab," she said. He winced – it was fleeting, and he hid it quickly beneath his composed, beautiful mask, but she caught it.

"Yes," he said quietly.

"And you're back in Faeortalam," she continued. "You're back in your world. I'd think that would be cause for celebration."

"Is it?" he said.

"Is it *what*?" she said in frustration.

"Is it my world?" Tyr murmured.

Vivian grimaced and rubbed one hand over her eyes. "Okay. Well. It's been an eventful day, and I'm pretty tired, so I'm going to head to bed." She tugged at a curl. "You're welcome to stay here, but you can't sleep in the bed with me."

He finally looked at her.

She snorted. "What a typical guy. That's the only thing that catches your attention?"

"I..." For a rare moment Tyr seemed at a loss for words. "I did not mean any disrespect," he finally said.

"I didn't say you did." She raised her eyebrows. "I'm just being very clear in what's going to fly."

He turned back to the fire. "I do not think I will sleep."

Vivian shrugged. "Suit yourself." She yawned. "If Niall stops by, wake me up so I can let him in."

She heard Tyr mutter something under his breath, but she ignored him as she turned to the bed. It felt just as deliciously comfortable as it looked and the sensation against her bruised and exhausted body was so amazing that she almost wanted to cry. It was strange how she went from completely amped and awake to crashing out in the space of an hour, she thought as she nestled beneath a soft blanket. One hand found the silver key at her throat, her fingers curling loosely around it. What door did it open? she wondered hazily as she drifted toward sleep. Her mind flipped through the images again: circular tower, gleaming table, scales flashing on the brow of a beautiful, fierce visage, strange silver instruments whirring on the shelves, curious young faces gazing up at her...

Sleep wrapped about her as she slipped into dreams so vivid that they could have been memories, none of which she would remember when she awoke.

Chapter 3

"There's a storm coming."

Mal sighed and straightened from the rail. Trust Hex to come and ruin a perfectly good sunset over the water. Pretending not to hear Hex never worked, and there was only so much avoiding someone that could be done on a ship at sea.

"You our weather-witch now?" Mal replied caustically. "Gonna whistle up a wind to whisk us away from the storm?"

Hex folded his arms over his chest. Mal didn't miss the flash of hurt in his dark eyes. "Thought you'd do that."

"I'm not a weather-witch," she retorted. "You'n I both know that."

"No, but you're something. We *do* both know that."

"Not this again, Hex." The words came out more of a groan than she'd intended, but she was thoroughly sick of his insistence that she was anything other than what she was – what she *wanted* to be – and that was a third mate on the *Dragonwing*. She scratched at a patch of skin that had been bothering her for a few days.

Hex's eyes softened. "You should get Jem to look at that."

"It's nothing," she growled. "Don't you have mainmast this watch?"

He shrugged one shoulder in that infuriating way of his that always made something odd happen to her stomach. "Kelor is letting us roam. It's calm...for now."

"Wish I had Kelor for my overwatch," she muttered. The second mates got to add a syllable to their names, but the thirds joked that the longer the name, the meaner the mate. Thirds only rated one syllable, a sound to be barked and shouted, used to summon and discipline. Seconds got one more, and the handful of firsts onboard had a full three. And the Captain had two names. Two whole names. The luxury of it, the elegance and excess of so many sounds to describe one person, sometimes made Mal dizzy with want. She already knew what name she would have when she was a first: Mallora. And she wished she'd been able to compose it herself in her hammock as she'd heard some of the other thirds do when they thought everyone else was asleep after watch. But that wasn't her lot.

"Telen isn't bad," Hex said, leaning his elbows on the rail next to her. She slid a glance toward him grudgingly, like a gold coin pushed across a table at the end of a game of dragon's tail.

"He isn't bad, but he isn't good," she said. Hex had filled out in the last year, his shoulders broadening and arms thickening with cords of muscle in a way that confused Mal. There were a few other women among the thirds: Sor, Oll and Iss. She'd heard Sor and Iss talking about Hex one night as she dressed in her red shirt and black breeches for watch. Thirds wore red so they could always be seen. Seconds wore gray, to blend with the sky and the ship (so they could prowl about and catch thirds unawares, the thirds muttered) and firsts wore crisp white, always spotless. The Captain wore blue, the color of the sky at noon and the sails of the *Dragonwing*.

In any case, she thought Sor and Iss ridiculous as they talked about Hex. She'd known Hex since the beginning of their lives – his mother had been a second onboard and they both vaguely remembered her. Neither of them knew anything about Mal's mother. Hex's mother had nursed them both.

They didn't have any little sparrows on the ship now. That's what they called the kids, sparrows, because they pattered about the deck and flew up the rigging light as little birds. They got to be free until they were seven, and then they either took their oath to the Captain and put on the black of a fourth – black so that they wouldn't be constantly upbraided for a dirty shirt, small mercies – or put ashore at one of the Isles, usually Haven or Horizon. Fourths didn't have names. They were all "you" and "boy," whether they were a boy or a girl.

"Telen doesn't let you roam on watch," agreed Hex with conspiratorial smile.

Mal scowled at him.

"Stop that," he told her mildly, grinning. He reached out with one hand and touched the crease at the center of her eyebrows with his thumb, like he could wipe it away. He'd done it since they were both sparrows whenever she was upset. Most of the time it gave her a feeling of warmth and comfort, but now it just annoyed her. She swatted his hand away, perhaps harder than she needed to. He raised his eyebrows.

"We're thirds," she said in irritation, as though that explained everything, but it didn't. It didn't explain anything at all about why she felt the way she did, and there was no one she could ask about it. Fat chance she'd ask Sor or Iss anything about being a woman. Oll wasn't bad. They'd once made a spit-solemn when they were fourths together that they would practice together until they beat all the boys at climbing the rigging – and they did. But they didn't share secrets anymore and spit-solemns were for sparrows.

They both gazed out at the ocean for a long while. Mal felt her heart expanding the way it only did when she looked at the sea, when she thought about the endless expanse of water surrounding them, its silken waves caressing the hull of the *Dragonwing*. The sunset bloodied the horizon and the shadows lengthened. Mal tipped her head back and watched the stars appear overhead, naming them quietly as they became visible.

She wasn't a weather-witch – one of the firsts, Kalinda, was their wind-whistler. Kalinda climbed faster than the other firsts, but Mal was confident she'd beat her. Firsts didn't have occasion to climb the rigging for actual work, though, so she'd never tested her skill against the small wind-whistler. She'd seen Kalinda work a few times, standing on the platform at the stern of the ship built especially for the task so that their weather-worker could see all the sails and adjust their enchanted wind with an eye to filling the canvas as the Captain directed.

Hex watched the stars come out silently. Mal studiously ignored him, resting her elbows on the railing again as she watched the last stains of sunset fade from the sky in the west. She rubbed at one of the patches of rough skin on her neck. Lately she'd noticed the red patches cropping up in odd places – behind her knee, on the back of her arm, on her neck, scaly and itching like she wore a fine-hair shirt against her skin. Just her luck to catch some sort of disease – they hadn't put ashore in weeks, though. Maybe it was something in the food, she thought, though they'd been eating the same fish and bread as they always ate.

"Jem might have an ointment," Hex said, his tone annoyingly helpful.

"I don't *need* to go see Jem," she snapped. "And even if I did, I'd go when *I* wanted to, not because you're playing mama and hovering over me like some sop!"

Hex straightened. She couldn't see his face in the shadows.

"Don't know why you're so prickly lately, Mal," he said. He tried to keep his voice light, but she could hear the hurt buried deep in it. Something squirmed uncomfortably in her stomach, but she pulled back her shoulders.

"I'm not prickly," she replied firmly. "I just don't need you trying to take care of me. I don't need anyone to take care of me."

"Never said you did," he said quietly.

The overwatch's whistle sounded from midships, summoning all the thirds on watch.

"Mal…" Hex started.

"Kelor's calling. You should go," she cut him off.

Hex tilted his head like he wanted to say something else, and then he walked past her, headed to muster with his watch mates. She told herself that it was better to gaze into the twilight alone, that she didn't feel a twinge of guilt at her harsh words. Hex had always been a constant in her life – he and the Captain and the *Dragonwing*. Once she became a second, she could move between ships, but she didn't want to. Captains could trade their thirds – reassign them if they weren't progressing, or if they'd gotten off on the wrong foot with a second or a first onboard. When they'd first put on the red shirts, Mal had nightmares that she'd been traded to another ship and had to leave the *Dragonwing*. The thought of it still made her breathless with dread, but she worked hard enough that she was among the top third of the fifty or so thirds they had onboard at any given time. She wasn't as strong as some of the lads, but she climbed the rigging faster than any of them and she'd go up in raging storms when others' courage deserted them.

She stood at the rail for a while longer. On the whole, more sen-ior thirds were left alone when they were off watch, not like when they'd been fourths and none of their time had been their own. The youngest thirds still had the worst jobs, like the scullery. Mal didn't miss the days when her hands were constantly chapped and blistered from scrubbing trenchers and cleaning Cook's pots.

A cool breeze ruffled her hair. She kept it short, though some of the other thirds grew theirs out. Iss could even braid hers now, but Mal thought that Iss would probably have a baby in her belly soon and be put off at Horizon. Thirds weren't supposed to have kids, not until they'd earned their place as a grayshirt. Iss would rather wear the shirt of a first after she'd lured him into bed than put on a grayshirt on her own merits, Mal thought scornfully.

"Hex said you needed some ointment."

Mal felt her face compress into a scowl again. "Hex says a lot of things he shouldn't say."

"And so do you," replied Jem, undaunted. He was the best among the thirds at doctoring, though if they were really sick their overwatch would take them to Bonesaw. None of them ever wanted to go, though. Bonesaw was a hulk of a first who looked like he'd rather break a limb than set it. He'd lost a leg to a kraken attack. There were rumors that Bonesaw wasn't much good at climbing anymore, what with his peg leg, and that was why he was the ship's doctor. Bonesaw wasn't his real name, either, and none of the thirds knew what he was truly called.

"Don't need anything," Mal muttered stubbornly.

"Then maybe you should stop scratching like you've got fleas," replied Jem with a grin.

Mal snatched her hand away from her neck, her face heating. Jem held out a little pot of ointment. She sighed and took it from him, twisting it open and sniffing its contents. "Ugh. Smells terrible."

"But it works," said Jem, leaning his slim frame against the railing. "Want me to put it on?"

"No," Mal said hastily. "Don't want you to catch it."

"I don't think it's something you can give to anyone else."

Mal narrowed her eyes at him, even though he wouldn't be able to see her in the shadows. "What makes you say that?"

Jem shrugged. "I just don't think it's contagious."

"Are you and Hex competing to see who can irritate me most?" she demanded as she dipped her finger into the ointment and slathered it onto the scaly patch on her neck. It burned for a moment and then a delicious cooling sensation soothed the terrible itch. "It does work," she admitted. "Thanks." She slid the pot into the pouch at her belt. "Need any rings for it?"

Each ship had its own currency. On the *Dragonwing*, thirds used copper rings, the seconds silver and the firsts gold. Fourths weren't allowed to trade anything but their own time, and the Captain had no need for rings at all. Some of the thirds wore their rings on their fingers and in their ears, but Mal thought that looked garish. Besides, why would you want everyone to know how many rings you had?

And if a bigger third wanted to corner you and take them from you, well, it was your own fault. She kept the majority of her rings in a hidden place, with a few stashed in her belt pouch for easy access. She even had a silver ring concealed in a different place, given to her by Telen after she'd dislocated her shoulder keeping him from being washed overboard during their last bad storm. He'd put her shoulder back in its socket with quiet efficiency when the squall died down, and slid the silver ring onto her finger while she was still white-faced and panting, gripping her good shoulder with his strong hand before walking away without a word.

"No rings," said Jem. "It's extra, really, of a batch that I made for one of the seconds."

"Let me guess," said Mal wryly as she patted the ointment onto another patch on the back of her arm, "one of the seconds caught a bad itch from one of the Nuremian girls on Horizon."

"I don't gossip," said Jem loftily.

Mal sniggered. "But you didn't deny it."

"You should just be grateful he paid me more than enough rings to cover it all," Jem said.

"And I suppose you think I should be grateful to Hex, too, putting you on my case," she said.

"Don't go sniping at him," Jem said.

"Oh, are you going to call me prickly too?" Mal crossed her arms over her chest, smearing the ointment she'd just applied.

"No. But I don't like being caught between you two."

Wiry Jem, with his quick hands and quicker smile, complemented her and Hex. The three of them hadn't been on a watch together for a while, but if they were battling a kraken or getting ready for a raid, the seconds almost always put the three of them together. The whole ship understood, from fourth up to first, that to take one was to take all three, whether it was in a fistfight or in a longboat.

She couldn't be irritated at Jem. "Sorry." She sighed. "Most of the time I don't realize I'm doing it."

"That's not entirely the truth, and you know it."

Jem also had a way of seeing through her that should have been annoying but, because it was him, simply kept her honest.

"I do," she admitted. Then she burst out, "I just...he just *irritates* me, Jem, I don't know *why* but he does!"

"Maybe because you're growing into a woman and he's a man," suggested Jem with a hint of humor.

"I'm not a woman, I'm a sailor," she growled. "I'm a third."

Jem chuckled. "Doesn't make you any less of a woman, Mal."

"You're ridiculous."

"So are you."

She snorted and turned back to the ocean. The waves glimmered under the rising moon. "Think we'll have another raid soon?"

Jem shrugged. "Depends if we can find a seam."

"It always depends if we can find a seam." She thought of the silver threads dancing in the air, the excitement and anticipation of the crew after a seam was sighted as they prepared for their raid into another world. "You know they say on Horizon that our Captain is the best at it."

"They also say on Horizon that you're a third who's spotted more seams than most firsts," countered Jem.

"I guess I just have better eyes for 'em," said Mal, shifting uncomfortably.

"And you seem to know when a kraken is lurking," Jem said.

"Not you too. I've had too many people harping on about how I'm *different* somehow," she said, her voice colored with frustration. "I just pay attention, that's all."

"And you're pale as a pureblood, with no gold ever from the sun," countered Jem.

"Oh, right, I forgot, you're of the opinion that my mother was some lost little Unseelie beauty who somehow ended up farther past the horizon on the ocean than any of her kind in centuries."

"Preferable to being Nuremian," said Jem.

"I don't know about that," retorted Mal. "And besides, the Nuremian women burn in the sun."

"Could just be your Seafarer blood coming through."

"I don't care who my mother was," she said, even though she did. She thought about it at night in her swaying hammock as she listened to the even breathing of the other sleeping thirds. She thought about it as she watched the horizon, perching on one of the ratlines highest up the mainmast. Jem knew it and she knew it. Somehow, she just needed to say that she didn't care. She didn't care about her mother and she sure as the ocean tides didn't care about the man who'd put a babe in her mother and then abandoned her. Her stomach clenched. Sometimes she imagined finding her father and confronting him, teaching him a lesson about leaving with her fists.

"Hex said that he thinks there's a storm coming," she said, more to change the subject than anything else.

"Kalinda moved her hammock up on deck," Jem said in agreement.

"Have you seen the Captain?"

"Not yet."

"He'll be up, if there's a storm," she said.

Jem didn't need to agree with that. A ripple caught Mal's eye. She straightened, and Jem glanced at her.

"What did you see?"

"Might be nothing," she murmured, settling into the quiet place where she let her eyes roam the waves, watching for another disturbance. Jem turned his eye to the sea as well.

"A storm *and* a kraken," he murmured, his whip-like frame coiled in interest.

"Maybe neither," Mal replied tersely.

"Storm'll stir up the water enough that our hull might not be enough," said Jem.

"Dragonbone isn't ever a sure thing," she said, feeling vaguely disloyal to the beautiful, sleek *Dragonwing*. There were only a handful of ships left with dragonbone in their hull. They'd been built in the early days of their people, passed down through families of Seafarers. It was thought that dragons once hunted krakens, so the scent of the dragonbone still deterred the giant sea creatures...but during a storm, the sea lashed with rain and wind, even dragonbone wasn't an effective deterrent against the monsters. Perhaps the Captain would try to provoke the creature before the storm, give them a better chance at driving it away before they were all fighting the ocean and wind, too. A little shiver wriggled down her spine. If a kraken were sighted, the Captain would invoke the law of the storm: No sailor washed overboard could be saved. It was the ocean's due. It was the price they paid to sail the wild seas, slipping through seams and raiding treasure in other worlds.

Mal felt her mouth go dry at the thought of the kraken and the storm both at once. Last kraken they'd fought had been a small one, and it had ripped away part of the port railing and damaged a few planks on deck. During the last storm, two of the thirds had washed overboard and the Captain had circled the ship, taking the helm himself, handling her brilliantly amid the driving rain and crashing waves. They'd hauled Kar out of the storm-lashed seas while the deck pitched and heaved, and one of the firsts had taken him to Bonesaw right away. They'd never found Vys, not even after the sea smoothed to glass under the pale pink of dawn.

"There," she whispered as she saw the unmistakable loop of a tentacle curving out of the waves.

"Maybe it won't go for the ship," Jem said hopefully.

"And maybe it'll give Bonesaw back his leg," Mal retorted. Krakens attacked ships. It was what they did. And it was the crew's job to fight them.

"We should sound a whistle," Jem said, but he didn't reach for the whistle that hung on a cord around his neck. He was waiting for Mal to do it, so she could claim credit for the sighting, she realized.

"Let me see it again," she murmured, her eyes skimming the dark waves. She gripped the rail with both hands, the strange patches on her skin forgotten along with her earlier irritation at Hex. Her scalp prickled.

Closer to the ship than before, another tentacle brushed the surface, barely breaking through the waves. Mal slid her whistle into her mouth and sounded the five short blasts that meant danger. Kelor appeared out of the shadows shortly.

"Kraken," she said calmly, pointing with a steady hand to the last place that the tentacle had broken the surface.

"You're sure? Not just a sea snake?" Kelor asked.

She turned and gazed up at the taller second, letting him see her eyes. "I'm sure."

Kelor nodded and disappeared again to tell his watch. Soon after, the bell sounded, calling all hands to their battle stations. It also signified that if they fell overboard, they wouldn't be recovered as the ship outran the kraken occupied with its meal.

Mal gripped Jem's forearm hard before they went to their separate watch stations. He went to the archers on the bow, and she took up her light spear from the rack by the foredeck and went to stand midships, ready to spring into the rigging with her spear slung across her back.

"Don't be kraken meat, Mal!" called out Oll as she passed, on her way to join Jem with the archers.

"Ah, I'm too scrawny for a kraken to eat!" Mal responded with a grin that she didn't feel.

"Third time you've been first to see the beast," said Telen as he counted his squad of spearmen. He looked directly at Mal. "Some'd say that's more than luck."

"Just sharp eyes," said Mal.

"Take those sharp eyes up to the platform," Telen ordered.

"Aye." She ducked her head and leapt into the rigging, climbing quickly to the platform that surrounded the mast about halfway up its height. There was no railing. She took her length of stronger-than-it-looked spidersilk off her belt and tied herself to the ring set into the mast. She'd paid ten rings to a one-eyed merchant on Horizon for her length of spidersilk, which most of the thirds thought was ridiculous; but she'd taken one of the heavy lines, longer than the spidersilk and what all the rest of the thirds used, and tied herself into it as a backup before throwing herself off the rigging. The spidersilk held her weight without any problem, and she didn't have to worry about the extra weight now when she climbed.

Lanterns burned fore and aft, ready to light the fire pits that the archers used for their flaming arrows. Fire onboard a wooden-hulled ship was a risk that they only took when they were preparing to fight a kraken. Mal looked down and watched the shifting shadows on deck, the crew small from her vantage point amid the sails. Her fingers found her knives, touching them for reassurance: a long one at the top of her boot, one at her waist and another strapped to her left wrist. She unslung her spear and settled down to watch. If she saw the kraken, she'd tell the rest of the crew with a series of whistles that they knew as well as words. The whistles and bells were their second language amid the salt wind of the sea.

She remained motionless, scanning the sea, for the next hours. The wind picked up, stirring from a breeze to a stronger wind that tasted of rain. Maybe there *would* be a storm. Her eyelids grew heavy – she hadn't slept since the night before, since she had the dawn watch; but she didn't move and she didn't sleep. The safety of the crew and the ship depended on her and the other lookouts posted among the sails. The archer firsts added more oil to their lanterns. No one questioned that she had seen a kraken. They were wily beasts, and the older and larger they were, the more unpredictable. Some krakens stalked ships for weeks before attacking. Mal sighed as she thought of standing battle stations for weeks. They could do it, but it would mean less sleep and little time to do anything but watch the waves for the next sighting of the beast. Her neck started itching again, but she didn't want to take her eyes away from the ocean long enough to apply more ointment.

"Captain's directed the station leaders to start rotation," said Ila, one of the seconds who was friendly with the best thirds. He pulled himself up onto the platform and handed Mal a steaming mug of broth. She took it gratefully, blinking as she finally drew her eyes away from scanning the waves. A few raindrops pattered onto the platform. Ila grumbled and pulled out his oilskin. Mal moved over to let him take his position as he liked, sipping at the broth.

"So, it's you and I on this station," Ila continued, his gaze focused on the ocean. "Six on, six off, so you'd better go grab some sleep. See you at dawn."

She nodded and finished her broth. If it was raining and cold, she'd want to wear her gloves and oilskin for next watch, she thought as she untied her spidersilk and coiled it, clipping the end to her belt. She slung her spear across her back and descended from the platform, the wind combing its fingers through her hair. The deck was quiet, only the sounds of the waves slapping the hull and the canvas creaking in the wind carrying through the dark air. Without saying a word to anyone, Mal found her way to her hammock in the dark, her steps sure. She knew the decks of the *Dragonwing* better than she knew her own body. Tying her spear to a crossbeam within easy reach, she slid into her hammock and fell instantly asleep, unbothered by the footsteps of other thirds coming into the berthing and their whispered conversations.

When she awoke, she knew before she regained conscious thought that a storm gripped the *Dragonwing*, her hammock swinging quickly from side to side as waves rocked the ship. She heard the howl of the wind and the creak of the hull, assaulted by the forces of nature. There were no whispered conversations now, nothing but grim efficiency on the faces of the thirds, lit by the dim *taebramh* light that one of them – probably Orr – had managed to conjure and stick to the ceiling of their berthing.

Mal pulled on her boots and checked her knives. She draped her oilskin around her shoulders and tied it at her waist, drawing the strings of the hood under her chin. On her hands she wore her thin sealhide gloves, flexible enough that she could still feel the rigging under her fingers as she climbed; and over those, thick, fingerless gloves with scored palms to grip her spear in the driving rain.

The wind made her stagger as she emerged on deck. Rain pelted into her face, cold and stinging. They'd rigged lines between the masts for transit, and she gripped one with a gloved hand. Smears of lantern light painted the fore and aft decks. She caught sight of a blue shirt through the driving rain: the Captain, a huge and impressive figure, standing at the helm. She shivered: he only took the helm in the worst storms. Their odds weren't good to face a kraken *and* this maelstrom. Her heart clenched at the unfairness of it. The *Dragonwing* was the most beautiful ship ever to sail the Unnamed Seas, her crew strong and brave and loyal, and she would go down in a raging storm, torn apart by a kraken and the unforgiving seas.

"Move along now!" shouted someone behind her. She recognized Telen's voice and her feet moved of their own accord, carrying her toward the mainmast. The ship rocked and pitched wildly, the deck surging beneath them one moment and falling away the next. Mal felt her heart leap into her throat. They'd never been in a storm this bad. Frothing waves washed over the side of the ship every few moments, slicking the decks with seawater. She felt like she couldn't breathe, the wind whipping rain into her mouth, but, somehow, she reached the mainmast and started the climb to the platform.

She was halfway to the platform when the kraken attacked.

A black tentacle reared out of the waves, crashing down onto the deck. The ship gave an ugly, terrifying lurch. Mal clung to the rigging, watching in frozen terror. By the size of the tentacle, this kraken was a monster, the suckers on its tentacle bigger than her head. The crew nearest the tentacle threw their spears and then hit the deck as flaming arrows arced toward the tentacle from fore and aft.

"Come on, Mal, get up here!" roared Ila from the platform, his face illuminated white in a flash of lightning.

The kraken screeched and withdrew its tentacle, the huge, slimy appendage rushing across the deck and back into the water, leaving a gaping hole in the rail. Water frothed across the decks and she saw at least two bodies that had been crushed by the kraken's tentacle. Mal forced her arms and legs into motion, tearing her eyes away from the scene of destruction.

"Good lass," yelled Ila approvingly, grabbing the back of her shirt and hauling her up onto the platform. She quickly tied her spidersilk onto the ring with shaking hands. "Now, let's see if we can get a clean shot next time!"

Their spears were tipped with poison. One spear wasn't lethal to a kraken, but dozens could be. The one attacking the *Dragonwing* now, though, was a monster, bigger than anything Mal had ever seen. She wished suddenly that she knew the names of the gods that some of the crew prayed to – maybe she wouldn't have felt so overwhelmingly frightened. The ship pitched and rolled through the foam-lashed waves at such an angle that the platform was nearly vertical, the mast suspended over the roiling ocean. She felt her spidersilk go taut, pulling on her belt, and there wasn't anything she could do except clutch her spear and wait for the ship to roll back the other direction.

A flash of lightning illuminated a hellish scene, not one but three tentacles now curling like monstrous snakes out of the water toward the *Dragonwing*. The kraken screeched again, an earsplitting cry that sent a sharp pain through Mal's head. She gritted her teeth and got her feet under her, pulling her spear out of its carrier and wrapping her other hand around her spidersilk line. To her left, Ila hefted his spear too, grinning against the deluge of the storm.

Two of the kraken's tentacles arrowed down toward the deck of the ship as a monstrous wave crested before the bow.

"Gods save us," whispered Mal, not sure which gods would even listen.

She saw Hex leap toward the tentacle on deck by the mainmast. She'd know his broad-shouldered silhouette anywhere, even through the dim light and driving rain of this storm. He carried two spears and thrust both of them deeply into the kraken's flesh. She stood and used her whole body as leverage to throw her spear into the same tentacle, yelling in triumph as her weapon struck home. The kraken thrashed, knocking Hex to the deck with bone crushing force. The *Dragonwing* plunged down into the trough of the massive wave, all of them suddenly sickeningly weightless for a long, suspended moment.

Mal saw someone grab for Hex's unconscious body, but then there was whitewater rushing across the decks and he was swept over the ruined rail shattered by the kraken. She felt the breath punched out of her with shock and anger. The sea would not take him. The kraken would not make him its meal.

The knife at her wrist was out of its sheath before she recognized her own intention. She cut the spidersilk near the brass ring, slid her knife back into its sheath, and when the ship rolled next, she dove from the platform into the roiling seas, Ila's yell ringing in her ears.

Chapter 4

"What do we need to do?"

Sayre ran one hand through his dark hair as he asked the question, looking painfully young and reminding Guinna of young Ramel. They'd barely recognize each other now, she and Ramel, with so many years and memories weighing them down.

"Are you asking what we need to do as two of our Queen's Three?" she said quietly. He sat in one of the chairs by the fire in her quarters. On Andraste's orders, they'd shifted the Unseelie quarters away from the frosted underground warren that Mab had favored. Ice had still encased the walls while they'd salvaged some of the furs and other items of comfort that had survived her brutal edicts. Their new quarters, closer to the center of the city, were serviceable for now, but chilly and damp when night fell over the White City. Guinna didn't know whether Andraste didn't bother with any enchantments to improve their lodgings…or if something of that magnitude was beyond her ability at the moment.

Sayre spread his long-fingered hands. "Yes. I'm asking…everything. I thought that we would have the answers somehow, but…"

"But that's not really how life works." Guinna finished his statement quietly.

"We're two of her Three," said Sayre, clenching his jaw and staring into the fire. "We should know what to do."

"You and I both know we were choices more born of necessity than any real talents that we have." Guinna smoothed the sleeves of her long, emerald green silk gown. She was not a warrior. She could fight well enough when the occasion demanded it, but she was no Knight. To her knowledge, it was the first time in their history that a woman, much less a woman not a Knight, had been made one of the Unseelie Queen's Three. It made her feel even smaller than her already diminutive stature. She would simply have to make it up to the Queen by providing steady and sage counsel. She would work thrice as hard as the other members of her Court who had trained with blades all their lives.

"You're sharper with words than some are with swords," said Sayre with a small smile.

"Don't pry," Guinna said mildly. She couldn't blame Sayre for hearing her thoughts occasionally, and she had been thinking with particular fervor. While they'd been exploring their own unconscious connection, their Queen had remained inscrutable. Most of the time they couldn't feel Andraste. Guinna wasn't entirely sure how it was *supposed* to feel, to be one of a Queen's Three. She vaguely wished that she could speak to Finnead, but he apparently was gallivanting around the White City like a hot-blooded squire, free of his memories and his angst. Then there was Ramel, but she sighed and didn't even pursue that line of thought.

"Why not Ramel?" Sayre asked.

"Ramel seems to think that *vinaess* and beautiful women are the best ways to drown his sorrows," replied Guinna, hearing the disapproval in her own voice. She felt old and severe, like one of the elders who'd taught the maidens courtesy and Court manners.

"I can't fault him for either of those," said Sayre, arching one eyebrow in consideration.

"In moderation, perhaps," said Guinna, flashing him a look. Stars, he was so young. His *father* had been younger than Guinna.

"Will you stop thinking about your age?" Sayre said with a hint of irritation. "It's going to be hard to get anything done if you keep obsessing over it."

"I am not obsessing. I am merely reflecting," Guinna replied with stiff dignity, smoothing an invisible wrinkle from her skirt.

"Well, if it means anything at all, I don't think you look a day over two hundred," said Sayre with half a grin.

Guinna sighed but couldn't help the smile that curved her lips. "You're a young scallywag."

"A young scallywag who is now one of the Unseelie Queen's Three," Sayre corrected her cheekily.

"Stars save us," muttered Guinna.

"So. What do we need to do? The Queen isn't herself. Anyone can see that."

"How do we really expect her to be herself, and what does that even mean?" Guinna said, shaking her head. "She has been through trials that most of us cannot comprehend, forced to do terrible things in the service of the Enemy…"

"Most of us were forced to do terrible things in the service of our Mad Queen," returned Sayre with calm logic. "And we are all bearing up. What can we do if the new Queen doesn't take up her mantle?"

"She's taken up her mantle," retorted Guinna. "She did not have a choice, just like she did not have a choice those centuries ago."

"There are always choices," said Sayre, his dark eyes reflecting the flames of the fire.

"We must be steadfast," continued Guinna as though he hadn't said anything. She paced in front of the fire. "We must help her see that the power to change our Court now rests with her."

"Not solely with her." Sayre shook his head. "We are all willing to do our part."

Guinna paused. "Perhaps that's exactly what she needs to see."

"How?"

Guinna took a breath. "Her memories were restored through the Lethe Stone, but perhaps they don't feel *real* to her yet. Perhaps the ghosts of her centuries with Malravenar still haunt her."

"I don't think there's any question about that," said Sayre somberly. They both fell silent. It had barely been a week since the battle in the icy throne room, and every night since then Queen Andraste had awoken screaming from nightmares that terrified both of them in their intensity. Sayre had enlisted the help of the head healer, Maeve, to concoct more of the sedative that had been used on Andraste during her captivity, but the Queen refused, wild-eyed, to allow them to dose her with it.

"We need to find a way to remind her of her life before the Enemy," said Guinna. She smiled. "I was one of her ladies then."

Sayre nodded. "I know." He grinned. "And I wasn't even born."

She slapped his arm lightly as she passed. "Don't be rude."

He chuckled.

"Perhaps some lessons as we used to do," murmured Guinna.

"Or will shooting a bow merely remind her of her time as Malravenar's assassin?" Sayre pointed out.

She sighed. "He twisted all that gave her joy. He tortured Finn and he broke her."

"Can we make her whole again?" Sayre asked earnestly.

"We have to try. No – not *try*. We must succeed, for our Court's sake," Guinna said fiercely.

They both stared into the fire for a few long moments.

"I asked Calliea to take me away, to take me to the Vyldgard," murmured Sayre. "I betrayed my Queen and my Court, and now here I sit, one of my Queen's Three."

Guinna stepped closer to him and placed a motherly hand on his shoulder. "I think we have both firmly established that we feel unworthy of the honor bestowed upon us."

"Honor, or death sentence?" Sayre said bleakly.

"None of that," she replied in a sharp voice. He looked at her in surprise. "You and I cannot afford to let dark thoughts overcome us. Andraste needs us. Our Court needs us." She nodded firmly, and after a moment he pressed his lips together and nodded as well. Squeezing his shoulder before releasing him, she turned back to pacing in front of the fire. "We have to help in any way we can. We must keep trying different approaches, even if it means reaching out to Queen Vell or Queen Titania."

"She wants to speak to Knight Finnead," said Sayre. "That much is plain."

"From what we have been told, Knight Finnead is perhaps not as amenable to that plan," Guinna said. "But I'll speak to Merrick. Perhaps he can help."

"Are you sure it is for the Queen's sake that you will speak to Merrick?" said Sayre innocently.

"You are impossible," said Guinna. "One moment you're morose, the next you're an imp."

"Ah, the fickleness of youth," he replied with a grin.

She waved a hand. "All right, all right, we really do need to discuss serious matters." She steeled herself. "The Queen still has not made a decision about the throne room."

"She would rather seal it off and forget it ever existed," replied Sayre.

"But that is not calling her sister's cruelty to full account," Guinna said. A flash of memory surfaced: Queen Mab sitting on her throne, talons carving into the stone as they always did those last months, her terrible, beautiful face impassive as she gazed down at her miserable subjects. When the cages had appeared in the throne room, Guinna had almost retched in disgust and horror at the Queen's intent. It had been much worse when the cages were actually filled with Unseelie flayed nearly to death for some small offense or no offense at all. The smell of blood had filled the throne room, punctuated by a gasp or moan from one of the cages at intervals, and the Mad Queen had relished it. Guinna clenched her jaw, cold disgust at her own weakness washing over her. "We should have fought harder."

"To fight her was to die," said Sayre firmly. "We saw that. We saw what happened to Bren and the other Scholar, and for stars' sakes, they were *librarians*."

Tears sprang into Guinna's eyes unbidden at the mention of her friend. Dear Bren, who had stayed fierce and defiant until the very end, trying to write messages to the Vyldgard or the Seelie using invisible ink that only fire revealed. The Mad Queen had been averse to any sort of flame after she'd lost her mind.

But none of Bren's messages had made it out of the Mad Queen's stronghold, and in the end, they were what doomed her. Guinna had tried to reason with one of the Mad Queen's Three, begging him to have mercy even though Bren held her head high and refused to say even a word in her own defense. She'd even worn the black band that had once signified loyalty to the Bearer to her execution.

"I did not mean to cause you sorrow," Sayre said in quiet apology.

"No." Guinna shook her head and choked out the word. "She needs to be remembered. To do anything less would be unworthy of her." A hot tear slipped down her cheek. So many had died. So very few were left from the days of her youth.

Sayre stood and folded her into his arms. It was not a romantic embrace. They had firmly established what they were to each other: brother and sister, bound in service to their Queen. She pressed her face into his chest and cried for all they had lost. He held her silently until she quieted, his arms firm and warm around her.

"I ran," she murmured into the cloth of his shirt, damp from her tears. "After Bren...I ran."

"You ran, and you escaped," said Sayre with a hard pride in his voice. "And it was your words that helped to bring the High Queen and the Seelie Queen to destroy the Mad Queen."

She swallowed. "It was all I could do."

"It was more than many did," he said firmly.

Guinna stepped back with a sigh and lifted her chin. "We should choose a delegation to pay proper respects to those killed in the throne room of the Mad Queen."

Sayre nodded. "I will speak to those I see at the practice yards today."

"And I will canvas those working in the healing wards," said Guinna. "Tonight, we should speak to Andraste about this." She pressed her lips together. "It cannot be put off much longer. It *should* not be put off much longer."

"And then it will be one more step," said Sayre with a nod.

She smiled at him. After her sister had been killed when Andraste was taken, she'd never thought she would feel so affectionate toward another young Sidhe. After the battle, when they'd been gore-stained and reeling with the weight of their new responsibility and power, after they'd settled Andraste in her chambers and staggered off to find their own, Sayre had said with defeat in his voice, "This is an impossible task set before us."

She had taken his beautiful face in her hands, both of them covered in dirt and blood, and she'd said to him gently, "How does the journey of a thousand miles begin?"

It was an old saying, one taught to children by their swordmasters and their Scholars. Recognition had flared in his eyes and the barest hint of a smile had curved his lips.

"With a single step," he'd replied, nodding.

And that was their prayer and their vow, the children's phrase taken by the two of them, shared between them to bolster their resolve and their heart.

"One more step," she agreed with a nod.

In the silence between their words, a knock sounded at the door of her chambers. She started slightly as she turned to the heavy oak door, not bothering to send her *taebramh* to investigate the identity of the person standing in the passageway. She already felt the *otherness* of her. She smelled the wild windblown kiss of the sky and the earthy scent of hay and *faehal*, mixed with a downy accent that tickled her senses like a feather.

"Valkyrie," murmured Sayre behind her, keeping pace with her as she crossed the chamber to open the door. She nodded.

When she drew back the heavy door, its hinges groaning in protest, Guinna found herself gazing up at the intimidating figure of the new Valkyrie commander, the one who'd lost an eye in the battle for the White City. Guinna lifted her chin. She was one of the Unseelie Queen's Three and she would not be cowed by this muscular warrior of a woman.

"Lady Guinna," the Valkyrie said with a respectful nod. She wore no eye patch and her blind eye looked like a pearl set into the socket, but Guinna had quickly learned how not to betray any interest in scars. "I was sent to ask a favor of you."

"Sent by whom?" asked Guinna. She tried to ignore the little spark of excitement in her chest: perhaps it was Merrick who'd sent the Valkyrie to ask this favor. Her heartbeat quickened traitorously at the thought of the dark-haired Arrisyn, now such a seasoned warrior. She remembered his days as a lithe page and then an apprentice in the Walker's guild. Experience had hardened them both, but she rather liked the look of it on him.

"The Seer," said the Valkyrie.

It took Guinna a breath to understand who the Valkyrie meant; then she remembered that the Bearer's brother, one of Queen Vell's Three, had some gift as a Seer. He was not a Knight or a Guard, so that was his title. The Seer.

"I see," she said with a nod. "And what is this favor that the Seer asks of me?"

"One of your Queen's Knights has spent much of his time since his return from the mortal world with us," the Valkyrie said. "For this we do not fault him. We are free to come and go as we please in the Wild Court." She showed strangely sharp teeth in a grin. "Always at the pleasure of our Vyldretning, of course."

"Of course," murmured Guinna, fascinated by the way that the Valkyrie looked so wolf-like and predatory.

"But the Seer thinks that perhaps this particular Knight is…close to the edge," continued the Valkyrie. Her good eye glittered. "He was your Mad Queen's Vaelanbrigh."

Guinna drew in a breath. "Knight Ramel." She nodded. "Take me to him."

"Shall I accompany you?" Sayre asked.

After a moment of thought, she shook her head. "Thank you, Sayre, but no. This is more a matter of an old friendship than official business for the Court."

"Is it not official business in your Court when one of your Knights is veering into darkness?" murmured the Valkyrie.

"I had not heard that lack of courtesy was an accepted behavior in your Court," returned Guinna icily, bristling at the tall woman's words.

"I mean no disrespect. I am merely making an observation. We are perhaps more open with our words in the Wild Court than is customary in your Court," the Valkyrie said smoothly.

Guinna wished she could remember the woman's name so she could issue a sharper rebuke, but she pushed down her irritation and took a long, slow breath. "Knight Sayre, if you would start the business which we discussed, I shouldn't be long."

Sayre nodded, his eyes not leaving the Valkyrie. "I shall tell Queen Andraste where you have gone, if she asks."

The Valkyrie grinned again. "No need to bristle, young Knight. I do not intend to keep your little wordsmith permanently."

"I doubt she would want to stay permanently," returned Sayre, softening his words with the hint of a grin. He'd adapted to interactions with the Vyldgard warriors much more easily during their time there, realized Guinna. She made a mental note of it.

"Unlike you," returned the Valkyrie with an answering grin. "I hear you handled your time aboard one of our mounts admirably."

Sayre chuckled. "As admirably as I could while I was terrified out of my wits."

"Oh, come now," said the Valkyrie, a purr in the bottom her voice. "A bit of terror makes life sweeter, does it not?"

"May we go to Ramel?" Guinna cut in before they could continue with their banter. She pressed her palms to the skirts of her gown, biting back her impatience. Ramel merited her time, since he was still a part of her Court, but she wished she didn't have to deal with these infuriatingly wild and unpredictable Vyldgard warriors. She felt ungrateful, since it was one of the Vyldgard who had rescued her from Mab's hounds and the Vyldretning herself who had protected her from Mab's wrath; but there was already so much work to be done in their own Court. She felt desperate and hollow, cold at the thought of how many good Unseelie men and women had died in the past years, first in the war against Malravenar and then at the hands of Mab.

"Of course, Lady Guinna," said the Valkyrie with a nod. She winked at Sayre, who grinned, and then turned down the passageway. Guinna stretched her legs to keep up with the warrior's long strides.

The passageways in the Unseelie's new home were not softly lit with *taebramh* like the corridors of the great cathedral in the center of the White City. Guinna hadn't seen the Seelie citadel on the other side of the City, but she heard tales of its elegance and beauty, airy pavilions and gauzy curtains as befitted the tastes of the golden Seelie Queen. They had larger concerns in the Unseelie Court, she reminded herself, pushing away the hint of embarrassment at the damp, cold corridors and the dark moss creeping through the cracks in the stone walls. They just had to give Andraste – and themselves – time to heal from the shock of Mab's death and the end of her reign of terror. They emerged from the dark passageway through an unassuming doorway into the bright sunlight of a warm day. Guinna blinked owlishly.

"And how have the days since the end of the Mad Queen treated you?" asked the Valkyrie conversationally as they passed two Unseelie Knights on their way to the practice grounds.

"It has been warmer," replied Guinna. Mab's icy grip had kept the Unseelie portion of the City in wintry snow and frost. Now the sun felt odd upon her skin.

The Valkyrie glanced down at her and arched an eyebrow. "You don't like me much, do you, Lady Guinna?"

Guinna felt a blush rising to her cheeks and told herself it was simply the warmth of the afternoon. "We have much to do in my Court."

"Aye, you have a new Queen and much healing to do," agreed the Valkyrie somberly. They walked in silence for a moment until she spoke again. "Trillian, by the way. That's my name. I can tell you don't remember it, and that's nothing to be ashamed of, but next time you might just ask."

"You are the one who came asking for my help," Guinna pointed out, though her argument didn't really make much sense. She tried to understand why she felt so defensive, and then she gave up and focused on keeping pace with Trillian.

"Yes," agreed Trillian, unruffled, "because one of your Knights is being eaten alive by guilt and sorrow, and he has perhaps slipped through the cracks with the rebuilding of your Court."

Guinna pressed her lips together. She couldn't think of a suitable reply, so she said nothing. Trillian's smooth voice contained no accusation that she could hear, but she felt her cheeks heating again all the same.

"I almost flew," said Trillian, glancing up at the blue sky, "but I did not want to make you uncomfortable with the prospect of another journey by air."

"Who said I would be uncomfortable with it?" Guinna asked. Her skirts tangled around her legs and she twitched them free with a practiced hand, barely breaking stride.

"No one," said Trillian with a casual shrug.

Guinna sighed lightly. They rounded the corner and the plaza before the great cathedral spread before them. The white stones shimmered in the sun. Flashes of movement near the roof of the cathedral caught Guinna's eye, and she couldn't help but stare at the spectacle of several winged *faehal* hauling blocks of white stone into the air, the blocks suspended by ropes and straps. Several other Vyldgard stood at a short distance, observing. Sun glinted off one Sidhe's silver hair. With a start, even at this distance, Guinna recognized Tyr. She'd glimpsed him from across the icy throne room in the aftermath of the battle, and she'd had the chance to see him at a closer range when they'd burned Mab's body. But it was still strange to see him again in Faeortalam.

"Repairs to the outer wall," said Trillian, pointing up at several blackened craters blasted into the wall. Guinna knew they were the work of Mab's vicious enchanted fire, launched by catapult in her attack on the Vyldgard. The Valkyrie commander slowed her pace and then paused as Guinna watched one pair of *faehal* bring a huge block of stone level with one of the blast marks. Their Valkyrie riders continually checked their positioning, and then one of them whistled to the Vyldgard on the ground.

Tyr stepped forward. Guinna recognized the short-haired smith Thea next to him, and on his other side stood a pale young woman with violently curly red hair. A familiar pendant glinted at the young woman's throat.

"Paladin Vivian," supplied Trillian. "She is learning much from Tyr."

"So, Tyr is Vyldgard now?" Guinna asked stiffly.

"He has not been baptized yet," replied Trillian with another little shrug. "It is not surprising that he needs time to consider his path in our world."

Guinna let her eyes wander down the line of those on the ground. Next to Vivian, there was a tall Seelie Knight who wore

Titania's sigil on his breast: her Vaelanseld, Knight Niall. How was it that the Summer Queen saw fit to continue their close friendship with the Vyldgard, without so much as an offer of assistance to the Unseelie? The Vyldgard and the Seelie *had* united to free them from Mab, at great risk to themselves, Guinna reminded herself. But she still felt like an outcast, watching the easy interaction between the Paladin and the Seelie Knight. Thea leaned around Tyr to ask Niall a question, gesturing up to the block of stone that Tyr was now moving into place with a complex series of gestures, sketching runes into the air that lit corresponding runes on the block of stone. Dust trickled down the wall as the stone slid into place. Even for someone who was not new to runes and *taebramh,* it was an impressive sight.

The pair of Valkyrie carefully adjusted the altitude and positioning of their mounts, slowly allowing slack in the ropes as runes nudged the straps down the length of the block. With a grinding sound, the stone slid fully into the wall, the lines falling free and the winged *faehal* wheeling away. Thea and Niall moved toward the other blocks of stone staged on the ground, stacked like child's blocks on the hard-beaten earth. With practiced efficiency, they looped the straps around another block. Thea produced a rune-stick and activated the runes on the new block. Tyr turned toward the Paladin, motioning to her. She grinned and nodded, clearly accepting his direction that she handle this next repair.

A sick knot tightened in Guinna's stomach at the camaraderie between the small group of Vyldgard and Seelie. She felt Trillian's gaze on her, and she carefully schooled her face into polite interest, but nothing more.

"If you would like any help in building in your part of the City, I'm certain Queen Vell would be open to the idea," said Trillian.

"I will mention it to Queen Andraste," said Guinna with false lightness. She turned away from the construction. "Where is Ramel?"

Trillian nodded at the cathedral. "Inside."

The Valkyrie commander led Guinna up the steps of the Vyldgard stronghold. "Maeve says your healers have been a great help in her ward."

"Eamon and his workers are very skilled," replied Guinna in agreement. She omitted the fact that they'd had reason to hone their skills over the past months: Mab had employed them to revive her victims, refusing to let those upon whom she wished to exact her twisted revenge escape her into death.

"This way." Trillian led her through several passages into the portion of the Vyldgard base which resembled their wartime accommodations on the journey across the Deadlands. Jewel-colored hangings separated the different compartments, and bright rugs covered the stone floor beneath their feet in an artfully haphazard riot of color. Though she'd stayed in the Vyldretning's own rooms in this very cathedral, Guinna still felt out of place, like she'd stepped into a foreign world.

"Knight Ramel has turned to bodily pleasures to distract himself from his sorrow," said Trillian softly as they continued down to passageway. "We do not judge anyone in the Wild Court for their private habits, and all his partners have been willing, of course. But Moira tells me that she believes he is mixing *vinaess* and white shroud in order to sleep."

"Dangerous," murmured Guinna.

"The Seer tried to talk to him," continued Trillian, "but the conversation did not go...well. He thought that, given your history, you may have better luck."

Guinna wondered what exactly about their history the Seer knew. Did his ability extend into the past, or had Arcana given him knowledge when she pulled him from the brink of death after Andraste stabbed him in the throne room of Malravenar?

Trillian stopped in front of a ruby curtain. Guinna heard faint voices, though the occupants must have been no more than a few strides away from them. She felt a grudging appreciation for the skill of the Vyldretning in the enchantment of the Wild Court's strong-hold.

"No point in asking permission," Trillian said, mostly to herself, as she swept aside the ruby curtain and motioned for Guinna to step inside. The chamber, while small, was much larger than it appeared on the outside, its walls delineated by more ruby curtains, the same rugs thrown over the floor in the chamber as in the passageway. A pile of furs looked to be a bed, and a table and two chairs sat in one corner. Guinna took in the disarray of the little room in one glance: several pewter jugs stood on the table, along with a myriad assortment of plates and stacks of different cups. A sword lay beneath the table half-sheathed like a forgotten child's toy. Bits of clothing littered the rugs. Guinna turned her attention to the occupants of the room. A woman with golden hair that coiled like a live creature about her head stood near the table, blocking Ramel from reaching it. Ramel, shirtless and barefoot, his trousers only laced halfway, leaned toward the woman as he spoke in a low voice.

"You've no right," he said to the woman, scowling at her. The expression looked strange on his handsome face. He'd always been so jovial, quick to relieve tension with a joke, thought Guinna. She caught a fleeting impression of a tangle of scars across his chest, red and angry, raised ropes twisting over his skin. He stabbed a finger into the air toward the Vyldgard woman.

"I've every right to step in when you might be killing yourself," the woman retorted, eyes flashing. Guinna saw she held a leather pouch in one hand.

"Why do you care?" demanded Ramel, narrowing bloodshot eyes. He seemed not to have noticed Trillian and Guinna, though they stood only a bit more than an arm's length from him, in plain view.

"There are more than just me who care whether you live or die," the woman said steadily. Ramel took a step toward her and she widened her stance, clearly ready to wrestle him if the need arose.

Ramel clenched his jaw. It looked as though he hadn't bothered to comb his auburn hair in days. He leaned toward the woman, reminding Guinna unpleasantly of a snake readying to strike. "You're nothing but a convenient lay," he sneered. "There were willing women before you and there will be willing women after you."

"Be that as it may," said the woman, unimpressed by his rude words, "I will not watch you kill yourself."

Ramel let loose a tirade of uncouth insults, covering everything from the woman's parentage to her skills as a lover. The growl of his voice didn't sound anything like the man that Guinna knew.

"Ramel," she said in shock and reprimand.

Ramel turned. Guinna had to stop herself from taking a step back at the force of the anger written across his face.

"Ramel," she said again. "Your behavior is hardly fitting a Knight of the Unseelie Court."

"Moira," said Trillian quietly, nodding to the woman, who grimly returned the greeting.

"My treatment was hardly fitting for a Knight of the Unseelie Court," retorted Ramel, his voice just short of a snarl. He motioned with one hand to the scars across his chest, the cruel rune that Mab had used to control him overlaid by mottled burn scars. Guinna saw that the skin at his wrists was still raw from bindings. She wondered when that had happened.

"You're right," she said with a nod, stepping closer to him. "You are absolutely right."

He chuckled humorlessly. "And your agreement is supposed to make it better?" He spread his arms to encompass the disorder of his little room.

"No," Guinna said calmly. She felt like she was trying to soothe a spooked *faehal*. "I don't know how to make it better, Ramel, but I know that I don't want you to put yourself in danger."

"In danger," he repeated scornfully. "I survived serving the Mad Queen. Being *bound* to her. Do you have any idea what that was like?"

"No," she said again. "But you are not the only one who suffered at her hands."

"*Not the only one?*" Ramel shouted, his voice fraying at the edges. Trillian and Moira both leaned forward, clearly ready to leap into action and restrain him, but he didn't close the distance between him and Guinna.

"You are not the only one," she repeated, her voice jarringly quiet after his outburst. "You are not alone."

Ramel laughed again, his eyes glittering above the bruised half-moons that stood out shockingly against his pale skin. "How wrong you are. My fate is to be alone."

Just as quickly as he'd shouted in anger, he looked forlorn.

"I could not save her then," he said, his voice barely louder than a whisper.

"She did not want to be saved," said Moira softly.

Ramel continued as though Moira hadn't spoken. "I could not save her then and I cannot save her now." He closed his eyes, swaying slightly. "But *he* survived, and he looks so much like her…"

Moira glanced at Trillian significantly. Guinna frowned. Something about Ramel's words made her uneasy.

"Ramel," she said gently but firmly. "Whom are you talking about?"

Ramel didn't reply, keeping his eyes closed. Trillian readied herself to reach for him – it looked as though he were about to collapse.

"Ramel," Guinna tried again. This time he opened his eyes and looked at her. "Are you talking about Molly?"

Ramel started. "Don't say that name to me," he growled. "I never want to hear it again."

"I don't understand, Ramel. Please help me understand. I'm confused." Guinna tried to keep him talking. "I thought you were speaking about – about the *fendhionne*, just now."

"She betrayed me," said Ramel, shaking his head. "She broke my heart long before she killed me."

"Killed you...?" Guinna looked hopelessly to Trillian and Moira, who both echoed her expression of confusion. "Please talk to me, Ramel. Tell me what happened."

Ramel's eyes went unfocused. "After she killed me, after she broke Mab's hold...her words were crueler than any pain she inflicted on my body."

A flash of understanding tore through Guinna's mind like lightning. *But he survived, and he looks so much like her...* "Ramel," she said, "what did the *fendhionne* tell you? Please tell me. Please tell *us*. We want to help."

"It's a cruel lie," whispered Ramel, his eyes haunted. "All I love turns to ash."

"Ramel, what did the *fendhionne* tell you?" prompted Guinna again.

He clenched his fists by his sides. "The bone sorcerer's apprentice told me after she killed me that Rye may still be alive."

Chapter 5

Quinn found Liam in the practice yard with Finnead. He hadn't realized how much time he'd been spending in the healing ward, even though Niamh had been healing well. He'd started helping with small tasks, some of the healers joking with him that they should make him an apprentice. But now he couldn't step foot in there, and he tried to avoid anywhere that Niamh might be. The practice yards weren't exactly a safe bet, but he'd heard that all the Valkyrie were tied up with repairing the outer wall of the cathedral.

"You're getting much faster, even without the First," said Finnead approvingly to Liam as Quinn approached their ring. "Have you had any luck in controlling the appearance of your Sight?"

Liam grimaced. "Yes and no. Just like before, it seems to still be tied to my stress level. I mean, it appears when I'm in a situation where my heart rate is elevated, things like that."

"And the remnant of Arcana still affects the power of your visions?" the dark-haired Knight asked in interest.

"It's about a fifty-fifty shot that she supercharges my Sight," replied Liam with a nod. "I've gotten used to the narration, but it's still weird."

"How do you still think things are weird after all our time here?" Quinn said with half a grin. Liam turned to him and for a long minute, Quinn thought that his old team leader would hold a grudge for the less-than-friendly exchange they'd had by the steps of the cathedral after the battle.

Then Liam shrugged his muscled shoulders and gave him an answering grin. "Some old habits die hard. It's weird to have another voice in your head other than your own."

"Come to practice with us, Quinn?" Finnead inquired brightly.

"If you don't mind me slowing you down," he replied with easy humor. He still felt frozen inside, but he was good at making others see what he wanted them to see. Right now, he didn't want anyone to know how badly Niamh had hurt him. He didn't want to display his weakness for everyone to see.

"You've improved as well," Finnead replied, his dark hair shimmering like a raven's wing in the sunlight as he executed a few sword strokes with lazy grace.

"Let's see if you still compliment me after I get my ass handed to me a few times," Quinn replied. He glanced around the practice yard and rubbed the scar on his chest, still pink and new. They'd rebuilt the practice yard and the forge with surprising speed after Mab's enchanted globes of fire had wreaked havoc during her attack on the Vyldgard. He remembered the impact, the sound squeezed out of the air by the force of the explosion, the dust coating all the survivors in white, like they were already ghosts. He took a deep breath and rode out the recollection for a moment, letting it wash over him, and then he carefully set it aside. Burying those things didn't do much good, but neither did wallowing in them.

"It looks good, doesn't it?" Liam said.

"Yeah." Quinn nodded and drew his sword from his sheath. Neither of them said something stupid like it looked like it never happened – because the section of the wall that had been blasted away looked slightly different than the rest of the wall, and the forge looked foreign, its roof higher and its walls protruding farther into the practice yard. Chael and Thea had taken advantage of the opportunity to rebuild the forge to their specifications. They'd made the best of a horrible situation, Quinn thought as he ran through warm-up drills, feeling the muscles in his arms begin to burn with the exertion.

"Shall we have another match while Quinn prepares?" Finnead asked Liam.

"By all means." Liam sketched half a bow to Finnead in invitation.

Quinn turned toward the practice ring so he could watch the match. He'd never seen Liam's Arcana-improved Sight in action. He switched his sword to his left hand to warm up that arm as well, even though he felt like an idiot when he tried to be ambidextrous.

Liam and Finnead stepped back to the edge of the ring, gazing at each other with calm intent from opposite sides. It didn't escape Quinn's attention that a few of the fighters in rings close to theirs paused their own training to watch the match as well. Quinn evaluated the two fighters with a detached eye. Liam had the height and reach advantage over the slimmer Finnead, but the Sidhe, though smaller, had the edge in speed. If Quinn were Liam, he'd try to keep the fight in close proximity, pin down the faster fighter and make him expend energy in fending off strong strokes at a close range.

Finnead nodded slightly to Liam, and at that signal, they both leapt toward each other, like a wolf and a lion rushing into a deadly fight. The speed of both fighters almost made Quinn dizzy. Their swords flashed, and snatches of color emerged from the whirlwind: the golden gleam of Liam's hair, the glint of Finnead's drowning-blue eyes, the paleness of Finnead's skin contrasting with Liam's tanned forearms. Liam moved faster than Quinn thought it possible for a man of his size to move, parrying Finnead's lightning-quick sword strokes, countering with his own attacks, adjusting the space between them fluidly. Dust rose around their feet and hung in the air, a dun fog reaching their knees. A few of the other observers murmured to one another as they stepped closer, drawn in by the magnificent display of speed and skill.

"The Seer will win this one," said a red-haired lad that Quinn vaguely recognized.

"You just think the Seer is prettier than Finnead," replied his companion puckishly.

"You know I have eyes for no one but Sage," said the redhead.

Now Quinn knew where he remembered him from: the healing ward. He'd seen the red-haired Vyldgard fighter sitting by the bedside of one of the wounded Seelie – Sage, as the Vyldgard had just said.

"I said it to the Bearer and thus I'll say it to you, my friend: Variety is the spice of life," retorted the Seelie, grinning devilishly.

"There's not many that can offend me, Ariel, and you're not on that list," said the Vyldgard lad coolly with half a smile.

Ariel laughed and they both subsided into silence, watching the match. The pace still had not slowed. Every time Quinn thought that Finnead would slide his sword through Liam's guard, the bigger fighter spun away with ridiculous alacrity. Several times Quinn even thought that Liam would overcome Finnead's defenses, but their swords arced through the air and clashed unabated.

The Sidhe observers felt it before Quinn did. He saw them straighten, Ariel cocking his head to the side and his companion taking half a step forward, eyes sharpening. Quinn took a breath and let himself go still, trying to detect what they were feeling. The hairs on his arms rose as his skin rippled with goose bumps. The air tightened, electricity building in the practice ring. A copper spark escaped Liam's mouth, glowing garishly as it whirled in the eddies created by their movement. For a reason Quinn didn't quite understand, he held his breath, reining in his instinct to step back from the ring. He'd never been near a lightning strike, but he somehow knew this was what it felt like in the moments before fire tore everything apart.

"This is certainly interesting," said a new voice next to Quinn. He managed not to jump in surprise.

The Bearer stood next to him, the Sword on her back and her plain sword at her hip, her golden hair braided in an intricate crown that reminded Quinn painfully of the Valkyrie's favored style.

"Yep," he replied, turning his attention back to the match as though something as simple as a girl's hair in a braid hadn't just punched the breath out of him.

Tess didn't say anything else, watching the match between her brother and Finnead with professional interest written across her face. Quinn remembered suddenly that Finnead had given up his memories of a certain time in order to restore Andraste's mind, and that time included when the Knight had fallen in love with the Princess destined to become the Unseelie Queen. Niamh had told him about it and added that some had sacrificed much more than memories, so she didn't understand the great fuss over the "noble" Knight.

The air tightened further, feeling as though it were actually pulling on Quinn's skin, as though a current funneled into the practice ring. Out of the corner of his eye, he saw Tess's hand move to her throat, press the skin there and then drift back down to her side.

Another copper spark emerged from the whirlwind of the two fighters. Somehow Quinn saw the final blows, despite the inhuman speed: Finnead lunged at Liam, his sword tracing a graceful, deadly arc toward Liam's unprotected side. Liam caught Finnead's blade with his own, twisting his wrist to lock the slimmer man into a body-to-body duel of strength. Quinn suddenly wondered if the two men were more evenly matched in strength than he'd thought, because Finnead was Sidhe after all, and one of the Vyldretning's Three. The dark-haired Knight held his own, grinning at Liam. Tess leaned forward from her position next to Quinn. He wondered briefly who she wanted to win.

With a heave that Quinn knew was herculean, Finnead created space between the two blades, forcing Liam back a step, his beautiful face alight with a fierce joy. Rather than continuing on the offensive, he circled Liam with sleek stealth, his movements deliberate. Liam moved forward for the stroke that in his mind would end the duel, and Finnead sidestepped neatly, his blade moving toward Liam's neck.

An invisible explosion shook the ground and threw Finnead to his back in the dirt with such force that his blade skidded out of his hand. The blast only manifested outside the practice ring as a push of strong wind that Quinn leaned into for a moment, and then it was gone.

Tess rushed forward into the ring as Liam dropped his sword with a curse, turning toward Finnead, who looked to be unconscious.

"Don't touch him," snarled Tess with a force that surprised Quinn. He stepped into the ring too, walking toward Liam and catching his team leader's eye.

"I didn't…I don't know…" Liam said, breathing heavily, sweat gleaming on his brow as he looked helplessly over at Tess, now kneeling next to Finnead.

"Take a step back, give 'em some space," said Quinn quietly but firmly, gripping Liam's shoulder.

"I'm one of the Queen's Three too," Liam protested.

"And she's the Bearer," countered Quinn. "She's none too happy with the whammy you just put on Finnead, so give her a minute."

"Should I go for Sage?" asked the redheaded Vyldgard fighter, his youthful face grave with concern.

"Yes," replied Tess shortly.

"I'll go, Robin," said Ariel. "You stay, you know more healing than me."

Robin nodded, and Ariel sprinted away on light feet.

"I'll get him some water," Robin said, moving quickly toward the fountain at the other end of the practice yard.

Most of the activity in the practice yard had ceased. It was mostly Seelie and Vyldgard fighters, with a few Unseelie. Quinn surveyed their faces, catching glimpses of curiosity, concern and condemnation before their inscrutable Sidhe nature rearranged their expressions into fathomless perfection, like marble carvings.

He stepped away from Liam. Crowd control—*that*, he could do. He took a deep breath and squared his shoulders. "Nothing to see!" he said, his voice just this side of a shout. "Back to your own business or leave!"

A few of the fighters looked at him in surprise, but to his gratification most turned back to their own practice rings. He looked around the yard for another moment, letting his expression turn challenging, but nobody contradicted him. He turned his attention back to their practice ring. Robin returned with the water and took a knee beside Tess, who pressed a gentle hand to Finnead's chest as he stirred and tried to rise.

"Give yourself a moment," she said.

To Quinn's surprise, Finnead obeyed her, resting his head back on the dirt again. He could see the glimmer of Finnead's half-open eyes and he knew that whatever Liam did, whatever that explosion was, it had frightening power. Not many things could knock a Sidhe Knight flat on his back and make him stay there for a few minutes.

Liam made a small sound, stepped outside the ring and retched. Quinn let him have a minute to do his business – no man really liked anyone hovering over him while he was busy being sick. As Liam kicked dirt over his mess in disgust, Quinn said in a low voice, "What happened?"

"I don't *know*," growled Liam.

"You do know," Quinn pressed. "What happened?"

Liam glanced at Finnead on the ground and grimaced. "I can't…sometimes *she* just…does things." He swallowed hard. Quinn saw the fear lurking in his friend's eyes. They hid it well most of the time, but they could see it in each other. It was easier to recognize in someone else if it was your own habit, too.

"Hey," he said. "You listen to me. You're in charge, not her. It's *your* body. It's *your* call."

"It doesn't feel like that sometimes," Liam said.

"I don't care what it feels like," Quinn snapped, hitting Liam's arm with an open palm. He needed to jolt his friend out of this stupor. "You're in charge. Got it?"

Liam still looked a little shaken, but he pressed his lips together and straightened. He nodded.

"Good," said Quinn approvingly.

Tess and Robin conferenced in low voices over Finnead. They seemed to reach an agreement, because they helped the Knight slowly sit up. Robin handed him a cup of water and Finnead drank it himself, though Quinn saw his hand shaking.

Liam winced at the same time that Finnead spilled what was left of his water.

"I have to go," Liam said. He ran one hand through his hair. "She's not happy."

"Liam," said Finnead from the ground. "I'm fine. I will tell the Vyldretning as much." The Vyldgard Knight even mustered a smile. "Truly, no worse a blow than I've taken in training before."

Liam smiled humorlessly. "You know as well as I do that's not true, Finn. And remember our connection works both ways."

"You don't want to keep Vell waiting," said Tess in a tight voice.

Liam nodded and sighed. He picked up his sword, sheathed it and walked away, passing Sage, who entered the practice yards at a run.

"I'm fine," repeated Finnead in protest as Robin went to meet the healer.

"If you were fine you'd be able to stand up on your own," retorted Tess with her no-nonsense voice.

"Liam did not strike me intentionally," Finnead pointed out.

Quinn stood to the side, wondering if he could offer to help without setting a match to the tinder currently stacked up in Tess's eyes.

"Intentional or not, it was a powerful blast," she said. "It's more worrying if it's *not* intentional." She sat back on her heels, falling silent.

Finnead reached for her hand. "This is not your fault."

Quinn frowned, trying to follow the conversation.

"If I hadn't bargained with Arcana, if I hadn't given her permission…" she said in a low voice.

"Then your brother would be dead," said Finnead firmly.

"If there's a deity inside him, if only a fragment of her can do that to him…" Tess began, but Finnead cut her off.

"No," he said with such vehemence that he winced. "Do not even think that he would be better off dead. The world would be less bright without him."

Tess narrowed her eyes, an unspoken question on her face.

"Your brother has become a brother to me," Finnead said. "He has helped me through dark times. I will not forget what he has done for me, nor what he has done for our Court."

"But it's getting worse," said Tess quietly. "The things that Arcana does…that the First does, using him as her conduit…if he can't control it, it could become…"

"Bad," supplied Robin. Sage knelt next to Finnead, beginning a healer's examination with clinical efficiency. Quinn remembered the way that all the humor would disappear from Duke's easygoing face when he transitioned into his medic duties. They'd needed him a few times, thankfully not for anything too serious. He missed his wiry teammate with a sudden fierce intensity.

Finnead stoically endured Sage's evaluation. Tess glanced at Robin when Sage's hands on Finnead's ribs prompted an intake of breath from the Knight.

"A few cracked ribs and most likely some bruises elsewhere, but nothing more," Sage pronounced.

"Nothing more," repeated Tess under her breath, shaking her head.

"Let us deal with this, Tess," said Finnead. "Please."

Her expression softened at his last word. Then she seemed to realize that Finnead still held her hand, and two spots of color appeared high on her cheeks. She cleared her throat and withdrew her hand from beneath his. "I'm not going to lie to you. I'm going to talk to Vell about it later."

"I wouldn't expect anything less," said Finnead with the ghost of a smile. He arched an eyebrow. "May I have your permission to stand?"

Tess chuckled. "You're beginning to sound like Robin."

"I'll take that as a compliment," Robin said cheekily.

"Can I help?" Quinn asked, stepping forward. He felt awkward next to all these luminaries of the Fae world: The Bearer of the Iron Sword, one of the Vyldretning's Three, a respected Seelie healer and a trusted Vyldgard fighter. In answer, Finnead reached up a hand and Quinn took it, pulling the Knight to his feet and pushing down the strange sense of gratitude that he felt at that simple action of acceptance. Finnead glanced down at Quinn's vibrant tattoos.

"Perhaps you can show us how to make such as these," he said.

"I'm no tattoo artist," demurred Quinn.

"But surely you know the method," said Finnead, still examining one of the tattoos on Quinn's forearm: a dagger through a heart, done in the traditional nautical style known as Sailor Jerry. "You must have observed them putting the tattoos onto your skin."

"Yeah," Quinn said, "but watching and doing are two different things."

"Indeed, they are," said Finnead with a catlike smile, releasing his hand. Quinn watched him to make sure he was steady on his feet, and then he stepped away.

Tess looked at Sage.

"I'll accompany you back to the hall," said Sage to Finnead.

"I would not mind the company," replied Finnead easily. Robin retrieved Finnead's sword and offered it to him hilt-first. After sheathing his sword with a nod of thanks, Finnead walked with Sage toward the entrance of the practice yards.

"You wanted to go with him," Robin said quietly to Tess, his voice uncharacteristically serious.

She sighed. "Yes. But I have to be…careful."

"And why is that?"

"You know why," she retorted, unsheathing her plain blade and beginning her warm up.

"He doesn't remember Andraste," Quinn said. He rubbed his chin. "Thought he seemed…happier."

"He is," Tess said, sending her sword singing vengefully through the air.

Quinn raised his eyebrows. "And that's a bad thing?"

"It's not a *bad* thing," said Tess.

Ariel made his way casually back over to their practice ring, and at a look from Robin the two of them diplomatically moved to another ring, discussing their next exercise in unconcerned voices. Quinn realized that maybe he *could* be useful.

"You've probably got a lot on your mind right now," he said to Tess, watching the younger woman as he stepped into the circle and began a series of more intensive drills. Handling a sword worked different muscles than pretty much any other weapon he'd handled, but he finally felt that he was starting to get the hang of it. He glanced at Tess as he finished his warm-up. She stared down at the hard-packed dirt as she rolled up her shirtsleeves, the emerald whorls encircling her hand and snaking up her right arm more vivid than any tattoo.

"Hey," he said, "maybe you'll feel better after you kick my butt a few times."

That comment wrung a weak smile from her at least. She arched an eyebrow.

"You're getting pretty good. I wouldn't say it's a done deal for every match now."

He chuckled. "Yeah, I might be getting pretty good, but that still doesn't mean much compared against all the fighters here."

Her smile widened. "Niamh well enough to hand it to you on a daily basis, eh?"

The dart of pain at the mention of Niamh caught Quinn unaware. He cleared his throat. "I mean, she's busy with other stuff." God, he sounded like a teenage boy trying to avoid telling his friends that his girlfriend dumped him. He stared at the gleam of sunlight on his sword, fighting the urge to break down and tell Tess everything. She had enough problems of her own. Everyone did. He didn't need to burden anyone with his stupid romantic troubles, even if it did feel like his heart was being wrenched from his chest when he thought about Niamh.

"Want to talk about it?" Tess said, her voice disarmingly gentle.

He didn't meet her eyes, because if he did he was pretty sure he'd start bawling. "Nah. I'd rather sweat it out."

She shrugged. "Works for me. Three to start?"

"Sounds good." He raised his sword.

Half an hour later, they finished the third of the three matches. Quinn straightened, wiping sweat from his forehead and trying not to pant. Tess looked annoyingly fresh, her golden hair still pinned up in its braid, though he did spot a glimmer of sweat on her brow as she turned.

"Let's get some water," she suggested. They walked toward the fountain at the other end of the yard, passing other fighters in their own rings, the clash of swords peppered with the occasional exclamation of triumph or dismay. Tess handed Quinn one of the cups hung by the fountain and filled her own. Quinn took three large swallows of the cold, fresh water and then poured the rest over his head, combing back his hair with one hand and sighing in satisfaction.

"You going to grow your hair long?" Tess asked as they stood and watched the activity in the practice yard.

Quinn shrugged. "Why not? Don't have any regulations I have to uphold anymore, since I'm technically dead."

Tess snorted. "Not like you guys ever followed the regulations for grooming anyway."

"Hey," he protested, "when in Rome, you know? Gotta look the part if we're out among the savages." He rubbed his chin. He'd stayed clean-shaven because that was Niamh's preference: Sidhe men didn't wear any facial hair. He wasn't even sure if they could grow beards on their annoyingly perfect faces. "Maybe I'll grow everything out."

Tess glanced at him. "So, is it a permanent thing, this...separation?"

He cleared his throat. "Looks like it."

"That sucks."

That surprised a chuckle out of him. "Thought you forgot how to talk like a normal person."

Tess grinned. "Sometimes it feels like it." She shrugged. "It comes and goes."

He took another sip of water. This was one of those days when the conversation at the practice yard was more important than the actual practice. "How're you doing, after the battle?"

Tess pressed her lips together in thought. Then she raised an eyebrow. "It sucks."

"That seems to be a general term of description right now."

Tess sighed. "There's a lot going on. It seems like no matter what progress we make, there's always more problems than solutions." She shook her head. "First it was defeating Malravenar. Then the bone sorcerer. Then Mab. Now... I mean, I don't know what the next challenge or who the next enemy will be. But I just feel like I'm constantly on edge." She took a draught from her cup and refilled it. Quinn waited. After a pause, she continued. "I didn't expect Molly to do what she did. That...hurt."

"I think that's an understatement."

Tess put her free hand on her hip. "And so is you saying that Niamh is 'busy with other stuff.'"

"Point taken."

She grimaced. "Sorry. That was mean."

"It wasn't mean. It was honest." At her probing look, he relented with a smile. "Okay, it was a *little* mean."

"There's just so much to sort through. And without a defined enemy, without a mission, I feel like I don't really know where I fit in," she said with an air of confession.

"Welcome to the club," he said dryly. "We should come up with a secret handshake."

"Or a password into a clubhouse where we throw our own pity parties." Tess glanced at him and smiled.

"Small violins and cakes," he agreed. "We can even play…what's that song…*It's my party and I'll cry if I want to* – hey, I'm a good singer!" he protested as she slapped his arm. A few of the Sidhe closer to them glanced over questioningly at his sudden burst of falsetto singing.

"Are you a karaoke champ?" Tess said, her voice choked with laughter.

"I mean, what if I am? You saying I don't have pipes? I should probably sing another song that's more in my range…"

"No!" she protested, breaking down in laughter.

He chuckled and finished his water, wiping down the cup with the cloth kept on hand for that purpose, and hanging it back on a hook by the fountain. "Up for a few more rounds?" He paused as he realized Tess was looking at him speculatively. "What?"

"You know, you should come talk to Liam a little more often," she said. "He needs someone other than me to remind him of who he used to be."

"Who he *used* to be?"

"I mean, he's someone else now. I'm someone else now, too. And you are as well, even though you don't want to admit it," she said as they began to walk back to their ring. "This world changes us. Not necessarily in a bad way, but…I'm worried about Liam."

"You're worried that the whammy Arcana put on him is getting worse," Quinn clarified as they reached their spot.

"I don't know how to help him," replied Tess, "and I know he doesn't want to worry me. I'm afraid that he's hiding how bad it is."

"Do we know that it's a bad thing? Just asking," Quinn said, putting up a hand as Tess looked at him sharply.

She took a breath. "I know. I've been talking to Vell about it. I think he doesn't want to show any one person how bad it is. She says that his Sight is getting stronger, but it's also taking a larger toll on him. While I was gone, he had a few visions that laid him out for the rest of the day."

"That sounds bad," Quinn said quietly.

"He puts so much time into taking care of others that I don't think he's taking care of himself. And I don't want it to get to a point where none of us can do anything to help because we didn't know the extent of the problem."

"Sounds a lot like what Finnead was doing before Vell took his memories," he pointed out.

"It's *similar*, but it's not the same. With Finnead, it was his own guilt, his own issues with what he'd experienced and what had happened in the past." A furrow appeared on Tess's forehead. "With Liam, it's that bit of Arcana that somehow survived and is inhabiting him. But I don't know how to get that out. I don't know if we *can*. Would it kill him, would he even survive?" She shook her head unhappily. "And I'm the one who made that decision."

"Now who's the one letting their own guilt get to them?" asked Quinn. "Seriously, Finnead had a good point. Liam's alive because of you. Don't question your decision. We've just gotta move forward and figure out a solution to the problem." He rested his hand on the pommel of his sword, a posture that reminded him comfortingly of resting his hand on the butt of his sidearm at his hip.

"And you'll help me?" she asked, looking up at him. "You'll help me to help Liam, even if he gets mad at us?"

"Of course, little boss," he said, using the nickname that all of Liam's team had teasingly called Tess during their first days in the Fae world. To his alarm, Tess's lips quivered, and her brows drew together like she was fighting the urge to cry. She lunged forward and wrapped her arms around him in a fierce hug, muttering a word that might have been "Thanks" into his chest. He circled one arm around her shoulders. She was the Bearer of the Iron Sword, and she was legendary in the Fae world, but Tess was still young. Her scars proved her toughness and the respect of the Sidhe proved her dedication to what was right, but she still needed friends to give her a hug every so often.

"Hey, I got ya," he said soothingly.

"Should I be worried?" said a familiar voice behind Quinn.

Tess straightened and peeked over Quinn's shoulder. The way her face lit up told Quinn that the voice could along belong to one person.

"Well, that depends," Tess said teasingly. "You go off into the wilderness and leave me without an adequate supply of hugs, I'll be forced to find them elsewhere."

Luca gave a mock growl as he strode over to their practice ring, still dressed for travel through the forests in a worn leather vest, a fur thrown over his shoulders. That phantom pain twisted in Quinn's chest again as Tess stepped away from him and Luca swept her into his arms, kissing her deeply. They gazed at each other like all the rest of the world had fallen away.

"How was the journey?" she murmured, reaching up to tuck a piece of his golden hair behind his ear. "You left so soon after the battle."

"Too soon," he agreed, catching her hand and kissing her palm. "But it is time for us to rebuild."

She nodded and then smiled up at him. "Just take me with you next time."

He chuckled. "I would not deny you anything, *anganhjarta*." He kissed her again and when he drew back said approvingly, "You have been hard at work. I can taste it on your lips."

"Quinn and I were sparring," Tess said with a nod, motioning to Quinn.

He raised his chin toward Luca. "Welcome back, man."

"I was not gone long," Luca said easily. He pulled the fur from his broad shoulders. "But thank you. Have you been practicing with axes lately?"

"Not as much as I should," Quinn admitted. Luca had taught them all the basics of fighting with the *ulfdrengr*'s preferred weapon back in the early days. "I've been slacking."

"Well, let us take away some of that…*slack*," said Luca with a lupine grin, pulling the two axes from his belt and tossing one to Quinn.

"You sure you don't want to take a minute to relax? You just got back," said Quinn, hefting the axe in his hand.

"We will have young *ulfdrengr* to train soon, I think. You are good practice," said Luca with a nod. Tess bit her lip to hide her grin.

"Then nothing to it but to do it," replied Quinn, grinning as they squared off against each other. He needed this, he thought. Pulling away wasn't the answer. And he made a silent vow that he'd help in whatever way he could – with Liam, with Tess, with all of them. He felt as if a weight lifted from his chest, and even though he knew he was about to be schooled by the best axe fighter in the White City, he felt better than he had in weeks.

Chapter 6

Vivian leaned back in her chair by the fireplace. She was still getting used to the casual opulence of her new surroundings. The Vyldgard weren't as glitzy as the Seelie, who sometimes reminded her of refined and elegant French courtiers. The Unseelie she hadn't quite been able to pin down. They were elegant as well, their beauty pale and shining like the moon, but they'd withdrawn into themselves after the battle. The Vyldgard reminded her a bit of what she imagined Vikings had been – the *ulfdrengr* certainly added their fierce Northern attitude to the mix, but the Sidhe who'd come to the Vyldgard, regardless of their Seelie or Unseelie roots, all exuded a sense of unbridled joy, reveling in every aspect of their beauty and their freedom, both their sensuality and their warrior spirit more evident than the Seelie and the Unseelie.

"Deep in thought?" said Niall from his seat opposite her.

She grinned. "Just finalizing my course of study in my head. I spoke to Thea and she said she'd teach me forge runes. I think I'll do that first thing while I'm fresh, at least for the first couple of weeks. I don't want to have any accidents because I'm tired."

Niall nodded. "Practical."

"Moira offered to help me with my riding and archery, so I think that will be after the forge lessons. Archery first and then riding." Vivian knew she didn't need Niall's approval, but she still wanted him to know her intentions when it came to her training. She wanted him to know that she was taking her studies seriously. No resting on laurels here. "That should take me to lunch. I'll take an hour to eat and then I'll go to the healing ward. Tess introduced me to a healer named Sage, and I'm going to apprentice with him to learn the basics."

"Sage is a good teacher and a good healer." Niall gave his taciturn seal of approval.

Vivian pulled at a curl. "Sage's partner Robin is about my size, so he'll be my sparring partner for a while."

"Be sure not to underestimate yourself," said the Seelie Knight. The firelight gleamed on his pale hair, pulled back into its usual neat ponytail.

Vivian felt color rising into her cheeks. A poker face was another thing she needed to work on. "I'm trying not to, but I don't have a baseline. I don't have anything to compare myself against except for Tess, I guess, and she's miles ahead of me."

"She has been here longer than you, and she is the Bearer," he replied, as though that explained everything.

"Right," Vivian said. She cleared her throat.

"And your evenings? How do you intend to spend them?"

"Well, first there's dinner," she replied. "Food is important. I pretty much plan my day around it." Niall chuckled, and she grinned, happy that he'd gotten the joke. "Other than that, I'll give myself an hour to wash up and stretch so that I can keep moving forward in training – reduce my chance of injury, I mean. And then... Tess gave me a few books to read, so I'll start with those." She pointed to a stack of leather-bound books over on her desk. "I'll also ask my other instructors for any material they think would supplement my practical lessons."

"You are disciplined," said Niall.

Her cheeks warmed at the note of approval in his voice.

"Just keep in mind that you should allow time for enjoyable pursuits," he said, his pale eyes gazing into the fire, his beautiful face unreadable.

"I...like what?" she asked lamely, tongue-tied, because her stupid brain was supplying some very explicit images of *enjoyable pursuits*, some of which involved Niall. Stop it, she chided herself. You're a Paladin – *the* Paladin, right now – not some star-struck, giddy teenage girl.

Niall gave his elegant little shrug. "Whatever interests you. Whatever will keep you from pushing yourself too hard. That's my concern. You might be *too* disciplined."

Vivian shook her head. "I don't think that's a thing."

"I think it is," said Niall in smooth disagreement. "And as your mentor, I want to ensure your success. You'll be a Paladin for the next century or more – "

"Wait, wait." She held up a hand to stop him. Her heart felt like it was hiccupping. "What did you just say?"

"You'll be a Paladin for the next century or more," Niall repeated patiently.

A little shiver ran through Vivian as she met his colorless gaze and recognized the surety there. "The next century or more," she said, her voice sounding strangled. She swallowed hard.

Niall leaned forward and covered her hand with his. "Accept my apology, Vivian. I should have approached that matter differently."

"No, it's okay," she said breathlessly, not sure if the swooping feeling in her stomach was from the magnitude of the revelation or Niall's touch.

"I did not know with full certainty that you would be accepted as a Paladin," said Niall, "and I also wished to speak to my Queen. I remember the Paladin, but I had no occasion to ask them such personal questions."

"So, you knew the doors would speak to me?" Vivian tried to focus on learning something productive from the conversation. She felt that if she let her mind wander she'd veer off into panic about *the next century or more*. She reflexively reached out for Tyr, but again she couldn't feel him, so she curled her fingers around Niall's hand.

"Again, I was not certain, but I knew there would be a sign," he said.

"I still don't know what the vision meant," she confessed. "I've been looking for the door this key opens, but I haven't found it yet."

"The White City will reveal its secrets to you in its own time," said Niall with a confidence that Vivian wished she felt.

"I mean, hopefully it doesn't take 'the next century or more,'" she retorted. "I still don't know entirely what you mean by that, but I still think in human years."

"That will fade as well in time," said Niall.

"Okay, okay." She waved her free hand. "Enough serious stuff. Does my training plan have your stamp of approval?"

Niall nodded. "Yes. With one addition."

"And that is?"

"I would like to continue our training sessions. I will not be able to do so every day, but I believe every third day will be sufficient and will allow me to monitor your progress."

"I...sure. Sounds great. Fantastic. Your room or my room? Or, er, someplace neutral, like the practice yards?" Vivian pressed her lips together before she could stumble even more.

"Here will be fine, unless you are not comfortable with such an arrangement," said Niall, glancing about her chamber. Vivian wished acutely that she'd made her bed, even though the pile of soft furs and blankets didn't really lend itself to neatness. Niall smiled slightly. "Or unless you intend to burn it down around our ears."

"In my defense, that was outside and that was my first time using that rune," said Vivian, feeling her ears heat as Niall referenced the incident in which she'd created a powerful fireball that nearly blasted both her and Tyr to oblivion. Only Tyr's quick reflexes had saved them both, and she'd walked away with nothing more than a few singed strands of hair. She sobered at the thought of Tyr. "I know you don't like him," she said quietly, glancing away from Niall into the fire, "but do you know anything that would help Tyr? I don't think he's handling the transition well."

"In what way?"

Vivian wasn't sure if she was imagining the coolness in Niall's voice. He always sounded very calm and collected, she reminded herself. "He just…disappears. I don't really know where he goes. And he…well, to be blunt, he hasn't fed. He won't answer me when I ask him whether he still needs blood."

She certainly wasn't imagining the look of faint disgust that crossed Niall's face, but she pressed on.

"I understand that he isn't your favorite person, but he helped us with the bone sorcerer. He helped us when we needed to understand Corsica. And he helped me to become a Paladin." She paused, acutely aware of the fact that Niall hadn't withdrawn his hand from over her own. "I'm not asking you to help him directly. Just…if you know anything, please tell me?"

"It is a reasonable request," Niall said finally. "Queen Titania bears no grudge against Tyr. He did not raise his sword against *her*, though he did entice some of our Court to follow him in his rebellion against Mab." He tilted his head. "Some even regard him as a kind of folk hero. He rebelled against Mab centuries before others recognized her for what she was."

"So, you think he'll be accepted back into the Unseelie Court?" asked Vivian.

"I do not know," said Niall. "We are about the same age, he and I, but he remembers much more than I."

"What do you mean, remembers much more?" Vivian couldn't resist asking, even though she felt like a parrot repeating Niall's words back to him. She had so many questions and so few answers.

Niall looked into the fire silently for a long moment before replying. "My Queen gives us many liberties, but in the end we are hers, body and soul. I choose it, and I do not regret it." He paused. "I have come to understand more and more the price of my loyalty. I accept that price. Ways of thinking and certain skills faded, and I do not remember them. I am a weapon continually honed by the demands of my Queen, and that is how it must be."

"Then Tyr remembers things that you don't because he was exiled?"

"Yes," agreed Niall without inflection. "And he studied in the North, in the days before the High Queen was even born."

Vivian felt again that disconcerting swooping sensation in her stomach as she tried to reconcile Tyr's age with what she already knew about the Fae world.

"No one would think less of you for feeling overwhelmed," Niall said almost gently. "To go from speaking in terms of days and months to centuries is not an easy adjustment."

"You can say that again," muttered Vivian. She took a deep breath. Focus. "Okay, so circling back. Tyr *might* be accepted into the Unseelie Court because Andraste is Queen now rather than Mab, but maybe she'd feel threatened because he's older than her and he rebelled against her sister." She thought for a moment. "Do you think Queen Vell would accept him into the Vyldgard?"

"Remember that in these times, it is also his choice," Niall said.

"That's what I'm worried about." She sighed.

"Perhaps you should ask him yourself. He…cares for you."

Vivian's mind immediately flashed to the brief but intense kiss that she and Tyr had shared in her bedroom back in the mortal world. "He's shutting me out."

"Perhaps in an attempt to protect you."

"Are you saying that because that's what you would do?" she said.

Niall withdrew his hand from atop hers, somehow making it seem as though he'd intended to do it before she'd made her comment. His face remained like a perfect marble carving. If anything, he'd become even more inscrutable since they'd returned to Faeortalam. "We are not talking about me."

"Well, then here's a question that *is* about you. How's your *taebramh*? Did it regenerate fully, or whatever you want to say, after you came through the Gate? I'd like to know for professional Paladin purposes, of course," she added.

"Of course," Niall said with a polite nod. "My Queen appreciated the necessity of my action, and so she chose to restore my *taebramh*."

There was something rigid in Niall's voice that Vivian didn't like, but she couldn't quite put her finger on what exactly it was. Then it hit her. "She...*chose*. Queen Titania might have chosen *not* to restore your *taebramh*?"

"It would have been within her rights," said Niall unflappably. "She is my Queen."

"But you did it to save Forin's life," protested Vivian.

"I made a decision that endangered my own life and thus the power of my queen," Niall replied.

Vivian blinked. "She could have *punished* you for trying to do the right thing?"

"It is my hope that you will soon understand that right and wrong are sometimes not clearly defined. Our existence is a series of choices. Each choice has a consequence. One must try to understand the ramifications of each choice, and evaluate that choice accordingly."

"You're sounding a lot like an unfeeling robot," said Vivian. How could she feel affection for such a being? Her mind immediately supplied the answer. Although Niall spoke coolly and smoothly about carefully evaluating choices based on logic, he'd still made the decision, in the moment, to save Forin's life. She swallowed. "You still did it, though. You saved Forin's life even though you knew Titania could have punished you."

"I have been told," said Niall in a soft voice, "that I am too soft-hearted." He smiled. "It is an accusation that I take as a compliment, but sometimes Queen Titania does not see it the same way."

"How does she feel about Andraste being crowned? That's a definite shift in the power dynamic."

Niall raised his eyebrows minutely. "You think I should be discussing the intimate details of my Queen's opinions on current events with someone who is not even of my Court?"

Indignation flared within Vivian, but she sensed somehow that he was testing her. Everything would be training now. Everything had a purpose and a meaning. So, she took a deep breath, folded her hands in her lap, and tried to look at it from a different perspective. "I would never ask you to speak of anything discussed in confidence. As a Paladin, I believe it is part of my task to understand the viewpoints of all three Queens and those within their Courts, and that is why I asked that question." She nodded in satisfaction at her own answer and then dared to glance at Niall.

He sat back in his chair and nodded, his eyes glimmering. "Very good. Always understand the diplomatic side of what you say, and what you don't say."

"Do I need to add lessons in diplomacy?" Vivian asked, trying not to let a despairing note enter her voice. There was just so much to learn. Now that the excitement and joy over her new path as a Paladin had faded into the daily reality of her life in Faeortalam, she felt like she had the first time she'd swam out past where she could stand at the seashore, and the swell of a wave had dunked her under, and then when she finally broke the surface again, another wave swept her under. She'd managed not to panic, holding her breath and figuring out the pattern so she wouldn't get a face full of water when she came up again. And then eventually she learned how to propel herself up high enough to keep her head above the waves, and how to dive below the waves to avoid them altogether.

She wasn't sure she completely understood how to navigate these new waters. The currents and swells felt foreign to her, despite her passion and her drive to learn. She took a breath and tried to calm the burgeoning panic rising in her chest, compressing her lungs as surely as deep water pressing in around her.

"Vivian."

Niall's voice drew her back like a rope thrown from shore. She swallowed and looked up at him. Treacherous tears gathered in her eyes and she clenched her teeth. He would think her a weak, useless little girl. Five minutes ago, she'd been fine, and now she felt all the aching homesickness that she'd never anticipated. Now she felt just how different she was in this new world of runes, spells, doors that gave visions, High Queens and warriors bound to wolves.

"Vivian," Niall said again, the gentleness in his voice unmistakable now.

She didn't want to blink because that would send tears falling down her cheeks. She couldn't see him clearly. It was like peering through goggles filled with water, colors blurred and lines distorted. But she still saw him stand from his chair and then kneel in front of hers. Her breath hitched at his closeness even through the piercing keenness of the homesickness coursing through her.

Niall placed his elegant, long-fingered hands on her shoulders. He was still nearly eye-level with her, though he was kneeling and she sitting. "From what I remember of the Paladins, none of them had to navigate all that you have at the very beginning of their time in this world. We have asked so much of you, and you have handled it so well, that it is easy to forget that you are young."

His palms pressed comfortingly into her shoulders. She resisted the urge to put her head on his shoulder and cry. Finally forced to blink, she clenched her jaw as two hot tears fell down her face. Niall wiped away one of them with his thumb. She swallowed past the hard lump in her throat and met his eyes, determined not to cry any more.

"But even though you are young," he continued, holding her gaze with his own, "you are strong. You will need your strength. I do not pretend to understand all the secrets of this world, though I have been one of Titania's Three for centuries." He paused. "I do not know what challenges lay ahead for you, Vivian. But I do know that you are equal to them."

He leaned forward, their faces separated now by a very small distance. Vivian could see each individual long lash framing his pale eyes, the lashes pale, pale gold just like his brows and his hair. He smelled faintly of something that Vivian couldn't immediately name, something that reminded her of bright, warm afternoons under a golden sun. It was like the memory of summer clung to him.

"But it is not enough that *I* know you are equal to them," he continued, his voice quieter but no less powerful.

Slowly, the panic crushing her lungs receded, ebbing away like the ocean retreating with the pull of the tides.

"*You* must know, in your heart of hearts, that you are equal to any challenge. That you will face any enemy and you will emerge victorious," he said. Something passed through his pale eyes, an emotion that Vivian didn't understand, even at this close proximity. "Doubt yourself, and you are already lost."

A bolt of panic arrowed into her at his last phrase: How could he tell her that he knew she was equal to any challenge, and then in the same breath speak of her downfall? She gazed at him, transfixed, waiting for his next words even as she struggled to understand the paradox of his last pronouncements. One of his hands moved from her shoulder to brush her cheek. If it had been anyone else, she would have thought the movement tender. With Niall, she never felt sure that she understood him.

"You are young and so fierce," he murmured. "So very determined. I have not felt a pull toward any other in so long."

Vivian took a breath. Clarity rushed back as though she'd just emerged from a dream. Somehow, she corralled her scattered thoughts, even as the magnetic pull of Niall's eyes threatened to overpower her, the very nearness of him making her feel a bit drunk, a bit dizzy with desire. "I think you are just fascinated because I am new," she managed, swallowing hard. "I don't want you to mistake that for anything but what it is." The words hurt to say, twisting something in her chest like a rope being tied into a knot, but she also felt better for saying them.

Niall withdrew his hand and then sat back on his heels, looking up at her with contemplation written across his face. "I do not think you will ever cease to surprise me."

Vivian didn't know if he meant that as a compliment, or as reassurance that, even if he *was* drawn to her for her newness, she would remain so to him forever. And until she puzzled through that, she knew what she had to do. "Niall. You are my teacher. My instructor." She smiled and tried to joke. "Don't you think it's a bit cliché to…have a dalliance?"

Niall stood abruptly. "A dalliance?"

Vivian felt sick. Maybe she'd completely read the conversation wrong. The Sidhe spoke in such vague terms, in such delicate metaphors! She stood too and walked over to the table, picking up the copper kettle to ensure it had water in it. Putting it on its hook over the fire required closing the distance between her and Niall, but she managed it, avoiding eye contact and maintaining what she hoped was a cool silence. Once the kettle was over the fire, she returned to the table to prepare the little silk sack of ground herbs that would go into the heating kettle. *Khal* reminded her a bit of coffee, but it was something completely different. Just another thing to emphasize her otherness in this new world, she thought with a hint of bitterness.

"You are right," Niall said finally. "It would not be considered wise for an instructor to conduct any…dalliance…with his student."

Vivian stared down at the pouch of herbs, her fingertips numb.

"But you are wrong if you think that what I desire – unwisely, but still – is simply a dalliance."

She forced herself to look at him. Don't be a coward, she told herself. Even though she could rarely read his beautiful face, now his expression was open, as though he'd given her the key to unlock his inscrutability. And what she saw in his otherworldly visage shook her to her core.

"Any sane being would say that I am far too old for you," he said with a hint of a smile, "but I would say to them that though you are young, you possess an uncommon...presence. You think yourself ignorant but you have learned with a speed that astounds me. Your determination and your dedication to mastering our lessons not for your own gain but to help those you loved...it is uncommon, Vivian, to find someone so selfless and so completely unaware of her own power."

"I though the whole point of our lessons was to help me become aware of my own power," countered Vivian, her voice hoarse but audible.

"Your *taebramh* is not your only power, Vivian," Niall replied. A flame burned in his pale eyes, and Vivian felt an answering heat kindling low in her belly. "And before you tongue-lash me for implying that your beauty is your other power, I am speaking of that which I just described: your selflessness, your dedication, your courage in the face of the unknown."

"Good, because I don't count beauty as one of my powers any-way," Vivian retorted acidly. She winced inwardly at the sharpness of her tone. She hadn't meant to sound so shrewish, but the needle on her emotional dial was jumping wildly.

Niall only smiled, and just like that he became unreadable once more. "I understand now that you do not fully trust me. It is something I will work to rectify."

Vivian felt a strange sense of loss, like the gates revealing a beautiful mansion had swung shut again, denying her entrance. Then she pulled back her shoulders, picking up the silk pouch of *khal*. Beauty. She resisted the urge to give an undignified snort. If Niall wanted beauty, she was sure he could have his pick of the stunning women of the Seelie Court. She navigated around him to deposit the *khal* into the now-steaming copper kettle. Out of habit, she glanced at her wrist, sighing as she remembered belatedly that her watch had stopped working as soon as they emerged through the portal into Faeortalam. She'd stashed it in her backpack, loathe to throw it away even though she knew its delicate interior had probably been melted into irretrievable oblivion after the spinning, whirling, gut-wrenching passage through the ether. Turning back to the table, she found the little silver hourglass that had come with the (in her opinion) exquisitely outfitted room. With a turn of her wrist, she flipped it over, watching the azure sand trickle down from the top chamber for a few seconds.

"I want to become the best Paladin I can," she said finally, finding it surprisingly easy to choose her words. "I believe that your knowledge and instruction will help me along that path. For now, I am going to focus on my studies."

"You would have been a good squire," murmured Niall, almost to himself.

"I don't exactly know what you mean by that," Vivian said, "but unless you have anything else to discuss, I think I'd like to start on my reading for tonight."

"Are you sure the ladies of my Court are not teaching you the art of dismissing a man from your rooms?" Niall said.

She knew he was trying to be playful, but she felt exhausted and irritated. "When would you like to have our first lesson?" Then she waved a hand. "Just send me a message, I guess."

As though summoned by the mention of sending messages, a knock sounded high up on Vivian's chamber wall, in a place that could only be reached by the Glasidhe. She took a deep breath, concentrated and pulled up a spark of her *taebramh* to open the invisible door that waited for her permission before allowing anyone access to her room. It was a pretty neat security system, she had to admit, but sometimes it struck her as a little impractical. A door with a lock had always been just fine, in her opinion…but then again, that had been in another world entirely.

"Lady Vivian!" said the Glasidhe messenger, bowing with a particular flourish.

"Farin!" Vivian said in delight, unable to stop the grin spreading over her face.

Farin zoomed down to hover in front of Vivian. She bowed to Niall and then turned back to Vivian. "I have been sent with a message!"

"And here I thought you were just visiting for old times' sake," replied Vivian, still smiling.

"You are not old," said Farin in a shocked tone. "You are very young, the youngest Paladin in a very long time."

"So I've been told," she said dryly, pretending to ignore Niall's soft chuckle. It was nearly impossible to feel annoyed at the buoyant and fierce little winged warrior who took words so literally. She gestured to the table. "Would you like to rest your wings for a moment and join me in a cup of *khal*?"

"Your courtesy is impeccable, Lady Paladin," said Farin approvingly as she alighted on the table. Vivian delicately picked up the thimble-sized mug reserved for Glasidhe guests. Farin bared her sharp, pointed teeth in a grin. "Though I do not set much store by courtesy."

Vivian smiled. "Let me guess, you set more store by skill with a blade."

"Yes!" crowed Farin delightedly, her aura sparking.

When the final grains of sand trickled down into the bottom of the hourglass, Vivian retrieved the kettle from over the fire, wrapping a thick cloth around its handle and setting it on a circular inset in the table crafted for the very purpose of setting down a hot kettle. The ingenuity of ordinary objects in the Fae world sparked appreciation within her at various moments throughout the day while she completed ordinary tasks such as this.

After pouring Farin's small mug of *khal*, Vivian filled two more cups, gesturing in invitation to Niall. He walked over to the table and took one of the chairs gracefully, as if they hadn't just had a very uncomfortable discussion. Farin produced a dagger and neatly cut a piece from a sugar cube nearly half her height. The Glasidhe handled their size with such alacrity, Vivian thought. They didn't complain about it and they didn't bemoan their ill fortune at being different by virtue of their birth – they just found solutions. Maybe she could look to them and learn from their example.

She added a cube of sugar to her own *khal* to tame the bitterness, blowing at the hot drink in companionable silence with Farin. After the Glasidhe had taken her first sip and flicked her wings appreciatively, Vivian asked, "How is your brother? I apologize that I haven't come to see you. I didn't know where the Glasidhe make their home here in the White City."

"Forin is doing quite well," said Farin. "He has regained use of his wings and can fly short distances now. My cousin Forsythe was not so fortunate, though he fights fiercely from the back of his hawk."

Vivian wanted to ask more about Farin's cousin, but she restrained herself. "I'm glad to hear it."

"Of course you are!" said Farin brightly. "You and the Bearer are much alike in your friendship with my people."

"I hope to emulate the Bearer in more than that, though it's a good place to begin," replied Vivian. She saw Niall's smile out of the corner of her eye, but she didn't give him the satisfaction of turning toward him.

"And speaking of the Bearer," continued Farin, setting down her mug of *khal*, "the message I have for you is from her. I do not bear messages for just anyone, you know," she said conspiratorially, her wings fluttering. "I am a scout and a warrior, not a messenger. When the Bearer asks, however, I am happy to be of service."

"Why would Tess be sending me a message?" Vivian asked blankly.

"Because you are the Paladin," replied Farin. She left the *silly girl* at the end of her reply unsaid, but her tone left no doubt in Vivian's mind that it was there. Farin flicked one wing with a hint of impatience. "The Bearer requests your presence for a meeting in her chambers in an hour's time. No reply is needed unless you require me to convey your regrets." Farin raised her slanted eyebrows. "And I do not think there is anything more important than this meeting."

"Who else will be there?"

"I do not know with entire certainty, but I believe it will be the three Queens and certain others. In addition to you," clarified Farin.

"Well, that does sound important," said Vivian. She raised her mug and took a fortifying swallow of hot *khal*, feeling its warmth spread down her throat and into her stomach. A spark of curiosity also kindled in the back of her mind. Perhaps it wasn't such a bad thing that she was the Paladin – if this was any indication, she wouldn't be kept in the dark about important events in Faeortalam. She nodded to Farin. "Thank you for bringing the message. I'd enjoy it if you stayed a bit longer."

"Of course, Lady Paladin!" replied Farin enthusiastically.

"And now that you have another guest, I regret to say I must take my leave," said Niall, standing smoothly. "My queen summons me."

"Perhaps I'll see you at the meeting," Vivian said, trying hard to keep her tone light.

"Perhaps," said Niall, giving her half a bow and then striding cat-quiet across the room. Vivian stared into her cup of *khal* rather than look at his tall, well-muscled form as he exited.

After he left, Farin cocked her head to one side. "There is…tension between you."

"Just a bit of a disagreement about my training," Vivian replied, though she felt vaguely guilty about not telling Farin the entire truth. But they weren't in her little house in Louisiana anymore.

"Well, I hope you set him straight," Farin said with a nod. She gestured with her small mug. "Men think they know everything."

Vivian chuckled. "That, at least, seems to have stayed the same between my world and yours."

"Oh, this is your world too, now," said Farin immediately and with absolute sincerity.

For some reason, that warmed Vivian. "Thanks, Farin." She took another sip of *khal*. "Would you mind telling me more about your cousin Forsythe? I don't think I've met him, but he sounds very gallant."

"Indeed, he is," said Farin, launching eagerly into a description of her cousin Forsythe. Vivian listened, glad for the distraction as curiosity and anxiety warred within her at the prospect of sitting at the same table as the three Fae Queens and the Bearer of the Iron Sword.

Chapter 7

Mal had never rightly thought about death. Oh, it had crossed her mind, the first time she nearly fell from the rigging, but she'd never truly tried to understand what death would *feel* like. Would her soul slipping from her body burn like fire, or would death scoop her up in silken paws, graceful and quick? Did souls even exist? Perhaps there was simply…nothing.

Her dive from the mast of the *Dragonwing* had rammed her heart up into her throat as she realized what she'd done, the absolute futility of her actions. But there was no way to take it back, no way to arrest her fall and clamber back onto the platform with Ila. Rain lashed her face and her body, the wind slamming into her with a ferocity that knocked the breath from her just before she hit the water.

Wave after wave shoved her down into the frothing sea. Salt stung her nose and her eyes. She started to fight but then remembered why she'd jumped: Hex. Hex wouldn't be battling the waves. Hex would be sinking, his lifeless body about to join the nameless skeletons whose bones the ocean ground into sand. Lightning tore the maelstrom in two and Mal stole half a breath before the next frothing wave slapped her down into the water. She dove and kicked, her heart hammering like a captured bird in her chest, urging her to go *up, up!*

But she opened her eyes and tried to see, shoving aside her sudden wild desire to claw for the surface; the salt water stung her eyes and she saw nothing but blackness, nothing but a void enveloping her. If not for the press of the water about her and the burning of her lungs she would have thought she was floating in a starless night sky. How poetic, she thought in disgust as her mind tried to make sense of her decision to dive into the maw of the storm.

Hex. Find Hex.

The scaly patches on her skin burned as though they'd been set on fire. She pushed aside that sensation too as she swam deeper, kicking her feet in their waterlogged boots, waving her arms blindly in front of her. A cold despair clenched her stomach, counterpoint to her lungs begging for air. Though she'd tried to jump toward where he'd been washed overboard, trying to find Hex was like tossing a ring into the waves and expecting to find it beneath the ripples.

She swam deeper, groping ahead with fingers spread wide, as though that small detail would let her find Hex. She knew dimly in the back of her mind that she didn't have much time left. She could hold her breath much longer than most – it had always been a talent, and she'd won a few rings betting against the older thirds when she was younger. But in the short and meaningless handful of time that was her life, she had merely an instant left. She saw it now. She understood how small and insignificant she truly was.

If only Hex didn't have to die, too. She closed her eyes, blind anyway against the salt of the sea. He would have made a good first one day, even if she found him supremely annoying.

Her chest began heaving as her body cried out for air. As she'd learned to do when the fourths were first taught swimming, she suppressed the instinct. She swam deeper with the last of her strength, somehow knowing that it was hopeless but still wanting to fight, to *try*, until the very end. Hex deserved at least that from her.

She felt a prickle of regret at leaving Jem behind. But if her body distracted the kraken and gave the *Dragonwing* a greater chance of escape, then perhaps it would have been worth it.

Colored lights began exploding behind her eyelids. Her chest felt as though she were a barrel about to burst its stays. She spread herself into the blackness and strange calm of the cold water, readying herself for that first stinging lungful of ocean. Whatever anyone said, drowning was not a peaceful way to die, though the sea surrounding her bore little trace of the raging storm gripping the *Dragonwing* above.

Her fingertips brushed something else – some*one* else – suspended in the void of the ocean, just as she parted her lips to accept the sea's cold kiss. Water rushed into her mouth even as she jerked and reached for whatever she'd brushed – her fingers closed around a sleeve, a wrist, warm but cooling, and she pulled herself toward Hex with maniacal strength. She'd found him. He wouldn't die alone.

As she clung to Hex in the blackness of the ocean, Mal realized with sharp clarity that she should have been busy drowning. Water filled her mouth. She tasted the ocean with sharp precision, her mind picking apart all the different subtleties as though they were scents for her to study: the warm trickle of water as it passed over Hex's skin, the fresher water churning down even into these depths from the storm above, the acrid, burnt taste of a creature that she instinctively knew to be an enemy…and the silvery coolness of something not living but once living, something that slid like cream across her tongue. She knew all this, felt it and tasted it, in an instant.

The kraken and the *Dragonwing*. She knew that the kraken still stalked the ship, but lurked below the surface, distracted now, trolling for the prey that it had scented in the water. She could sense it coming closer, rolling the salt of the sea across her tongue, letting the ocean whisper its secrets to her. She opened her eyes in surprise.

And she could *see*.

Goose flesh erupted on every inch of her skin, even the parts of her still burning with that harsh fire. She saw the world beneath the waves as though illuminated in silver light, all in tones of green and black and hints of silver that she somehow knew would lighten to delicate blue and white and gold beneath the light of a noon sun.

Hex's slack face glowed white a mere hand's breadth from her astounded gaze. She stared at him for a moment, mesmerized by the beautiful planes of his high cheekbones and the strong line of his jaw, just beginning to darken with the shadow of a beard. A string of bubbles trailed from his parted lips. Those lips…she touched them with the pad of one finger. So full and luscious, like they belonged to a woman…

And then Mal realized that whatever witchcraft gripped her, whatever spell had snatched her from death, it hadn't touched Hex. She pulled him closer, pressed her ear to his chest, even though she could taste in the warm water around him the faltering of his heart. She breathed faster in panic – she *breathed*.

Mal froze again. *She was breathing seawater.* Breathing the stinging salty ocean as though it were cool night air. Sucking it into her mouth as though she'd been doing it all her life. It felt *different*, thicker, but a strange new strength coursed through her body with every breath. It felt *right*, like she was remembering some long-forgotten skill.

But now was not the time to marvel at this sorcery. Hex was dying – *not dead yet, just almost*, she thought fiercely as she caught him around the chest and kicked hard, pushing up toward the surface, swimming with a speed she didn't know she possessed. He was heavy, his muscular form dragging through the water with a weight that made her grit her teeth, but she kicked faster, pulling with one arm and gripping him with the other.

The surface wasn't far. She tasted the metallic sheen of the rain that had journeyed through lightning-kissed skies. Her sharpened vision picked out the silhouettes of flotsam outlined starkly against the surface of the water, the churning sea oddly beautiful from below, a mosaic of light and dark laced with silvery foam.

But even if she could get Hex onto one of those pieces of flotsam, even if she managed to get him to breathe again and kept him from capsizing, the *Dragonwing* wouldn't pick them up. Not until the kraken had ceased its attack – and that was never a sure thing. Sometimes it took days for the Captain to declare the end to a kraken battle.

Mal pulled Hex up toward a particularly large piece of wood, grim determination taking root in her mind even as she knew she was still as doomed as when she'd first dove into the storm-lashed sea, never mind the miraculous spell that allowed her to breathe underwater.

She reached the piece of wood, recognizing it as one of the large crates that held the blue hens the Captain so prized. She spied their sodden, drowned little bodies tossed about within the crate, pitifully small with their soaked feathers. Grimacing, she grabbed the crate from beneath and *held her breath* – or water, she thought with dizzy amazement – as she heaved Hex up onto the large crate. It pitched and then righted itself, but Mal knew it was a fool's errand to expect it to stay upright on its own. She kicked and scrabbled until she managed to scramble onto the sodden boards of the crate, hauling Hex farther up onto it beside her, barely enough room for them both despite her slim build.

She blinked hard: Her improved vision had disappeared, leaving her to stare into the darkness dizzily. By feel, she pulled Hex onto his side, found his cheek and slapped it hard, flattening herself against the crate as a wave picked them up and tossed them. Somehow, they didn't capsize though these were the same waves throwing the *Dragonwing* about like a child's toy.

A sleek black tentacle broke through the wind-raked waves a ship's length away. Mal's throat constricted. She slid her hands around her belt until she found the length of spidersilk still trailing from her...but she tugged, and the free end had somehow become wrapped around Hex's belt.

She didn't have time to question it and she didn't have time to waste on the waterlogged knot. Her fingers found the knife in her boot and for the second time she cut her spidersilk, looping it through the slats of the crate with an alacrity borne out of fear and necessity. After she finished tying Hex to the crate – maybe sealing his fate, maybe saving his life – she gripped her dagger in her hand and slid silently off the crate into the water, her sight crystallizing as she kicked toward the kraken.

A tentacle curled lazily toward her, thicker than her waist and studded with suckers as large as her head. Disgust warred with terror inside her. Sailors met death at the grasping tentacles of the kraken, and here she was swimming toward it. Her mind shied away from the scale of the beast as she spied another tentacle drifting through the water what seemed like an impossible distance away. She palmed her second dagger from the sheath at her waist, grateful that this one was a bit longer at least. The tentacle drew nearer, her sharp vision throwing it into horrifying relief.

But she got the sense that the kraken expected an easy meal. It was old – it hadn't grown this large without years, maybe even centuries, passing as it expanded in the deep of the ocean. It was old, and it expected an easy meal, sailors washed overboard, delicate morsels no more than a mouthful but so very delicious, tasting of sky and sun.

Mal realized she had bared her teeth as these realizations about the kraken filled her head, and something very much like a growl issued from her. She propelled herself forward with a powerful kick and stabbed into the tentacle, ripping and gouging at the kraken with a savage fury that erupted from her without warning. She lost all the control that their knife-master had tried to beat into them during their lessons. She felt like the maelstrom above them replicated in miniature, whirling and stabbing, kicking and rending and cutting with animalistic pleasure at the kraken's shriek of pain. Inky blood clouded the water around her and the foul taste of it registered in the back of her mind, but her desire for revenge overpowered her disgust.

Mal didn't know what event had planted that desire for revenge so deeply in her breast, but she let it fuel her, urging her faster and faster through the water until she found another tentacle, her blades flashing and cutting and shredding –

Another tentacle slammed into her, knocking her away from the beast. She snarled, the sound high and otherworldly to her ears. The pain of the blow receded beneath the bloodlust. This one was ancient, but so was the blood that ran through her veins. She arrowed in again, weaving between the creature's seeking tentacles, until she saw its massive, misshapen head and its gnashing beak.

She would end this threat once and for all, for Hex and for the *Dragonwing* and for the nameless thirst for blood raging through her. The kraken fixed her with one huge, hateful scarlet eye. She swam faster, and then something caught her by both wrists with bone-wrenching suddenness. Thrashing and twisting furiously, she saw behind her the figure of a man, blue scales shimmering in patches on his skin, his hair a delicate silvery green.

"You've wounded it enough," he said, his voice wavering through the water but reaching her ears all the same.

Mal snarled at him, lashing out with her feet. He avoided her blows easily and shook her by her wrists like a cat caught by the scruff.

"Come now, cousin, show some dignity," he said, raising his pale brows.

As though they weren't drifting amid a nest of kraken tentacles, the man easily transferred both her wrists to one hand and gripped her chin with the other, turning her face first to one side and then the other.

"You should not have forced the change." He shook his head.

The kraken gave a groan and slid down toward the darkness of the ocean's depths, an inky trail of blood trickling after it. Mal twisted to watch it go, and the pale man released her chin. She glimpsed a few other figures prodding the kraken along with long, shining blades.

She turned back to the strange man before her. Maybe she was dead, and this was some twisted underworld. Perhaps she'd been knocked out by a blow from the kraken and even now she lay in a hammock in Bonesaw's cabin. But the throb of her ribs where the kraken had struck her felt too real, and she became once again aware of the strange burning at her neck and behind her arm, those patches on her skin that had itched fiercely for weeks.

"Do not stab me. I am going to release you," said the man.

Mal felt as though she'd been rolled in a sealed barrel, shaken and dizzied. What was happening to her? What had she just done? Her head began to ache and her eyes widened as the absolute *impossibility* of the scene in which she found herself pressed in on her. Maybe this was what going mad felt like.

The man with the glimmering scales on his brow released her wrists. Her daggers – prized possessions both – fell from her nerveless fingers as panic bubbled up in her chest.

"Too young," said the man, shaking his head again.

"Are you done berating her for what she does not understand, Calinth, or shall you wait 'til she's drowned herself with her own disbelief?"

Another being, this one indisputably female, emerged from the murk to swim next to the one she'd called Calinth. Mal blinked at her dazedly: she had long, vibrant azure hair that spread in a cloud about her head. The woman wore nothing but a kind of token wrap about her waist made out of some silver fabric that Mal wanted to touch. The woman held one of the long silver blades that Mal had glimpsed in the hands of those shepherding the kraken.

"You have always been softhearted, Serena," said Calinth.

Mal thought muzzily that she must be his first. Serena: three syllables. And he with only two: Calinth.

"No, I am just quicker to act," replied Serena, taking Mal by the arm and swimming upward.

Moments ago, Mal had been fighting a kraken. Or had she? If this was all a dream, none of it mattered…yet the woman's grip on her arm felt bruisingly real, and she kicked her feet weakly, trying to help. Serena didn't even notice, her luminous eyes focused up toward the surface, reading the underbelly of the sea.

"You have a good wind sorceress, for all she's not Kin," said Serena with a note of approval in her voice.

Mal felt her lungs tightening and her head going heavy on her neck. Serena gave her a little shake.

"Almost there. Push it away until we get to the surface."

Push what away? Though she didn't completely understand, Mal tried. Years aboard the *Dragonwing* had conditioned her to obey orders, even when they made little sense to her at the time. So she gathered herself and tried to *push it away*, and it seemed to work because Serena made a small sound of approval.

"Here we are, little one."

With no ceremony whatsoever, Serena flung Mal out of the water onto the crate, which somehow still held Hex's unmoving body. Mal convulsed as she tried to breathe. Somehow the air felt like water once had to her, wrong and repulsive. She slithered on her belly, the rough wooden planks scraping her as she tried to return to the water. But strong hands flipped her over onto her back – and then closed around her throat.

Mal thrashed with the desperate strength of a fish caught on the line. A sharp slap stung her cheek.

"You'll spill you both back in. Lay still. I know it hurts."

Tears squeezed out of the corners of Mal's eyes at the painful grip around her throat, but if she had to die to give Hex a chance – if she had to lay still while this strange creature strangled her so she didn't capsize them both, then so be it.

Then something deep in her throat shifted, something near the base of her skull that she'd never felt move before, and pain shot down into her lungs. She rolled and retched, brine burning her nose and throat.

"There," said Serena in satisfaction.

Mal felt the woman-creature shift.

"Oh, he's a beauty," she purred.

If Mal had been able to move, she would've tried to get between Hex and the beautiful woman with scales and the sword in her hand. But as it was, paroxysms rocked her, rippling through her painfully as she retched again and again, one hand gripping the rough wood of the plank beneath her.

"As a favor, little one," came Serena's voice, smooth and silvery as moonlight on a calm sea. Then she was so close that Mal smelled her faint salty scent, her breath brushing Mal's ear. "Be careful not to misplace your playthings. Next time they may not be returned."

And with that, Serena was gone. Lost as she was in her own misery, Mal's heart nonetheless stuttered with joy when she felt Hex lurch and heard him add his retching to hers. She felt a vague gratitude to the azure-haired woman, though she still felt like the woman could have just as easily gutted them both with her shining silver blade.

Her entire body hurt, pain screaming through her with an intensity she'd never before experienced. But Mal still pushed herself onto her side, tried to roll over to see Hex, to make sure he was all right. Rain still pattered down on them, but wind no longer battered them, and the waves swelled beneath them but no longer crashed down with foam-capped ferocity. Serena had been right. Kalinda *was* a good wind-witch.

"Hex?" she rasped. Her lips felt swollen and salt-stung. She couldn't see very well but focused on the pale smear of his face. She pulled herself closer with one arm. Something shifted and grated within her side, and then a new, fierce agony punched the breath from her. She tasted blood.

Maybe the kraken had really hit her harder than she'd thought. Maybe she would still die.

But at least Hex had a chance. And the *Dragonwing* was safe. Jem would take care of Hex. They'd have each other.

Blue sails tugged at her fading vision. She turned her head with the last of her strength, and thought that the *Dragonwing* sailing toward them, her sails full-bellied with Kalinda's whistled wind, was a fitting and beautiful last sight for a sailor to see. Her body hurt too much. It felt like she was on fire and yet she shivered.

She didn't hear the whistles from the lookout and the roar of the Captain at the helm as they spotted the crate with its unlikely cargo, bobbing in the dregs of the storm. She let her eyes slide closed, welcoming the velvety darkness.

When she realized through the haze that she still felt the ache of her body, she knew she wasn't dead. Sounds returned first, gruff voices that she didn't immediately recognize. After a while she heard an adamant speaker, younger than the others, that finally drew closer. Jem's voice drew her closer to the surface and the light. Cool water wet her lips and gratitude rushed through her. She struggled for the surface just as she'd fought the ocean with Hex's unconscious body.

Hex.

Her skin felt too tight for her body, her eyes full of grit as though she'd gone to sleep on the white strip of deserted beach on Horizon after drinking too much ale at one of the taverns. Her head pounded just as hard too, and her tongue felt like a roll of cloth shoved into her mouth. But she forced her eyes open, whimpering against her will at the sting of peeling back her eyelids.

"Mal," said Jem, "hold still, let me help."

And he was there with steady hands and a cool washcloth, dabbing gently at her eyes, helping her unseal them. She glimpsed smears of color before a shard of light stabbed into her head.

"Go slow," advised Jem. "Let yourself adjust."

Mal wanted to ask him why Bonesaw had let him attend to her, where she was – because she wasn't in her hammock down in the berthing with the other thirds – and, most importantly, where Hex was. But her tongue felt like a huge caterpillar, like one of the acid green quilled ones that crept across the leaves of the bread plants on Haven, fat and squiggly. Actually, she amended, her tongue felt like a huge *dead* caterpillar. She tried to swallow and succeeded only in making herself nearly retch as her movement needled her dry throat.

"Easy," said Jem, an edge of exasperation to his voice. "I know you don't know what *slow* means, Mal, but we nearly lost you."

We. Jem made it sound like there were others who cared whether she lived or died. If she'd been able, Mal would have snorted. Fat chance. Thirds were expendable. They were *all* expendable, really. She tried to blink again. This time her eyelids moved a bit more easily, and the light didn't spear her eyeballs quite so painfully. She left her eyes as slits and then cautiously opened them wider. The blobs of color resolved into a blurry image: Jem, busy mixing something on a little table by her bedside, brushing his unruly dark hair out of his eyes with the back of one hand. His movement made her dizzy, so she shut her eyes again.

She was lying in a bed. That meant they'd taken her to Bonesaw. That meant she was in the cutter's cabin, so called because Bonesaw used it to amputate limbs that had been crushed or destroyed like his. Most who went into the cutter's cabin didn't come back out. A shiver ran through her as she wondered how many loyal *Dragonwing* crew had rasped their last breaths in this very bed.

"Think you can drink this?" Jem asked.

Mal opened one eye. The prospect of something cool to soothe her parched throat sounded heavenly, but drinking meant moving enough to sit up, at least a little, and opening lips that felt as though she'd been out in the harsh sun for days without shade. Why did her body feel so abused? Yes, she'd dived into the stormy seas, and yes, she'd fought a kraken – she winced at the memory of its tentacle crashing into her – but other than her ribs, she should have been mostly fine. Why did she feel like she'd been keelhauled?

"Mal," Jem prompted patiently.

She opened her other eye and nodded minutely. Even that motion sent nausea rolling through her and stabbing pain into her side. Jem didn't have to tell her to move slowly – she couldn't have moved faster if she tried, but after a few moments of careful, concentrated effort she propped herself up against the wall, two pillows wedged behind her. Jem brought the copper cup to her lips and slowly tipped it into her mouth. For once, his concoction didn't taste like he'd taken the worst parts of Cook's spices and mixed them all together.

"Just water," he explained with a wry smile, "and a bit of mint and honey."

As she finished her first sip, a bitter aftertaste assailed her mouth and she cut her eyes at him accusingly.

"And a bit of blackfin root to help with your healing," Jem added.

For all the terrible taste of the blackfin root – it reminded her of the time that she'd licked a patch of pitch heated by the sun as a fourth on a dare – Jem's elixir seemed to loosen her tongue and shrink it down from dead-caterpillar size to something manageable. Still thick and unwieldy, like it was twice its normal size, but Mal thought she could probably talk when she finished.

As her immediate thirst and the ache of her bone-dry throat receded, she became aware of the patches of skin that had burned like fire in the sea. They felt raw and painful, as though flame had truly touched her skin. She grimaced but then focused on finishing the cup of water. She wanted more but her stomach felt too full already. She leaned her head back against the wall for a moment and then opened her eyes, looking at Jem intently.

"Hex?" she croaked.

"It was touch and go between the two of you for a bit," Jem said, his eyes darkening. "But he's fine now. Still not on full duty, but well enough to stand watch."

If she could have laughed, she would have. Trust Hex to go back to his watch as soon as he was able. He had the most misbegotten sense of obligation, especially when it came to his own health.

"I know," Jem said, nodding. "I told him he should give it a few more days, it's barely been a week, and he just shrugged. I'm beginning to agree with your assessment that he's quite irritating."

Mal felt her eyes go wide. "A week?" she rasped.

"Six days," clarified Jem, "though it could be five since you two were fished out near dawn."

"How?" Her voice came out a whisper.

Jem shrugged. "The lookout saw you. Captain was on the helm, and he made the decision." He shook his head. "The kraken had retreated but we thought he'd wait. He didn't."

"Why?"

"Bugger me if I know, Mal." Jem shook his head. "Though there's an interesting rumor sweeping through the thirds."

She didn't think she could talk anymore, so she just raised her eyebrows in question. The movement sent little needling pains through her skin.

"There's a rumor that you're – "

"That's quite enough."

Jem immediately shut his mouth as the smooth voice of their wind-whistler, Kalinda, filled the cabin. Mal felt a spark of irritation. Blast the woman's timing, even if she was a first! Now curiosity scratched at her insides while her thrice-damned skin felt like a whole army of fleas burrowed into her. Or maybe those little comet worms, maybe those would be a better metaphor. She'd never had them, but they slid under your skin and left bright red trails, like a small, bloody shooting star.

"The Captain will want to know she's awake," said Kalinda, walking across the cabin with authoritative strides. She was not a large woman – her head barely reached past Jem's shoulder, and he wasn't one of the taller thirds. Kalinda had skin that turned a deep shade of gold in the sun, like a proper Seafarer, and her dark hair lightened to chestnut at the ends.

Mal knew that all Jem could do was obey, but she still felt abandoned as he left the cabin. He glanced over his shoulder at her, taking the risk to reassure her. She read the worry in his eyes. There was something wrong, she'd bet her last ring on it. He'd been about to tell her something about it, but Kalinda had silenced him.

The door closed, leaving her alone with the wind-whistler. Kalinda wore a long jacket with many pockets, tied with a white sash around her waist. Her pockets held all the sundry instruments of her trade: little bits of silk and feathers in various colors, bones of birds and other things that Mal didn't rightly know what to call. Being this close to the wind witch sent little shivers across her skin…or maybe that was just the ripple of heat from her still-burning, thrice-cursed patches of disease.

Mal tried not to show her discomfort. She glanced down at her hands. Her fingers looked like sausages shoved into a ball of dough, her joints red and swollen. The sight unsettled her. How could she climb with such hands?

"Brave," said Kalinda, her face unreadable.

Mal blinked.

"Foolish, but brave," the wind witch elaborated, crossing her arms over her chest.

Before Mal could say anything to this surprising compliment – it *was* a compliment of the highest order, even tempered by the rebuke – booted footsteps sounded in the passageway. The door burst open as though blown by a gale, a huge silhouette blocking the light.

Mal's bones turned to ice. She felt like she couldn't breathe. The Captain of the *Dragonwing* walked into the cabin, and it seemed that all light and all air swirled toward him. Kalinda moved with silent precision behind him, shutting the door and taking station by it, her hands clasped neatly at the small of her straight back.

Mal had lived her entire life on the *Dragonwing*, and she'd never been this close to the Captain. He addressed the crew at intervals, after a successful raid and at the solstice, before putting in to shore and when they returned; but the thirds always climbed the rigging for a better view, that was how far back they were pushed on the decks. Now she felt as though she'd burst into flame at the intensity of his presence and her embarrassment that she could not properly show her respect. She struggled as upright as she could and raised a swollen hand to her forehead and then her lips, ignoring the lance of white-hot pain in her side.

"Third Mal," he said in a deep voice.

"Sir," she whispered, staring at his boots. They were black and well worn, just like those of his crew. Somehow she'd always imagined him to wear immaculately polished boots.

"Look at me," the Captain commanded.

As though compelled by a force beyond her control, Mal felt her chin rise and she shifted her gaze upward. She noted distantly that the Captain's face was weathered but handsome, much *younger* than she'd thought him to be. A silver scar ran down one cheek and crossed just the corner of his full lips. She swallowed. There was something achingly familiar about those lips…an echo of something in the planes of his face…

"You disobeyed orders," the Captain said.

She couldn't look away, though all she wanted was to disappear, burrow into the bed or throw herself overboard because she couldn't bear the disappointment in his level voice. Shame coursed through her, even as a small voice in the farthest reach of her mind protested that she'd done what she had to save Hex, and she'd do it again.

The Captain's dark eyebrows raised fractionally. "You will answer me when I speak to you, Third Mal."

"Yes, sir," she whispered, her voice still deserting her.

"You disobeyed orders," he repeated.

"Yes, sir." Her skin burned but her soul felt seared. She'd failed her Captain.

"Why?"

She blinked. "Sir?"

"Why did you disobey orders?" he said.

"You'd best answer the Captain, Third Mal," said Kalinda with a low growl in her voice from her post by the door.

Mal gathered herself and swallowed. "Sir...I could not bear to see...Third Hex...overboard. I thought to save him."

"You thought to save him, even though you know the law as all on my ship do?" The Captain's eyes glinted. They were blue, like the ocean under a noon sun.

"Yes, sir," said Mal. "I decided...if I could not...save him..." She had to pause and swallow. "Then he would not die alone." She paused again. "And perhaps we would give...the ship a chance." Her tongue felt like it had been filleted with a dagger, cut by even those few words.

The Captain looked at her for a long moment. "I cannot tolerate those who disobey orders, Third Mal."

Her throat constricted. Her lips formed words, but no sound came out. She nodded, relieved at least that her battered body had for the time being forgotten how to produce tears.

"You saved...Third Hex. But I must still mete out a punishment befitting a third who disobeyed me."

The Captain's hesitation before saying Hex's name made Mal think that he was about to say something else, but he recovered so smoothly, and Kalinda gave no sign that she'd heard anything odd, that she thought she must have misheard.

"A fortnight from now, you will stand mast."

Mal couldn't control the tremor that wracked her body. Standing mast before the Captain meant lashes or keelhauling. Even hanging, if the Captain decreed it.

The Captain's fierce face softened slightly. "Five lashes, Third Mal."

Her stuttering heart started to beat again. Five lashes was a light punishment for mast, especially for one who'd broken such an ingrained order.

"Five lashes with the cat o' nine tails." The Captain pressed his lips together as though the words left a bad taste in his mouth.

Mal was proven wrong as treacherous tears filled her eyes. It would be quick, but just as brutal as forty-five lashes with the bullwhip. But she clenched her jaw. It was worth it. She'd live – probably – and Hex was alive. "Aye, sir." This time some ragged sound emerged from her swollen lips.

The Captain looked down at her for another moment. He nodded. "A fortnight, Third Mal. Regain your strength."

And before she could say anything else, he turned on his heel and strode from the room. Kalinda followed him like a small, silent shadow, but not before her glittering eyes had fixed on Mal with unreadable intensity.

The door of the cabin clicked softly shut. Mal swallowed, tried to breathe, tried not to think about the cat o' nine tails' terrible barbs biting into her flesh. The Captain could have keelhauled her or hung her from the mast as punishment for her disobedience. She was lucky it was only lashes. She clenched her jaw. She'd get through it.

With an effort, she turned her mind to examining the Captain's visit. Why had his face tugged at her memory so? She frowned as Jem slipped back into the room, white-faced. Then she blinked as the pieces slid together in her head.

"Jem," she croaked. "The Captain."

He nodded, seeming to be shaken as well by their proximity to the man who was a god on this vessel at sea.

Mal licked her lips with her unwieldy tongue and said the words aloud. "The Captain looks like Hex."

Chapter 8

Firelight danced on the walls of the Bearer's expansive chambers, augmented by small *taebramh* lights hung from the ceiling in beautifully crafted little globes of colored glass. Somehow Guinna felt comfortable here despite the fact that it was not Darkhill. Maybe it was the fact that she'd known Tess since she was a white-faced mortal girl who'd been looked upon as the price to pay for bringing the prophesied *fendhionne* into Faeortalam. Sayre walked beside her, both of them half a step behind Andraste.

The Bearer had requested this meeting – not a formal council at the Queen's Pavilion, but a gathering in her chambers that would hopefully allow them to remain more relaxed and open to cooperation. Guinna admired the neat trick of diplomacy. Tess was certainly no longer the young mortal who'd been carried through the Gate by Finnead.

"Welcome, Queen Andraste," said the Bearer. She didn't wear the bandolier of the Caedbranr across her chest; Guinna spied it looped over one of the chairs at the long table set up in the center of the room.

"Lady Bearer." Andraste greeted her coolly.

For all the memories Guinna had of Andraste's wild, playful spirit, none of that had reemerged after the death of Mab. She felt Sayre glance at her, but she said nothing. It wasn't her place to force friendship between the Bearer and the Unseelie Queen. And there was the matter of Finnead that complicated the two women's interactions, though Guinna was fairly sure that Tess laid no claim to the dark-haired Knight. She'd glimpsed Tess interacting with the big, golden-haired *ulfdrengr*, and though it had been years since she'd allowed herself any dalliances, she still recognized the signs of infatuation.

"Please, have a seat. Would you like some *khal*?" Tess asked, moving to a little table by the fire bearing a full set of mugs and a steaming kettle.

Guinna felt her mouth twitch in the beginning of a smile. Oh, how much Tess had learned. A little spark of pride glowed in her chest at her old friend's casual skill in guiding the interaction. When she'd first come to Darkhill, Tess had a tendency toward blunt words that hadn't endeared her to some.

"I would rather stand," said Andraste in that same cool tone. Guinna sighed inwardly; she understood now that it was going to be one of *those* days with the Queen, in which she tried entirely too hard to be icy and detached so as not to give any inkling of weakness.

"Well, you can drink *khal* while you're standing," pointed out Tess with a small smile. Andraste didn't reply, and the Bearer shifted her attention to Sayre and Guinna. "Three cups of *khal*, then?"

"Thank you, Lady Bearer," said Guinna.

Tess raised an eyebrow but didn't correct her in the use of her title in front of the Unseelie Queen. She handed Andraste a steaming mug with a polite nod, and then she turned back to the table to pour mugs for Sayre and Guinna. "Queen Titania will be arriving within a few moments, I think, and the Vyldretning shortly after. I appreciate your willingness to come and share part of your evening with us."

Andraste nodded stiffly, her blue eyes hooded as she regarded the Bearer.

It must have been the Valkyrie Moira who'd spoken to the Vyldretning and the Bearer about Knight Ramel's wild behavior and ramblings about Rye. Guinna hadn't spoken to anyone but Andraste, and the Queen had slowly withdrawn from her openness of those first few days after the battle in the icy throne room.

Tess handed Sayre's mug to him, and she turned to Guinna, sobering. "I'm going to add Bren's name to my sword tonight."

Guinna accepted the mug of *khal*, its warmth seeping into her cold fingers. Guilt stabbed into her as it did with every mention of their friend's name. "She would have thought it a great honor."

A sad smile curved Tess's mouth. "No, she would have had some choice words about the stupidity of symbolic actions, I think."

"Or she would have wanted to study the origin of a tradition such as that," countered Guinna, fondness overriding her sadness.

"Probably would have found three tomes on it and read them all overnight," agreed Tess.

A Glasidhe flew into the room through a small door cut into the wall above one of the beams that crossed the ceilings. Guinna made note of that convenience for the messengers: perhaps it was something they could implement in their own quarters.

"Lady Tess," said the messenger, who wore a blue feather in his hair, "the Seelie Queen approaches with her Three."

"Goodness, I hope I have enough chairs," murmured Tess, raising one eyebrow. Then she said louder, "Thank you, Haze."

"It is always my honor, Lady Bearer," said Haze, bowing deeply. The feather fell from behind his ear and he snatched it from its leisurely drift, flying up to perch on the crossbeam, his aura leaving a bright trace through the air.

Guinna had deliberately chosen to wear a gown for this meeting. When necessity dictated, breeches and shirts were all very well, but she was not a Knight or a Guard. She was an excellent archer and good enough to hold her own with a blade, but that was not her chosen profession, unlike all the rest of the Queens' chosen Three.

She thought she would have felt like an imposter if she wore a blade at her hip and tried to look like them. She'd chosen a gown of deep blue, understated but regal, a sprinkle of glittering gems at the neckline and waist bringing to mind the night sky. Andraste wore a shimmering silver gown that looked like woven moonlight. Her splendid dark hair cascaded down her back in loose ringlets, the only adornment her diadem with the glittering star set into it. Sayre wore a shirt made of the same material as Andraste's gown, a dark vest and dark breeches. Guinna wondered briefly when Sayre had found the time to coordinate his wardrobe to that of the Queen, and she pushed aside the slight feeling of exclusion—why had Sayre or the Queen not given *her* any chance to match their dress? Such thoughts were childish, she told herself firmly, and she had no time for them now that she was one of the Queen's Three.

Her musings were cut short by the arrival of Titania and her Three. As always, the Seelie Queen radiated her own light, dressed simply in a gown the color of a bright spring sky, a delicately woven golden belt shimmering at her waist. Her Three all wore plain white shirts and fawn breeches. None of them wore weapons. Guinna thought that perhaps the odd coloring of the Seelie Queen's Three, their golden skin and hair leached to white and silver by their struggle to save their Queen from Malravenar's imprisonment in the ether, might help Andraste to feel less conscious of her own scars.

"Welcome, Queen Titania," said the Bearer, motioning to the table. "Please, have a seat."

"With such hospitality, you could be mistaken for Seelie," said Queen Titania with a brilliant smile, gracefully moving to choose a seat at the far end of the table. Her Three chose seats around her, two to her right and one to her left, arraying themselves about her with unconscious precision. Guinna felt a little rumble of envy at their effortless coordination. She and Sayre felt nothing like that with Andraste.

"You know as well as I do that I belong to no Court, Queen Titania," replied Tess, her voice light but her words serious. She brought two mugs over to the table. One of Titania's Three, the shortest and slightest of her warriors, rose from his seat to help her. "Thanks, Ailin," the Bearer said easily. Ailin set one mug before Titania and then in front of the tall, broad-shouldered man at her right hand. Niall, Guinna remembered. Ailin followed Tess back to the little table by the fire. Titania fell into easy, murmured conversation with Niall.

"So, I take it your sword arm is well recovered from the Dark Keep?" Tess asked Ailin as she poured two more mugs of *khal*.

Guinna felt like an eavesdropper, still standing silently behind her Queen who had refused to relax her guard, the camaraderie between the Bearer and the Seelie in striking contrast to Andraste's icy silence. Had they traded one frozen Queen for another?

"Quite well, Lady Bearer," said Ailin.

"I thought you didn't put stock in titles among friends in your Court," replied Tess, her green eyes alight with enjoyment at the conversation.

"You're quite right, Tess." Ailin grinned. "We can always count on you to remind us to abide by our own words."

Tess chuckled. "I hope that's not a veiled complaint."

"We don't believe in titles among friends and we certainly don't believe in veiling complaints," replied Ailin, raising his colorless eyebrows. "If you'd do me the honor, I can show you just how well recovered my sword arm is at the practice yards."

"Certainly," agreed Tess. "I'll be glad of the challenge."

With two mugs of *khal* in his hands, Ailin turned back toward the table, pausing to incline his head respectfully to Queen Andraste. She returned the nod stiffly.

"My queen," said Guinna quietly, stepping closer to Andraste, "perhaps you would be more comfortable seated at the table."

Andraste glanced at Guinna, hesitated, and then nodded. She glided toward the table, choosing the seats closest to the fire, the farthest from Queen Titania. Guinna took the seat to her right and

Sayre the one on her left. They still faced the door, so she saw the second Glasidhe messenger zoom through the small circular entrance.

"The Paladin, Lady Bearer," said the female Glasidhe, baring pointed teeth in a fierce grin of pride.

"Thank you, Farin," said Tess. She smiled fondly up at the Glasidhe. "Would you like anything to drink?"

"Lady Vivian and I had *khal* just moments ago, but I thank you for the offer," Farin said. She flew up to join Haze in the rafters.

The Paladin stepped through the wall of Tess's chambers with her eyes screwed shut, hands clenched into fists at her sides as though she were bracing herself for something unpleasant. She opened her eyes belatedly and smiled sheepishly. "I'm still not used to walking through walls that look solid."

"It took me a long time too," said Tess with an air of solidarity.

Guinna noticed with a start that the Paladin wore the pendant of the last Bearer, Gwyneth, at her throat. It depicted the river tree in which Tess had found the Sword. Behind it, on the same cord, glimmered a silver key that Guinna had never seen before.

The red-haired Paladin, though she looked young, must have won the Bearer's respect for such an emblem to be given to her as a gift. She looked at the Paladin with a more critical eye: She stood nearly as tall as the Bearer, her build a bit slimmer, but looking as though she had some skill as an athlete. She wore an odd belt with pouches and loops holding various tools that Guinna thought must be from the mortal world, though she recognized a pair of rune-sticks, one white and one black. Her pants and shirt were similar in style to the clothing that the Seer's team of mortal fighters favored. The Paladin and the Bearer, though Guinna couldn't say that they looked like *sisters*, certain looked as though they could be cousins. It was more a similarity in their stance and attitude than their actual physical appearance that suggested a relation.

"Lady Paladin," said Titania graciously, smiling in welcome.

"Please, call me Vivian," said the Paladin, her cheeks reddening even as she returned the Seelie Queen's smile.

Titania laughed, the sound brightening the room like the merry burble of a brook. "Ah, you are very much one of Gwyneth's children, that I can see."

Titania's words only seemed to make Vivian more uncomfortable. "Ah, yes, I suppose so." To her credit, she kept her smile from wavering. "I take that as a compliment."

"You should," said Tess, a glimmer of humor in her eyes. "Here. *Khal.*"

"Thanks," said Vivian, a look of relief crossing her face as the mug occupied her idle hands.

"I do not know how you drink so much *khal*!" piped Farin from overhead.

"It's not nearly as strong as coffee, and I drink a *lot* of that," replied Vivian.

"What is *co-ffee*?" queried Haze.

"You were not paying attention in the mortal world if you do not know about coffee," scolded Farin.

Guinna missed Bren fiercely. Her friend would have been able to elucidate the origins and traditions surrounding coffee in the mortal world. She swallowed hard. Now was not the time to let emotion overwhelm her.

A third Glasidhe messenger entered the room. "The Vyldretning!" he announced with a flourish.

"Thank you, Wisp," said Tess.

"Your messengers seem to be a family affair," said Vivian with a genuine smile as she watched Wisp enthusiastically greet his cousins on the rafter, complete with Farin chiding him for his lack of armament.

"We are among friends, Farin," Wisp replied easily.

"But we have other enemies, too," said Farin staunchly. "Just yesterday I saw a spider bigger than you and Haze put together in the western tower! Just as well no one uses it!"

Guinna noted Vivian straightened at Farin's words. The Paladin must not like spiders, she thought. She had no love for the creatures either, but after time spent in the forest in her younger years, she'd learned that most often even the most intimidating creatures were also frightened of her as well.

The Vyldretning entered the Bearer's chambers with no fanfare, dressed in the understated and functional yet elegant attire that had become somewhat her signature style. For this meeting, she'd chosen a silken scarlet tunic over black breeches and knee-high black boots, polished to a gleam but undoubtedly practical with their low heel and lack of ornamentation. A black leather belt encircled her waist, worked with accents of gold. The plain gold circlet constructed by the Crown of Bones gleamed against her dark hair, which was braided and pinned in a coronet about her head. The Vyldretning's eyes echoed the gold of her crown.

She walked with the easy grace of a predator who knew that none could challenge her. Guinna had seen her in battle at the icy throne room, and she knew the confidence of the Vyldretning was well earned. Behind her walked her Three: Calliea, the Valkyrie commander with the golden whip coiled at her side, her blue eyes scanning the room; Liam, the Seer and brother of the Bearer who'd been pulled through a tear in the veil with his companions by Malravenar's creatures, a gambit that had failed when Tess and Luca had rescued them; and Finnead, once an Unseelie Knight and Mab's Vaelanbrigh, now one of the High Queen's Three.

Guinna pushed away the unexpected prickle of jealousy that curdled her stomach at the sight of Calliea, so tall and muscled, golden-skinned and beautiful. It was no wonder that Merrick loved this warrior woman. She looked...unassailable. And then she swallowed against guilt. It had been Calliea who'd saved her from the Mad Queen's hunting hounds, descending from the sky on her winged mount like an avenging goddess, plying her golden whip against the ferocious hunting hounds about to tear into Guinna's flesh.

Calliea's eyes locked with Guinna's for a moment, and something unreadable flashed through them. Guinna went cold and looked away. She was no coward, but neither was she so foolish as to challenge this vaunted warrior – *and* one of the High Queen's Three – in the presence of those who held the fate and future of Faeortalam in their hands.

Titania rose from her seat and rendered a small, graceful curtsy to the High Queen, her Three echoing her movement and bowing from the waist. Sayre and Guinna stood, and a breath later, Andraste did as well, but she looked pained as she curtsied.

"Titania. Andraste," the Vyldretning said, greeting each in turn. Then authentic warmth entered her voice as she turned to the Bearer. "Lady Bearer."

"High Queen," replied Tess with a nod, her eyes dancing as though they were sharing some private amusement. It was well known that the Bearer and the High Queen were fast friends. They'd journeyed across Faeortalam together in the quest to enlist Seelie aid in the final battle against Malravenar. Guinna had heard more than one ballad describing their adventures, though she questioned the accuracy of some details. She doubted there were truly sirens living in the Darinwel after all these years.

Then her Queen demanded her attention: Andraste stiffened as Finnead followed the High Queen to the table, taking a seat next to Liam. Calliea sat closest to the Seelie and Finnead sat closest to the Unseelie. Guinna wondered whether they'd discussed the seating arrangement beforehand, or it had just occurred naturally. So many events that she'd once thought were happenstance, both large and small, had been revealed to be carefully orchestrated after she peeled back the air of casual indifference.

And though Andraste kept her veneer of indifference, Guinna felt the maelstrom of emotion surging through her, so strong that it burst through the barriers normally erected by the young Queen against the two of her Three. She resisted the urge to reach over and take Andraste's hand like a sister: though they were much the same age, Andraste's time spent as a slave to Malravenar rendered her much younger in her mannerisms. The Enemy had stolen her freedom and her innocence, and he'd also robbed her of centuries of living her own life, gaining experience and wisdom to use now that she was Queen.

Guinna felt Sayre settle into the steady foundation that he'd become in the days after Andraste's crowning. Despite his youth, Sayre had quickly understood that Andraste needed a calm, unmoving, dependable Knight. Sometimes Guinna felt that he recognized their Queen's needs faster than she did, just by merit of his age. Andraste had been much his age when she had been captured and enslaved.

Over Sayre's steady, reassuring presence, Guinna added her soothing touch. She drew on her memories of her time as one of Andraste's ladies during the golden years of Mab's Court, when Finnead had been a new-baptized Knight and Ramel his squire. She had truly loved the young Princess, and loved her still now as Queen; but she had to practice sifting through those memories, careful not to let Andraste glimpse her sorrow at the death of her sister Rose during that fateful attack on their camp all those centuries ago. That had happened once, that first night when they'd all been trying to find their footing in this intimate new construct, emotions tangling and overlapping like a skein of knotted thread. Andraste had gone white, the scars on her cheeks standing out like brands, staggering as the force of Guinna's remembered grief hit her as though new – because it was, to her. There were so many things Andraste didn't know, things that had happened as a result of her imprisonment.

Guinna didn't know if protecting Andraste was the right choice, and she knew she couldn't protect her from everything – that was a fool's errand if ever she'd heard one. But *she* wouldn't cause her Queen pain, not if she could help it. Rose had been dead for centuries. There was no need to dredge up that grief, long since accepted.

As the Bearer returned to the little table by the fire and the low murmur of quiet conversation rose again, Guinna watched Finnead. She'd known him since they were young, and if she hadn't had the presence of the Vyldretning and the star diadem on Andraste's brow to anchor her to the present, she would have sworn that she was looking at a younger Finnead, a newly minted Knight, in that brief but happy time before he'd been captured with Andraste by Malravenar's forces. The lines of strain had disappeared from around his mouth, the deep shadows beneath his eyes gone, his dark hair gleaming with that beautiful raven's-wing sheen once again. His sapphire eyes, so changeable and stormy, fixed on the Bearer, following her as she walked to the table with three mugs of *khal* skillfully balanced in her grip. Guinna heard Andraste take in a shuddering breath.

The Seer glanced between Finnead, his sister and the new Unseelie Queen. He smoothly diverted Finnead's attention with conversation, their words too low for Guinna to hear. The Bearer placed the mugs of *khal* on the table in front of Finnead, allowing him to pass them down to the others. Guinna recognized that walking the long way around the table would have made Tess's avoidance of Finnead insultingly obvious, and she didn't meet the Knight's eyes; but Finnead brushed his hand against hers, seemingly by accident, as he went to grasp one of the mugs.

The Paladin took a seat to the right of the Bearer. Tess sat down and picked up her own mug of *khal*, taking a contemplative draught as the murmured conversations died into silence.

"Once again, thank you all for coming," said the Bearer, the *taebramh* lights glinting off her golden hair. The emerald war markings bestowed on her by the Caedbranr wrapped around the wrist and hand that held her mug. "I know there's much to do and many demands on your time, so I'll dispense with any unnecessary words. I wanted to introduce you all to our Paladin, Vivian."

The young woman seated at Tess's right side nodded to everyone.

"I know some of you have already met her, and I'm sure that

you've at least heard of her, but I wanted to make the formal introduction. The Paladins were an important part of the White City in ages past. Just as I'm proud to be the Bearer, I'm also proud to welcome Vivian into Faeortalam. When I journeyed back into Doendhtalam to fulfill my oath of killing the bone sorcerer, Vivian proved a crucial part of our success."

Guinna noted the small smile of approval on Calliea's lips, and the look of pride worn by Titania's Vaelanseld, Niall. They'd both been part of that expedition, and it was clear they held Vivian in high regard.

"So, I trust you will welcome her and help her in what ways you can in her journey as a Paladin," concluded Tess. She turned to Vivian expectantly.

"Thank you," said Vivian, her voice uncertain at first but then gaining strength. "I appreciate the welcome and the opportunity to meet such legendary warriors and rulers." She nodded to Titania and the High Queen, and then turned to nod at Andraste. "I've spoken to a few members of your Courts during the past days, and a few of them have graciously agreed to take part in my training. I thank you in advance for allowing them to help me become a Paladin worthy of the name."

"You are more than welcome at any time in my Court," said Queen Titania warmly.

"And you may find some different styles of fighting that are to your liking in the Vyldgard," said the Vyldretning, her golden glinting as she gave a wolf-like smile. "My fighters won't coddle you, but if you don't mind a few bruises, I recommend you train with them."

"Bruises are reminders to move faster and get stronger," replied the Paladin immediately.

"I like her," said the Vyldretning to the Bearer, her grin widening.

Guinna felt the silence of her own Queen like frost radiating from their end of the table. She actually glanced down to ensure that no ice crystals were creeping across the floor or the wood. The Mad Queen's penchant for mirroring her moods with icy blasts had created an expectation in Guinna's mind, one that she was relieved to find unfulfilled at the moment. It was just her connection to Andraste that let her feel that frost...she hoped...until she saw Finnead glance at Andraste, a small crease on his brow.

What was the use of restoring Andraste's memories and bringing her back from the brink of madness – no, from the *depths* of madness, if one was to be truthful – if they could not convince their Queen to act differently than her sister? Guinna pressed down her frustration. It was not productive and would only push Andraste farther away. She focused her attention back on the conversation as the Bearer spoke again. Finnead, too, shifted his gaze back to Tess.

"That isn't the only reason that I asked you all to meet," said Tess. One finger decorated with green whorls traced the rim of her mug. "There are many challenges that face us in rebuilding after Malravenar...and rebuilding after Mab." She nodded to Andraste, the motion emphasizing the tone of her words. She wasn't accusing or blaming, just stating the facts. "As the Bearer, I believe it's part of my duty to help all three Courts work together, to bridge any gaps between them and to help the Paladin in her mission to work alongside us as well."

"Hear, hear," piped Wisp from the rafters.

"So," Tess continued, a hint of a smile in her voice now, "I'd like to discuss a piece of information that recently came to my attention. *Our* attention," she amended, nodding first to the Vyldretning and then to Andraste. "It was said that the bone sorcerer revealed to the *fendhionne* that Lady Rye, once of the Unseelie Court and captured by Malravenar's forces, may still be alive."

"And how do we know this?" asked Titania, her mellifluous voice devoid of humor now.

"Knight Ramel told one of my Valkyries," said the Vyldretning.

"The *fendhionne* used Ramel in a Dark ritual to forge her black blade," said the Bearer.

"She killed him," added Vivian softly, "and brought him back. Farin showed Ross."

Guinna wondered briefly who Ross was, but then followed the gaze of the Paladin as she glanced up at the ceiling.

"It is as the Lady Paladin says," confirmed fierce little Farin, leaping from the rafter to hover over the table. "I watched the ritual."

"And did you hear the *fendhionne* tell Ramel that Rye may be alive?" Calliea asked.

"No," said Farin. She flicked her wings. "I was captured by the Exile Corsica and put in a cage."

Wisp and Haze hissed their disapproval, their auras brightening in anger at the mention of such indignant captivity.

Guinna felt a disorienting rush of emotion from Andraste. She straightened in her chair, trying to keep her expression unreadable even as she helped the young Queen wade through the flood of sentiment.

"So, it is possible she told him," said Tess.

"He said that she wanted to torture him beyond his physical wounds," said the Vyldretning thoughtfully. "Could it be a lie?"

"It could be," admitted Tess, settling back in her chair.

"What would she gain by such a lie?" asked Titania's Vaelanseld.

"Nothing beyond gaining a hold on Knight Ramel even after her death," replied Calliea.

"That in itself would not be out of character," remarked Niall.

The Bearer winced almost imperceptibly at the harsh judgment of the *fendhionne* who had once been her best friend, but she nodded. "Especially at the end, she was driven by the thought of revenge."

"Why would she want revenge on Ramel, though?" pointed out Calliea, shaking her head. "If we're to believe what we knew before you ventured into the mortal world, Tess, they were in love."

"They were in love," Tess agreed, "but Mab's cruelty tore them apart. Maybe she blamed Ramel for not fighting hard enough against her."

"He already blames himself for that," said Guinna, slightly surprised at the sound of her own voice. She thought back to the little compartment with Moira and the one-eyed Valkyrie, Ramel's disheveled clothes and bloodshot eyes.

The Vyldretning turned her head, looking at Finnead. "What do you think?"

Finnead thought for a moment, his beautiful face unreadable, and then shook his head. "I do not remember." Oddly, he looked at the Bearer's brother, as though for help.

"You said that Rye saved your life," the Seer said calmly. "She fought the bone sorcerer and allowed you to escape."

"But you did not see her die," prodded the Vyldretning, addressing Finnead but looking to Liam to answer. Guinna realized that they must have prepared somehow for Finnead's loss of memory. He'd probably told his story to Liam.

Andraste clenched her jaw, her hands tightening on the arms of her chair. Guinna sent calming thoughts toward her mistress. It would not do for her to lose her temper here.

"No, he didn't," replied the Seer thoughtfully.

"This would not be the first time Finnead pronounced someone dead and they were alive," said Queen Andraste in a tight, cold voice.

Guinna took in a deep breath and let it out slowly, trying to ignore the sinking feeling in the pit of her stomach. Some would say Andraste had a right to be angry at Finnead. But Guinna also knew that Andraste still loved Finnead, and the Queen only stood to hurt herself by alienating him farther.

"There is no apology that would erase the hurt I have caused you, my lady," said Finnead after a long moment of tense silence. The sincerity and detached courtesy in his voice made Guinna's chest ache for Andraste.

"Always the perfect picture of courtly decorum, Finnead," said the Unseelie Queen bitterly.

"Knight Ramel is an Unseelie Knight, and Lady Rye is Unseelie," cut in Sayre firmly, leaning over the table from his seat at the end. "Perhaps the Unseelie should handle this matter."

"Knight Ramel brought this concern to one of my Valkyrie," pointed out Calliea.

"Knight Ramel is free to bed whomever he likes," Guinna replied coolly, before she could properly assess her response. "But that does not change the fact he is Unseelie."

Calliea raised her chin, meeting Guinna's gaze challengingly. "Perhaps he wishes to change the fact he is Unseelie. He was abused by your sister, so it is no wonder he chooses to escape to the Vyldgard."

"Enough," said the Vyldretning with firm finality, glancing between the two women. "Regardless of personal sentiment or loyalty to one Court, we have seen in the recent past that isolation is not the answer."

"Indeed," agreed Titania softly. The Seelie Queen looked at the Bearer. "What is your proposed solution, Lady Bearer?"

"A small expedition to determine the truth of the *fendhionne's* claim," the Bearer said, her eyes sweeping around the table. "It may also function as a survey of the Deadlands, and a mission to establish diplomatic relations with any beings that were once in thrall to Malravenar." She lifted an eyebrow. "Or to establish that there is no wish for diplomacy, if that's the case."

"Do we have a location?" asked Ailin, leaning back in his chair and propping his ankle on his knee, as though they discussed the possibility of a tournament or a spring day's ride.

"We're working on that," said Calliea. "The Arrisyn's scrying glass is damaged, but he's been working with Thea and Tyr to try to repair it."

The Bearer looked directly at Andraste. "Queen Andraste, what are your thoughts?"

A little knot of anxiety lodged in Guinna's throat as the entire room waited for Andraste's reply.

"If Rye is truly alive," said Andraste in a low, measured voice, "then we owe her our best effort at freeing her." She paused. "Rye was one of the truest friends ever to enter my life. If there is even a chance that she needs our help, I believe it is our duty to provide it."

Finnead gazed at the Vyldretning, his eyes darkening as some silent communication passed between them. The High Queen nodded. "It is only right that you wish to join this expedition, Finnead."

"I'd like to go," said the Paladin unexpectedly. She colored as all heads turned simultaneously to her. "What better way to see Faeortalam and learn about it?" she explained.

"It isn't a bad idea," murmured Tess, looking at the High Queen. "After all, we had *our* journey."

The Seelie Queen turned her golden head to her Vaelanseld, touching his arm with a graceful hand. "You have been gone from me far too long, Niall, but I would ask this of you."

Guinna thought she saw something like gratitude in Niall's eyes as he bowed his head in acceptance of his Queen's edict.

"I'll speak to my Valkyrie," said Calliea. "I'm sure that a few will want to join, and it would be an advantage to have them in the air."

"We don't need to have a final roster right at this instant," said the Bearer, but she looked satisfied that the Queens had taken up her idea. "I think with the help of our very capable Glasidhe messengers, we can work on having the composition resolved within a few days."

"Knight Ramel will want to go," said Sayre.

"Of course," said Tess, but Guinna saw the hesitation written in her eyes. She actually agreed with Tess: Ramel was in no shape to go on some wild expedition across Faeortalam. He couldn't even keep himself sober and groomed as befitted a Knight of the Unseelie Court, much less one who had once been his Queen's Vaelanbrigh.

"Is there any other emergent business which requires our attention?" Titania asked.

Tess smiled at the Seelie Queen's courteous nudge to draw the meeting to a close. "No. Thank you again for coming."

"Of course. It is always a delight to see you, Lady Bearer," purred Titania, rising from her chair. The Bearer stood as well and accepted Titania's sisterly embrace. The Paladin shifted in her chair, no doubt wondering if she were next, but the Seelie Queen settled for brushing Vivian's shoulder with one graceful hand and favoring her with a smile.

The Seelie entourage left the Bearer's chambers, and it felt as though some of the light in the room exited with them. Guinna took a swallow of her cooling *khal*.

"We must go," said Andraste stiffly.

"Thank you for your hospitality," Sayre said with a bow to the Bearer, trying to make up for their Queen's abruptness.

"And thank you for your time," replied the Bearer.

"Please let me know if there is anything I can do for the Unseelie," said the High Queen, watching Andraste rise with perceptive golden eyes. "Your people and mine share some of the same tragedies. It is not an easy path after such a thing."

Andraste said nothing, managing only a jerky nod.

"We will send a messenger," said Guinna, ignoring the irrational urge to glare at Calliea as she spoke to the High Queen.

The Vyldretning inclined her head. Andraste walked forward quickly. Conversation began again behind them as they passed through the wall back into the passageway beyond. Guinna stretched her legs to keep up with the Queen even as she wondered what the Bearer and the High Queen would discuss now that the Seelie and Unseelie had left.

Andraste turned to Sayre. "Find Ramel. Bring him to me," she said, her words terse and voice clipped.

"Aye, my Queen," replied the young Knight. He turned down a passageway that would lead him to the sleeping compartments Ramel was known to frequent.

Guinna let Andraste sweep down the hallway in icy silence, hoping that her Queen would come to her senses before she validated the quiet rumors that she, too, was destined to rule the Unseelie with a cold, harsh hand. She sighed and steeled herself for a long evening, hoping that she and Sayre could help balance their volatile new monarch's emotions, as yet another drama unfolded before them.

Chapter 9

Quinn stretched the muscles that he'd taxed the day before, pulling one arm across his chest and slowly increasing pressure. He'd let the deal with Niamh get into his head way too much, and now he felt like was finally regaining his footing. For the past few days, he'd met Luca, Tess and a rotating cast at the practice yards in the morning right as dawn lightened the sky and again in the late afternoon.

He stifled a yawn. He'd always had some trouble getting up before the sun, even though he'd spent years doing pre-dawn training and executing raids under the cover of darkness. Losing sleep for a mission was one thing, but losing sleep to train was another. Still valid, but sometimes his tired body didn't quite agree. Right now, how he felt reminded him of his first days in the military, every day of training leaving him feeling like he'd been on the losing end of a fistfight with three guys bigger than him. To be fair, sometimes that had actually been the case.

Gray light washed over the practice yards as Seelie and Vyldgard began to fill the rings and line up at the archery range. Thea waved at him and then stifled a yawn under one hand as she made her way toward her forge. For a while, Quinn would've sworn that Thea slept at the forge, but maybe training and some distance from the constant stress of conflict and looming battle had done them all some good.

"Ready for this session?" said a voice close to his ear.

Only Quinn's experience with prank-happy teammates saved him from jumping like a frightened rabbit. As it was, he turned his head slowly and leveled a hard look at Ariel. The Seelie man grinned puckishly.

"I'm always ready," Quinn replied, returning his attention to his stretching.

"I think, technically speaking, that you aren't *quite* always ready, because that would imply that you are infallible, which you are most definitely *not*," mused Ariel as he began to run through his own routine.

"Too early to talk that much," muttered Quinn as he transitioned to a simple yoga routine that he'd used for years to ensure that a lack of flexibility didn't cause injury during training or combat.

"It is never too early for intelligent discourse," returned Ariel.

"If that's your logic, then maybe you should be silent," said Tess drily as she approached.

Quinn chuckled. Liam's sister had certainly sharpened her tongue in the days since she'd become the Bearer. Or maybe it was just that she'd grown up, he thought. She certainly wasn't a kid anymore, unsure of herself and trying to find her place in the world. He watched her out of the corner of his eye, saw the calm confidence in her movements and the surety in her expression as she unsheathed her plain blade, the Iron Sword secure in its sheath on her back.

"Lady Bearer, you wound me," said Ariel, brushing one hand over his chest.

"You've tougher skin than that, Ariel," retorted the Bearer with a smile.

"True," admitted the Seelie fighter, "though if I did not, I would still accept your barbs with a grateful heart. 'Tis an honor to be mocked by the Bearer." He grinned.

"Is it an honor to be beaten by the Bearer?" Quinn asked, raising his eyebrows. Tess gave a surprised chuckle and looked at Ariel questioningly.

"For a mortal, you are very cheeky," Ariel said, pointing his blade at Quinn.

"Only in the best way," replied Quinn.

Something flashed in Ariel's eyes and a strange heat passed between them. Tess cleared her throat and hummed tunelessly to herself as she extended her blade and traced slow patterns in the air, warming up her sword arm. Her war markings glimmered in the dusky half-light. Quinn tore his eyes away from the handsome Seelie now observing him with an uncomfortably keen interest. He walked his hands out into a plank position and pressed up into downward dog, studying the hard-packed dirt in front of his face with determination. He would not look up to see if Ariel was still watching him….and he would not admit that there was a part of him that wanted the Seelie man to be ogling him. Of course, the Sidhe didn't ogle, they weren't that blatant…but there had been no mistaking the spark.

Swinging one leg forward into warrior pose, he stood and caught Tess's contemplative look. He didn't owe her any explanation, true, but he counted her as one of his friends in this world. Then he pulled back his shoulders. There wasn't any shame in what he was. It had taken him so long to accept himself that he wasn't about to let anyone take that part of him away. He'd fallen in love with a woman – a beautiful, fierce, stubborn woman who rode a winged mount like an avenging Norse goddess – but that was over. He was free to pursue whatever and whoever interested him.

"Lady Bearer," said a new voice.

"Ailin," replied Tess with a smile. "So, you really did want to show me how well healed your sword arm is."

"I don't say such things lightly," said the Seelie Vaelanbrigh. "Gawain might join us as well, but he has less tolerance for early morning training."

"Him and me both," muttered Quinn, transitioning back to plank and swinging his other leg forward.

"Vaelanbrigh," said Ariel with a respectful nod to Ailin.

Ailin acknowledged his sign of respect and then turned back to Tess. "Do you think your *ulfdrengr* will favor us with their presence this morning?"

"I don't own them," said Tess lightly. "But I think Chael and Luca might make an appearance."

"I had the opportunity to spar with Luca during our journey to the White City," said Ailin. "He was quite a warrior."

"Still is," corrected Tess with a smile. Quinn thought he saw some discomfort behind her smile, lingering after the battle in the Dark Keep where she'd thought that she'd lost Luca forever, though in reality he'd only been sucked through the damaged Great Gate into the mortal world.

"Of course," Ailin agreed easily. An aquamarine jewel glinted in the hilt of his sword as he unsheathed it.

"Do you all get to choose your power colors?" Quinn asked, squinting at the gemstone. "Or is it something you're assigned?"

Ailin chuckled. "It's something of an inheritance, I suppose you could say." He turned his attention back to Tess. "Have you thought more about the expedition? I'm surprised you don't want to go yourself."

Quinn and Ailin glanced at one another at the mention of an expedition. It was an unconscious reaction, but it felt like a thread had pulled at both of them, their eyes meeting with the same question and thirst for adventure hanging unspoken between them.

"Just because I didn't volunteer doesn't mean I don't want to go," said Tess. "But I have to realize that I can't go on every quest now. I can't drop everything and rush into the wilderness."

"You could," said Ailin with an elegant half-shrug. "You are the Bearer. You determine your own fate."

"That's true," admitted Tess, "but I also think it wouldn't be a good decision...based on who's already going."

It was hard to tell in the shadowy predawn light, but Quinn thought that Tess was *blushing*.

"What expedition?" asked Ariel finally, looking between the two of them expectantly.

Tess busied herself with weaving a *taebramh* light for their practice circle, leaving Ailin to answer the question. The Seelie Vaelanbrigh unconcernedly brushed a lock of his pale hair away from his eyes.

"The *fendhionne* told Knight Ramel that the other lady captured with Knight Finnead and Queen Andraste may still be alive. The Paladin, Knight Ramel and Knight Finnead are gathering an expedition to verify the claim."

Quinn frowned. "Didn't all that happen centuries ago? How would Molly know any of that?"

Tess tossed her *taebramh* light into the air. It hovered over their practice circle, casting a warm glow down on them, sharpening the shadows. "I think that when Molly took the bone sorcerer's power, she also took – or experienced – his memories. She wanted to suck every bit of knowledge from him. He was the one who captured and tortured Finnead, Rye and Andraste."

"And he planned the destruction of the *ulfdrengr*," added Ailin in a quiet voice.

"Sounds like the bastard deserved to die," replied Quinn.

"He did," said Tess firmly. She pressed her mouth into a thin line and raised her sword. "Anyone ready?"

Quinn glanced at Ailin and Ariel, neither of whom immediately volunteered, and then shrugged. "I'll go."

Tess gave him a hard, glittering grin that Quinn knew didn't bode well for him, and they stepped into the practice ring.

Ten minutes later, they stepped out of the ring, Tess having beaten Quinn to first touch three times in a row.

"One of these days," Quinn promised, taking long, slow breaths through his nose and out his mouth, calming his racing pulse. He plucked his shirt away from his sweaty skin.

"You're getting better," said Tess without any pretense. "That second bout, if you had been more aggressive, you might've been able to catch me in a cross-body lock. That would be your advantage, since you're bigger than me."

"Bigger doesn't always mean stronger," he pointed out. Honestly, he thought that Tess might beat him in pretty much every category at this point. Liam had told him that both he and his sister weren't entirely mortal anymore, and superhuman strength and speed seemed to be part of that package deal.

"True," admitted Tess. She smiled and tucked an errant strand of hair behind her ear. "But you *are* getting better." Then she caught sight of someone over Quinn's shoulder and her face brightened. His heart squeezed at the expression on her face: it was the expression of someone completely and totally in love. He'd once looked like that, mooning like an idiot over Niamh.

"Care for a round, Vaelanbrigh?" Ariel said, inclining his head to Ailin.

"Certainly," said the other Seelie, and they stepped into the ring.

Quinn steadfastly watched the two Seelie as they began their bout, but he still heard Tess greet Luca with a murmur and the unmistakable sound of a kiss. He swallowed hard. He wouldn't go crawling back to Niamh just because he missed having someone to kiss. She didn't want him. She'd made that abundantly clear both during that conversation in the Valkyrie paddock and the days following, when she'd avoided him just as studiously as he'd avoided her.

"Get a grip on yourself," he growled, crossing his arms over his chest.

Luca and Tess walked over; thankfully, the two of them weren't prone to ridiculous displays of public affection, so he didn't have to endure watching them cuddling into one another by the side of the practice ring.

"Quinn," said Luca, extending his big hand.

"Luca," Quinn returned, gripping the other man's forearm in the gesture of kinship common between the *ulfdrengr* and, by extension, the Vyldgard.

The huge blonde warrior watched Ailin and Ariel for a moment, his ice-blue eyes following their elegant, graceful movements. "I'm going to go throw some axes," he announced with a nod. He raised an eyebrow at Quinn and then Tess. "Care to join?"

"I need to get some blade work in," said Tess.

Quinn fell into step beside the bigger man. "I'll take you up on that offer."

They walked across the practice yards to the newest area, marked out after they'd repaired the damage from Mab's attack weeks before. Three targets stood side-by-side, about the same size as their archery targets but constructed with more bracing in the frame so the targets could handle the force of an axe or a throwing blade.

"Chael says that he and Thea have finished a few axes in the past days," Luca said conversationally as Quinn chose an axe from the rack on the white stone wall.

"I don't have any gold coins or whatever it is that I need to pay them for their time," replied Quinn, settling on a mid-sized axe that felt balanced in his grip.

"There's no real need for gold. Not in the White City, at least."

Quinn glanced at the wolf-warrior. "You saying you approve of me getting an axe of my own?" He hefted the axe in his grip and adjusted his stance, focusing on his target as he drew back his arm. The blade of his axe thudded into the target a little low, but it still hit sharp-edge first and buried deeply.

"You are as competent as I would expect our striplings to be," said Luca with a nod after considering Quinn's throw.

It took Quinn a second to translate: *stripling* wasn't really a word in his normal vocabulary, but he remembered that it meant something like *boy* or *youth*. He laughed. "Well, that's a ringing endorsement."

Luca threw his own axe, his aim perfect as always. Quinn thought that the stationary targets didn't really challenge the *ulfdrengr*. As they both walked to retrieve their weapons, Luca said, "I meant no insult. My people are – were – taught to wield weapons as soon as we could hold them. It isn't a fair comparison."

"Life isn't fair," replied Quinn. "Doesn't matter when you know it or not, that's just the way it is." He yanked his axe out of the target. "And I'll take it as a compliment." He grinned. "Just thought it was a little funny. I've been a soldier in my own world for most of my life now, and I start over at square one here."

Luca shook his head. "No. I don't believe you started…*at square one*." He hesitated on the unfamiliar phrase and then continued. "You and the others on your team have good instincts. The basics remain much the same between our two worlds. You just need time to become comfortable with our weapons."

"I think that's an accurate assessment."

They threw their axes for a while in companionable silence. Quinn liked the almost meditative feeling of throwing the axe, walking down to the target to retrieve it, and lining up again. It reminded him in a good way of shooting rifle on the range. Rifle had always been his favorite, the prone position specifically. He'd learned how to regulate his breath, pause at the exhale, squeeze the trigger slowly until the rifle fired. Contrary to what most people thought, good rifle marksmanship was all about calm, collected movements. It was almost Zen. The end result was undoubtedly violent, but there were few things he enjoyed more than the slow, sweet lineup of the sights, the feel of the rifle against his cheek, the delicious anticipation as he exerted pressure on the trigger with the pad of his index finger.

Finally, curiosity got the better of him. "So," he said conversationally to Luca, "what do you know about this expedition?"

Luca grinned. "You wish to go?"

Quinn shrugged. "Not really doing much good here." He threw his axe and grimaced as the blade didn't rotate enough to bite into the target, falling to the ground with a disappointing clang. "You going?"

"I think that Chael and I will be journeying with the expedition for a while, but we have our own task to attend," replied Luca.

Quinn heard a murmur pass like a ripple through the courtyard. He checked his surroundings and his heart jumped when he spotted the huge tawny wolf prowling along the wall closest to them. He knew that Kianryk was bound to Luca, but something primitive within him still shuddered at the lethal predator's graceful silence.

"Something to do with the wolves?" he guessed.

"Yes," replied Luca.

"Finally getting to rebuild, huh?"

"If we find the right companions," said the bigger man. The newly risen sun gleamed gold on the braids in his hair.

"That would be something," murmured Quinn to himself as he watched Kianryk. He'd always loved working with the dogs, even thought about putting in for the school to become a handler, but he'd known even then that it would gut him if his dog were killed in the line of duty. What would it feel like to be bound to one of these Northern wolves? He'd glimpsed Vell's black Beryk a few times, his golden eyes just as searing as those of the Vyldretning. The wolf bound to Chael, Rialla, was more elusive and aloof. He'd seen her once near the forge as Chael cleaned up for the day, but she'd quickly slid into the shadows, as though she didn't want to be seen.

"It is going to be more than just something," replied Luca with a smile. Resolve shone in his eyes. "It is going to be a long and difficult journey to restore our people…but after the destruction of the North, Vell thought she was the last of us."

"You and Chael survived," said Quinn with a nod.

"Thanks to Vell and Tess." Luca's gaze went distant for a moment. "There was a time when I thought all hope was lost, when I longed for death…not because I did not want to live, but because I was being used for such a hideous purpose." He flexed his scarred hand, the brutal marks rippling. "Tess brought me back into the light. She saved me, body and soul."

Quinn thought of the days he'd spent by Niamh's side in the healing ward, reading to her until his voice gave out, and then just sitting with her hand in his. He'd poured all his love into helping her heal. He pushed down the tide of bitterness that threatened to overwhelm him. "Did you ever think of making the choice not to accept her love?"

Luca chuckled humorlessly. "My first words to her urged her to kill me. It took me some time to understand that I was free. And that she chose to love me, not out of any sense of obligation, but for me."

Suddenly Tess's earlier comments made a lot more sense to Quinn. "She's not going on the expedition because Finnead is going."

Luca shrugged, unbothered by the mention of his one-time rival for Tess's affection. "Finnead is no longer burdened by the guilt that kept him from truly loving Tess."

"Because of the lethe stone?"

"From what I understand, yes. Vell took a great portion of his memories, almost all of those memories of Andraste. He fully understood what he gave up, but I don't think anyone thought that he'd be…" Luca trailed off, searching for the right word.

"Happier?" suggested Quinn.

"Happier," confirmed the *ulfdrengr*.

"Guess it just goes to show that self-loathing is definitely not the way to go," said Quinn. "So…you worried?"

Luca looked at him in puzzlement. "Why would I be worried?"

"Well, if good old Finnead isn't in love with Andraste anymore, does that mean he's going to fall back on old habits? His involvement with Tess," Quinn clarified. He knew he was probably venturing onto thin ice, but he couldn't quite bring himself to care. Besides, Luca didn't offend easily. Despite their reputation as fierce warriors, the Northmen displayed the kind of unshakeable calm that only those who'd seen death and fought hard battles understood. Most things that irked people seemed silly little details after you'd been through hell and back.

Luca grinned and shook his head. "No. I am not worried. It is Tess's choice as well. If she wishes to become his lover, I ask only that she is honest with me about it."

Quinn blinked. "Well that's…progressive."

"Not all people expect their partner to be everything to them," said Luca. "In fact, my people thought it unwise to think such a thing. In some cases, yes, it happens. But it is difficult to find a partner who is all things: lover, friend, partner, teacher, student…there are many roles to fill in a person's life."

"So…" Quinn stopped himself before he crossed the line.

"You were about to ask if I would be jealous," said Luca with a chuckle as they walked to retrieve their axes. He shrugged his massive shoulders. "In all likelihood, yes. But jealousy is simply another negative emotion to master, is it not?"

"I…guess so," said Quinn. He felt like he'd been thrown into the deep end of the pool with his ankles tied together and hands tied behind his back, like during his drown-proofing class. All he could do was kick his way back up to the surface, grab a breath and accept the fact that he was in over his head. Flailing and panicking certainly wouldn't help.

"Have you ever held a bird in your hands, Quinn?"

"Uh…" The unexpected question caught him off guard. "No, I guess not."

"It is a lesson we teach – *taught* – our young ones," continued Luca. "Their task is to catch a snow bird and bring it back alive to their training master."

"I can see how it applies to hunting, but I'm not sure where you're going with this," admitted Quinn.

"You must hold the snow bird tightly enough so that it does not beat its wings and break them in its bid to escape, but if you hold it *too* tightly, it will let you suffocate it. It feels safe and secure in your hands at just the right amount of pressure, so it will not struggle." Luca cupped his hands around an invisible bird, as though he held it around its belly and wings. "But if you squeeze it too tightly, it will die. It won't make a sound. It won't fight. It will just…" He spread his hands. "Die."

"That's…dark," said Quinn. He considered for a moment. He never claimed to be the sharpest tool in the shed, but he was pretty sure he could figure out this metaphor. "So you're saying if you hold the one you love – or your relationship – too tightly…"

Luca nodded. "Yes. You can strangle it."

Doubt immediately assailed him. Had that been his mistake with Niamh? Had he held her too tightly, tried to cling to their relationship with such force that he smothered it? He took a deep breath and ran one hand through his hair. He'd need to learn how to braid it soon, or maybe he could beg an elastic hair band from Tess or Vivian.

"My words upset you," said Luca, a crease appearing on his brow.

Quinn chuckled. "You know, I don't care how intimidating you look, I think you're just a big teddy bear."

Luca's frown deepened. "I don't believe I bear any resemblance to a mortal child's toy."

His chuckle expanding into a laugh, Quinn slapped Luca on the arm. "It means you actually care about people. You're a good guy."

The look of puzzlement faded from the *ulfdrengr's* face. "Ah, I see." He raised an eyebrow. "As long as it is still known that I will rip my enemies limb from limb." Without turning his head, he threw his axe at the target, the blade burying itself deeply in the center.

"I don't think anyone doubts that," Quinn reassured him.

Luca grinned wolfishly and Kianryk yawned from his vantage point against the wall, showing his long white teeth.

"I think you would be a good addition to the expedition," said Luca as they retrieved their axes and Quinn replaced his on the communal weapons rack.

"Depends on who else is going," Quinn amended hastily as he realized that he could be backing himself into a corner. But then again, maybe being forced onto the same team as Niamh would be a kind of cleansing. Maybe it would force them to either rekindle their relationship or move past it, and he didn't think the odds of rekindling were good. He cleared his throat. "But thanks for your vote of support."

"Oh, we aren't voting," Luca replied seriously. "It will most likely be the Queens who decide. Or maybe the Paladin, since she's going. Perhaps the Queens will decide the leader and delegate from there."

"I didn't mean...yeah, gotcha," said Quinn with a smile. The Northmen were also infallibly logical in their interpretation of slang. It reminded him a little bit of the Vulcans from Star Trek...always logical, always immutably literal, though Luca at least didn't display the emotional detachment that he'd expect from a Vulcan. He chuckled to himself. They even had pointed ears like the Vulcans.

"Did I say something amusing?" asked Luca guilelessly. "Sometimes my grasp of this language is...less than ideal."

"No, it was just my own thoughts. Scout's honor," replied Quinn, holding up three fingers.

Luca narrowed his eyes. "I did not know you were trained as a scout."

Quinn suppressed another laugh. God, he was so bad at not tripping over his own feet these days, even in something as simple as a conversation where he *knew* his turns of phrase would be taken literally. "Yep, you could say that."

Well, it wasn't *not* true, he thought. He'd been a Boy Scout for a few months before he'd been kicked out of the troop for convincing five of his fellow eight-year-olds to paint their faces and go hide in the woods under cover of darkness during their annual camping trip, successfully sending three of their parent escorts spiraling into panic attacks. Now he smiled at the memory...if only those indignant Boy Scout parents could see him now...

Luca nodded. "That only reinforces my thought that you'd be good for the expedition. Merrick is a scout as well, and he might go, but Vell hasn't spoken to us about her intentions."

Quinn nodded. "I understand."

They walked back toward the sparring ring. Tess and Ailin locked blades, meeting and then dancing away in a fast-paced bout that sparked a bit of envy in Quinn's chest. Though he knew he was making progress, he still felt clumsy beside these preternaturally gifted warriors.

"Tess scored a touch and then Ailin scored a touch," said Ariel to them as they approached, with the air of someone updating their friends on the score of a football game. "He has the reach on Tess, but she's really focused on her footwork the past sessions. It's harder to catch her off balance."

Tess tossed her sword into her left hand but Ailin adjusted seamlessly to the switch. They spun and leapt at dizzying speeds. Quinn only kept track of Tess by the Caedbranr on her back and the darker gold of her hair compared to Ailin's nearly silver head. The clash of their swords rang out and mixed with the echoes of other fighters sparring, creating an undulating ocean of sound around them, ebbing and flowing with the pace of the matches.

Finally, in a movement too quick for Quinn to properly see, Ailin executed a complicated pattern with his blade, and the match came to an abrupt end, Tess standing stock-still with Ailin's blade at her throat. She grinned at him, panting. He lowered his sword and bowed to her, returning her smile.

"It's been a long while since anyone scored a touch on me," he said conversationally as they exited the ring.

"Well then, perhaps you aren't as well healed as you boast," retorted Tess lightheartedly.

"Perhaps," the Seelie Vaelanbrigh replied with easy grace.

"Has throwing axes tired your arm too much?" Ariel asked Quinn, mischief glinting in his eyes.

"Oh, it takes a lot to tire me out," replied Quinn. If it had been a few weeks before, he might have winced at the subtle flirtation in their words, the spark of interest and undercurrent of heat. But now he grinned at Ariel. He liked the way that his words kindled a response in the Seelie man.

"Well, let's put that to the test, shall we?" Ariel raised his eyebrows and his blade, motioning to the ring in invitation.

Quinn smiled and stepped into the ring as he unsheathed his sword. Between word of an expedition that seemed right up his alley and this intriguing, unexpected encounter, today was shaping up to be very interesting, indeed.

Chapter 10

"For the past century or so, most didn't really want to learn runes," said the smith Thea, her face gleaming in the light of the forge. "It became...*fashionable*...to use *taebramh* without runes. Some saw it as a way to demonstrate their superior power and control." She shrugged. "But I think for some it was just a way to avoid the work of studying."

"Runes have always been our tradition in the North," said Chael from his shadowy corner where he sat and drew a whetting stone down the length of a recently finished blade.

Vivian tried not to let surprise at his words show on her face. She wasn't surprised by the *content* of his words...she was just surprised he spoke at all. This was her third lesson with Thea, and the first time that Chael had uttered a sound. She caught his lips move in a smile even through the shadows.

"Yes, I can speak," he said, a black humor coloring his words. "I just choose not to most of the time."

"Well, I value the words of anyone more experienced than me," said Vivian truthfully. "And here, that's pretty much everyone."

Thea grinned as she selected a smooth board for their next rune.

"In some ways," said Chael. "But you have done things that some of us have not." He shrugged one shoulder. "I have never traveled between the worlds. I have never fought a bone sorcerer." He paused. "And I've never faced one of the Exiled in single combat."

Vivian felt the blood rush to her cheeks as Thea looked at her sharply.

"You dueled one of the Exiled? Which one?" demanded the smith, hands on her hips.

"I only met two," Vivian said. "Corsica and Tyr."

"So which one did you fight?"

"I...how do you even know about it?" Vivian asked, frowning and fixing first Thea and then Chael with a searching gaze.

"You'll find it's very difficult to keep secrets around here," replied Thea.

"What, do you lurk in the shadows and eavesdrop?" demanded Vivian, directing the question toward Chael.

The enigmatic *ulfdrengr* chuckled. "Eavesdropping is for children, Lady Paladin." He held up the blade and sighted down its edge. "I merely listen and gather information."

"Right," muttered Vivian. She sighed at Thea's insistent, curious gaze. "I fought Corsica." She swallowed, remembering the fear that had choked her as she faced the fierce – and more than likely insane – Sidhe woman who'd spent centuries in the mortal world honing her thirst for revenge.

"And obviously you won," said Thea approvingly.

"I didn't really have a choice."

"What did you use to fight her?"

Vivian wondered if there was a polite way to change the subject...but then again, she was among warriors. Of course they'd want to talk about past battles, dissecting fights like football players watching film of opposing teams and talking about strategy before a big game. "At first just my sword. The place we were fighting was unusual. It was her lair in New Orleans – that's the city near where I live…lived. Anyway," she rejoined, "I tried to be…unpredictable." She shivered as she remembered the maniacal bloodlust gleaming in Corsica's eyes as the Exiled woman advanced on her, grinning like a cat who'd caught the canary. "Forin and Farin taught me a lot in a short amount of time, but I knew I didn't stand a chance if I just followed the usual playbook, so I tried to keep her off balance, and then I…" She smiled. "I used a spell-orb and a shield rune."

"You had time to inscribe the rune in the midst of the fight?" Thea asked, her eyes alight with interest.

"It was close," admitted Vivian, "but I managed it. And I also dove behind this statue, that helped too." She cleared her throat. "So, I guess I can say that I'm decent at shield runes, but I'd still like to get back to learning about forge runes."

Thea chuckled. "So young, yet so serious. I think you should tell me about that spell-orb sometime. Sounds interesting." But she picked up the clean board and her rune stick. Vivian leaned close, watching the order with which Thea inscribed her precise strokes as she drew a complex rune in the center of the board. "All right. We need to increase the temperature of the fire substantially, but remember that one of the marks of a good smith and one of the hardest things to do is keeping the temperature of the forge consistent…"

Vivian took out her little notebook and made careful notes with one of the pencils she'd brought along in her backpack. Thea had spent a good ten minutes inspecting her yellow No. 2 pencil during their first lesson. Vivian had explained to the smith some of the different writing instruments available in the mortal world. It was fascinating to realize how such mundane details caught the imagination and the interest of her Sidhe tutors.

They discussed the technical details of the rune and the activation procedure, as well as safety procedures, which was rather a big deal for forge runes.

"Make sure you're ready to put it directly in the forge after marking the activation, because you'll have exactly ten seconds," warned Thea.

"Otherwise, you might burn the forge down," said Chael, still sitting in his corner. His amethyst eye gleamed. "And we've just finished rebuilding this place, so I'd prefer that didn't happen."

Not for the first time, Chael's scars and silver hair reminded Vivian of Tyr. A wave of heat washed through her that had nothing to do with her proximity to the glowing forge. Almost unconsciously, she reached out for their invisible connection. Tyr hadn't talked to her for days now, and she knew he was avoiding her. Perhaps his tolerance of her in the mortal world had only been for his own benefit: she'd been able to speak for him, and she'd willingly given him her blood so he could heal and grow stronger. Perhaps now he didn't need her, and that was why she always found the connection blocked, like a solid door separating them.

"Something on your mind?" Thea asked mildly as she slid her rune into the belly of the forge and donned her heavy gloves, pushing the glowing metal of the blade she was crafting farther into the glowing embers as the heat intensified.

Vivian peeled her curls off the back of her neck as she started to sweat in earnest. She busied herself by pulling the elastic from her hair and scraping her heat-wild ringlets into a bun on the top of her head.

"That's why I keep my hair short," said Thea with a grin, examining the metal and then pulling it from the forge with just a gloved hand. Runes crawled over the black leather of her gloves, sparking a bit where the hot metal challenged their protection.

Thankfully, Vivian's bid to buy time had worked, and Thea turned her attention to selecting a hammer for the blade. Vivian tried to study the rune as she'd drawn it in her little book of notes, the final stroke to activate it written at a safe distance to the side in a small circle, a habit she'd begun to ensure she didn't accidentally complete any runes even though they were only written in pencil. But her mind refused to focus on the lesson at hand, instead veering first to Tyr and then to the silver key bequeathed to her by the last

Paladins, flitting between those two subjects like a hummingbird between two blossoms.

Perhaps Tyr really *was* just that self-centered. Could she really blame him, after all he'd endured during his centuries of punishment? But after sharing his thoughts for weeks, after being his conduit to the others as they planned their defeat of first the bone sorcerer and then Mab…she felt like she'd known him. Bitter disappointment rose within her, even though she tried to push it away. She was a Paladin. She had bigger fish to fry than crying over hurt feelings because a five hundred year old Fae didn't return her affection.

At least, that was what she tried to tell herself.

The musical ring of Thea's hammer pounding on the metal of the new blade filled the forge. Instinctively, Vivian touched the rune she carefully inked behind each ear before her lesson. It was the first rune that Thea had taught her, a rune to protect her hearing from damage by the loudness of the forge. Most forge runes were eminently practical – as was Thea. It wasn't difficult to understand why the Vyldgard warrior had been drawn to her craft.

"I get to forge weapons," she'd told Vivian on their first day. "There's beauty in the ferocity of a fighter who's defending something she loves…and my blades become a part of that beauty. Poetry, really," she'd mused, running her fingers over the hilts of the finished blades that stood in a rack along one wall, awaiting their warriors.

She watched Thea swing her hammer down onto the dull red metal, striking sparks from it as she shaped the new weapon. The sinewy strength in Thea's frame differentiated her from most of the other Fae women, though Vivian had glimpsed a few of the Valkyries – especially their one-eyed commander – who looked particularly Amazonian. She flexed one arm idly and wondered whether supermuscles were part of the whole Paladin package.

"You're distracted," said Chael. His voice reached her through the din of the forge courtesy of the runes, though they wriggled and tickled her skin at exerting themselves. She suppressed the urge to scratch, because that might smear the rune and then she'd be deaf after five minutes.

Chael beckoned her. She glanced at Thea, immersed in her work. That was how their lessons had gone: Thea teaching runes and then crafting her blades. Vivian used the time to observe and then to study. Though they'd only had a handful of lessons, they'd fallen into an easy camaraderie. Chael had silently moved in and out of the forge like a shadow…and now today he not only spoke to her, but showed some interest in actually *conversing* with her? Would he *teach* her? Curiosity bubbled up as she obeyed his summons, sliding her little notebook back into its pouch at her belt. She had the feeling that whatever lesson Chael was going to impart, it probably wasn't going to be the type that she would be able to capture in her notes.

She walked toward Chael and then stopped uncertainly about an arm's length away. He looked up at her from his seat, his single amethyst eye searching her face.

"Is it true that your eyes match your wolf's?" she blurted, unable to contain the question.

"Yes," he answered, his eye glimmering with something like amusement…but Vivian didn't feel like he was laughing at her.

She stood awkwardly, not sure what to do with her hands or where to look, though she solved the latter dilemma by deciding to boldly meet his evaluating gaze.

"So, you are the Paladin," he said in a low voice.

Vivian spread out her hands and arched an eyebrow. "Ta-da," she said. "A live Paladin, here for your examination and perusal…" He clearly didn't understand her reference to a circus barker, so she let her hands fall to her sides and tried not to give in to the blush beginning to suffuse her cheeks. She cleared her throat and tried a different tack. "And you are an *ulfdrengr*."

He smiled slightly. "You pronounce the word well."

"I have an ear for languages."

"One that has probably been enhanced by your Paladin heritage," said Chael.

She blinked. "I haven't really tested that out."

Chael narrowed his eye. "Perhaps tomorrow we will test it."

"You don't think Thea would mind...I'm supposed to be learning forge runes," said Vivian.

"You should learn whatever you deem important and interesting," countered Chael.

"It's a self-guided curriculum," she acknowledged, "but I can't just go changing it whenever I want, willy-nilly, no discipline or order..."

"You're going on the expedition, are you not? That will require some flexibility in your training." Chael set the tip of the sword he was sharpening onto the floor. Its silver length gleamed in the reddish light from the forge.

"That's true." She couldn't help the grin that curved her lips at the mere thought of the expedition. Tess had decided on giving the other Courts a week to make their final decisions on their representatives, and to ensure those representatives were fully prepared. Seven days seemed like an eternity to Vivian – she wanted to go explore this beautiful, magical world *now*. But she treated the waiting as another training opportunity: Patience was not her strongest virtue, and as Niall had mentioned, the Sidhe thought of time differently. She'd have to get used to their time frames.

"Tess was the first mortal in our world in centuries," said Chael. He brushed his fingers over the scars on his face, lightly touched the eye-patch he wore over one eye. "She saved our people from extinction."

"She did?" Vivian felt her eyes widening at the promise of a tale from the Bearer's adventures. Yet again she felt like a child next to Tess, already legendary in this world, but she pushed the feeling aside. She'd have time enough to prove herself.

Chael nodded. "She did. Luca and I were captured by the Enemy during the destruction of the North. There were many of us captured, actually." He took a breath. "We just happened to be the strongest, though we would not have named ourselves so at the outset."

"How did you find out you were the strongest?" Vivian asked quietly.

"We did not die," replied Chael simply. "The bone sorcerer and other instruments of the Enemy tortured us. Time meant nothing. They killed most of the full-grown warriors, because they knew they would not be able to break them. And then, one by one, those we had known since birth, those we had trained with and had grown up beside us, hoping to be worthy of being chosen by a wolf…they succumbed." Chael paused. Vivian shivered despite the heat of the forge. "Some died because they were not strong. Some chose death willingly because they despised the thought of being used as a tool by the Enemy."

"But you didn't choose death," she said softly. Once again, she felt that strange similarity to Tyr as she looked down at Chael. The men could have been brothers…hair turned silver by the pain of their past, faces scarred by circumstances beyond their control…

He shook his head. "No. I did not. Somehow, I still clung to hope."

"Hope that was eventually fulfilled."

"Eventually." He nodded. "But not before we were used for terrible purposes."

"That's not your fault," Vivian said immediately. She wished she'd found more eloquent words, but pressed on. "If you were forced…that's not your fault."

Chael smiled, his expression humorless. "You sound like Tess trying to convince Luca that the crimes he committed were caused by the cursed dagger."

"Sounds like they were," she replied staunchly.

"Do you understand what I'm trying to tell you?" Chael asked in a soft voice. He leaned forward, and she took half a step back to preserve the distance between them. Thankfully, he didn't seem to notice.

"You were telling me about how Tess saved you and Luca," she said with a frown.

"And I am also telling you that there is always a choice, Paladin," said Chael. He leaned back in his chair. "We survived. Tess freed us. Too many people look upon that and do not see the other outcome."

"If you hadn't been freed," Vivian said slowly, trying to follow his logic, "then you and Luca would have been enslaved and compelled to do evil things, maybe forever."

Chael nodded. "I always remember that. We were separated from an eternity of serving the darkness by a margin as thin as the edge on one of my blades."

"You were separated from an eternity of serving the darkness by the Bearer," retorted Vivian.

"The Bearer is not an infallible goddess," replied Chael, unmoved. "She could have failed. And then we would have been lost."

Vivian took a breath. "I don't quite understand your point in telling me this."

"There is not one specific point, Paladin," said Chael. "There are always things to learn from the past. But I do think it is important to remember that there is always a choice."

Somehow, he knew her thoughts about Tyr. Vivian felt suddenly and viciously exposed, but she drew back her shoulders. "I'll remember it."

He nodded. "Good."

And then he lowered his silver head, drawing the whetting stone down the length of the blade. Vivian glanced at Thea, who paused in her hammering and arched an eyebrow, giving her a little nod as though to encourage her to continue the conversation.

"Are you coming on the expedition?"

It was a stupid question, really, but it was all she could think of to change the subject, so she couldn't help the surprise that flared across her face when Chael answered without looking up: "Yes."

"I...did not expect that answer," she admitted.

Chael glanced up at her. "I know I have a reputation as a recluse."

"More of a ghost," said Thea from her anvil.

"Maybe a shadow," said Vivian at the same time.

Chael raised his eyebrows. "Then this expedition will be good for me."

"And…why are you going?" Vivian asked, feeling daring as she pressed her luck. Continuing this conversation with Chael felt like walking a tightrope, a delicate balancing act that could end either in glory or humiliating defeat.

"Rialla does not like the White City," he replied. "And it is time to…find more wolves."

"Find more wolves," breathed Vivian. "You know, my roommate Ross, she has a dog, a retired working dog named Mayhem, only everyone calls her May, mostly, and I just absolutely…" She trailed off as she realized that she was rambling, and Chael was staring at her. "…love her," she finished dumbly, pressing her lips together.

Chael smiled and arched an eyebrow. "I knew there was a reason I liked you."

Vivian smiled sheepishly. "Well, hopefully that's not the *only* reason."

Chael's smile widened. "There's a certain kinship between those who understand what it is to be only one or two of their kind."

She felt as if he'd plucked a chord deep within her; she felt it resonating through her as the truth of his words sank into her mind. "I never thought of it that way before. But I'm not really –"

He held up a hand. "I'd suggest not trying to equivocate. You are the only Paladin, currently, and it may be years before you find another."

"Right." She toyed with one of the pouches on her belt. "In that case, I'd better get back to the runes lesson. If it's just going to be me, I have to be…well, the best Paladin I can be."

Chael nodded and turned back to sliding the whetting stone down the sword. She opened her mouth to thank him for talking to her, but thought better of it. Maybe that would just make him feel awkward, and she didn't want to discourage him from speaking to her when she had her lessons with Thea. She turned back to the shorthaired Fae woman, focusing her full attention on absorbing everything that Thea could teach her.

After filling her notebook with two more pages of runes and notes, Thea concluded her lesson for the day when Moira leaned against the open door of the forge.

"I might come by for a blade soon," the Vyldgard scout said with a nod.

Thea sighed with envy and then grinned. "You're going, aren't you?"

Moira grinned in reply. "Only debate is whether I'm going as a Valkyrie or as a scout."

"Well, I've been making some new silver-tipped arrows either way. The new head should increase the range and speed significantly."

Vivian watched the exchange between Thea and Moira, noting the light in Thea's eyes as she discussed the advancements in the weapons she'd forged, and the passion in Moira's voice when she uttered the name of the Valkyrie.

"Come on then, Red," said Moira, hefting her bow. "Time for archery."

"That's a good nickname," said Thea approvingly as Vivian groaned melodramatically.

"It's not a very creative one," she pointed out as she followed Moira into the practice yard.

Moira chuckled. "Well, I'm sure you'll have another before long, especially since you're coming on the expedition."

Vivian tried not to stare at the beautiful bodies in motion across the expanse of the practice yard. At least they all had the decency to keep their shirts on, she thought as she watched one pair of Seelie men.

"Have you heard of who else has been chosen? I've been told some names, but I don't know whether they're just gossip."

"I don't know," Vivian replied truthfully.

"Well…I suppose we'll find out soon enough." Moira shrugged as they came to a stop at the line nearest the archery targets.

Vivian selected the bow that she'd come to think of as hers from the communal rack. She strung it neatly in one fluid motion and Moira nodded approvingly. By the end of the hour and over thirty shots into the target later, sweat slid down Vivian's back and she felt her arms shaking.

"That's enough for today, I think," Moira said, brushing a curl out of her face. She smiled at Vivian's stubborn look. "When we start out training, I promise it's like this. We don't shoot all day and spar all night. We're Sidhe, but we're not gods."

"Right…just supernatural beings who live for centuries and possess magic and stuff like that," replied Vivian as she unstrung her bow with a grunt of effort. It was always harder to take the bow apart than put it together, but she managed it without letting the suddenly released stave hit her in the face, so she counted it as a win.

"It's all relative," replied Moira cheerfully. "And you have *taebramh* as well, so I don't technically think that counts as an ability solely relegated to Sidhe."

"If you want to nitpick," conceded Vivian, massaging one arm and then the other.

"Nitpick," Moira repeated with an air of thoughtfulness. "You have such *interesting* words." She tilted her head. "We'll have to get you a bow of your own before the expedition. I expect Queen Vell would be just fine with outfitting you from the Vyldgard armory, though I'd guess that Queen Titania would be quite amenable too…"

Moira turned on her heel and began to weave her way through the practice yard, her curls swaying about her head like a living creature. Vivian patted her own curls to verify that her hair hadn't been animated by some unseen force in a similar fashion. She suspected it was just another part of the mystery that still shrouded the Sidhe, though she'd already learned so much about them in the past week.

The riding instruction with Moira left Vivian's legs just as sore as her arms were from archery. She surreptitiously tried to stretch the tightening muscles as she finished rubbing down her *faehal*, who flicked her tail and fixed her with one liquid eye. Vivian smiled and scratched the mare behind her ears, which she'd learned that her mount enjoyed. Moira had said that it made sense for her to have a consistent mount, and she'd chosen a black mare for Vivian whose former owner had been killed in the battle for the White City. At first, Vivian had tried not to think about the grisly circumstances that had landed the beautiful *faehal* in the communal stables, one of the mounts that any in the Vyldgard could use. That proved impossible, and she'd lain awake for a few hours one night, trying to envision the Sidhe who'd ridden the black mare into battle, never to return.

"I think I have a name for her," she said to Moira as she picked up the brush to work a snarl out of the *faehal's* tail.

"If you name her, she's yours," Moira cautioned.

Vivian blinked. "Just like that?"

"Almost. I'll just have to tell Liam or one of the ones he's assigned to care for the communal mounts." Moira grinned. "Get used to the fact that you're the Paladin and if you ask it, most likely it will be given."

"I don't want to ask for too much," Vivian replied immediately. She felt her cheeks flushing. "I mean, I haven't *done*...much."

"You helped the Bearer in the mortal world," Moira pointed out. "You assisted the Vaelanseld of the Seelie Court *and* the Vaelanbrigh – former Vaelanbrigh – of the Unseelie Court. You've already won the trust of a few of the Glasidhe scouts, who are notoriously skeptical ever since the Enemy destroyed the Three Trees."

Vivian waved a hand, her entire face burning now. "Okay, okay. I get it. I'll try to use the privilege...sparingly. But I do need a *faehal* for the expedition, don't I?"

"You do," agreed Moira. She leaned against the wall of the stables. "So I think you should name her and be done with it. You work well with her. She'll understand as you progress in your skill as a rider and respond to that."

Her embarrassment at being told that a Paladin could commandeer whatever she wanted faded as she finished combing out the last small snarls in the *faehal*'s tail. She moved to the front of the stall. The mare met her gaze with an eerie intelligence shining in her dark eyes. Vivian admired the colors playing upon the mare's dark coat: she was not only black, but gleams of deep sapphire and peacock green and bright azure shone in ripples as the *faehal* shifted. The colors reminded Vivian of the Northern Lights.

The mare was not the largest *faehal*, nor was she the flashiest: Vivian had seen one with a fiery red coat, and another that gleamed silver with a black mane and tail. But she had been patient with Vivian for the past days – there was no other word for it when the mare helpfully slowed as she sensed Vivian losing her balance, speeding up again when she thought her rider was ready.

"If I remember correctly," Moira said, "she's descended from one of Knight Finnead's mounts, Midnight."

"Maybe he can tell me about Midnight during the expedition," murmured Vivian, stroking the *faehal*'s silken nose. The *faehal* didn't feel like horses; their skin was smooth and slightly cool, as though they were partially reptilian. Details like that served as constant reminders to Vivian that she was, indeed, in another world, exploring another reality and another set of cosmic rules.

"Her name?" prompted Moira.

"Nyx," Vivian said quietly. A smile curved her lips as she said it, and the *faehal* tossed her head and snorted as though she approved.

"Goddess of night from one of your older civilizations," mused Moira.

"Greek," Vivian agreed, glancing at the scout in surprise.

"We have Scholars devoted to mortal studies," said Moira with a shrug. "When I was younger, I loved to read, and I found the tales from your world most fascinating."

"I guess I never thought that Sidhe would find mortals interesting," confessed Vivian as she gave Nyx a farewell pat.

"The strange is always interesting," said Moira as they left the stables. Then she grinned. "For a time, it was very fashionable to have mortal lovers, you know."

"I read about that in one of the histories that the Bearer recommended to me," said Vivian with a nod. She found she was looking forward to her break for lunch, though now she debated whether she had the time to take a bath before her afternoon lessons in the healing ward with Sage.

They reached the front steps of the cathedral and Moira looked at Vivian. "Know your way back from here?"

"Yes," Vivian said, mostly truthfully. She *had* gotten lost a few times in the hallways of the cathedral, but she was sure that they shifted, changing at certain times at the bidding of the High Queen's enchantment. But she'd discovered that if she held her destination firmly in mind, most of the time the passageways aligned very quickly and obligingly.

"All right then. Tomorrow, I think, we will start working with your bow, so we'll go choose that first thing."

Vivian nodded. Moira gave her a nod and then went on her own way, stopping to talk to several Vyldgard who had gone hunting outside the city by the looks of the brace of rabbit tied to one's belt and the small deer slung over the shoulder of the other. Vivian jogged up the steps, grimacing at the burn of exertion in her already-sore thighs, but she didn't slow down. The Fae world was so wondrous that she felt like she had to travel quickly so she didn't miss anything.

At the top of the steps, the pendant at her throat heated suddenly. She swallowed a gasp, one hand grabbing the Bearer's pendant to keep it from scorching the delicate skin just above her collarbone. Something compelled her to turn, her feet pivoting as if moving of their own accord. She didn't resist – the pendant didn't feel menacing or even very bossy. It felt as though it was trying to help her somehow.

She stared at the great door and realized that she'd been standing in much this spot when the last Paladins had spoken to her and bequeathed her the silver key. Frustration tinged with a bit of shame rippled through her. It had been nearly a week since she'd been given the key, and she'd looked for references to the Paladin's tower in all the historical texts that she could find, but she was still no closer to puzzling out the location of that fantastic circular room that soared up into the sky, shelves filled with whirring instruments and stacks of books and scrolls.

The great door depicted the same battle scene that it had shown when she'd first arrived: Life-sized Valkyrie swooping down on the White City, with warriors mounted on *faehal* below fighting ugly, demonic creatures at the outskirts of the citadel. Vivian waited and stared, but the figures didn't move. She pressed her lips together, steeled herself and pressed her free hand to the door.

Nothing happened. The pendant still glowed just this side of burning-hot in her palm. She gritted her teeth. Objects imbued with power that spoke in riddles were fast becoming her greatest pet peeve in this new world. She stepped back and looked up and down the door, muttering to herself.

"What is it I'm supposed to see? Not the Valkyrie, not the battle scene itself…the door. Is it a reference to the key? Does the key fit in *this* door somehow?"

She searched for the lock on the great door, but the grand portal into the cathedral did not have a lock, only supports for a long crossbeam to barricade the entryway should the citadel come under attack.

The pendant blazed in her hand. She hissed at it, sure that it was going to leave at least a first-degree burn on her palm.

"What is it I'm supposed to see?" she repeated, mystified and now a bit irritated. She was pretty sure the pendant could just show her an image or give her a vision. But that would be too easy. Instead it had to scorch her hand until she figured out what it wanted.

"Not the doors themselves…" She let her eyes go slightly unfocused, roaming over the doors, but she still couldn't see anything noteworthy. Then she frowned. "But what if it's not…*noteworthy*?"

The pendant pulsed as though to encourage her to pursue that line of thought. She scanned the door and spotted a small black spider industriously weaving a web in the crook of a bronze Valkyrie's elbow.

Just yesterday I saw a spider bigger than you and Haze put together in the western tower! Just as well no one uses it!

Farin's words echoed in her head. She'd felt a spark of interest at the time, sitting in Tess's chambers, but then her enthusiasm for her lessons had washed over that momentary recognition, burying it deeply.

"The western tower," she repeated to herself in a low voice.

The pendant's heat faded to pleasurable warmth, and she smiled, her annoyance forgotten. She fairly ran back to her chambers, her purpose so clear that the passageways didn't send her down even one wrong turn. She'd have to find Farin – and to do that, she'd have to find someone who knew how to summon one of the Glasidhe messengers. Maybe Sage would know. She sent a spark of *taebramh* ahead of her, traveling at such a speed that the wall barely accepted her token before she hurtled through it.

As there had been each of the past days, a simple meal waited on her table: bread and a hearty stew filled with meat and vegetables. Her mouth watered at the smell, but she was too excited to eat just yet. Perhaps she could go straight to the healing ward and ask one of the other healers to help her send a message – she made a sound of frustration at her own inability to plan, since she'd been standing right next to the healing ward at the entrance.

"What has excited you so?" Tyr said from his chair. He stared into the empty, cold hearth as though a fire leapt there.

Vivian couldn't even muster annoyance at him. She took a few breaths to steady herself before answering, and then she held up the silver key hung around her neck.

"I think I know where the Paladin's tower is."

Chapter 11

The other thirds were avoiding Mal, and she couldn't rightly blame them. She lay miserably in her hammock, too ill to stand watch and too healed now to sleep all day, though Jem had offered to brew her something to make her do just that. Even Hex hadn't said much to her, other than a gruff greeting when she'd returned to her hammock in the third's berthing with small, stiff steps, Jem hovering over her like a mother bird ready to defend its hatchling. She hadn't had the energy to say anything tart, and besides, she'd been a bit worried that she'd need him to catch her when her legs gave out.

It was almost high noon now. They'd strike the bells at any minute after the second manning the watch received permission from the Captain. They'd had smooth sailing since the storm, but they hadn't sighted a seam. Mal thought maybe the crew was getting restless as sometimes happened on long stretches at sea without much to occupy them. She shifted and pressed her face against her arm. Well, in five days they'd have some entertainment when she went to mast.

Her stomach turned over. She felt sick every time the thought surfaced, even though she'd tried to force herself to get used to it by thinking of it constantly for the first day after the Captain's harrowing visit. She hadn't told Jem, not out of any misbegotten sense of self-pity or secrecy, but because she thought that he might do something as crazy as her dive off the mast in the storm. He'd told her more than once that he was proud of her. She squirmed at the brotherly affection in his eyes.

Hex seemed well, but he'd moved his hammock to the other side of the berthing from their little corner. She thought that maybe she reminded him of almost dying. She'd wanted to ask him what it felt like, but he hadn't so much as given her the time of day in ages. At first, she'd wondered if he'd seen anything – whether he'd glimpsed Corinth or beautiful Serena – but she combed over the memories and realized that he'd been mercifully unconscious the entire time. The blow from the kraken had been hard enough to knock him senseless, but he hadn't broken any bones. Jem had told her that Hex had gotten sick with wet lung for a few days, but that was to be expected after drowning in cold water. She remembered the ocean water as cool and caressing, silken and filled with scents she wanted to experience again.

Scents. Tastes. She wasn't sure how to fit words to the strange experience beneath the waves. It felt almost like a fever dream now, but she clung to it all the same. She remembered Serena's pale hair and Corinth's fierce handsome face in the dimly lit greenish water. She relived the feeling of breathing in the seawater, placing a hand on her chest as she took deep breaths to reassure herself that she could in fact still breathe air. She pressed her fingers to her throat, trying to find the invisible trigger that had shifted that mechanism near the base of her skull.

She hadn't walked topside since she'd awoken because she was afraid that if she saw the azure expanse of the ocean from the deck, she'd dive in again. She didn't know how to explain this to Jem, so she didn't, turning her face into her arm when he suggested that a bit of fresh air may do her good. She hated the sadness of his sigh but she didn't trust herself not to go in search of those beautiful creatures that had saved her and Hex.

Mal ran over their words in her mind like some of the thirds counted their rings in their palms, caressing each of them with fond ownership.

You have always been softhearted, Serena.

Had Calinth wanted her to drown? Did her existence offend him somehow?

You have a good wind sorceress, for all she's not Kin.

How had Serena known about Kalinda....and kin to whom? Mal stared up at the boards overhead, her hammock swaying gently in the calm seas. The mate of the watch struck the bells, their clear tones reverberating down to the very bones of the ship. She shifted her gaze to the obsidian bone running through the hull of the ship beside their berthing. Centuries of thirds rubbing the dragon bone for luck had imparted a delicate silken sheen to the black bone. Mal had touched it once when she'd first been made a third and for some reason she couldn't articulate she hadn't liked it. She'd been a silly sparrow so she'd never touched it again.

As far as she could glean from the scraps of conversation she heard in the berthing, the *Dragonwing* had miraculously come through the maelstrom with no major damage, just the shattered rail, some damaged deck planks and a few tears in one of the smaller sails that had been whipped out of its bindings during the storm. That storm had been a ship-killer, but somehow they'd made it through. Mal remembered the silhouette of the Captain at the helm, his strong figure solid against the flashing lightning and impervious to the bellowing thunder and driving rain. A little shiver ran through her.

"Are you feeling feverish?" said Jem, his quick eyes catching the small movement as he entered the berthing.

"No," she replied in a flat voice. Her skin itched, but that had become a constant. The swelling had mostly gone down, but she still felt like she was a too-ripe fruit about to burst open. It was not a comfortable feeling. She knew if she mentioned it to Jem he'd spend all night trying to brew a tisane to help, so she kept her mouth shut. She didn't need to worry the one person who could still look her in the eyes.

"Are you sure you don't want to go topside, Mal?" Jem said gently. The hopefulness in his voice lanced into her.

"It's a beautiful day," he continued. She heard him turn and address someone behind him. "Isn't it, Hex?"

Her stomach clenched. Hex, who looked like the Captain who could very well kill her. But that wasn't his fault, she reminded herself. What fourth hadn't dreamed of being the Captain's sparrow? Not that it much mattered until you were a first, you still had to work your way up, but the Captain of the Shadowheart hadn't known she was the Captain's daughter until she made second. Seafarers did not countenance favoritism. Blood inheritance they understood, as long as it was earned.

"It is," Hex said. Though his voice was subdued, she knew from the sound that he stood to the left of Jem. There was a scuffling sound that made her think Jem had kicked Hex – or tried to. Hex cleared his throat. "You should come topside, Mal."

She stared up at the ceiling and felt the ship move beneath her gently, borne by a natural wind in her sails.

"Mal," said Jem, an edge of frustration to his voice. "You could at least answer."

Mal swallowed. "Why?" Her voice was still hoarse. She thought it might have to do with Serena's hands around her throat, or the fact that she seemed to be host to some devilish disease burning her up from the inside out.

"It's…it's a beautiful day," Hex said, repeating Jem's earlier words.

She snorted. Apparently, she disgusted Hex so completely that he couldn't think of anything to truly say. The snort hurt her throat. It felt like she'd been coughing for hours, even though she hadn't.

Jem walked closer. His worried face filled her field of vision as he leaned over her hammock. "Mal, I don't know what else to do. What's wrong?"

The Captain is taking me to mast for saving my best friend's life, and now that best friend avoids me like a leper. That best friend is also the Captain's son. None of the other thirds think I'm worth anything because they haven't said a word to me. I think I may be dying of some strange disease. I breathed seawater under the waves and I tasted the silver scent of the ship on my tongue and I want to go back.

"Nothing," she whispered, staring through him.

Jem scowled at her. "If you weren't still recovering, I'd shake you!"

She didn't reply. Why bother? Jem had clearly dragged Hex here against his will, and Jem was only there because of his blasted healer's sensitivity. Jem disappeared, and she heard him murmuring to Hex. Footsteps sounded from the ladder down into the third's berthing.

"Telen wants all thirds on deck to man the sheets on the main-mast," said Iss from halfway down the ladder.

Mal heard one of them sigh, it might have been Jem or Hex, and then they were both gone, summoned away. Good riddance. She turned her face into her arm. She would have told them to go away anyway. Her body throbbed, and she let herself slide into half-dreams of swimming through the silken sea, watching moonlight filter through the calm water, following the shadowy trail of a ship as it glided overhead, a long silver blade glimmering in her hand…

When she opened her eyes again, she didn't know if it was still day or she'd slept the last of the sunlight away. It was impossible to tell such things below decks in their berthing. When they were fourths, Jem had a theory that the Captain's cabin had a porthole, which Hex had roundly denied; Mal had shimmied out over the rail on the stern under the guise of investigating something caught on the rudder, and she'd swung out far enough to see that the Captain did indeed have a porthole, larger than even Jem had thought, the solitary window set into the ship at the stern.

Had the Captain ever seen the beautiful creatures of the water following the ship? Did he know of their existence? Mal supposed he would, having lived his entire life on the ocean. She didn't know how the older sailors kept such wondrous things from the thirds and fourths…though if Hex was his son, the Captain was capable of keeping secrets that would have burst Mal's chest like a bad barrel.

Mal didn't even know what the creatures were called. They certainly weren't Sidhe, at least not wholly. She'd heard tale of sirens, but never a male siren, and they had tails of great fish. Calinth and Serena had legs – scaled and finned, from what she could remember, but legs. Maybe they were related to sirens somehow. The purr in Serena's voice as she warned Mal not to *misplace her playthings* certainly fulfilled the seductive and deadly traits of the sirens in lore.

Her stomach rumbled. She sighed. Despite the fact that she did nothing whatsoever to encourage it, her body insisted on healing and getting stronger, with the exception of those cursed patches on her skin that itched like the blazes. Hunger pains clenched her midsection. With a growl, Mal gave in to her body's demands. She swung her feet out of her hammock, wincing as the tender soles touched the deck for the first time in a few days.

She wasn't as sore as she expected, though stiffness limited her movement until her limbs properly warmed to their task again. She muttered a curse every few moments as she wincingly pulled on a clean red shirt, brushed her trousers and stuffed her feet into her boots. For a moment, she stood flummoxed, trying to remember where she'd stowed her daggers, and then she remembered that she'd lost them both in the ocean.

No matter. She probably wouldn't need daggers in a few days anyway. The familiar tide of despair gripped her at the prospect of mast. The whole crew would be there by Captain's orders. She'd lose any respect she'd gained through the sweat of her brow and the strength of her back over the last dozen years of her life. A shudder ran through her. Maybe it would be better to give in to the call of the sea. If she drowned, she wouldn't have to stand mast. She wouldn't have to give up her red shirt and face the lash.

"If you're going to get food, you'd best hurry," said Oll from near the ladderwell. "Almost time for Cook to secure midday rations."

Mal decided that didn't need a reply. Besides, she didn't know what to say. Oll didn't move, though, as she walked toward the ladderwell.

"Do you need help?" the other woman said, her eyes shifting as though she were embarrassed to ask.

"No," Mal replied shortly.

Oll nodded but still didn't move.

"What?" barked Mal, her voice breaking. She felt too tired to be angry, but the alternative was giving in to that tidal pull of despair. Even though she felt hopeless, even though she felt betrayed and worthless and sad, she still didn't have it in her to give up. That was their chant on most raids: *Never give up, never give in! No quarter asked, no quarter given!*

"I'm not afraid of you," said Oll. The flicker in her dark eyes said otherwise. "Even if the others are, I'm not."

"Bully for you," replied Mal crossly. She felt her legs starting to tremble minutely and knew she had a limited window to climb the ladder and make it midships to the galley. She took a step forward, and Oll darted away. Mal shoved her irritation into the back of her mind. She had to focus on practical things, like food.

But as she emerged from the berthing onto deck, the late gold of the afternoon sun dripping like oil from the wood of the *Dragonwing*, Oll's words echoed in her head as nearly every crew member in her vicinity averted their eyes, suddenly busy with other tasks.

I'm not afraid of you.

Even Telen wouldn't look at her as she passed the mainmast. She spied Hex's broad shoulders over near the starboard rail, but he was on watch. She wouldn't bother him.

Even if the others are, I'm not.

Why would anyone at all be afraid of her? Mal wondered fruitlessly as she walked the deck toward the ladderwell that led down to the galley. She didn't have to alter her course at all – no sliding between two other thirds or hopping out of the way of a brisk-paced second. There were others on deck, others headed toward the galley, but they parted around her like water flowing around a rock. She kept her gaze down on the deck rather than risk looking at the blue expanse of the ocean, which tugged at the edges of her vision temptingly.

A feminine laugh echoed from Hex's direction and as other sailors moved out of her line of sight, Mal saw Iss leaning on the rail next to Hex, stroking her fingers through her long hair and gazing up at him with dewy eyes. Mal snorted. So that's why Hex had moved his hammock. He probably slept next to Iss now. Or slept *with* her.

She told herself that the pain in her chest was really from the hunger in her belly. Her body didn't know itself anymore. *She* didn't know her own body anymore. The patch of rough skin behind her left elbow cracked and bled as she slowly traversed the ladder down to the galley. No one barked at her to move her red-shirted self quicker, as she was used to. She *did* have to wait for her food like everyone else – apparently their fear of her didn't extend to giving up their place in the mess line, she thought wryly as she idly pressed a finger to her bleeding arm.

The younger third serving the mess line spilled the first bowl he tried to give Mal, jumping nearly out of his boots when he glanced up at her and realized who he was serving. Mal blinked. Did she look hideous? Was there a terrible scar that she'd somehow acquired? Iss had a bit of polished silver she used as a mirror, maybe...she shoved that thought away. She wouldn't ask any favors of Iss.

Bowl of stew in hand along with her crust of bread, Mal un-hooked the copper cup from her belt and held it up for the third on water-barrel duty. He ladled her allotment of water into the cup, slopping some over the sides. She pressed her lips together but before she could say anything, he glanced down the line and gave her an extra half-ladle to make up for it.

Perhaps being feared had its advantages, she thought as she found a shadowy corner to sit and eat. She drank the broth of the stew and scooped out bits of salted meat with her bread. As she ate and the pain of her empty stomach receded, her mind continued to try to make sense of Oll's words, gnawing on them like a mongrel with a bone.

Her skin still felt tight, but the swelling had mostly gone down. She flexed her fingers. They didn't look like sausages anymore. That was good. She wished briefly that she could take a bath, but that was fancy at its finest. Even the Captain only washed once a week underway while they were searching for a seam. Water was more precious than even food on a ship sailing the Endless Seas.

Maybe they wouldn't find a seam. Maybe this would be one of those times where they would put back into Haven without any spoils to trade. It had happened only a handful of times that Mal could remember, but she'd only started really paying attention to things such as that when she made third.

She finished her stew and drank the rest of her water, which tasted coppery and somehow green to her. She winced. Cook paid attention to the fresh water, knowing that the Captain would hold him responsible if the crew fell ill from a contaminated barrel. And no one else seemed to notice. Mal took her bowl up to the scullery. The third working there snatched her bowl out of her hand when she was still three paces away like he was afraid that he'd catch fire if he got too close to her.

She leaned on the port railing to rest for a moment after climbing the ladder from the mess decks, shutting her eyes against the inviting glimmer of the ocean. The dark current pulled at her soul again: she couldn't even walk from mess decks to berthing, and she had Captain's mast in five days. Or was it four? A crushing panic grabbed her, squeezing her ribs like a vise. She gripped the railing with both hands, trying to breathe, feeling another patch of skin near her right wrist split open. The bright, immediate pain anchored her.

"Are you ever going to tell me what happened down there?" asked Jem from beside her.

She didn't open her eyes. "Why?"

"Because I'm your friend," said Jem, sounding a bit wounded. "Or I thought I was. Something happened to both of you down there, and I can't help you if I don't know what happened."

"You helped enough," said Mal wearily. She'd meant it to be a compliment, her acknowledgement of all Jem had done for her over the past days, but her words came out tired and bitter.

"What happened?" he pressed.

"Oll said everyone is afraid of me," she countered.

"Why won't you open your eyes?" Jem paused. "Does the light hurt? That could be symptoms of – "

"It's not that," she snapped more harshly than she intended.

"Then *what is it*?" Jem said in frustration. "Hogs' balls, Mal, between you and Hex it's like trying to work out a constantly changing riddle!"

She opened her eyes and stared a Jem. "Hogs' balls?" She raised an eyebrow. "You never swear, and the one time you do, that's the best you've got?"

"Well, apparently I need to swear to get you to answer me, because that's the most you've talked since we fished you out," retorted Jem, crossing his arms over his chest. He was nearly the same height as Mal, so they stared at each other for a long moment. Mal noted that Jem's hazel eyes were more green than brown, and the brown was really closer to gold in the afternoon light.

"Well?" he prodded.

"I don't want to talk about it…here," she replied, hoping he'd just let it drop and knowing he wouldn't.

Jem spread his arms. "Where do you suggest? We're on a ship at sea. There's no such thing as privacy."

Mal suddenly wondered if she'd hear Hex and Iss enjoying each other in the berthing – it happened occasionally, and she'd never paid it much mind, but then again she was younger than Iss and hadn't ever shown any interest in such things. She gritted her teeth.

"You look like you want to stab something," Jem observed un-helpfully.

"I always want to stab something," she replied, feeling the loss of her beautiful hard-earned daggers all the more keenly. Jem waited silently. She stared out at the ocean. "Don't let me jump, all right?" she said suddenly as its pull crested, like a hook behind her breast-bone, urging her to kick her heels over the railing. It would be so simple…the water was so close…

She felt a tug at her belt and found that Jem had taken a firm grip on it. His unquestioning loyalty broke through the gray haze of her apathy in a way that little else had. That and the sight of Hex standing near Iss on the railing…

"You jump, I jump after you," he said.

"You hate swimming." She shook her head.

"But I do know how to swim." He looked at her expectantly and then gave her belt a little tug.

She swallowed, resisting the urge to scratch her elbow. It was already bleeding, she reminded herself. "I…saw Hex go down after I threw my spear into the kraken. And then the wave washed him overboard." She shrugged. "I jumped. I…got lucky. I found him. Swam up to the surface. Lashed him to the crate." Her mouth felt dry and her heart pounded. She'd never lied before. Lying was not a vice tolerated on the *Dragonwing*. Lying, stealing or cheating another out of his due were all offenses that earned fourths a thrashing and everyone else mast.

"If you tell me what really happened," said Jem in a low voice, "maybe I can help."

Jem *did* know herbs and healing. Maybe the sea creatures had given her some disease…but no, she'd had those patches on her skin before she dove into the storm-lashed seas. "You'll think I'm addled."

"Maybe you hit your head and you don't remember," he replied with half a shrug. "But whatever you *think* happened, that's the reason for your black mood, far as I can tell."

"No." She shook her head, even though that was only partially true. "Well…a bit. But…mast." She choked on the word.

Jem's face darkened. He didn't reply.

Mal took a breath and pushed away the whirl of darkness. "I…when I was underwater…I found Hex. And I was drowning. But I…didn't."

"Obviously," said Jem with an air of patience.

"I breathed," said Mal, staring out at the ocean. "It was…wondrous."

"You breathed underwater. Like sorcery?"

"Like sorcery," she agreed. The line of the horizon shimmered with heat and gentle waves lapped the hull of the ship. "And I could see. Everything was silver and green. And then…" Her throat closed. Somehow, she knew deep in her bones that she wasn't supposed to utter a word about Calinth and Serena. "Then I swam Hex to the surface. I lashed him to the crate. And I…I went back to fight the kraken."

"You fought…the kraken," repeated Jem.

She tore her eyes away from the beauty of the ocean and looked at him searchingly, but her friend didn't seem disbelieving, just repeating it for clarification. "Yes." She shrugged. "I could see, I could breathe, I could swim and I had my daggers. Why not?"

"And you're sure you didn't hit your head."

She narrowed her eyes and then caught the spark of amusement in Jem's gaze. She shrugged. "Believe me or not, doesn't matter."

"Why wouldn't it matter?" said Jem sharply, tightening his grip on her belt.

"Mast," she replied with a grim finality. Yet however terrifying the prospect of mast seemed, the sun's warmth still felt good on her skin, and the sea breeze washed over her, its briny embrace welcome after the stale air of the berthing.

"You'll survive," Jem said firmly.

She shrugged one shoulder. "Let's talk about something else." She slid a glance at him. "Does everyone know about Hex?"

"Know what? Oh." Jem pressed his mouth into a line. "I don't know. I think most of the seconds suspect. Definitely the firsts."

"Bastards," muttered Mal. It felt like Hex was slipping further and further away from her: First she'd seen him in the Captain's face, or the other way around, she supposed. And now he'd outgrown her, instead preferring Iss and her long hair. Her stomach clenched. "I should've been nicer," she said to herself. Hot shame rolled through her. "That's why I jumped, you know," she said louder, looking at Jem.

"What was?"

"The last words I said to Hex. He was just trying to help, and I said I didn't need anyone to take care of me. Then he was washed overboard."

"That's not why you jumped," said Jem. The quiet confidence in his voice stirred something deep within her. How could he be so sure that he knew her so well?

"Then why did I?" she asked a bit tartly.

"You love him," said Jem.

Her heart stopped and then leapt into her throat and started beating wildly like a captured bird. But before she could choke out any words, Jem continued calmly.

"You love him as I love him, and as I love you," he finished.

She looked away. "I suppose you're right."

They stood in silence for a moment, watching the sun gleam on the gentle roll of the waves.

"Let me put some ointment on your arms," said Jem finally.

They started back toward the berthing. Mal knew he walked close to her in case she fell, but she didn't much mind. Somehow after their conversation she felt lighter, even though a prickle of some hot emotion jabbed her when she glimpsed Hex and Iss again at the rail. She followed Jem across the decks, glad that at least one person on the *Dragonwing* didn't fear her. As she obediently held out her arm for his doctoring, Mal thought for the first time since she'd awoken that perhaps everything wasn't lost after all.

Chapter 12

"The Paladin will have the Vaelanseld of the Seelie Court," said Queen Andraste, "as well as Knight Finnead, one of the High Queen's Three."

Guinna had to credit the young queen for keeping her composure at the mention of Finnead.

Andraste's full lips twisted. "And we are sending Knight Ramel." She glanced first at Guinna and then at Sayre, a question in her eyes.

"I've spoken to Ramel," said Guinna, "and while he has not been the model of decorum these past weeks, I believe that being a part of the expedition will do him good."

She *had* spoken to Ramel, hauling him out of his mess of a room smelling of *vinaess* and possibly stronger spirits, pretending she didn't see the tawny glow of the naked Seelie woman still sleeping amidst the furs.

In the corridor, Ramel had the gall to act offended and put-upon. "You said before that whom I bed is my own business."

"I didn't say anything at all about who you're bedding," Guinna had retorted sharply. She searched the face of the Unseelie Knight. He still looked youthful, so much like the brave squire who had obeyed his Knight – Finnead – and fought his way through the forest in order to send a message to Darkhill after the Princess' capture those centuries ago. He'd rescued her from a *garrelnost* and ensured she reached safety, nearly at the cost of his own life. "What *is* my business," she continued, pushing those memories away, "is the fact that you are still carousing about like a dandy and a lush. It is not befitting for a Knight of the Unseelie Court, much less one who was once the Vaelanbrigh."

His eyes, once so full of laughter, sparked with anger. "The Vaelanbrigh to the Mad Queen, don't forget," he said bitterly. "Useless in protecting anyone at all, even myself."

Guinna raised her chin. He was nearly a whole head taller than her, but she glared up at him challengingly. "I should slap you. You're here wallowing in your own self-pity when you *could* be doing something useful." She shook her head and crossed her arms over her chest. "Perhaps I should suggest to the Queen that she takes your Knight's sword. It's obvious you care nothing for it." Though she winced internally, she let scorn seep into her voice. Empathy had done nothing to change Ramel's behavior, so perhaps this was the way to reach him.

But Ramel laughed, a hard, brittle sound with an edge of anger. "You do that, Guinna. Everything else has been taken from me, why not that?" He spread his hands and unwillingly drew her eyes to the scars visible on his left hand and arm, the remnants of his foray into the mortal world at the bidding of the Mad Queen.

"Stop feeling sorry for yourself," she said, holding her ground even as Ramel took half a step toward her. "You must have heard by now that the Queens are assembling an expedition to investigate the possibility that Rye is alive."

Ramel froze, his eyes glinting with suspicion. Guinna's heart twisted. What had Mab done to him, this Knight who she remembered as puckish and valiant, loyal and fierce, that he questioned everything now?

Much the same as was done to many others, she reminded herself sternly, thinking of Bren. She pressed onward. "I'd think that you would want to be a part of that."

"No one could keep me away," Ramel said.

"Only yourself," she replied. "If you aren't fit to serve as one of the Queen's Knights, how will she send you on this expedition?" She gestured to his wrinkled and stained shirt, his unlaced trousers hanging from his hips haphazardly, his sallow skin, bloodshot eyes and unkempt hair. "You and I both know that appearances aren't everything, but please." She caught his eyes. "Make yourself present-able. Go to the practice yards. Stop drinking."

He flinched minutely at her last suggestion. Her stomach dropped. She'd failed him as a friend, to let him sink this far into the morass of his own self-hatred. Between him and Andraste, she felt as though she were trying to pull two drowning swimmers to a shore that drifted farther and farther away. Sometimes she wondered if she had the strength to save them both.

She drew back her shoulders. Whatever the strength required, she would find it. She had to believe there was a reason she'd survived the reign of the Mad Queen, just as she'd had to believe there was a reason she'd lived and her sister Rose had been killed all those centuries ago on that fateful night in the forest.

Ramel ran a hand through his hair. "How long? And who else?"

"A week, maybe a little more time," she replied. "I believe the Bearer and the Paladin will preside over the final composition."

"The Paladin," he murmured, as though to himself.

She nodded. "Yes." She cleared her throat. "So…if you need help…I am sure Healer Maeve would be happy to assist you. Or Eamon, if you would prefer someone of our own Court."

"I would prefer someone outside of our own Court," he said darkly, scrubbing one hand across his eyes.

"Then perhaps Sage or even the Lady Bearer," Guinna continued inexorably. She had to know that he'd take this step. She couldn't drag him the entire way.

Ramel stared at the rich carpet beneath their feet. "Tess has other worries."

"For stars' sakes, Ramel, will you *stop* that?" Guinna exclaimed, stamping one foot for good measure.

He raised his eyebrows in surprise at the vehemence of her reaction. "Stop…what?"

"Thinking that everyone has something better to do than helping you," she said crossly, narrowing her eyes at him and jutting out her chin, challenging him to contradict her. He opened his mouth and closed it again without uttering a word. "There are people who care about you. People who *love* you," she clarified. "Me. Tess. Finnead. Vivian. Others I can't think of right now, but who do exist." She took a deep breath. "Andraste cares about you as well. She knows that her sister treated you unjustly. She needs all the loyal Knights in our Court to help her rebuild, and that includes you."

"You don't understand what she did to me," Ramel said in a low voice.

Guinna wasn't certain if he was talking about Molly or Mab, but it didn't matter. "You're right," she said. "I don't. No one will ever truly understand, Ramel, because *they're not you.* They didn't experience it. They didn't feel what you felt. But that's not an excuse to shut everyone out and drink yourself to death." She swallowed. "We all suffered. I'm not comparing. It isn't about who carries more pain or who was wronged the most." She paused, took a few more calming breaths. She could feel Sayre in the corner of her mind, checking on her – he'd felt her agitation. "Do you know what Sayre and I had to do the other day?" she asked softly, holding Ramel's gaze.

"No," he admitted warily.

"We had to go to the throne room," she said in that same quiet voice, "and lay the bones of those that Mab had killed to rest. Sayre discovered a rune that recreated the faces of the dead, when drawn on the skull." She'd already relived that day many times, with Sayre and on her own in her dreams, and its chill horror no longer touched her at the memory. "Tess came with us." Her throat clenched when she remembered Tess's anguished cry when Bren's face materialized in a swirl of ghostly rune-magic. The Bearer had shoved her knuckles into her mouth to stifle her grief, and after a few moments she'd taken the small skull from Sayre's hands, staring at its empty eye sockets for a while in silence.

"Who else?" Ramel said solemnly.

"Donovan came. He thought it his duty." Guinna thought of the charismatic Knight who'd been baptized Mab's Vaelanmavar in the throes of battle at the Dark Keep. He'd been quiet and none of them had remarked on the scars across his face, though by the end of those draining hours, he and Tess had talked in low voices as they walked somberly back through the fading light of evening.

"I heard he was injured during one of the raids," said Ramel.

"More than once," replied Guinna. "You'll have to ask him yourself if you want the details." She refocused on the grisly topic at hand. "We went to the throne room and we stayed there for hours, Ramel."

He wouldn't meet her eyes now.

"She killed so many," she continued in a gentler voice. "None of it was your fault. None of it was anyone's fault." She reached out and touched Ramel's arm. "Don't give her the satisfaction of keeping any sort of hold over you."

At that, Ramel looked up. He swallowed hard, his throat bobbing several times; and then he nodded. "You're right." He tugged at the hem of his wrinkled shirt. "I'll…start to make changes."

"I'll know if you don't," she cautioned him, holding up a finger.

He chuckled. "Of course you will. You were always something of a mother hen, Guinna."

"Lucky for you that I am," she replied dryly, but relief blossomed in her chest at the sound of his chuckle. Surely that meant that she'd broken through the cocoon he'd spun for himself from his apathy and self-pity. Hesitantly, as though they were two strangers – because sometimes it felt as though she didn't know anyone anymore after the upheaval of their Court – she stepped forward and embraced him. After a suspended moment in which she thought that he might shove her away, he rested his arms delicately around her.

She drew away and wrinkled her nose. "Take a bath, Ramel."

He waggled his eyebrows. "Is that an invitation?"

She rolled her eyes. "No, it's a friendly suggestion."

And with that, she'd left him to sort himself out, hoping that he'd been honest in what he said. Now she stood before her Queen and steeled herself to answer questions.

"If I remember," Andraste said slowly, "Ramel loved Rye, though I do not think it was ever…"

"Consummated?" suggested Sayre.

Andraste blushed, her cheeks turning a delicate shade of rose. Guinna reminded herself that Mab had guarded her sister's virtue quite seriously, though she had been certain those centuries ago that the Princess and Finnead had secret trysts of some description.

"Consummated," affirmed the Queen. "Not that the act of physical consummation is any true measure of how deeply one loves." The blush in her cheeks, rather than fading, flamed higher.

"I believe I sufficiently motivated Ramel to change his ways," Guinna said. She thought she detected a hint of gratitude in the Queen's lovely face at the graceful change of subject. "As I said, I think it will do him good."

"Would that be sufficient for our contribution?" Andraste asked, her blue eyes searching their faces once again. She tilted her head slightly. "Guinna, do you feel any desire to join in the expedition?"

"My place is here with you, my lady," Guinna replied instantly.

"Thank you," said Andraste with a nod. "But if you wished to go and you asked it of me, I would consider it."

Guinna shook her head. "I can defend myself well enough and I have ridden out to battle before, when it was necessary, but I am not a Knight or a Guard. My place is here with you, to offer what counsel I may as you make decisions about the future of our Court."

"You are ever loyal, Guinna," Andraste murmured. One hand

drifted up to her pale cheeks and traced the brutal scars left by the bone sorcerer and Malravenar. "Even when others draw back in fear, you are ever constant."

"How could I fear someone I love, my lady?" said Guinna truthfully. Perhaps if she reminded Andraste often enough that she was loved, she, too, would allow others close again.

"Oh, that can happen quite easily," Andraste replied, a hint of sadness in her voice. She smiled. "I loved and feared my sister."

"Queen Mab was magnificent, yet terrifying," said Sayre. His youthful, earnest words sometimes resonated with Andraste more than an older, level approach, Guinna thought, perhaps because while Andraste was just as old as Guinna, she hadn't truly *lived* these last centuries. It was as if she'd gone to sleep and then awoken in a different world…except Andraste's nightmares had been very real. At first Guinna hadn't been sure of the wisdom of Sayre as one of the Unseelie Queen's Three, but he was young and resilient enough not to have a heart hardened by bitterness and anger. He drew them both back toward gentler, more forgiving versions of themselves.

"What else have you heard about the others going on the expedition?" Andraste said. "Do you think the Arrisyn or the Laedrek will take part?"

Guinna thanked the stars that her centuries of experience helped her to suppress the blush that tried to rise to her cheeks at the mention of Merrick…and his lover, Calliea.

"The Arrisyn, perhaps," replied Sayre, saving Guinna from implicating herself with any inflection in her voice. "The Laedrek will stay here, I think, or perform some other task for the High Queen as one of her Three. With Knight Finnead already part of the expedition, I doubt that Queen Vell will send the Dragonslayer as well."

"Dragonslayer," Guinna muttered to herself with a little huff. How could she compete with a *dragonslayer*?

"Do you have something to say about the Laedrek, Guinna?"

Andraste asked mildly, the mischievous gleam in her blue eyes belying her calm tone.

"Nothing at all, my lady," Guinna replied in a voice smooth as silk.

Andraste smiled and Guinna felt herself smiling in return.

"Sharing private jokes is all well and good until you're the one who doesn't understand the humor," commented Sayre.

Andraste laughed – *really* laughed – and Guinna felt a surge of affection for the dark-haired young Guard who was now one of the most influential individuals in the whole of their Court.

The conversation turned to simple matters of lesser importance for a while, and then Guinna gathered herself. Time to start asking difficult questions again.

"My lady," she said, "we should discuss the plan to rebuild."

The sparkle of laughter faded from Andraste's eyes, but she nodded in agreement. "Yes."

"Do you intend to move us back to Darkhill?" Guinna continued.

"I know that was my sister's intention," replied the Queen.

"It does not matter what your sister intended," Guinna said boldly. "It matters what *you* intend, my lady."

Andraste took a deep breath and nodded. Her hands found her long dark braid, her fingers running down its length and then starting at the top again, as though she were stroking a small animal as she thought. Guinna thought of Rye's faithful hound, Mira, sired by one of the *ulfdrengr* wolves on one of the Unseelie hunting hounds. Though Guinna shuddered at the thought of hunting hounds because she'd narrowly avoided death at their gleaming teeth, she watched Andraste's unusual habit and thought that perhaps a pup or a kitten would steady the Queen's hands, take her mind off herself sometimes.

"Darkhill is the seat of our Court," Andraste said finally. "But I worry that the centuries of my sister's rule will forever be imprinted upon its halls." She stopped stroking her braid as if she'd suddenly realized the motion of her hands, clenching her fists instead in her lap. "I do not know if I can contend with the ghosts of the past in that place."

"Most of Queen Mab's cruelties were inflicted here in the White City," pointed out Sayre guilelessly. Guinna winced but Andraste only looked at Sayre in appreciation.

"I...had not quite thought of it that way," said the Queen.

"I think it would give those who survived a sense of comfort to return to Darkhill," Sayre continued, his voice thoughtful.

"And do we leave a delegation here in the White City? I believe that the Vyldgard will be here for a while yet until the High Queen makes a decision on the location of *their* seat of power. And the Seelie seem committed to the restoration of the City, especially now that there is a Paladin."

"Indeed," said Guinna, nodding. She thought for a moment. "I think we still may be a few weeks, perhaps even a few months, away from those who were – injured – healing enough to make the journey to Darkhill."

"You mean those who my sister tortured," said Andraste darkly, touching her scars again.

"Yes," Guinna replied.

"How many are still in the healing ward?"

"I would have to verify with Eamon, my lady, but at least two dozen," she said.

Andraste closed her eyes briefly but then drew back her shoulders. "Keep me updated on their condition."

"You could visit them yourself, my lady," Guinna ventured, feeling as though she were toeing out onto new ice at the onset of winter.

"I do not want to distress them," the Queen replied, an edge to her voice.

Sayre took up the cause. "Distress them, my lady?"

Andraste scowled at them both. "Do not think I am immune to observing the discomfort that my appearance provokes."

"Are you speaking...literally?" Sayre said, stars bless him.

The Queen leveled her blazing eyes at him. "Yes, Sayre, I am speaking *literally*. Not only do I bear a strong physical resemblance to the Queen who tortured them, I am also..." She clenched her jaw and then finished the sentence, gritting out the word. "Disfigured."

Ah, now they were getting somewhere. Guinna felt a spark of hope leap within her chest, just as she had when Ramel had chuckled. It was the first time that Andraste had spoken in plain language about her scars. She held her tongue, hoping that Sayre would continue to take the lead. His approach seemed to be working, after all.

The brave young Guard met his Queen's eyes without flinching. "Yes, you bear scars, my lady. But seen or unseen, all of us do."

Guinna marveled at Sayre's tact. She wouldn't have thought the younger man capable of telling the Queen to stop wallowing in self-pity so neatly and courteously. Andraste flushed, the lines carved across her cheekbones standing out starkly.

"And yes, you resemble Queen Mab." Sayre shrugged one shoulder, still holding the Queen's gaze steadily. "I look like my brother, but no one has ever accused me of his crimes."

Andraste drew in a deep breath and let it out slowly. Guinna tensed, thinking that maybe the young Queen would lose her composure – she felt Andraste's anger like a coiled muscle at the edge of her awareness. But despite the tense, uncomfortable feeling, Andraste looked at Sayre and said levelly, "Thank you."

A small smile touched Sayre's mouth. "You're welcome, my lady."

Andraste sat for another moment and then encompassed both of them with a look of consideration. "I have not been fair to either of you. To both of you." She held up a hand to cut off both their protests. "You know it as well as I do." She swallowed. "And now it's been made clear to me that the only way I can be the Queen that my people – *our* people – deserve is to let you be the two of my Three that I need you to be."

"That you deserve," Sayre said quietly.

The hope in Guinna's chest quickened along with her heartbeat. This was what they'd been waiting for. This was what they'd been striving toward – Andraste realizing that she and Sayre were there to *help* her, that they passed no judgment and they asked nothing other than the privilege of being two of her Three.

"It has been…difficult," admitted Andraste. "After Queen Vell used the Lethe stone on me to restore my memories…I've felt out of place. Nothing is as I remember it. Nothing is as I expect it to be. It is…" She closed her eyes briefly. "Dizzying."

"We have seen that it is not easy for you," said Sayre. "All we ask is that you allow us to be what we are meant to be."

The Queen twisted her hands in her lap. "It is not easy," she repeated softly. "In the first hours after I was crowned…everything seemed effortless. I had this new power coursing through me and I felt like anything was possible. And then, somehow, that feeling slowly faded."

"The euphoria wore off and it was time to do work," Sayre contributed.

Andraste accepted his explanation with a small smile. "Something of that nature." She carefully unclasped her hands and smoothed her skirts, resting her fingers tranquilly on her knees. "And now you have allowed me to see that it is time I accept that there is work to be done." She nodded. "I've allowed myself to become mired in my own self-pity and trapped in self-doubt. That does our people no good at all."

Guinna almost laughed at the distinct similarity between this conversation and the words she'd shared with Ramel only hours before.

"Something amusing about that admission, Guinna?" Andraste asked dryly.

Guinna started guiltily. "This just reminds me very much of the conversation I had with Ramel. I was not half so tactful as Sayre, though."

"I heard you pulled him from his room by his ear and gave him a proper tongue lashing," replied the Queen with an amused smile.

"I have no idea how you heard that, my lady, but I assure you that I am the very soul of courtly comportment," Guinna said.

"The very soul," agreed Sayre gravely.

Andraste laughed. "Well, I cannot deny that. You keep us all acting civilized, Guinna, that I can't deny."

"It depends on your definition of 'acting civilized,' my lady," Guinna said. She cleared her throat and arched an eyebrow. "For example, I seem to remember that you were rather fond of wearing breeches. There is no one now to tell you that you cannot do so."

Andraste's eyes widened almost comically. "Wouldn't it cause a scandal?"

"My lady," said Sayre, his voice rich with held-in laughter, "you are the Queen. You decide what is scandal and what is not."

The Queen settled back in her chair. "I suppose I am," she said musingly. Then she grinned and looked at Guinna. "I could even go to the practice yards."

"You could," Guinna agreed with a nod and a smile.

"It might inspire our Knights and Guards to practice more regularly with those of other Courts," said Sayre thoughtfully.

"Our Knights and Guards have not been to the practice yards?" Andraste said with a hint of outrage, raising her dark eyebrows.

"They have been keeping mostly to themselves, and not interacting with the Vyldgard and Seelie Knights and Guards," replied Sayre.

"Well," said Andraste, "if their Queen is seen in the practice yards, then that will certainly encourage them to take up the habit themselves, would it not?"

"It would indeed, my lady," agreed the Guard. He glanced at Guinna, his excitement reflected in her eyes as well.

Andraste straightened, thought for a moment, and then stood. "No time like the present."

"I – *now*, my lady?" Sayre scrambled to his feet.

"I see no reason why not." She nodded. "And then I shall visit the healing wards."

"Aye, my lady. I shall go to the smith to procure you a suitable sword."

"No need," said Andraste, waving a hand, already halfway across the room toward her wardrobe. "I'll do it myself." She glanced over her shoulder at Sayre. "Would you be my sparring partner for today?"

"As my Queen commands," said Sayre with a grin and half a bow.

"Your Queen might command you to let her win a few rounds," said Andraste under her breath as she threw open the doors of her wardrobe and considered the selection, "because she will most certainly be out of practice."

"I'll…wait outside," said Sayre.

"Guinna, do I *have* any breeches?" Andraste asked with a hint of puzzlement.

"Yes," she answered promptly, walking briskly across the chamber.

"Good," Andraste replied, putting her hands on her hips.

As Guinna pulled out the breeches from where she'd carefully folded them weeks before as she'd helped prepare the then-Princess's chambers, she didn't suppress her smile. Today had certainly surprised her. It was a day of new beginnings for more than one beloved friend, and it wasn't even noon yet.

Chapter 13

"Mind if I join you?"

Quinn turned at the question and grinned when he saw Liam trotting down the steps in front of the cathedral. "That's a stupid question. You don't need to ask."

"I know." Liam shrugged. "Just being polite."

Quinn snorted. "Are you getting all domesticated and stuff?"

"And stuff?" His former team leader raised an eyebrow. "I wouldn't say so."

"I mean, just make sure you're not *too* polite."

Liam's grin reminded Quinn of the wolf-like expression that Vell wore sometimes. "Never." He surveyed Quinn's outfit. "Nice shorts."

"You know it," replied Quinn easily. He'd always been the handiest one with a needle and thread on their team, able to fix just about anything they tore and modify their uniforms to fit more comfortably and practically. The lack of an actual sewing machine here had reduced his speed, true, but he still remembered the stitches that his grandmother had taught him decades ago. She'd been very forward-thinking, his *abuela*; she'd insisted that both her grandsons and granddaughters knew how to cook, sew, throw a punch and hide a knife on them no matter what clothing they wore.

He struck an exaggerated pose to model the shorts that he'd made: loose trousers cut and hemmed mid-thigh, nothing complicated. "Want me to make you a pair?"

"Maybe," said Liam. He shrugged. "I'm getting used to trousers all the time though."

"Guess we could actually go on supply runs to our world now that there's a Gate open all the time," mused Quinn. He ran his hands through his hair as he stretched his hamstrings.

"I'm fine staying here," replied Liam, starting his own stretches. "How far you going?"

"'Til I get tired, I guess," said Quinn. "My tracker on my watch doesn't really work anymore, you know…I've just been gauging by time and effort."

He'd added runs to his training routine as a way to expend some of the restless energy that he found building up after being suddenly cut loose from his apprenticeship as a healer and taking care of Niamh. Thinking about her didn't hurt anymore…or rather, it was the ache of a healed scar rather than the sharp pain of a fresh wound.

"Want to take it easy on me and keep it at a conversational pace?" Liam asked.

Quinn eyed him suspiciously. "Luck, are you actually suggesting we take it easy? I don't think I've ever heard that from you before. Are you *sure* you're not going soft?"

Liam chuckled. "Pretty sure. I just want the chance to talk. We've both been busy."

"Fair enough." Quinn shrugged and finished stretching. A few passing Sidhe glanced at them with mild curiosity. He wondered if they used running as conditioning or if that was a purely mortal phenomenon, and he asked Liam as much.

"From what Finn has told me, they do a lot of conditioning as pages and squires," said Liam as they started out at an easy jog. A light mist still wreathed some of the darker corners of the white-paved streets, and a cool breeze washed over them. "They have a sort of Hell Week style test called the gauntlet that's run by their instructors as well as the Knights who sponsor them as squires. It's not uncommon for there to be deaths."

"Wait, they have a whole system of pages and squires? I don't see any of that happening now."

"Finn says that once the threat of Malravenar started becoming apparent, most Sidhe made the decision to stop having children. They're long-lived enough that they don't necessarily worry about extinction if they don't reproduce."

Quinn chuckled. "You were a biology major, weren't you?"

"Pre-med," said Liam. He grinned as they turned a corner. "Until I figured out that I was meant to be a guy with a gun, not a doc in a lab coat."

"You'd've made a good doc," Quinn replied. He took a few breaths, enjoying the feel of the easy pace gradually warming up his legs and the sweat beginning to prickle on his forehead. "So, they just decide not to have kids and that's that?"

"Pretty much."

"Have you turned your expertise to thinking about, oh, what would you call it, cross-species reproduction?" Quinn raised one eyebrow suggestively.

"I don't think it's *cross-species*," repeated Liam dubiously. He shook his head. "Besides, we're nowhere near that."

"That's what you're saying today, but wait 'til she turns those pretty golden eyes on you and says she wants a mini-me," warned Quinn. He leapt to the side to avoid Liam's good-natured swipe at him.

"Yeah well," his former team lead said a bit gruffly, "that wouldn't be too bad."

Quinn gave a huge, overly dramatic gasp. "*You want to make babies with the wolf queen!*"

"Dude, shut *up*," replied Liam, but he was laughing. "How're things with Niamh?"

"Well, there's no *things* with Niamh anymore," he said. "She cut me loose a few weeks ago."

"And why didn't you tell me?" demanded Liam.

"Dude, you've been busy with your own stuff." Quinn shrugged as they turned another corner, heading vaguely in the direction of the Queen's Pavilion. Navigating cities was second nature to them at this point. He just let his mind mark off the turns as they made them. "I'm not gonna go crying to you about a split."

"Alright, man, it sounds like you've got it under control."

"I do," Quinn said. He knew he sounded a bit stiff and he increased the pace, the burn in his legs chasing away the vague ache in his chest. When they slowed again, he said, "Are we allowed to talk about this expedition or is it considered secret squirrel stuff that can only be discussed in rooms warded by runes or something?"

"You're blatantly changing the subject, but I'll allow it," said Liam. "There's no one around. We're fine."

"So, Finn is going, huh?"

Liam nodded. "It makes sense. Rye is the one that engineered his escape way back when. He thought she died."

"Finn's really not good at the whole casualty assessment thing, is he?"

Liam, in a voice thick with a suppressed laugh, told Quinn in some very choice words not to act like a particular portion of his anatomy.

"Hey, I'm just speaking truth to power. Isn't that part of my jo – oof." This time, Quinn failed to avoid the elbow that Liam angled into his ribs.

"Everyone knows it. You don't have to say it out loud."

"I mean, I'm just saying, if there's anyone else that Finn declared dead…we might want to go look at those records, because if his record is any indication…"

Quinn trailed off and launched into a sprint to avoid Liam's reach, both of them suppressing laughter as they rocketed down the deserted streets. Sometimes it felt like they were both fresh out of school, all hopped up on patriotism and those hooyah lines the instructors force fed them, ready to head overseas on their first rotation. You could always tell who hadn't been on deployment; they laughed more easily, and the horseplay was more often and more violent, like they were still testing their limits, toeing the line as though that would prepare them for actual combat. Most guys who'd actually gone overseas just rolled their eyes, like an experienced hunting dog turning its nose up at the antics of half-grown pups.

They reached the Queen's Pavilion and slowed out of their sprint, both of them winded but still with gas left in the tank.

"That was good," panted Liam, nodding.

"Needed it," agreed Quinn, lacing his fingers behind his head to counter his bad habit of bending over and putting his hands on his knees when recovering from sprints. He watched the breeze pluck at the gauzy curtains of the pavilion, the sheer material waving gently in the morning light. "So," he said finally. "This expedition."

"Yeah," said Liam, but it was more of a question. He glanced at Quinn, wiping the sweat from his forehead with one sleeve. "You want to go?"

"I did originally, but I've been thinking it over," he said slowly. "At first I just wanted to get away from the city because the break with Niamh was still fresh. Running away, you know?"

"Understandable," said Liam, his green eyes unreadable.

"But then I thought more about it. I think I'd be a liability more than anything." Quinn shrugged to signal that he wasn't really too put out by that idea, that he'd accepted it as a sort of fact.

"You're only a liability if you let yourself be," said Liam.

"All well and good to say to someone who's been through the training and is on our level," replied Quinn. "I mean, in our world, we're the apex predators. We're *it*, you know? But here, they're on a whole different plane. It's not even a comparison."

"Tess and I have made it work," pointed out Liam.

"You and your sister both have some extra juice from your superpowers," countered Quinn. He motioned with one hand, and they eased into a jog again, heading back toward the practice yards.

"I wouldn't call them *superpowers*, but I guess you're right."

"Of course I am," said Quinn.

"Don't say that like your batting average is perfect."

"Better than Finn's, I'd bet," muttered Quinn.

"He's already beating himself up about it enough. Don't make him feel worse."

"I'm not saying it to him, I'm saying it to you. Or does your weird mind-meld thing make it one and the same?" Quinn hadn't honestly considered that.

"It's not one and the same," sighed Liam, "but I'm just saying, he's a good dude, he doesn't deserve an extra helping of crap for the decisions he's made in the past."

"Duly noted." Quinn shrugged. "Thought the Lethe stone wiped his hard drive, anyway."

"You are just hitting all the bases when it comes to being insensitive this morning," Liam said.

"And you're overusing baseball metaphors," returned Quinn drily. "I never claimed to be sensitive. What's your point?"

"My point is that maybe you should try to put yourself in someone else's situation before you pass judgment."

"Relax. I'm not passing judgment. Just making observations." Quinn raised his eyebrows. "That ancient goddess in your head making you feel some kinda way about being nice to people?"

Liam rolled his eyes but pressed his lips together and didn't reply. Quinn's skin prickled, and it wasn't from the breeze swiping over his sweaty body.

"Hey, speaking of…you doing all right with that particular situation?" he asked. He'd learned that sometimes the only way to approach a subject was head-on, especially if it was a difficult one. No sense in dancing around the darn thing.

"Doing as all right as I can, I guess," said Liam. "There's not much I can do."

"Couldn't you maybe take her out? Like...extract her somehow?"

Liam winced. "The First isn't a splinter that I can dig out. I don't know why there's still a fragment, because Tess told me that she made a deal with Arcana, her life for mine. Maybe it's the immortal part of her that can't die."

"What does that mean for you?" Quinn tried to understand the implications, but his mind kept skipping like a scratched record, still unused to grappling with such questions even after the time he'd spent in the Fae world. Maybe it meant that Liam couldn't die? Or would the fragment just hop into another host like it had between Arcana and Liam? "I have very little experience with the whole playing-host-to-a-deity thing."

"Yeah, well, welcome to the club," replied Liam with such weariness in his voice that Quinn looked sharply at him.

Maybe there was more than one good reason not to go on this expedition. Despite the tense conversation with Liam that had left a sour taste in his mouth after the battle in the frosty throne room, Liam was still his friend. More than his friend – the word wasn't adequate to define their bond. *Brother* was closer, but even more than that. The whole 'blood is thicker than water' didn't apply sometimes when it came to the guys who did what they did for a living.

"So, you're staying here," he said as they slowed to a trot, the grand cathedral coming into view as they turned the last corner.

"Yes." Liam nodded and then grimaced. He glanced about to see that no one was within range to overhear him – which was a greatly expanded range, considering the infernally sensitive hearing of the Sidhe. He lowered his voice anyway. "I don't know whether Vell is keeping me close out of love or worry."

"What's she worryin' about?" Quinn kept his voice just this side of neutral, curious but not overbearing. He was good at getting most people to talk to him, when he set his mind to it.

"You saw in the training yard," muttered Liam as they began to stretch.

The prickle of unease returned in Quinn's stomach. He widened his stance and bent at the waist, pressing his palms to the still-cool paving stones, the pull in his hamstrings a good background for thought and conversation. He pitched his voice to match Liam's words. "Has that happened more than once?"

"In different ways, but yes," Liam said. He scowled at Quinn. "How are you so flexible? It's unnatural."

"If you learned a little bit of yoga like I keep trying to teach you, it's *not* that difficult. And don't change the subject," he replied mildly. "What's happened the other times?"

Liam thought for a moment as he sank into a squat, pressing his elbows into the inside of his knees. "At first I thought it was an advantage. The First – Arcana – whatever it is now…she supercharged my Sight." A wry grin twisted his lips. "I beat Finn, first time I'd ever beat him in the practice ring. It was like I knew what he was going to do before he even did it…like everything was happening in slow motion almost."

"That sounds…handy," commented Quinn.

"Until I lost control and hit him too hard. That first time was just with the flat of my blade. You saw the last time."

"Is it…centered on Finnead, somehow?"

Liam blinked. "I hadn't really thought of that." He stood and swung one leg forward into a lunge. "No. It's happened other times, but I've managed to keep it – her – from causing any real damage."

"Causing any *real* damage?" repeated Quinn, raising an eyebrow.

"To anyone else," clarified Liam without meeting his eyes.

Quinn digested this new piece of information. "Have you talked to Vell about it?"

He nodded. "She knows."

"Tess?"

He shook his head. "No."

"Don't tell me…you don't want to worry her," guessed Quinn.

"I *know* it's a ridiculous excuse, you don't need to remind me," Liam said with a sigh. "She's…well, she's a warrior now. She's grown up and she's gone through almost as much as we have."

"I'd say more," Quinn replied seriously. "I mean, think about it. She got dropped in the middle of this new world with really no guidance, she figures out that she's the heir to the Sword…and she was carrying out her own quest pretty darn well by the time we came along."

Liam smiled fondly. "You're right about that." He slid a glance in Quinn's direction, his green eyes speculative. "You think I should tell her?"

"I'm not telling you what to do," said Quinn with a shake of his head. "I'm not in that business. But I'll tell you what I think. Tess is your sister. She's the Bearer. Both those things mean that what's going on with you is important to her…because she loves you, and because you're one of the High Queen's Three."

"I think the Sidhe underestimate you," commented Liam as he rubbed the back of his neck.

"I don't know whether that's a compliment from you or an insult from them."

"A little bit of both." Liam grinned at him. "Want to come grab *khal* and breakfast in my room?"

"Ooooh, you have one of those nifty food-magically-appears tables, don't you?" Quinn said enviously. "How does that work? Does it listen to you if you tell it you want something different?"

"You can try," Liam said with a shrug. "I usually just take what's there."

"See, you're settling. Don't be a settler."

"That word doesn't mean what you think it means."

"Don't stifle my creativity!" Quinn retorted with mock seriousness.

Liam chuckled as they walked up the steps of the cathedral. The shadow of a Valkyrie overhead rippled over them like dark silk.

Quinn didn't miss the glance from Liam. He kept his eyes focused on the flight of stairs.

"At first, the urge to look up was like…" Quinn shook his head. "Every time, man. Every single time one of them flew overhead, it was like this *need*. I had to see if it was her, even though I knew that seeing her would hurt." He shrugged as they reached the great doors. "Now it's just a thought that crosses my mind. Something I can control."

"Good for you," Liam said in quiet approval.

Quinn shrugged again. "Not like I want a medal or anything for it."

"You went through a lot with her, after the battle," said Liam. He nodded to two Vyldgard women who saluted him with grins and flashing eyes.

"You and I both know that's no guarantee of anything at all," he replied, and he was mystified to hear that there wasn't any bitterness in his voice at all.

"True," Liam allowed.

"Speaking of going through a lot…how's Tess?"

"What do you mean?"

"Dude, her best friend crossed to the Dark Side and then died. That's some heavy stuff to unpack."

"Okay, first of all, I don't know whether you or Vivian is the bigger dork," Liam said as they navigated the passageways, Quinn following his lead.

"We prefer the term nerd," Quinn replied archly. "Dork implies that we're not cool. And we are *definitely* cool." He nodded definitively, managing to keep his serious expression for a few moments before grinning.

"Sure. Nerd. Wouldn't want to offend you by calling you something other than your preferred descriptor," quipped Liam.

"So, have you talked to her about it?" Quinn directed the conversation back to Tess.

"She hasn't talked to many people about it."

"That's a no, then."

Liam sighed as they rounded another corner and reached a tapestry, emerald green with a golden wolf on it. Quinn gave a low whistle.

"You guys have matching tapestries," he said, wiggling his eyebrows.

"It's her *sigil*," replied Liam.

"Still. First matching tapestries…then, next thing you know, Beryk will be having wolf cubs, they'll be toddling about, then Vell will get all googly-eyed and – "

"Pups," interrupted Liam.

"Pardon?" Quinn raised his eyebrows, blinking.

"They're wolf *pups*, not cubs. Cubs are bears."

"Fine, fine. Wolf *pups*. Then Vell will get all googly-eyed, and I'm not saying it's a bad idea, you two would make beautiful man-cubs…or woman-cubs. Girl-cubs? I don't know. Anyway, they'd be pretty, but I'd think there would be some – "

"Please stop talking, or you don't get to see the magical table of food," Liam said.

Quinn shut his mouth and cleared his throat, looking at the tapestry and then at Liam, who rolled his eyes.

"After all these years, food is still your primary motivator."

"There are worse things to use as motivation!" retorted Quinn indignantly, following Liam through the tapestry. He immediately located the aforementioned magic-food-table sitting by the fire, already loaded with a plate of meat and cheese, some green leafy stuff that smelled kind of like basil, and half a loaf of bread.

"I do have to make the *khal* myself, so there's that," said Liam.

"Who do I have to kill to get one of these?" Quinn said, immediately starting to build a sandwich. His stomach rumbled ravenously at the smell of the fresh-baked bread.

"You could probably just ask around and see who inscribes the runes. Merrick tried to explain it to me. Apparently, it doesn't make the food appear, because there are actually some loose rules with *taebramh*. It's difficult to create something from nothing, so these runes just pull the food from the kitchens to here."

"Okay, more important question," said Quinn around a mouthful of sandwich. "Do they have a rune to summon donuts?" He widened his eyes. "I just realized *they don't know what donuts are.*"

"What a travesty," commented Liam as he put the copper kettle over the fire.

"Yeah it is," agreed Quinn seriously. "Do you know how much *happier* they'd be if they had donuts?"

"Or fatter."

"I don't think they're physiologically capable of getting fat, Luck. Seriously. It's their genetics, along with the beautiful immortal stuff."

"Maybe it'll give you a donut if you ask," suggested Liam. "Like I said, I've never tried."

Quinn took a few steps back from the table and looked at it sternly. "Donut," he said in a firm voice.

Nothing happened.

"Maybe you need to show it who's boss," said Liam, pressing his lips together and squinting at the pouch of *khal* to keep from laughing.

"What, like intimidate it? I always intimidate people when I'm shirtless." Quinn nodded. "Makes total sense."

And that was how the High Queen walked in on her Seer laughing so hard there were tears in his eyes as a shirtless Quinn performed some sort of tribal dance around the table, shirtless and bellowing *"Donuts! I demand donuts!"*

She crossed her arms and stood by the wall, watching with golden eyes that began to glimmer with amusement.

Quinn went into an imitation of the Australian *haka* dance. He'd seen rugby players do it once before while they were on a port call to Sydney. Except he decided he needed to work donuts into it – that was what he was cajoling the table into providing, after all. Liam nearly fell off his chair, his shoulders shaking in silent mirth.

"Is this some mortal tradition that I haven't seen before?"

Quinn nearly knocked the table over as he spun around, the improvised words to his donut *haka* dying on his lips. He cleared his throat. "I…wanted donuts."

Vell narrowed her eyes. "What are do-nuts?"

"Only the most heavenly pieces of fried dough that exist," replied Quinn, his voice muffled as he pulled on his shirt.

"You could probably just describe them to one of the cooks," she said dryly, lifting an eyebrow.

He grinned at her. "Now what fun would that be?"

"Apparently less than shouting at inanimate objects."

"To be fair," said Liam, his voice still laughter-choked, "I encouraged the experiment."

"Why does that not surprise me?" Vell murmured, a smile turning up one corner of her lips, unmistakable heat in her gaze as she looked at Liam.

"Should I…leave you two?" Quinn asked, taking another bite of his sandwich.

"Don't be silly," Vell said, still holding Liam's eyes. "You can't have breakfast without *khal.*"

"In that case…" he muttered, finishing off the sandwich in his hand in three more bites and industriously assembling another one. He waved his free hand in the general direction of Vell and Liam. "You want one?"

"Don't want your dirty paws all over it," said Liam.

"I'm quite capable of getting my own food," said Vell at the same time.

"Suit yourself." Quinn shrugged and took his second sandwich to a seat at the table.

"Is there something urgent?" Liam asked, a slight frown marring his brow as he looked at Vell.

She shook her head as she sat down, taking the seat opposite Quinn and promptly propping her boots up on the table, leaning her chair back on two legs. He was immediately reminded why he liked the High Queen so much, even if she was intimidating sometimes.

"Nothing that requires us to skip breakfast," she replied. "Though I think we will go north soon. The wolves are restless, Rialla especially."

Liam retrieved the kettle from over the fire and poured them cups of *khal*, passing the first one to Vell.

"I don't think it would be wise to wait much longer. From what I remember, she will start to have the urge to build her den soon." Vell grimaced. "I confess I didn't pay much attention to the mating and whelping when I was younger. It didn't much interest me."

"Let me guess, you were more interested in beating the boys at archery and blades," said Liam with a fond smile.

Quinn frowned, trying to catch up. "Why would you need to know about mating and…*oh.*" He blinked and looked questioningly at Liam.

It was Vell who grinned and answered him. "Rialla is carrying pups. It hasn't been long, but Chael says he's sure." There was a certain proud glint in her eyes that Quinn realized he usually associated with men announcing that their wives were pregnant. He blinked again and put together the pieces: It was either Beryk or Kianryk who'd sired Rialla's litter, and Vell had that gleam of satisfaction about her that made him think it was Beryk.

He opened his mouth and then closed it, deciding it was probably rude to ask. Instead, he raised his cup of *khal* and said, "Congratulations."

"We will still need to find more wolves," said Vell. "It will be a long process."

"Whatever needs to be done, we'll do it," said Liam firmly. Quinn wondered whether the conviction was part of Liam's love for Vell or if his former team leader was thinking about having a wolf of his own.

"Who can be bound to wolves?" he asked. That was, presumably, a safer topic than who sired Rialla's litter.

Vell turned her sharp golden gaze to him. After a moment, she said, "Whomever the wolves choose. It is not up to me to dictate their partners."

"So, there's some sort of ceremony where they choose?"

"We call it the *Kjosa Dreyr*. The blood choice." She smiled. "It occurs only after the candidates have proven themselves worthy."

"But the candidates were usually kids, right?"

Vell chuckled. "We hold blades before we walk. I was riding in front of my father before I could speak in words that anyone could understand."

"Thinking of you as a child is vaguely terrifying," Quinn said, narrowing his eyes.

She chuckled. "As it should be. I was a hellion."

"A hellion," repeated Liam musingly. "You don't say."

Quinn nearly choked on his *khal* at the charged glance between Liam and Vell. He recovered and swallowed the rest of his drink. "Hey, just realized I gotta go…check on stuff." He waved the remaining half of his sandwich at Vell. "Congrats again."

"Thank you," she murmured as he stepped around the table. She'd gone very still, like a predator about to pounce on its prey, her gaze fixed on Liam. For his part, Liam leaned back in his chair and surveyed her with glittering eyes.

"Have fun, you two," Quinn said, unable to help himself as he stepped through the invisible exit back into the passageway. He chuckled as he took a bite of his sandwich and started back toward his own room, looking forward to a bath and some time to absorb the news that they would indeed have wolf pups underfoot after all.

Chapter 14

Vivian slid the leather cord holding the silver key over her head, staring at the nondescript door in front of her. Her heart beat faster. Despite the grime coating the dull metal, something within her quickened at the thought of putting the key into the lock and opening this door. She brushed a cobweb away from her face.

"Let me examine it," said Tyr, moving past her before she could answer. His mellifluous voice still caught her off guard sometimes...and if she was honest with herself, she missed the closeness of their silent communication.

Tyr had insisted that she allow him to accompany her to this far reach of the cathedral, a place beyond the High Queen's bespelled passageways. She'd known that arguing wouldn't do a thing to change his mind; despite the fact that words had risen to her lips questioning why exactly Tyr felt so driven to protect her when he barely spoke to her even during their lessons, she held her tongue. Instead, she'd been noting every detail of their journey into the dusty passageways. The thought that they were most likely the first living beings to walk these halls in centuries sent prickles of awareness down her arms.

As Tyr silently scrutinized the door, Vivian ran her eyes over the elaborate sconces in the stone of the wall, the filigree draped with cobwebs. The ceiling over their heads did not soar into distant heights as it did in other parts of the cathedral. Vivian thought that this part of the cathedral seemed older, built in a different time than the grand, cavernous main body of the building – not just because it was now cloaked in dust and the elaborate webs of industrious spiders, though here beyond the first two sets of doors, even the spiders were long since dead. The blocks of stone in the walls were smaller, the edges rounded as though time had softened the hard edges of the perfectly cut building materials.

Tyr stood stock-still in front of the door, the only movement his lips as he whispered a word every now and again. With his silver hair and ethereal aura, he could have been a ghost among the ruins of a long-forgotten civilization. Vivian touched the different tools on her belt for reassurance, letting her hand settle on her rune-stick. The silence enveloped them like velvet, none of the background noises of life in the cathedral existing here.

It was practical, Vivian thought as she turned her attention back to the High Queen's strategy, to build an enchantment only over the dimensions which one expected to occupy. Maintaining the spells must take some energy, even if it was of little concern to someone as powerful as the High Queen. Vivian swallowed as she thought of how effortlessly the Vyldretning wove such complex workings. She'd also heard the tale of how the High Queen had woven her *taebramh* into delicately crafted wings that had, in turn, been transformed into flesh and blood, knitted to the frames of the magnificent *faehal*. The High Queen had created a different kind of creature altogether, and the reality of such skill and power stole Vivian's breath…while also igniting a very small, but very real, flame of want in her chest. Someday, she wanted to wield those kinds of enchantments. Someday, she wanted to change the very fabric of the world with her *taebramh*.

Finally, Tyr turned and said, "I do not think there are any runes of ill intent." His voice fell oddly flat into the silence, swallowed by the dust.

"I'd hope not," Vivian said, rubbing her thumb over the edge of the silver key. "That would be a foul on the play, don't you think, if this is really what we think it is."

"The Paladins went to great lengths to preserve and protect their knowledge," replied Tyr. "It would not surprise me if they had wards on their stronghold."

Vivian smiled and raised an eyebrow. "But those wards shouldn't be against another Paladin."

"Perhaps we should ask the Bearer or the High Queen for assistance," Tyr said grudgingly.

"Why?"

"Because I cannot be sure that I have not missed something, and I do not want to endanger you."

"I have the key." She held up the silver key. It gleamed even in the shadows. "And at the end of the day, this isn't your decision. The last Paladins recognized me. They gave me the key, and I'm opening this door."

Tyr didn't reply, so she stepped past him, ignoring the shiver that ran down her spine. She brushed away the cobwebs beneath the elaborate doorknob, expecting to find a keyhole, and instead revealing only more grime-darkened bronze. She frowned and ran her gaze over the rest of the door. No keyhole.

"So, it's not a typical door," she muttered to herself, very aware of Tyr watching her. She forced herself to stay focused. No matter what Tyr thought, she was a Paladin. This door would open for her. "What would they want?" She tilted her head and thought back to the vision that the last Paladins had embedded in the great doors, trying to recognize any clues. "Paladins aren't necessarily related by blood, but I *am* of the Bearer's blood…or would that just confuse it?" She shook her head and took a deep breath. "There has to be something…else."

What other than her blood would the door recognize? She pressed her lips together, glancing at the key in her hand and then at the door. A rune could be written by anyone…so that wouldn't do the trick, she didn't think. Then she straightened.

"Of course," she said,. "Just like in the High Queen's enchantment. Our chambers only open to our *taebramh*." She frowned. "But the key must mean something still…"

Tyr stood by her elbow, noiseless as a ghost. She pushed down her irritation at him: What good was an ancient Sidhe with so much knowledge if he maintained his surly silence? Vivian took a breath. She concentrated and called up a small drop of *taebramh*, reaching out toward the door and watching as her *taebramh* manifested in a glow at the tip of her forefinger. The pendant at her throat warmed, and then the key in her hand *jumped*. She reflexively closed her fingers around it, but its sudden movement halved the distance to her other hand, and it strained toward the shining swirl of *taebramh* beginning to separate from her finger.

Her breath caught in her throat. She delicately held the key with her fingertips and slid the blossoming drop of *taebramh* onto it. The key shivered as it absorbed the bit of blue-tinged fire. A corresponding glow appeared in the center of the door, pulsing beneath the grime like moonlight through a dirty windowpane. Vivian watched in fascination, her heart beating faster as the key settled back into her hand, just ordinary silver. But the light in the door expanded, tendrils spiraling outward like cracks in ice, the pulsing of the light matching the tempo of her heart. Dust rose in small fingers from the floor as the ground beneath their feet began to vibrate. Pieces of dirt flaked from the door, revealing a coppery sheen. Vivian heard Tyr say something beneath his breath. He put his hand on her shoulder as though to pull her back, but she shrugged him off, instead stepping closer to the door.

The spiraling fire that her *taebramh* had sparked reached the outer edges of the door and leapt to the walls, racing down the passageway and sweeping the cobwebs away from the intricate fixtures, lighting them with a dancing pale fire. A cool wind swept away the rest of the dust and the door shed the last of its centuries of filth. The vibrations settled into a quieter hum that sang through Vivian's bones, and with a soft click, the door opened inward, its hinges silent despite the centuries of disuse.

Excitement coursed through her. This was part of her inheritance as a Paladin. Her mind traveled again to the vision of the circular tower, shelves of books and enchanted objects stretching upward as far as the eye could see. Armed with the knowledge contained within that vast library, she would be able to learn what the last Paladins had known. She would be able to be the Paladin that the Fae world needed.

Shadows lurked in the room beyond the open door. She swallowed – it was certainly far from inviting, but she could at least take care of the illumination. She quickly wove a ball of light and activated it with a touch of *taebramh*, sending it spinning beyond the door. Sudden wariness seized her, and she sketched a shield rune on the back of her hand, holding it before her as she stepped across the threshold.

Her *taebramh* light soared up into the reaches of the tower. No other light illuminated the circular room. Vivian moved slowly, scanning the darkness for anything alive and finding nothing but shadows. She walked to the center of the room, her footsteps echoing. Something flickered beneath the dust on one of the flagstones. She knelt and brushed away the dust, finding a rune twisting and quivering on the stone, activated but damaged. One of the lines had faded beneath the onslaught of dust and the passage of time.

Her breath stirred the dust as she reached out and, with one stroke, restored the rune. Instantly, wind blasted out from the rune. She fell backward with a yelp, the sound turning into a sneeze at the dust thrown into her face. Regaining her feet, she sneezed two more times as the wind scoured the room. When she finally opened her eyes, blinking back tears from the reaction to the dust, she gasped, nearly dropping her rune stick.

"You did not know that rune," said Tyr. "You should not have completed it without knowing it."

"I knew what it would do," Vivian replied absently, her eyes widening as she took in the tower.

She had acknowledged the possibility that the Paladin's library no longer existed as she had seen it in the vision. Over the centuries without a Paladin to see to its upkeep, there could have been damage to the tower itself, or plundering of its contents. She'd thought of all the different threats to such a magnificent collection of books and enchanted objects: floods, fire, ravaging creatures from Malravenar's army bent on destroying the Paladins' legacy.

She had not allowed herself to dwell too long on the *other* possibility: that the Paladin's library existed *exactly* as she had seen it in the vision. She had tamped down the bubbling excitement she felt at that prospect, talking to herself about the logical chances that the tower had survived the centuries intact, especially considering the upheaval within the Fae world.

And now she stood in the center of the most beautiful, fascinating room she had ever seen, countless books of every shape and thickness lining the shelves, interspersed with those odd objects that had caught her eye in the vision which even as she watched began to spin and whir to life. A knot formed in her throat and she swallowed thickly as she stared at the tower, barely blinking – there was so much to see, so much to absorb. Despite her best efforts at self-control, tears pricked at the corners of her eyes. It very much felt like someone had reached into the back of her mind and pulled out one of her dreams, incarnating this room that spoke to her as though she'd chosen every book and designed every object herself.

With a flutter, a robe lifted of its own volition from one of the tables, shaking itself slightly like someone emerging from a long slumber. Runes swirled over the dark fabric, giving the robe a liquid shimmer. A silver fog coalesced at the cuffs of the robe's sleeves and above the collar, creating a vague sketch of hands and a face. Before Vivian could properly absorb this strange sight, the robe – or the being wearing the robe – flew past her and began attempting to push Tyr from the room with the air of an indignant schoolmarm ushering a student from a restricted area. Tyr's eyebrows shot upward in surprise as the fog-creature flapped the robe's arms at him and then resorted to physically prodding at him, looking a bit like a sparrow swooping around a larger bird.

Vivian cleared her throat. "I – wait, it's all right!"

The fog-creature wearing the robe paused, turning its torso back toward her questioningly even as it poked at Tyr with one arm. Tyr muttered something under his breath as he batted away the rune-infused fabric, prompting the fog-creature to redouble its efforts.

"Hey," said Vivian, "please stop doing that!"

The being wearing the robe immediately dropped its arms. It seemed like it didn't want to completely abandon what it viewed as its duty to evict Tyr from the tower, but Vivian saw that it was compelled to obey her voice. It settled for drifting a few feet away from Tyr, angling its sketch of a face toward Vivian but turning back at intervals to check that Tyr hadn't moved.

"Hello," she said cautiously. "I'm sorry I don't know your name, I'm a very new Paladin and there are no other Paladin here to teach me."

The fog-creature drooped conspicuously at her last words, as though she implied that it was somehow its fault that there were no Paladins in the Fae world except her.

"No, no," she quickly amended, "I'm not – I don't really know *why* there aren't any other Paladin. I just – I just found the tower. So…could you…is there a *guide* or something of that sort?"

The silvery creature turned fully toward Vivian and bowed to her.

"Oh, I meant…like a book?" she clarified hopefully.

It cocked its head to one side and brought one hand to where Vivian imagined its chin would be if its face were not composed of constantly evanescing silver mist.

"Or anything that you think would be helpful to a brand new Paladin," she added.

The robe-wearing mist-creature zoomed away, hovering by a section of the shelves and running its silvery appendages over the spines of the books until it found the object of its search, pulling it out and then zipping over to the next shelf. Fascinated, Vivian watched it progress higher and higher up the tower, gravity no match for the runes animating it. It stopped to wind a mechanism on one of the whirring silver globes, as though it couldn't help itself, and then turned back to its mission.

Vivian tore her eyes away from the levitating robe. She looked at Tyr, grinning. "Isn't this amazing?"

He surveyed the magnificent tower with a closed expression. "It is a good resource for your training."

She didn't miss the lack of enthusiasm in his voice or the guardedness of his face. "Well, I think it's fantastic. It's like…it's like the library at Hogwarts and the one in the castle in *Beauty and the Beast* had a love child, and it's *mine*." She swallowed again, struck by the enormity of it. This tower full of centuries of knowledge and priceless magical objects was entrusted to her guardianship.

"It belongs to the Paladin," replied Tyr neutrally.

"That's what I mean," Vivian said, frowning at him. She glanced upward and checked to see that the mist-creature was still gathering books – it was so high up now that Vivian hoped it didn't drop any of the books balanced precariously in a fold of its robe, since from that height it would most likely kill her. Death by falling book, right after she'd discovered this amazing place – no, thank you. She called up a spark of *taebramh,* ready to activate the shield rune still inscribed on the back of her hand.

She turned back to Tyr. They gazed at each other for a long moment. His expression didn't change, and she knew better now than to prod at their silent connection. It had withered away to a bare thread, ready to snap.

"Why did you follow me here?" she asked finally, crossing her arms over her chest.

"I told you, I wished to ensure that there were no malicious spells in this portion of the cathedral," Tyr replied.

Vivian raised an eyebrow. "That's very noble, considering the fact that you barely talk to me even when you're teaching me."

Something flickered through Tyr's eyes, but he shrugged one shoulder in elegant disdain. "I fail to see the correlation between wanting to ensure the safety of the Paladin and my apparent failing as a garrulous companion."

"Don't hide behind fancy words," she retorted, an edge to her voice now. "I know what they mean." She raised her chin. "So, I'm just the Paladin to you?"

He didn't answer her. The light from the filigreed sconces highlighted the silver scars on his face.

She sighed. Time to try a different tactic – maybe if he didn't respond to anger, he'd respond to a softer approach. "Tyr, look, I'm…worried about you. I know it can't be easy, being back in this world again after so long."

A wry smile twisted his lips. "You know nothing about it."

"Mostly because you won't *tell* me anything," Vivian replied almost gently, using all her self-discipline not to run over to him and shake him senseless. Why was he being such a stubborn mule? "Look, if you're fine, if you don't want to talk to me…I understand. If it was only a matter of convenience, talking to me in the first place…well, I can't say I like it, but I can understand that too. It would just be easier if you'd just *tell* me."

"And burden you with things you cannot change?" Tyr lifted one silver eyebrow and shook his head. "No. *That* I will not do."

"That's what you're supposed to do with the people you care about," Vivian said, taking a step toward him. "Or was that all just a lie too?"

"Please do not press me on this, Vivian," he said softly.

"Why?" She spread her hands. "I just don't understand, and to me that's worse than being told something I don't want to hear." She tried to steer the conversation back into safer water. "Are you able to eat, or do you need blood? There aren't many mortals here, though I suppose the Bearer and her brother, and Quinn…" She stopped and swallowed. For some reason, thinking of beautiful, self-assured Tess offering her wrist to Tyr made her stomach turn with sickening jealousy. She blinked.

"I have not accepted blood from anyone," said Tyr finally. "The Vyldretning has been…helping me. And Queen Titania as well," he added grudgingly.

"Not your own Queen?"

"She is not my Queen," said Tyr in a low, bitter voice.

"Okay," said Vivian slowly, "but you helped put her on the throne, so I think she'd be…"

"Do not mince words." Tyr wouldn't meet her eyes. "I am a Queenslayer."

"Technically speaking, yes, but the other Queens had agreed that Mab needed to be taken down," pointed out Vivian.

"She allowed the Enemy to take my sister," said Tyr in a voice so quiet that Vivian almost didn't hear him. "And now that Rye may be alive…she cares nothing."

"I don't think that's quite fair," said Vivian. "Queen Andraste spoke in support of the expedition – "

"And what support did she offer?" Tyr demanded, his eyes snapping with a fury so intense that Vivian took a step back.

She let his words fade into silence before she answered, measured and careful. "I don't think you should let anger consume you." She gestured to the library. "Help me explore this. I think there's a good chance we could find something useful to take with us on the expedition."

The robed silvery creature descended from the far reaches of the tower, its arms overflowing with books large and small. It spilled its bounty onto one of the tables artfully scattered around the room and then immediately began stacking the books, a tessellation of different sizes and colors. Vivian pulled out a wooden chair, eyeing it for a moment and then shifting over to the plush velvet armchair at the other side of the same table. A thrill coursed through her as she surveyed the bounty of books.

"Thank you," she said honestly to the fog-creature. "Do you have a name?"

It finished stacking the books and tilted its head questioningly at her, as though it didn't understand.

"Well," she said, thinking, "I'm guessing you're a servant to the Paladins, right? Or a kind of butler in the Paladin's Tower."

The silvery creature nodded its shifting head so enthusiastically that it lost a good portion of the incandescent mist composing the right side of its face.

"As long as you don't mind," Vivian continued, a smile spreading across her face, "I'm going to call you Alfred."

The Tower servant, newly christened Alfred, bowed deeply to her.

"In my head, you just said something like *Very well, Master Bruce*," she said, imitating a stiff British accent and chuckling at her own joke. "I'm such a nerd." She picked up the book closest to her, a small volume with a title embossed in gold on the bottle-green cover. "Oh," she said in disappointment, "I don't speak…whatever this is."

She squinted at the flowing script: It looked a bit like French, but she was fairly certain that some of the letters on the pages of the book didn't actually exist in the English language. She turned a few pages, marveling at the thickness of the vellum and the construction of the binding with small, precise stitches. "Should I even be touching this?" she murmured, thinking of the old books in cases that one had to don gloves to handle.

"There are preservation runes," Tyr said.

She looked up and saw that in his noiseless, graceful fashion, he'd taken the wooden seat that she'd rejected, and he was examining another book, his long fingers turning the pages slowly.

Alfred reappeared at her elbow, offering her a small wooden case. She set down the book and took the case from him, opening it and blinking in surprise at the strange little golden spectacles sitting on a cushion of velvet. Alfred gestured with his diaphanous hands for her to put them on. She slid them onto her nose, feeling slightly ridiculous – but then she looked back at the small green book, and *she could read the cover.*

Vivian couldn't say whether she saw the strange language in English, or whether the spectacles somehow enabled her to just understand it as it was written, but either way, she *understood* it.

"Thank you," she said again to Alfred. The servant bowed and then glided off. She looked at Tyr. "How can you say this isn't fantastic?"

He raised an eyebrow at her. "I never said it was not." A real smile tugged at his mouth. "Those spectacles make your eyes look twice their usual size."

Vivian chuckled and blinked owlishly at him. "What, this doesn't count as the 'sexy librarian' look?"

Tyr looked back down at his book, and she very nearly didn't hear his reply, but he murmured, "Oh, you do not need spectacles for that."

Even as a blush rushed to her cheeks, she sighed internally. She hadn't had a great handle on understanding Tyr before they'd come back into Faeortalam, and now it felt as though she'd give herself whiplash if she tried to follow his changes in mood. One moment he was surly and silent, the next radiating fury, and now the spark in his hooded eyes ignited a little flame low in her belly. She pressed her lips together and bent her head over the book again. Maybe she could learn something useful that would help them on the expedition. "Has Merrick been able to repair his scrying glass?"

"He and Thea have been working on it."

"That's not what I asked," she replied. "Did they fix it?"

"Not to my knowledge."

She paused and looked for Alfred, who appeared by her chair as though he could read her thoughts. "Do we have any books that would help in the repair of a damaged scrying glass?"

Alfred put his hand to his chin in his thoughtful pose and then zoomed off, spiraling upward until he reached a shelf at least fifty feet above their heads. He returned with a volume bound in soft white leather. Vivian set aside the green book for a moment and opened the white book. She raised her eyebrows and held up the book for Tyr's inspection, showing him the detailed diagrams of a scrying glass that looked nearly identical to the damaged one that she'd seen on Thea's work bench. "Now are you convinced that we might find useful things here?"

"I said it would be a useful resource," replied Tyr, arching one eyebrow.

Vivian scowled at him. Alfred flapped a robed arm at Tyr, apparently thinking it his duty to emphasize the Paladin's displeasure. Tyr raised both eyebrows and looked at Alfred. The Tower servant crossed its arms defiantly, as though to tell the silver-haired Sidhe that he wasn't intimidated.

"I've taken apart enchantments like you three times before breakfast," Tyr said mildly.

"Don't you dare threaten Alfred," Vivian responded immediately. She found herself feeling absurdly protective of the mist-creature. "It's not his fault that he's bound by certain rules."

"Which, for the most part, we do not know," said Tyr.

"I'll figure it out," muttered Vivian. "Should we get this book to Thea and Merrick now, or can it wait?"

"The scrying glass has been broken for weeks. I am sure it can wait until we are ready to leave the Tower for the day," replied Tyr.

Vivian nodded. "Makes sense." She surveyed the pile of books and pushed the golden spectacles farther up the bridge of her nose. "All right. What else do we think we'll need to know?"

"Everything," said Tyr seriously.

"Well, you already act like you know everything sometimes, so…"

He chuckled at that, paused and then spoke. "Vivian, I have missed talking to you. I simply did not want to…tie your fate to mine, as I am unsure about my own future."

"Well," she said without looking up from the green book, "you forget one very important thing, Tyr. A lot of people do."

"And what is that?"

She met his eyes. "I have a choice in this, too. So, don't hide behind this notion that you're trying to protect me. I may have a lot to learn, but I don't need protecting."

He blinked and then inclined his head. "Very well."

With a nod, she turned back to her book, devouring the pages hungrily. After a moment, she retrieved her little notebook from the pouch on her belt and started taking notes. She had a lot of ground to cover in the coming days, both literally and metaphorically, and she couldn't afford to waste another minute.

Chapter 15

For a moment after Mal woke, she lay in the haze of a new day, feeling the sway of her hammock and the gentle rock of the *Dragonwing* as she prowled the seas in search of a seam. And then the realization hit her like a slap across the face: Today was the day she would stand mast.

In the days since her conversation with Jem, she'd done her best to regain her strength. The bruises on her throat and side had faded, though her ribs were still a mottled shade of yellow. She could move almost as quickly as before, her joints worked back into smoothness. Those blasted patches of skin, though, refused to go away. In fact, she had two particularly bothersome new spots that itched like the blazes at the nape of her neck and on her right ankle. No matter what ointment Jem concocted, the red, bubbling patches never went away. Some of his remedies helped with the itching, and for that she was grateful.

She stared up at the ceiling as her hammock rocked. Calm seas had meant that the ship was making good time, but they hadn't found a seam. It was the longest she could remember the Captain not being able to navigate the *Dragonwing* to a raid. Though most of the crew wouldn't meet her eyes and avoided her like she had a particularly dreadful case of Nuremian pox, she still heard the whispers.

Most thought that the gods of the ocean were punishing the ship for denying the kraken its due – for *Mal* denying the kraken its meal. A few held the opposite thought: that the gods of the ocean were punishing the ship for their treatment of Mal, who'd saved them all from the kraken.

Admittedly, those who thought she was a hero still avoided her. They just didn't go out of their way to make her feel even more like a stranger on the ship that had been her only home for as long as she could remember. Jem, of course, still talked to her. Hex uttered a few words every now and then, though she'd determinedly made it a point to leave the berthing whenever he or Iss entered, because while she loathed herself still sometimes, she didn't need to hear *that*. So, she didn't see Hex often anymore, to say the least.

She'd taken to climbing up onto the mainmast platform in the hour before sunset, watching the bloody sun dip into the horizon, washing the rest of the ocean orange and gold. Sometimes she thought about never seeing such beauty again. Sometimes she thought about diving from the platform again. But mostly she watched the silken surface of the water, hoping to see one of the beautiful creatures who had saved her from the kraken. Her memories of Serena and Calinth faded until she thought that perhaps they'd been a dream. She whispered their words to herself, turned them over in her mind like she turned over rings in her palm when she thought hard.

You have a good wind sorceress, for all she's not Kin.

What did Serena mean by Kin? *Who* were Kin?

You should not have forced the change.

What change? Why had Calinth then told her that she was *too young*?

Mal sighed in her hammock, fighting against the current of hopelessness that threatened to pull her into the cold depths of despair. It didn't matter what the glimmering, beautiful Serena and Calinth had said, because who knew if she would survive until tomorrow. She wasn't *dense* – she thought that the patches on her skin somehow *meant* something, but she didn't know what. The craziest idea that had floated to the top of her mind was that perhaps *she* was one of those glittering creatures swimming beneath the waves, but that was patently ridiculous. She snorted. She wasn't graceful and gorgeous. She was a third with hair that she chopped off herself every so often with the edge of one of her daggers. She had scars on her hands and knees and elbows from working the decks of the *Dragonwing* since she could walk.

And besides, the voice in her mind said as her thoughts came full circle, she could be dead in a few hours. Some people just couldn't withstand the shock of a lashing. Their bodies just quit. She shivered and wrapped her arms around herself, wincing as one of the scabs on her left elbow broke open at the sudden movement.

It would certainly be ironic if she died from her punishment after she'd survived her dive into the raging seas and battled a kraken. Ironic or not, though, she'd still be dead. They'd tip her body overboard, a weight tied to her feet so that they didn't sail past her bobbing corpse a few weeks later. That had happened once, and the Captain had nearly sent the second in charge of that burial to join the bloated, fish-eaten body that had bumped gently, sickeningly, against the hull of the *Dragonwing*.

Maybe she should have gotten up early to watch the sunrise.

"Morning," said Jem. "Hurry up or you won't get breakfast."

She swung her feet out of her hammock and combed her fingers through her hair.

"Some of your hair is turning silver," said Jem. "Did you notice?"

"I don't really pay attention to my hair," she replied, voice still thick with sleep. She glanced around the berthing – the dozen or so thirds who stood night watch were still fast asleep in their hammocks, but even they would have to be up and on the decks at noon to witness mast. Her stomach clenched. "I don't think I'm going to eat breakfast."

"You're going to eat," said Jem firmly, grabbing her arm and pulling her with surprising strength toward the hatch.

"Fine," she grumbled, "you don't have to drag me."

"If you'd stop feeling so sorry for yourself, I wouldn't have to," Jem said implacably.

Mal opened her mouth to tell him that maybe if he were facing mast for saving someone's life, then he'd feel differently, but she decided it wasn't worth the effort. She didn't want her last words to Jem to be angry – that hadn't turned out so well for her last time during that sunset conversation with Hex.

"I'm not saying that you don't have a *right* to a little self-pity," Jem continued as he followed her up the ladder onto deck. "But the wallowing gets old."

Mal found herself only half hearing Jem's words. The thought of Hex had touched off what felt like a thousand sparrows inside her rib cage, swooping and diving from her heart down into her stomach and back at dizzying speeds. She swallowed and let herself scan the decks for him. He'd be up, probably, because he had the noon to sunset watch now…

"Hex is busy," Jem said softly, taking the lead as they slipped amidst the bustle of the morning watch. A few of the younger thirds were already scrubbing the decks near the mainmast with soapstones. The weathered boards closest to the mast gleamed a darker shade of gray than the rest of the decks, permanently stained with the blood of all those who had endured the lash at mast over the centuries of the *Dragonwing*'s long life.

Jem touched her shoulder as she slowed, staring at the decks and thinking about how her blood would be added to those stains in a few hours' time.

"Stop dwelling on it," he advised in that same quiet voice. "You'll only suffer twice."

Mal snorted at that. "Easy for you to say."

"I have to watch," he pointed out.

She frowned as they reached the ladder down to the galley and mess decks. "You said Hex was busy?"

"That's what he told me," replied Jem.

The hum of conversation on the mess decks died into silence as Mal got in line for breakfast. Even though her stomach clenched again, she stared straight ahead and refused to let the crew see her afraid. Let them look their fill now before the Captain plied the cat o' nine tails on her back. She drew back her shoulders.

Whispers buzzed like flies among the crew eating their breakfast. Mal resisted the urge to glare at them, instead staring at the back of the second in line in front of her – until he stepped aside, and the two thirds and the first in front of him did as well. She looked at them in confusion.

"Third Mal," said Cook, holding up a bowl.

Jem poked her in the back. "Go," he whispered.

Her feet moved. She walked woodenly down the mess line, her cheeks burning at the attention. Why did they want to humiliate her further than what was already coming?

And then she realized as she reached Cook that his stern face looked unusually gentle, and he held a bowl separate from the stack that the third on kitchen duty was filling from the pot.

"Third Mal," he said again with a nod, handing her the bowl.

She stared down at a portion that looked fit for the Captain himself, and definitely not a third like her: porridge with a fat slab of golden butter melting a pool in the middle of it, one side of the bowl occupied with thick chunks of pork belly. The steam rising from the bowl smelled as heavenly as the best food Mal had ever had at the tavern on Horizon.

Cook reached over and slid a slice of brown bread into her bowl. Then he nodded as though that had been the finishing touch, and pressed a tankard into her hand. Mal immediately knew from the smell of it that it was ale – and *good* ale at that, not the stuff usually reserved for the thirds.

"From the firsts," Cook said with a nod, crossing his brawny arms. The line had started moving around her, the others accepting their bowls without so much as a word of complaint.

"I…don't understand," said Mal, even though her mouth watered at the delicious scent wafting into her face from the bowl she held.

"What's there to understand?" Cook raised his eyebrows. "This is your food, go eat it."

Jem tugged at her elbow, his own bowl and copper cup of water balanced in his other hand.

"You'll pull through," said Cook, in a gruff voice so low that Mal almost didn't hear him as she let Jem guide her toward a table in the corner.

"What *is* this?" she asked him, flummoxed. She took a swallow of the ale as she sat down and closed her eyes at the cool bite of it on her tongue. "Mmm. This is strong."

"From what I've heard," said Jem, taking the seat opposite her, "it's something of a tradition."

Mal raised her eyebrows as she picked up her spoon and examined the bowl, trying to decide what spoonful would be best first.

Jem leaned across the table. "The firsts will deny it all day. But I heard one of the seconds saying that they all contributed a few rings to make sure you were well fed."

Mal blinked. Now that Jem mentioned it, she remembered some uncommonly rich broths during her convalescence. She hadn't thought twice about it at the time, mostly because her body had felt like one huge bruise and her fingers were still as big as sausages, but now she wondered if that had been the firsts too.

"If you would've lifted your head out of your cloud of misery, maybe you would've seen that there are more that care about what happens to you than you think," Jem commented between bites of his breakfast.

Mal didn't know what to say, so she scooped up a hefty spoonful of her porridge and shoved it into her mouth. An involuntary groan of ecstasy escaped her – this was actually better than any food she'd had on Horizon or Haven, better than any food she'd ever had in her life.

"Try not to make everyone else jealous," said Jem drily, but he smiled.

She pushed the bowl toward him as she took another bite, motioning that he should try some. He shook his head.

"No. That's against the rules."

"Rules," she snorted.

"You may not care, but I'd rather not have my hide tanned by Cook," replied Jem as he finished scraping the sides of his bowl. He leaned back against the bulkhead, lacing his fingers behind his head and settling one ankle on the opposite knee.

Mal tried to strike a balance between savoring her meal and taking Jem's advice. Far from feeling sick, her stomach felt full and satisfied after she finished the bowl, and she picked up the tankard of ale to wash it down.

"I think they put a pinch of something else in there," said Jem conversationally. "That bit is from the seconds."

Mal eyed the ale suspiciously. "Put *what* else?"

"Something to ease your mind," he replied. "That's the best we could do."

"We? You're not a second." Mal took another swallow of the ale, paying close attention to the flavor, and she thought she tasted something vaguely bitter at the very back of her tongue – but she didn't drink the ship's good ale every day, so it was difficult to say.

"Well, the seconds don't have anyone who's a hand at herbs and healing," Jem said, addressing his empty bowl.

"Jem," said Mal, "you can't get in trouble for it, can you?"

He shrugged and brushed an unruly strand of dark hair away from his eyes. "Not unless someone squawks about it, and I've only told you."

A lump formed in Mal's throat, and that made it very inconvenient to drink the good ale still left in her cup. She snuck a glance out at the rest of the mess decks, where everything seemed to be back to the normal morning meal routine: Yawns and bleary eyes intermingled with jibes and wisecracks, the contrast of those who hated morning and the spry sailors who were up with the sunrise colorfully apparent.

"Drink the rest of that," said Jem, tapping her tankard with a finger. "Needs a bit to set in."

Mal obediently raised the tankard to her lips. Maybe the rest of the crew hadn't been ostracizing her after all, she thought. Hex's words surfaced in her mind. "Jem," she said slowly, "have I been…*prickly*, lately?"

He choked on a swallow of water. "Stars, Mal, never thought you were slow in the head until now. You're really asking that?"

She colored and took another swig of ale.

"When you glare at everyone like you're going to punch them, that's a pretty good deterrent," Jem elaborated. "Plus, there was a bit of speculation after you pulled off saving Hex in the middle of that storm."

"We don't need to go over this again," muttered Mal, shifting. Serena and Calinth's faces appeared in her mind's eye. She resisted the urge to scratch one of the peeling, bubbling patches of skin. Jem had said that some on the ship thought she had some sort of mystical heritage. Well, what good was mystical heritage if there was no one to explain it to you and nothing to gain from it?

"You asked, I'm telling you," replied Jem with a shrug.

"Speaking of Hex," she said, seizing on the distraction even though she felt a stab of discomfort as she brought up the third member of their trio, "what's he doing?"

Jem wouldn't look at her. "Don't know. He didn't tell me."

She stared into the ale, swirling it in her tankard and watching the bubbles race in circles. "He's been avoiding me."

"You've been alternately mired in misery and spitting fire," Jem retorted. "He was giving you space, and then you rabbit from the berthing every time he steps into it. He thought you didn't want to see him because he reminded you of…well, everything."

He did. She'd dreamt of him underwater, painted in green and silver, shadows carving ethereal beauty into his already handsome face, a trail of bubbles emerging like pearls from between his half-parted, full lips…She shook herself and blinked. "Not entirely true."

"And you waited 'til now to try to clear this up?" Jem looked at her incredulously. "I love you more'n the Captain loves Kalinda's wind-whistling, Mal, but stars, you're ridiculous sometimes."

She drained the rest of her tankard so she didn't have to look at him as she gathered her thoughts. "You're right," she said slowly. "I curled into myself. I let despair drag me down." She shook her head. "I should have forced myself to shed that self-pity earlier."

Self-pity and jealousy, whispered a small voice inside her, poking at her memory of Iss and Hex standing by the rail, so close they were almost touching. She shoved it away. What did it matter now? She had a few hours before mast, and then stars knew what would happen after that.

"You'll survive," Jem said, relinquishing his relaxed pose and leaning forward, focusing his intense gaze on her face. "You hear me? You'll survive." He pressed his lips together. "For a few minutes in that storm, I thought I'd lost both of you, and I never want to feel that again."

Her lips twisted in a wry smile. "Well, it's only me going to mast, so there's no danger there."

"Right," he said.

There was something about the way Jem wouldn't meet her eyes that sent prickles of foreboding down her arms.

"Jem," she said, echoing his earlier motion as she leaned forward, "what aren't you telling me?"

He sighed and ran one hand through his hair. "I can't tell you something I don't know, Mal, but I just have a feeling that Hex is doing something cracked."

"Why?" she demanded.

"Because you saved him, and you're being punished for it," he said with an air of impatience. "If the opposite had happened, what would you do?"

Mal squinted as she thought for a moment. Whatever they'd put in the ale began to send tendrils of warmth from her stomach into her limbs. It was an altogether comforting feeling, like being wrapped in a finely woven, warm blanket. "I'd probably go pound on the Captain's stateroom door," she said, with a chuckle to show Jem that she understood just how ridiculous she sounded.

"Exactly," Jem said grimly.

She narrowed her eyes at him. "What, you think Hex is fool enough to go and...do that?" she finished weakly, sitting back in her chair as the realization hit her. "Does he know he's the Captain's son?" The words came out in a whisper, even though the mess decks were emptying as sailors turned to for their watches and other duties. Jem stood the sunset to midnight watch, and he'd worked out some kind of deal with the seconds to have more time with her while she healed.

"I think so," Jem answered. "This is only my guess, but..."

"Tell me!" Mal insisted, though her words came out more of a squeak than a firm order. She blamed whatever they'd put in her ale. Good for easing anxiety, not good for sounding authoritative, she thought a bit dizzily, trying hard to focus.

"I think that Iss found out from one of the seconds, or maybe even one of the firsts. Who knows with her," Jem said. "She held it over Hex's head for a while, made it sound like she knew some sort of secret...which I guess it was, in a way, but it was only a matter of time before he found out." He shook his head. "She was using it to try to trade with him."

"Trade for...what?" Mal managed.

Jem slanted a gaze at her. "I don't have to spell that out for you."

She told herself firmly that she didn't care a whit about Hex's choice of partner for a bit of fun, though the idea of Iss using the knowledge of his paternity to get him into a hammock rankled her. She knew better than to ask whether it had happened – Hex knew, after all. It felt like she'd swallowed a stone, even through the warm haze of the herbs from her ale. "Why didn't you *stop* him?"

"I can't stop either of you from doing anything, mostly because you don't tell me these things until after they're done," replied Jem. "I'm still waiting for the two of you to learn that I'm the sensible one."

"We know that," she said. "We're just too stubborn to actually ask you for help."

"That also," Jem said, drinking the last of his water.

Mal put her head in her hands and tried to think, which was becoming increasingly harder. Maybe she shouldn't have accepted the drugged ale…but it was so *nice* not to break into a sweat at the thought of mast. It didn't distress her at all anymore, though she knew in the back of her head that she should really be afraid of the wicked cat o' nine tails.

"Come on," Jem said, gathering up their bowls. "It wouldn't do for you to sleep away your last few hours before mast on a table in the corner of the mess decks."

"But it's *comfortable*," murmured Mal, pillowing her head on one arm. Jem left briefly to deposit their dishes in the scullery, and then, with more finesse than earlier in the morning, he levered her out of her chair and guided her toward the ladder to the weatherdecks.

"Put a bit too much in," he said mostly to himself. "Thought you'd need almost a full dose, but I should have gone with the half…"

"Are you saying…I can't handle my ale?" Mal asked, raising an eyebrow as they emerged into the sunlight. She tipped back her face, feeling the blossoming warmth on her skin.

"Not at all," said Jem blithely. He took a deep breath. "Would you like to go sit on the bow?"

Mal nodded happily – the bow was her favorite place on the ship that didn't involve climbing up among the billowing blue sails. They passed a couple of seconds on the way up to the foredeck, and both nodded to Mal gravely. She chuckled. "Funny. Mast is a good way to get noticed."

Jem sighed even as he smiled. "I definitely dosed you a bit too heavily. You'll settle out by noon."

"How much time?" she murmured, sitting by the rail and feeling the wind comb its fingers through her hair.

Jem glanced up at the sun. "Two hours, give or take."

"Good," she said. "Don't let me fall asleep."

He sat down next to her, leaning against her shoulder comfortably. They sat in companionable silence for a while, and then he asked, "Anything you want to talk about?"

She smiled hazily. "Remember the first time we were able to drink ale on Horizon?"

Jem chuckled. "How could I forget? The two of us had to carry Hex because he bet one of the older thirds that he could outdrink him."

"Which he did," said Mal with a grin. "Lucky for him he was a lot smaller then and we could carry him."

"Or unlucky for him that he was a lot smaller then," rejoined Jem. The wind carried a light sprinkling of sea spray over the rail as the *Dragonwing's* bow nosed into a wave.

Enveloped in that warm, herb-induced cocoon, Mal leaned against Jem and they recounted the many adventures they'd had over the dozen years since they'd been made fourths on the ship together. Jem had actually been taken onboard a year after Hex and Mal had started, but he was about their age and he was a hard worker who didn't get them all in trouble, so they hadn't held it against him. They even tried to remember details of the previous Captain, who'd been killed in a raid before they'd even made third. Mal realized through the haze that they were talking about Hex's grandfather. She squinted.

"Jem, Hex'll be Cap'n one day," she murmured, watching a cloud scud by in the slice of sky between two sheets on the foremast.

"It might be a very long time until that happens," he said. Then he straightened and looked past Mal to the ladder leading down to the main decks.

Kalinda stood at the top of the ladder. Today she wasn't wearing her full wind-whistler's coat, just the bandolier across her chest holding the absolute necessities of her trade. She'd braided her long hair in an intricate design that reminded Mal of a sea snake twisting through the water. Her brilliantly white shirt made Mal's eyes hurt. She managed to get to her feet without Jem's help.

"Third Mal," Kalinda said, her dark eyes glinting in the bright sun, "I've come to escort you to mast."

Mal nodded. "Aye, First Kalinda. May I have just a moment?"

"Only one," said Kalinda, and she turned her back on them to give them privacy.

Mal threw her arms around Jem's neck, clutching him like she'd grasped at the floating bit of flotsam that had saved her and Hex's lives in the storm.

"Easy," he murmured comfortingly, rubbing his hand in circles on her back. "Get it out now, can't let them see you shaking."

She buried her face in his shoulder, took a deep shuddering breath and then stepped back. With a glance at Kalinda, she told him quickly, "If I…don't make it, I want you and Hex to have my rings." She whispered the two hiding places she used in his ear.

"You know you'll have to move them now," he said with a smile, "once you've gotten through this."

She smiled crookedly. "I trust you, Jem."

"Never trust a sailor with your treasure." He recited the well-known saying with a wink.

"Third Mal," said Kalinda again.

She straightened and turned away from Jem. Even through the warm haze of the seconds' gift, she still felt her stomach clench and a strange flutter in her chest. "Aye, First Kalinda."

"Follow me closely," said the wind-whistler.

Mal fell into step behind her, close enough that they were almost touching.

"The Captain has decided to use the seawater," said Kalinda, her lips barely moving as she walked briskly across the deck toward the mast. The gathered crew made a path for them so neatly that the first didn't have to pause once.

Mal's breath hitched. 'Using seawater' meant that there would be two firsts stationed on either side of the Captain. After every lash, they would douse her torn flesh with seawater and pass their empty bucket back to the rail to be refilled by the thirds stationed there. On the one hand, it was literally rubbing salt in the new wounds, adding to the already excruciating pain of the whip. On the other hand, Jem had told her that dousing new wounds in seawater usually helped speed the healing, so some took that as a sign of favor from the Captain.

Kalinda didn't seem to expect an answer, because she continued in her low voice, "Remember your bravery, Third Mal. You'll need it."

The ship was unnaturally silent, the only sounds the canvas of the sails creaking as the wind filled their bellies, the swish of the waves against the hull, the distant call of some seabirds as they dove for fish in the glittering curves of the ocean. Mal breathed deeply, trying to calm her racing heart. She wondered where Jem would watch – maybe from the mainmast rigging, if he could still find a place this late.

The final row of sailors, all white shirts, parted before Kalinda's brisk steps, revealing the mainmast. Mal swallowed the cry that tried to crawl up her throat: Hex knelt before the mast, his hands bound behind his back and his face bloodied. His dark eyes blazed as he looked up at the imposing figure of the Captain.

"You will not be bound," said Kalinda to Mal. She led her to a spot even with Hex on the opposite side of the mast, still facing the Captain. "Kneel here."

"What happened? What did he do?" Her voice came out as a whisper.

"Kneel," repeated Kalinda, steel in her voice now. "If you make me tell you again, you *will* be bound."

What had Hex done? Mal knelt and glanced desperately at him, taking in the bruise blooming along his jaw and the black eye beginning to show darkly against his tanned skin. She fought the urge to run to him. Maybe she should have made them bind her.

"We are here this noon," boomed the Captain, his voice expanding in Mal's head, crowding out all other thoughts, "for the mast of Third Mal."

A spark of relief kindled somewhere near the beat of her heart. Perhaps there was some mistake. Perhaps Hex had already received his punishment and he was here just as a measure of shame.

"You know why she is kneeling before me. She broke the rule of the kraken, a cardinal rule ingrained into every member of this crew from the day they step onboard as a fourth."

A murmur of agreement rippled through the crew.

"For her transgression, she will receive five lashes."

The wind sighed through the sails of the *Dragonwing*. Mal felt the warm boards beneath her knees and drew up all her resolve. She would not cry out. She would let death take her before she let any sound of weakness pass her lips.

"And then," continued the Captain, his voice darkening. Fear bloomed in Mal's chest, cold as the winter sea. "Third Hex will stand mast."

She felt as though the breath had been punched out of her. The firsts standing in a ring around the Captain shifted as they heard questioning mutters slide through the crew, fluttering like moths about the rigging and the sails where the thirds perched.

"Third Hex thought it his right to challenge my authority," said the Captain, his voice soft and deadly now, "to mete out such punishment as I see fit to those who choose to break the rules onboard this vessel."

"There is a difference between knowing transgression and a choice to save the life of a fellow sailor," Hex said loudly, his words slurred slightly by a swelling lip.

The moth-wing mutters transformed into buzzing akin to a nest of mud bees, even as the Captain signaled one of the larger firsts, who stepped forward and hit Hex in the face, knocking him to the deck. The humming only grew louder. The Captain stood unmoved, waiting until the swell of muttering died down, though Mal thought she saw a flash of something like regret cross his face quickly as he looked down at the third who was his son.

Mal could hear Hex's labored breathing. She wondered how badly they'd beaten him. Gods, why had he tried to reason with the Captain? Why hadn't he just let her take her punishment and let them all get on with their lives?

Because he cannot stand the thought of your life ending in trade for his, whispered that voice in her mind.

"I will take her lashes," Hex yelled, raising his head.

She bit down on a shout of protest.

"That is not the law of the sea," said the Captain in that quiet, terrifying voice, his eyes glittering icily. "But since you are so bent on suffering more than Third Mal..." He raised his voice for the whole crew to hear. "For his transgression, Third Hex will receive ten lashes."

If Mal had been standing, she probably would have needed to grab onto something. She felt the shock course through her body. Ten lashes. That was very nearly a death sentence. She almost missed the second part of the Captain's pronouncement amid the outcry from the rigging.

"And banishment."

A few of the seconds, the gray-shirted rank behind the firsts, looked uneasily at each other. Mal couldn't see much from her vantage point on her knees, but she saw boots shifting, heard the thirds scurrying through the rigging like spiders rushing with deadly speed across their webs. The firsts closed the circle tighter about the Captain, their gazes sharpening at this unexpected response.

The Captain looked unmoved by the outcry. Mal wanted to shout at him – how could he mete out such a punishment to his own son, his own flesh and blood? But she knew that he would probably reply that such was the law of the sea.

"Third Mal," the Captain said, shifting his dark gaze to her, "will you kneel or stand?"

She drew back her shoulders. "I will stand, sir." Her voice rang out over the assembled crew. A hush fell over them, though an angry hum could still be heard shifting among the sails.

The Captain held out his hand. One of the firsts placed the grip of the cat o' nine tails into his palm. The small blades affixed to the end of its tails glinted in the sun. Kalinda stepped forward as Mal stood and walked to the brass ring set into the mast.

Mal heard her own breath, oddly loud in her ears, as she gripped the sun-warmed ring. The breeze played on the bare skin of her back as Kalinda cut the back of her shirt open with a single swipe of her dagger. The other woman neatly tucked the edges of Mal's shirt into her breeches, preventing the breeze from catching the front and exposing her to all watching. It was a small gesture and took no more than a heartbeat, but Mal knew she would remember it forever.

"Stand ready with the buckets," Kalinda ordered.

Mal tensed as she heard the Captain's heavy tread approaching. She clenched her jaw and braced herself.

She heard the whistle of the whip through the air an instant before it bit into her flesh. The force of the blow nearly knocked her from her feet, but she clung to the ring doggedly, clamping her jaw shut so hard that her teeth ached. Pain roared in the background and black spots dotted the edges of her vision. She noted with strange clarity the droplets of blood spattering the deck, knowing they were hers.

More footsteps, and she rallied her self-control in preparation for the seawater. The water sluiced down over her back, and fire bit into her flesh…but then instantly cooled, as though Jem had just applied his best salve to her skin. She swallowed and thanked whatever gods there were for such a small mercy.

The second stroke of the whip was much like the first. She shuddered at the pain, its enormity beyond the grasp of her conscious mind. She pushed away the darkness pressing at the edges of her vision. The second bucket of seawater chased away the pain, leaving her gasping in relief.

"What is this sorcery?" growled the Captain.

The third blow knocked her against the mast, her shoulder hitting the wood beside the ring and stars bursting behind her eyes. She slipped on the deck slick with water and her blood, but didn't fall, hauling herself back into position with single-minded focus. As she gazed down at the soaked boards, her mind supplied a strange hallucination: it looked as though her blood shimmered golden in the seawater. She very nearly laughed but remembered she wasn't supposed to make a sound.

The darkness nearly rushed over her head at the fourth stroke, but something seemed to be wrong. She felt the pain of each lash, the blades woven into each of the nine strands slicing into her flesh…but with each dousing in seawater, something strange was happening. She could feel it, she couldn't quite describe it, but she *knew* it was strange because even through the roaring in her ears she heard the murmurs and then shouts from the crew.

"No seawater for this last one," said the Captain.

Her knees gave out at the ferocity of that last blow, and she almost opened her aching jaw to beg for the relief of the seawater…but the water rushed over her flesh nonetheless, despite what the Captain had said.

"My apologies, sir, didn't hear," said Kalinda in a serious voice, though Mal thought disjointedly that she didn't sound sorry in the least.

After a pause, the Captain's booted steps carried him away from Mal. She stood shivering, clinging to the ring, not sure at all if it was really over.

"Let go, girl, let go," said Kalinda into her ear, her small hands prying Mal's fingers free from the brass ring.

"Hex," she gasped. She heard the Captain asking Hex the same question he had posed to her, and Hex answered the same. He'd take his lashes standing.

"Nothing you can do for him now," said Kalinda grimly.

Mal released her hold on the ring and her knees gave out. Kalinda muttered a curse but kept her from falling, though the first's grip on her arm was sure to leave bruises. Mal slid to her knees on the wet deck. She touched the glimmering golden sheen in the water, now darkening to something like bronze.

"I don't know what spell that was, but it was a hell of a casting," Kalinda said into her ear. "You're not bleeding." Then the other woman was gone, taking her position once again with a bucket of seawater by the Captain's side.

Mal pressed her hands to the deck, her mind torn away from contemplating her miraculous healing and molten-gold blood. She turned her head just in time to see the brutal first blow land on Hex's bare back.

His blood did not glimmer gold, and seawater did not heal him. He doggedly held his silence beneath the brutal strokes of the whip. Rage glinted in the Captain's eyes, and Mal felt a deep hatred for the man surging up within her, a welcome distraction. After the seventh blow, Hex collapsed soundlessly. Mal stuffed a fist into her mouth to keep from crying out as two of the firsts hauled him up and bound his hands to the brass ring on the other side of the mast.

Hex's ink-dark blood crept across the deck, a tendril reaching Mal. She fought not to retch, breathing hard.

Finally, the tenth blow landed.

"Anyone who tends to him joins him in banishment," said the

Captain in a steely voice, throwing the bloody whip down onto the deck. He pointed at one of the firsts. "Set a watch on him."

The circle of firsts parted, Jem wriggling through the close-packed throng, his healer's satchel over his shoulder.

"No need to set a watch to see who will help him, sir," he said with a deep bow. The buzzing in the rigging sounded as though someone had kicked a nest of mud bees.

Mal's heart swelled at Jem's unflinching loyalty. Without waiting for a response from the Captain, he turned to Hex, taking his dagger from his belt and working on cutting through the rope that bound Hex's wrists to the ring.

Mal stood, stumbled, and righted herself, gritting her teeth. If she had to crawl over, so be it. But she managed the walk. Her voice didn't work when she tried to ask how she could help, but Jem glanced quickly at her and knew what she meant to say.

"Hold his head and try to take some of his weight when I get through these," he ordered tersely.

Mal immediately obeyed, trying not to look at the mess of torn and bleeding flesh that had once been Hex's back.

"Impertinent whelp," she heard the Captain growl, and then he stalked away.

Mal swallowed down bile and told herself firmly not to shake. Mast was over, but Hex needed her. Hex *and* Jem, because they had been banished, and they would need all their wits to survive as Seafarers with no ship.

Chapter 16

At first, the Seelie and Vyldgard fighters practicing in the training yard did not recognize Queen Andraste. Dressed as she was in breeches and a dark blue shirt, no star diadem upon her brow, the Queen nonetheless drew curious glances as she strode across the yard toward the smith's forge. Sayre flashed a grin at Guinna, the two of them following half a step behind the Queen. Guinna had decided to change into breeches as well in a show of solidarity, but she missed the comforting weight of her skirts against her legs. She stretched her paces to keep up with Andraste, raising an eyebrow at Sayre's youthful enthusiasm.

The Queen hesitated slightly at the door of the forge, seeming to consider knocking. Then she drew back her shoulders and pushed the door open, stepping confidently into the red-gold light beyond.

"If you want a weapon, you'll have to wait at least a week," said the shorthaired smith as she pulled a cherry-hot piece of metal from the forge with a rune-inscribed glove. Sweat gleamed on her brow and Guinna glimpsed the cords of muscle in her back and arms as she brought her silver hammer down upon the blade, sparks spraying in a magnificent, fiery display.

"All of these are spoken for?" Andraste asked between the ringing strikes of the smith's hammer, stepping over to a rack of blades in various styles. Some were clearly meant for Seelie hands, slender and gold-tinted, their hilts embossed with sun and trees. Others Guinna imagined in the hands of Vyldgard fighters, the designs fiercer somehow but no less graceful, some of the blades wider and a few curved strangely. Guinna remembered Rye wielding such a curved blade once, the memory as vivid as though she'd just watched Tyr's twin jesting with Ramel yesterday as she tried to teach the Unseelie squire how to throw an axe properly.

"Told you," said the smith, raising her voice in irritation as she thrust the blade back into the forge. She turned, flicking damp hair out of her eyes with her gloved hand, leaving a smear of ash across her forehead. "Wait is at least a…" She stopped, tilted her head, took in the dark-haired woman and the two Unseelie behind her.

Guinna met the smith's questioning eyes and nodded in confirmation.

"Well," said the smith, clearing her throat. "Wait is *supposed* to be a week, but I'll make an exception for you, my lady." She bowed from the waist, not quite as deep a bow as Guinna would have expected to the Queen of the Unseelie Court; but then again, the smith was Vyldgard now.

Andraste smiled. "There are a few benefits to being a queen, I suppose."

The smith didn't reply. She glanced at the blade in the forge and apparently decided it would be fine for a few moments. Then she looked at Andraste appraisingly, her frank gaze evaluating the Queen's stature. "Looks like you'd want a slim blade."

"Slim," agreed Andraste, "but on the heavier side, if you please." She smiled at the smith's badly hidden look of surprise. "What's your name? I'm sorry, I haven't been – back – long."

"Thea, my lady," the smith replied.

"Thea," Andraste repeated, still smiling. "You see, Thea, before I was imprisoned I trained with the pages and then the squires of the

Unseelie Court. At first, I'd disguise myself as a boy and sneak down to the practice yards, but of course that only worked for so long before someone unmasked me."

Guinna watched Andraste's face, waiting for the telltale spasm of pain, but either the Queen had taken her words to heart and endeavored to move past self-pity, or she'd simply decided to hide it. Either way, the Queen actually looked happily wistful as she recounted the memory. The smith Thea listened respectfully but there was an edge of wariness to her gaze, as though she couldn't understand the end game of the Unseelie Queen in this visit to her forge and now this personal recollection.

"I was determined to learn, but there were a few squires who took me aside and explained to me that I was putting them all in danger by practicing in disguise. My sister would have had them all flogged and maybe some of them banished if she'd ever gotten word that they'd struck me, even within a practice ring."

Guinna glanced at Sayre. The younger Unseelie gazed at Queen Andraste, enraptured with the tale. She smiled, feeling a surge of affection for the Guard and tamping down her own sudden feeling of world-weariness. She'd been a part of the young Princess's schemes, though Rose had always taken more delight in the deception. And she'd also learned how to wield a bow and a sword alongside her mistress, first to merely provide companionship to Andraste and then out of genuine enthusiasm.

They had been so young and untroubled, those centuries ago.

"So, I struck a deal with one of the young Knights. Well, he'd just been made a Knight, actually, and I suppose I didn't so much strike a deal as I browbeat him into teaching me." Andraste smiled fondly.

Inexplicably, Guinna felt her own lips curve in an answering smile. Some of Thea's wariness faded, and the smith looked genuinely interested in the Queen's tale.

"I practiced endlessly in my own chambers, and then sparred with him during outings that were *supposed* to be very proper, very boring hours of painting flowers and landscapes, with the Knight and his squire standing watch as we discussed the composition of the sketches."

Thea chuckled. Andraste grinned, her blue eyes sparkling. She turned to Guinna.

"Lady Guinna is also a fair hand at wielding a blade thanks to those sessions," she said, arching one dark brow.

"I wield a blade when I must," replied Guinna with a smile.

"Deadlier with words," murmured Sayre in a voice pitched only for her and the Queen's ears.

"So, you see, Thea, I'm used to a real blade. One that I can use to defend myself or anyone else should the need arise."

"Aye, my lady," replied Thea with a nod, "though I hope the need never arises again."

"As do I," replied Andraste, "but we must all prepare for the dark day when we are called to arms again."

"Wise words indeed." The smith crossed her arms over her chest and walked over to the rack of weapons, murmuring to herself as her eyes traveled over each individual sword. Finally, she reached out and drew a sword from the middle of the rack. Somehow Guinna felt as though that blade had been hidden, because how else could her eyes have missed the gorgeous silver sword wrought with delicate blue stones of every hue, from the deep blue-black velvet of a starless midnight sky near the hilt to a cluster of nearly white stones at the pommel, scattered like a spray of blossoms against the shining silver.

"I did not know who would claim this one," said Thea, a note of satisfaction in her voice. She held the blade on her flat palms, offering its hilt to the Queen. Andraste took it from the smith's hands, drawing in her breath as she wrapped her fingers around the hilt. Guinna felt the Queen's pleasure as strongly as if it were her own – she swayed against the dizzying sensation, suddenly unsure where she ended and Andraste began. She felt Sayre's steadying hand on her shoulder, though he too breathed heavily, feeling the same rush of emotion from the Queen.

"You like it, my lady?" Thea asked, though by the slight smugness joining the satisfaction in her words, she already knew the Queen loved the blade. Guinna narrowed her eyes. She certainly needed to become used to the Vyldgard habit of showing so much emotion.

"Do you have a scabbard for it?" Andraste asked, turning the sword in the flickering light of the forge's fire. To Guinna's eyes, it looked like blue and white fire licked the hilt and Andraste's hand.

"Yes, though it isn't the original, I fear," Thea replied. She disappeared for a moment into another room and returned with a plain black scabbard in her hands.

"Sometimes the greatest treasures are concealed in plain sight," said Andraste enigmatically, accepting the scabbard from the smith and sliding the magnificent blade into it with a silvery hiss.

Thea looked at Guinna. "Do you need a blade, too?"

"No," Guinna said.

"Yes," said the Queen at the same time.

Guinna cleared her throat and resisted the urge to smooth her palms down the thighs of her breeches; if she'd been wearing skirts, she would have been able to smooth them, but in breeches the habitual motion just looked crass. "I...had not intended on entering the ring, my Queen."

"And why not?" asked Andraste. "Guinna, you just gave me that lovely speech about starting anew. That goes for you as well."

"I confess that I do not see how that relates to my picking up a blade again," Guinna said, settling for linking her fingers together demurely in front of her. Perhaps if she relied upon those courtly habits...

"Nonsense," said the Queen firmly. "You see very well how it relates to it, you just choose not to."

Sayre pressed his mouth into a line to avoid grinning outright.

"I only pick up a blade when necessity warrants," Guinna tried.

"Again, nonsense." Andraste unbuckled her belt and slid the scabbard onto it, testing its weight against her hip and nodding in satisfaction. Her gaze pierced Guinna. "I need you alive for many more centuries to come, Guinna, and that means I need to know that I've ensured you're given every tool to return to me."

Guinna took a deep breath. Centuries of polite conversation, words wielded just as handily as blades, had taught her when she was going to lose an argument. Sometimes it was simpler to admit defeat gracefully. "As you wish, my Queen."

Andraste grinned.

When they left Thea a quarter hour later, the smith had outfitted Guinna with a plainer but well-made blade a bit lighter than the one at the Queen's hip, taking Andraste's request for a set of throwing knives with only a hint of surprise. Sayre had asked about the time required to forge a properly balanced battle-axe.

"Thinking about asking the Bearer's *ulfdrengr* to teach you to fight in their style?" Thea had replied. "Chael forges all the axes, you'll have to come back and ask him."

"Chael," said Andraste thoughtfully as Sayre scanned the yard for an open practice ring. The murmuring sweeping through the yard like an ocean wave told Guinna that the Queen's identity had been discovered, but Andraste was magnificently unaffected, tossing her dark braid over one shoulder as she followed Sayre toward the selected ring. "Have I met this Chael?"

"You would probably remember him if you had, my lady," said Guinna truthfully. "Silver hair and sometimes wears an eye patch, scars across his face."

"Not unlike Tyr," said Andraste, almost to herself.

"Besides the fact that Tyr is not bound to a Northwolf," Guinna agreed with a smile.

"Tyr bound himself to the Paladin," replied Andraste without skipping a beat. "I think that is somewhat similar."

Guinna chuckled at the Queen's lighthearted yet apt comparison:

There was indeed something fierce about the young mortal Paladin that brought to mind a creature of the forest, wild and untamed. "I've never seen a red wolf, my lady."

"Maybe she'd be better described as a fox," said Sayre, unsheathing his blade and beginning to run through a warm up routine. Andraste watched him for a moment before drawing her own sword. The Queen tested its balance with a few strokes and then, taking a deep breath, she began her own calisthenics, the blade arcing in precise patterns, painstakingly slow at first and then faster as she warmed to the feel of a weapon in her hand again.

Guinna stood at the edge of the ring and crossed her arms over her chest, glancing around the training yard. She caught the curious gazes of a few of the Vyldgard, and a few of the Seelie openly conversed about the Queen, their eyes glittering with interest. She raised her chin and turned her attention back to the Queen. If Andraste did not care, then neither did she. Let them stare and whisper.

As Andraste began running through faster drills, Guinna marveled at the change in her. She had not seen Andraste after Finnead had rescued her from the Dark Keep, other than a glimpse as he rode through the White City with the Princess' limp form in his arms. While Ramel had withdrawn after Mab threatened the *fendhionne*, he'd still spoken to her about the efforts to heal the Princess from the madness still gripping her after the centuries of enslavement. Now Guinna watched the Queen whirl through a complex set of movements, her blade flashing and her feet tracing elegant, quick steps on the hard-packed dirt. She wondered suddenly if Andraste had been forced to use a blade on anyone during her enslavement; most knew that their now-Queen had been called the Dark Archer for part of the war against Malravenar. She'd killed dozens of Sidhe fighters with her poisoned black arrows, though the fault lay with Malravenar, not her.

A chill ran through Guinna as she considered this new line of thought. She tried to think of it as though she were not one of the

Queen's Three…or two, as it was for the moment. They still felt the absence of their third like an ache that never fully went away. How would she regard the new Queen if she were just another member of the Court she glimpsed from afar every now and again? A knot formed in Guinna's stomach as she realized that some would not have such loving and charitable views of their new Queen. Guilt pricked her. She should have thought about this long before a bright morning in the practice yards, but then again, she and Sayre had been fighting to keep the Queen from descending into the darkness of despair or withdrawing completely.

Andraste stopped her drills, her skin glowing and eyes flashing as she motioned Sayre into the ring. The younger man grinned and bowed deeply to the Queen before stepping across the inscribed circle. Andraste was Queen, Guinna thought, but perhaps not all accepted her as such. What of those who had loved the ones she had killed as the Dark Archer? What of those who saw her as having a choice in her enslavement, wrong as Guinna thought that opinion was? She pressed her lips together. She'd been spending far too much time worrying about the Queen, and not enough time paying attention to the whispers of the Unseelie Court.

Andraste leapt toward Sayre with her blade raised, a flinty look of concentration in her blue eyes. Sayre met her attack with a measured, careful defense, though he did raise an eyebrow at the intensity of the Queen's attack. A frown wrinkled Andraste's brow as she launched into a second offensive. She was moving quickly, but not as quickly as Sayre, who danced away from the attack with ease. Guinna could see that Sayre was tempering his speed and skill to match the Queen. He forced her to shift into a defensive stance as he tested her knowledge of blocks and parrying strokes, calm focus on his face. His look reminded Guinna of the old sword master who had taught their Court's pages long ago.

The match lasted for a few more minutes. Andraste began flagging, though she narrowed her eyes and fought to keep the speed of her sword and the quickness of her feet. Guinna wondered suddenly if Sayre would end the match in the typical way: a sword-point pressed to the throat of the weaker opponent. She reached out through their connection and felt his calm, steady presence, centered by the focus of the blade practice, and the knot in her stomach loosened a little. When Andraste danced back to the edge of the circle in a bid to snatch a moment of respite, Sayre lowered his sword and inclined his head to her.

"Well fought, my lady," he said.

Andraste gave a very unqueenly snort. "You barely broke a sweat, Sayre."

Sayre raised one eyebrow. "Shall I explain myself, my lady?"

The Queen blew out a breath and sheathed her sword. She waved a hand at Sayre. "No, no, it's very obvious that I'm out of practice."

"I wouldn't so much say out of *practice* as out of *conditioning*," said Sayre.

Guinna winced as Andraste looked sharply at the dark-haired Guard. Sayre unconcernedly sheathed his sword, gazing steadily back at the Queen.

"You are fortunate that one of your duties is to speak truth to power," Andraste said dryly. "Otherwise I might have taken offense."

Sayre grinned. "My lady, you are free to take offense if you choose."

"No," said Andraste with a sigh, shaking her head. "If I am so harsh and capricious as to punish those closest to me for speaking the truth, then I'm no better than my sister."

"You are far better than your sister," Sayre said immediately, his voice serious.

"In more ways than one," Guinna agreed. She gently pushed away the thoughts that had occupied her during the sparring match, herding them into a neat little group to be shepherded into a corner of her mind and examined later.

"Something concerns you, Guinna," said Andraste, brushing a damp tendril of dark hair away from her face.

"I will speak of it to you later, if it pleases you, my Queen," Guinna replied. The training yard was no place to talk of discord within their Court.

"Very well," said Andraste with a nod. "While I catch my breath, perhaps you can provide Sayre with more of a challenge than I did."

Though sweat dampened the Queen's shirt and she seemed out of breath, Guinna thought that she seemed a bit distracted, like a person who was trying to remember some half-forgotten thing just out of their reach. The Queen looked down at the blade in her hand, her eyes distant.

"Are you certain, my lady?" said Guinna. "I do not wish to take away from your time in the ring."

"I…need to think," said Andraste vaguely.

"We can start with some basic drills," said Sayre encouragingly to Guinna.

She drew her sword and stepped into the ring. Though she was no Guard or Knight, a little thrill of anticipation coursed through her. She felt a smile curve her lips. "Thank you for the generous offer, but I think we should see how it goes."

He grinned, adopted the starting stance and nodded to her. Five minutes later, they were both breathing hard and whirling through a fast-paced match. Guinna watched Sayre's chest for his next movements, though his skill bordered on the level at which he betrayed no sign of his intentions, even as his body began to execute the next stroke. She tried a tricky little combination that Bren had taught her, and Sayre barely blocked it. He regained his balance almost instantly, flashing half a grin at her creativity.

Guinna found herself reaching for the space between breath and heartbeat, sliding into that strange half-trance where her body moved without conscious direction, the sword in her hand becoming an extension of her body, her mind emptying of all thought save for the immediate moment. She almost slid her blade through Sayre's guard, but he caught her sword crosswise and with a sharp twist of his weapon deftly disarmed her. As the hilt of her sword left her hand, Guinna dropped to the hard-packed dirt and thrust out one leg in one fluid movement, neatly sweeping Sayre's legs from under him. He turned his fall into a graceful roll while she leapt for her sword; as her fingers brushed the hilt, she felt the cold prick of his blade against the side of her throat.

She pulled her hand away from her weapon, swallowing down disappointment. Though she put less stock in her fighting ability than most, it was still difficult to accept defeat amidst the heady, pulse-pounding whirl of a bout, even if it was only a sparring match in the training yard. The cool, careful touch of Sayre's blade disappeared, and she turned her head to look at him. He brushed dirt from his knees, standing from a wide lunge. A little bud of satisfaction bloomed into something like pride as she realized that he'd actually had to *work* to end the duel with her.

"You learned some lessons from the Vyldgard," Sayre said, a note of approval in his voice. He offered her his hand, pulling her to her feet.

"After Calliea rescued me from Mab's hounds, I had to do *something* with my time," she replied lightly, though she heard the tremor in her own voice at the mention of the great black beasts that had very nearly killed her.

Sayre looked thoughtfully over at other fighters sparring in the training yards. "We can learn from each other."

"Now that Malravenar is gone, what incentive do the Courts have to work together?" Guinna asked honestly, retrieving her blade and carefully wiping the dust from it with the edge of her shirt.

"We saw it with the bone sorcerer," said Sayre. "And with Mab. Just because the threat is not to our whole world does not mean that we should retreat to that state of casual enmity that once existed between us."

"Casual enmity," repeated Guinna, turning the phrase over in her mind. She looked at the Queen, realizing that Andraste had remained silent for a long while. "My lady, what do you think of some incentive to promote training between all the Courts?"

Andraste blinked and took a deep breath, shuddering slightly as though waking up from sleep. "That sounds like an idea with merit, Guinna." The Queen looked down again at her sword. "Sayre, when you are sufficiently recovered, I would like another bout."

Sayre brushed a curl of unruly dark hair from his forehead. He bowed to the Queen. "Whenever you are ready, my lady."

Guinna raised an eyebrow at Sayre. He seemed to be a bit over-confident, accepting another bout mere moments after they'd finished theirs, but then again, he was a full Guard with decades of training, despite what she saw as his youth. Not for the first time, Guinna felt the centuries pressing down on her as she stepped out of the ring, sheathing her sword. She had to admit, its weight at her hip *did* feel reassuring.

Andraste stepped into the ring and raised her blade. For a reason Guinna couldn't quite name, the Queen looked *different* from the first time she'd sparred. A prickle of premonition swept down Guinna's spine, and she tensed as Sayre adjusted his grip on his weapon. The dark-haired Guard nodded to the Queen and the match began.

Guinna felt herself take another step back from the ring instinctively, her eyes widening at the ferocity of the Queen's attack. One of the pairs in an adjacent circle paused in their practice to watch, such was the difference in skill displayed by Andraste and met by Sayre. Guinna felt the flare of Sayre's surprise and then his pleasure at unleashing his full abilities. She could not feel anything from the Queen.

Another pair of fighters stopped to watch the match, Seelie and Vyldgard forming a small, loose crowd of onlookers around the circle. Guinna wondered briefly if she should disperse them somehow, but it was all she could do to glance away from the sparring match that had turned into such a staggering display. As the match continued, she could see that Sayre was using all his considerable talent simply to defend against Andraste's quicksilver blade, barely going on the offensive himself. Murmurs began rising around the ring, counterpoint to the clash of swords and the occasional sounds of effort from the Guard. The Queen fought with an icy silence and a steely composure that sent another chill across Guinna's skin.

Andraste pressed Sayre's defenses with inexorable speed, her beautiful face showing no trace of effort save an occasional flash of her blue eyes. A look that might have been fear crossed Sayre's face fleetingly, so fast that Guinna thought she had been the only one to catch it, because she felt the jump of Sayre's heart as he realized that some force within the Queen had been unleashed, something wild and perhaps dangerous – something from the centuries that she had spent enthralled under Malravenar's Dark power.

The Queen moved with ferocious, swift intent, her blade now a blur. Sayre blocked it twice more, leaping away with admirable quickness, but somehow she was there again, as though he'd not moved at all. His eyes widened fractionally as he barely avoided a thrust of her gleaming sword, and Guinna's mouth went dry. Would the new Unseelie Queen drive a blade through one of her Three here in the practice yards, overwhelmed by whatever force within her that had been let out of its cage? A sense of helplessness gripped her – what could she possibly do? If she stepped into the ring, she felt certain that she'd only make things worse, because while she'd acquitted herself well, there was no way she could stand up to that whirlwind of skill and speed.

Sayre maintained his composure as he danced around the ring, blocking the Queen's blade and then slipping away, though the Queen's speed gave him little relief despite his talent at evasion. A small smile appeared on Andraste's lips. The Queen looked like a cat playing with a mouse as she stalked Sayre around the ring – there was no doubt she could have ended the match at any point, but she seemed to be *enjoying* Sayre's increasingly desperate defense against her onslaught. Guinna jumped as a hand landed on her shoulder.

"Do you need help?" Ramel said quietly into her ear. For the first time since he'd returned from the mortal world, his breath didn't stink of liquor.

Guinna nodded and smiled – the nod for Ramel, the smile for the dozen or so Sidhe now watching the match. For some reason, she didn't want them to know that the new Unseelie Three didn't understand their Queen's darkest secrets.

"Try to catch her attention when I do," Ramel said quietly to her. He took a breath and drew back his shoulders as though he didn't hear the new note of surprise in the buzz of commentary around the ring, as though he didn't see the raised eyebrows as the onlookers noticed his presence. Sayre stumbled, and the Queen advanced on him relentlessly. Guinna reached for her connection with the Queen, grasping it as though it were a thread she was about to pull.

Ramel stepped into the ring, prompting a rush of voices: Though sparring matches were by design casual events, they still adhered to the rules of courtesy which dictated that none should intervene unless absolutely necessary. Sayre fell to one knee. The Queen drew back her blade, terribly beautiful, like an avenging goddess about to sweep down upon an unrepentant world.

"My Queen, forgive me," said Ramel in a clear, carrying voice.

Guinna pulled hard on the invisible thread, gritting her teeth at such rough handling of that precious connection to her Queen. The arc of Andraste's sword paused, her back arching and head turning as she sought out the source of the voice.

"My Queen," Ramel said again, his voice powerful yet soothing, commanding yet respectful. Guinna felt the Queen's awareness turning, changing from the strange, icy composure to something more like what she had felt from the Queen in the days since the restoration of her memories and her sense of self. Sayre used the time to rise gracefully to his feet and sheath his blade, as though the interruption had not saved him from the possibility of harm at the hands of his Queen.

For a moment, Guinna thought that Andraste was going to leap at Ramel with her sword raised, but the Queen finally nodded to Ramel, sheathing her blade. "Yes, Knight Ramel?"

"There is a message for you," Ramel said in such a way that Guinna knew all those assembled would assume that it was a message of importance, meant for the Queen and her Three only. Mercifully, Andraste accepted the premise with an elegant nod, stepping regally from the circle. Sayre followed close behind, and Guinna fell into step as they walked toward the gate of the training yard. She studiously ignored the voices rising behind them. It was a good thing that Andraste had come to the training yards, letting the other Courts see that she was not her sister.

Or at least that was what Guinna told herself as she thought about how to broach this difficult subject with Andraste as they walked back toward the cathedral, the sun warm on their backs, glittering on the stone of the White City.

Chapter 17

"The expedition is leaving in four days," said Liam without preamble as he brushed aside the curtain and entered Quinn's small tent-like room.

"Tell me what you *really* want to talk about," Quinn replied without even looking up from where he sat cross-legged in one corner of the room, his blades laid out beside him as he'd once done with his guns, each one awaiting its turn for a careful inspection and cleaning.

Liam prowled around the room rather than sitting on one of the cushions that served as seats at the low table. Quinn glanced at him and then picked up one of his daggers, reaching for his whetting-stone with the other hand. Finally, Liam said, "I don't like being left behind."

"Vell's not going," pointed out Quinn. "And unless something's changed, neither is Tess. I'm staying here too, so that's most of the people that rank high on your list."

Liam shot him a look. "You seem to think you know a lot about my list."

Quinn shrugged as he ran the stone down one side of the blade. "I think I do, all things considered. You're on mine – all the boys are. You know that and I know that. Most of the time family makes it, and

Vell is, well, whatever you two are at this point." He paused. "Do they have marriage here? Guess I never thought about it all that much."

"That's a lie if I ever heard one," replied Liam.

Raising his eyebrows, Quinn said, "If you meant that I thought about the whole marriage thing with Niamh, you're mostly wrong. It crossed my mind, but there was so much happening that I didn't really dwell on it. I was just happy with what we had."

"That was below the belt. Sorry." Liam ran one hand through his hair.

"It happens." Quinn thought for a moment as he methodically sharpened the dagger. The repetitive motion settled him in a way that he recognized from cleaning his weapons and gear both in training and on deployment. Preparation was just as important as the actual mission. "Who're you worried about, then?"

"Feels like I'm worried about everyone. Like things are too quiet and I'm just waiting for something to happen."

"Like it can't be real that all the battles have been won and everyone is living happily ever after," Quinn said quietly.

"Exactly," Liam agreed. He finally stopped pacing and settled onto one of the low cushions. "I feel like I'm...off-balance."

"A lot of things have changed pretty quickly around here."

Liam leaned back on his elbows and stared at the *taebramh*-lantern on the table. "How do you have one of these things in here?"

"Thea rigged it for me. It's like an oil lamp, the way she explained it. She put a certain amount of taebramh in there and I just have to touch the activation rune. Every so often I bring it back to her for a refill."

"Clever," said Liam approvingly.

"Better than having an open flame," replied Quinn. He gestured to the brightly colored hangings, rugs and furs surrounding them. "I have the feeling that this isn't really up to fire code, and I don't have the whammy to put it out instantly like everyone else."

"I think you overestimate the extent of most Sidhe's abilities," said Liam.

"I really don't think so. And besides, better to overestimate than underestimate."

"That's usually applied to adversaries."

He shrugged. "Hard to know who's who in the zoo sometimes, and that can all change. We just fought a battle that's proof of that."

"If you're trying to help me with my balance problem, you're doing the opposite," Liam said drily.

"Sometimes the truth doesn't help." Quinn set aside the dagger and picked up a slightly longer blade, sighting down its length and looking for any damage to the cutting edges. "So, spill it. Who else are you worried about? You won't do anyone any good if you bottle that stuff up."

"Says one of the masters of it," muttered Liam.

Quinn only grinned as he picked up the whetting stone again.

"Finn's been...different," said Liam finally.

Quinn grunted. "You guys got pretty close while I was away. If I were the jealous type, I'd have my panties in a bunch."

"I'm not touching that one with a ten-foot pole. The last part of it, anyway," said Liam, raising one eyebrow. "But yes, we did get...pretty close, like you said. Part of it is because of the bond through both of us being one of Vell's Three. We lost Gray, and we gained Calliea. That brought us closer, in a strange way."

Quinn shook his head. "Nothing strange about it, really. Loss either pushes people apart or draws them together."

Liam looked at him as though he wanted to say something about that particular observation, and then he sighed and shook his head instead.

"Look," said Quinn, "talking about Niamh doesn't really hurt anymore, so you can say whatever you want to say." A small voice in the back of his head whispered that he was a liar, that it still hurt but he was just able to ignore it now because it wasn't the gut-wrenching pain of a freshly broken heart.

"I was just going to say that I know the feeling," Liam said finally.

He stared into the softly pulsing light of the *taebramh* lantern. "After our dad died, Tess and I became a lot closer. I didn't really understand it at the time, but the opposite happened with our mom. She pulled away from us, so I've seen it go both ways."

Quinn nodded. "Remember when Starling was killed? His wife wanted nothing to do with us."

Liam sighed. "Man, that was a rough one. They'd only been married what, two years?"

"Something like that. First deployment and he catches a shot to the neck." He stared down at his blade, transported back to that dark night. "Remember how it always smelled over there?"

Liam provided a few choice words describing the odor of manure, livestock and unwashed bodies that had permeated most of their deployments.

"He wasn't even point, just got hit with a ricochet," Quinn said, throat tightening. Why had he brought this up again? He'd been six-man in that stack, he'd seen Starling go down and they'd finished the push into the room, clearing the building and establishing security. The kid had tried to do what he'd been trained, pressing the heel of his gloved hand to his neck to try to stop the flow of blood. He remembered Duke's low, encouraging voice as he worked over the kid.

"Sometimes I can't See everything," Liam replied, his voice tight with emotion.

"Wasn't implying that you should've Seen it," Quinn said. He felt tired, bone-weary from the weight of that memory. They'd made it onto the evacuation helicopter and Starling had still been alive, just barely, but they'd lost him as the bird sped through the dark skies toward base, the gunners at their open doors staring down into the hostile moonscape below. Duke hadn't given up on Starling, because that wasn't what they did. Once they got him off the chopper, the docs had needed Quinn's help to pull Duke away. The wiry medic hadn't talked to anyone for almost three days.

They sat in silence for a few moments. Liam finally spoke.

"Gray's death drew us closer," he said. "And gaining Calliea…she didn't replace Gray, because that's impossible to do. But she brought us closer, too."

"It's like magnets," Quinn said.

"Say again?" Liam replied, unconsciously reverting to their military-speak.

"Magnets," he repeated. "Except you don't know which side is which, which people and events are going to draw you together and which are going to force you apart."

"I guess it's something like that," Liam said thoughtfully.

"So why are you worried about Finn? Seems like he's better off without all those memories."

"If someone told you that they could take away all the painful memories you have, most of what causes you guilt and makes it hard to sleep at night, would you do it?"

After a moment of consideration, Quinn shook his head. "As much as it sucked to go through the experiences, they're a part of who I am. You can't just depend on the happy times. It's the bad ones that forge you into a stronger person."

"My point exactly," said Liam.

"So…" Quinn put all the pieces together. "You're worried that Finn's not the same person he was before his memories were taken."

"Do you think you'd be the same person if a huge chunk of your life were ripped out of your head?"

Quinn thought back to the few times he'd seen Finnead since the battle. "I mean, I don't know him as well as you do, but he seems…happier."

"He *is* happier, and I don't honestly know what to do with that."

"So, you'd rather he be the brooding, inscrutable tragic hero?" Quinn raised his eyebrows.

Liam scrubbed his face with one hand. "That's not what I'm saying."

"Sounds an awful lot like it is."

"It's not just that he's happier, Quinn. It's that his experiences shaped him. He gave up so much of what shaped him because it was the only way that he could help bring Andraste back."

"And he made that choice, didn't he? He knew what the consequences could be."

Liam snorted. "That's like saying you know what selection is going to be like before you experience it. It's one thing to talk about it. It's another thing to go through it."

"Fair," allowed Quinn, "but you still go into it knowing that it's going to be tough and it's going to challenge every part of what you think about yourself." He shook his head. "I think you're not giving Finn enough credit. He's centuries old. He's survived more than most of us can imagine."

"With this possibility that Rye may be alive...I just worry that it's going to go badly for him. And for Ramel," Liam added.

"I'm not a particular fan," Quinn said carefully. "All I know is he got blown up by Vivian and everyone worked to save him. I guess he's a decent guy because they were all pretty committed to making sure he survived."

"He was one of Tess's first friends in this world, and he taught her how to use a sword. Just for that alone, I at least owe him the benefit of doubt."

"You try to be all hard, but really you're a teddy bear," muttered Quinn.

"When it comes to people who help the ones I love, I take it seriously."

"Well, this has been a great kumbaya session," said Quinn, setting his last dagger down, "but what can you *do* about any of this?" He stretched his legs and imitated Liam's posture, leaning back on his elbows. "Finn's going on the expedition and Tess is staying here, so that nixes a lot of the conflict that could be there. Plus, Tess seems perfectly happy with Luca."

"First loves can have a lot of pull. And the *ulfdrengr* don't quite adhere to what you and I would think of as traditional relationships."

"Look, man, I'd hesitate to call it 'love' between Finn and Tess. It was a lot of longing and lustful thoughts, sure, but from what Tess told me, it was always just this push-pull of wanting and then being rejected. Finn was kind of a jerk to her."

"He had a lot of guilt, and she was really new to this world," said Liam.

"I don't know whose side you're on here."

"I don't understand why you think I have to pick a side," Liam replied.

Quinn hummed thoughtfully. "You're feeling caught between the two of them."

Liam shifted. "Maybe. But you're right, there's not going to be anything to be caught between soon, because Finn is leaving with the expedition and Tess is staying here."

"And I'm staying here. Don't forget about me," Quinn pointed out. He watched his old team leader's face, gratified when Liam smiled and it looked genuine…but when the amusement faded, his friend just looked tired.

"You're staying here to keep an eye on me," said Liam. "Don't think I don't know that."

Quinn shrugged. "So what if I am? There's going to be lots of other interesting things going on here too." He waggled his eyebrows. "I still think I can get that table in your room to give us donuts."

"Because you've been teaching the cooks how to make donuts and asking them to put them on the plate that transfers to my table," replied Liam.

"Still a victory." Quinn straightened and resettled, folding his legs into a sort of modified yoga pose that made Liam shake his head. "Don't be jealous. Strong and bendy, man, that's where it's at."

"Keep telling yourself that."

"So, are you going to sit at my table staring at the lamp all day or are you going to tell me what else is on your mind? Clearly we haven't covered everything."

"There's another expedition," Liam said slowly. "One that hasn't been discussed very openly yet."

"The wolves," Quinn said, remembering the conversation in Liam's quarters after the unsuccessful donut *haka* dance.

"Sometimes I forget that you're smarter than you look," Liam said drily.

Quinn grinned. "Hard to believe someone this pretty can keep up with a conversation, I know."

"They'll be heading into the wilds. Definitely Luca, Chael and Vell, and I think Tess will be headed that way as well." Liam paused. "Vell hasn't spoken to me about it yet, nothing beyond what she's already hinted at in conversations with everyone."

"Are you feeling like you're not as close as you were?" Quinn ventured.

"It's not really a matter of closeness. It's more that I think she sees what Arcana is doing to me, and she's…cautious."

"Cautious about what she tells you," he said.

"Yes."

"Because of the fact that Arcana is surfacing more often these days?"

"Surfacing more often and more…violently." Liam swallowed. "I'm losing control. I need to find a way to…take her out. Take *it* out."

"What'll happen when you do that, though?"

"I don't know."

"You could die," Quinn said. He forced himself not to wince as he said it. Today, apparently, was a day for remembering gory battlefield scenes involving his teammates, except the one at the forefront of his mind now had taken place in Malravenar's Dark Keep after they'd battled through hordes of his creatures and Tess had driven the Iron Sword through the Big Bad himself.

"I *did* die," Liam said, as though he was thinking the very same thing as Quinn.

Quinn looked at his friend solemnly. "It's really that bad?"

"It's really that bad," Liam affirmed seriously, his green eyes grave. He swallowed. "I'm starting to have nightmares about hurting people, and when I wake up I can't remember if it's real or not."

"Why would Arcana want to hurt people?"

"She was tortured by Malravenar," said Liam softly. "I think she was a little bit insane to start out with, and I only have a fragment of her in me. She was an immortal goddess, yes, but at least part of her chose to stay in a Sidhe body."

"Vell's sister," said Quinn, remembering the strange, puppet-like movement of the young girl who bore such striking resemblance to the High Queen.

"Yes. And Vell's sister endured…a lot. Too much. I wonder sometimes if Arcana had to take on any of her memories."

Quinn tilted his head as a thought occurred to him. "Is that because *you* inherited some of those memories?" The pieces started to fall into place. "You said that Vell's sister was forced to torture *ulfdrengr*. That she hurt people. Do you think your dreams are her memories?"

"I don't know," said Liam, "but I can tell you that they're pushing me toward the edge."

"Hey," Quinn said fiercely, standing and crossing the room with quick strides. He sank to his haunches by Liam's chair and gripped the other man's shoulder. "You listen to me. You're not gonna go over that edge, all right?"

The doubt in Liam's eyes scared him more than anything he'd seen since being pulled into this unpredictable world of darkness, beauty and magic. Even when he'd seen Niamh for the first time in the healing ward, he'd known that she'd fight to make it back to him. But to see the doubt in the eyes of a man he loved like a brother and had followed through hell and back…that sliced into him with a deep and searing alarm. He shook Liam's shoulder a little. "You're not going to because I'm not gonna let you. Got it?"

Liam drew in a shuddering breath. "Don't let me hurt anyone, all right?"

"You wouldn't hurt anyone who doesn't deserve it," Quinn said firmly.

"*Her* definition of who deserves it is much different than mine," Liam replied, his voice strained.

"Okay, well, we'll work through it." Quinn said the words with a confidence he didn't feel. How was he supposed to understand how to help Liam if he didn't understand what exactly was happening to him? "Have you talked to Vell about this?"

"I haven't told her everything. She can feel some of it."

"She doesn't know about the dreams," Quinn guessed.

"Not the dreams," agreed Liam. "I don't want to do that to her."

"She's strong."

"I know. It has nothing to do with her strength. It has everything to do with me loving her too damn much to hurt her with the knowledge of what her sister did."

"That bad?"

"That bad," Liam affirmed.

"Okay." Quinn took a deep breath. The dreams on top of Liam's Sight and his responsibilities as one of Vell's Three…it would be a lot for anyone to handle. "I'm here for you, okay? Don't you ever forget that. We've been through a lot together." They'd shared funerals and homecomings, the rush of battle and the agony of losing teammates, the thrill of a successful mission and the frustration when their strike missed the target. They'd watched each other's backs in every sense of the word for years now, and that wouldn't ever change, not even if they were in another world.

"You don't have to remind me," Liam said. "I know. That's why I'm here. I need you to…I don't know what it is I need you to do."

"You need me to be there for you, and that's what I'm going to do." Quinn nodded. He'd had versions of this conversation before with other friends, other teammates who couldn't shake the demons that had ridden them home from war. "We'll figure it out. We always do."

Liam nodded. Quinn reached his arm around the other man in a brotherly embrace. It was a sign of how much Liam needed it that he rested his forehead on Quinn's shoulder and gave a shuddering sigh. Quinn patted his back reassuringly. "We got this, man."

Liam drew back with a tired smile. "You can stop being so encouraging. I'm not going to go jump off a bridge or anything."

"No bridges around here, but that's a good thing," said Quinn.

Liam stiffened and grabbed the edge of the table, his knuckles whitening at the strength of his grip.

"Hey," Quinn said quickly, "what is it? Vision or crazy urges?"

"Vision," Liam gritted out before his eyes rolled back in his head.

Quinn swore as Liam collapsed, thankfully missing the table and landing on the rug. He didn't remember the Sight being this violent with Liam – now it looked more like a seizure rather than a temporary loss of balance or spell of dizziness. Liam's body went rigid and Quinn quickly shoved the table away from him so that if he started thrashing, he wouldn't hurt himself. He spared a quick glance away from Liam to rescue the *taebramh* lamp from crashing onto the floor. Even Thea's sturdy runes might not have survived, and he wanted to stay in the good graces of the smith.

The vision ended a moment later. Quinn knew it hadn't been long, but he still had to swallow down his concern, his heart beating as hard as if he'd just run sprints. He took a cushion and slid it under Liam's head, checking the other man's pulse – slow and steady as though nothing had just happened. Weird, but then again weirder things happened all the time here. He rifled through his things until he found his canteen, shaking it experimentally and nodding when he heard the water sloshing in it.

Liam grimaced and shifted, bringing one hand up to his face and shielding his eyes as he slid them open. He sat up stiffly, swallowing a groan.

"Want some water?" Quinn offered him the canteen.

Liam took it wordlessly. A swig of water seemed to help him shake the lingering torpor of the vision. "That sucked."

"Why are some like that and some not as bad?"

"I think it depends on how far away the subject of my Sight is," Liam said, his voice raspy. He raised the canteen to his lips again. "That one was pretty far away."

"How do you know? Is it like you're zooming over the landscape, like from a bird's eye view?"

Liam shook his head. "Most of the time I just have to puzzle it out based on the surroundings."

"So how do you know this one was far away?"

The other man finished off the water in the canteen and set the empty container on the table. "Well, for one thing, it was a ship."

"A ship like…a ship on an ocean?"

"That's usually how it works," Liam said drily. He shifted and winced as though the vision had left him with bruises. "The only ocean that I know of in Faeortalam is at the edge of the Seelie kingdom."

Quinn gave a low whistle. "Far seems like an understatement."

Liam gave a raw chuckle and ran a hand through his hair. "That's the first one I've had in a while where Arcana didn't hijack my Sight."

"That's a good thing, isn't it?"

He shrugged. "Neither here nor there." He swallowed and then levered himself to his feet using the table.

"Whoa there," said Quinn, reaching out to steady him. "What do you think you're doing?"

"I've got to go start figuring this one out," said Liam.

"Who do you need to talk to? I'll send a message, and you can rest for a bit. I'll get some food from the kitchens too," said Quinn, pushing down lightly on Liam's shoulder. His concern deepened when the other man let himself be guided back to a sitting position.

"I think perhaps Tyr," Liam said thoughtfully. "I haven't heard of anything involving a sea-going people from either of the Courts. Maybe it was something that was erased from their memories like the Exiles. That means Tyr would be the best bet."

"Send a message to the creepy white-haired guy, got it," said Quinn with a nod.

Liam chuckled. "That's unfair."

"Okay, creepy *silver*-haired guy," he amended. He pointed at Liam. "Stay."

"Only because you asked so nicely," Liam replied, making no move to stand again.

"Jess and I trained you well," said Quinn with a nod. "I'll go find one of the little guys, see if I can get a message to Tyr."

"You are so…" Liam trailed off, searching for the word.

"Perfectly impolite? Endearingly impudent? Adorably impertinent?" Quinn supplied.

Liam chuckled. "Sure. Let's go with that."

Quinn grinned back. He grabbed one of his daggers, slid it into the sheath at the top of his boot – always have a weapon, that was an indelible truth no matter what world you were in – and stepped through the curtain into the passageway. His grin faded, and he walked quickly toward the common room where the Glasidhe always had a messenger posted. Whatever Liam's Sight had given him, that puzzle paled in comparison to the question of how exactly he was going to help save his friend from the fragment of a deity that once saved his life but was now slowly poisoning him. He took a deep breath. Just another day in the land of magic and mayhem.

Chapter 18

"Four days," Vivian muttered to herself. She reached for another of the books stacked on the table by the armchair that had become one of her favorite places to read in the Tower. Flames danced in the nearby fireplace. Beside the fireplace on a lacquered black pedestal stood a silver arm that twitched to life every few hours, picking up a log and placing it into the flames, poking at the embers with its fingers and then returning to its pedestal. Vivian had spent the better part of an evening trying to decipher the runes that animated the silver arm, in an attempt to both overcome her own feeling of unease at its lifelike appearance and motion, and because she thought that it might be useful to know how to make such limbs for Sidhe who had lost theirs in battle. It was still beyond her level of rune knowledge, though, and she hadn't mustered the courage to ask Tyr or Niall to take a look at it.

She knew she didn't have enough time before the expedition left to decipher all the secrets of the massive library that spiraled up into the dimness overhead. She pushed the golden spectacles up higher on her nose with two fingers. It would take her years to even begin to scratch the surface of the knowledge that the trove of books and objects offered, but she felt like it was her duty to at least *try* to grasp as much as possible before the expedition departed. She'd still kept up her lessons with Thea, Sage and Moira, though she'd shortened her time in the healing ward and had spent most of her time at the forge helping decipher the white book with the diagrams of the scrying glass. That very morning, Thea had finally replaced the last tiny knob, and Merrick had inscribed the scrying runes with a tiny brush dipped in ink made in part from his own blood.

The look on Merrick's face when he turned the knobs of his scrying glass and the thick glass in the center turned opaque with the mists of his *taebramh* made all the hours of translating that arcane book worth it in Vivian's eyes. While they would have probably figured it out on their own eventually, even without the white book, the fact that she was able to help warmed her with satisfaction. Alfred had even had a glass of something like wine waiting for her by the armchair when she got to the library. That made her wonder how exactly the rune-animated servant had known about the success of the repair. She added it to the list of questions she wanted to ask Niall or Tyr.

A rapid little knock sounded at the door of the Tower. Vivian marked her page in her book with a strip of silk – the last Paladins had favored bookmarks as well, it seemed, because there were gorgeous little pieces of cloth stacked at the edge of nearly every table in the library, some embroidered and some plain. Vivian had even found a few under the cushion of the armchair. She still felt a little thrill when she touched them, thinking that the last Paladin and all the Paladins before them had touched the very same strips of cloth, just as they'd sat in the same chair as she and gazed into the same fireplace.

Alfred bowed and motioned to her, indicating that the guest who sought entrance to the Tower was diminutive in size. Vivian smiled. "It's a Glasidhe messenger? They're always welcome."

Alfred bowed again and zoomed off to open the door. On the first day, Vivian had tried to open the door with her *taebramh*, just as she did in her chambers, but Alfred had seemed genuinely affronted that she had attempted to bypass him and his butler-like tendencies. So, from then on she'd allowed Alfred to tell her in his sign language who the visitor was – for Tyr he swept a hand over the silver mist of his head to indicate silver hair, and for Niall he stood very straight like a soldier and mimicked Niall's courtly bow. She hadn't had any other visitors yet, but she thought that it would be interesting to see how Alfred interpreted other members of the Seelie, Unseelie and Vyldgard.

"Good evening," she heard a familiar Glasidhe voice say courteously to Alfred.

"Forin!" she exclaimed, setting her book on the table and standing as the Glasidhe zoomed into the room. "It's good to see you carrying messages again."

"Only doing my proper duty," said the Glasidhe who had been one of her first sword teachers. That had been after he'd nearly been killed by Corsica as she'd broken the rune trap that held the bone sorcerer. His unabashedly outspoken twin Farin remained one of Vivian's favorite Glasidhe, even though sometimes she felt guilty about having actual favorites.

"Welcome to the Paladin's Tower," said Vivian. She'd meant it to come out grandly, but instead she thought she sounded more like a college kid proudly showing off her first apartment, and it made her feel slightly ridiculous.

"It is a sight to see," said Forin with an air of politeness, turning in midair as he surveyed the shelves of books and magical objects.

"And this is Alfred." She gestured to the rune-animated robe with its cluster of silver mist at the collar and hems. Alfred swept an elaborate bow to the Glasidhe messenger.

"He is very courteous," Forin said, returning the bow gravely. "Now, if you please, Lady Paladin, I have a message."

"Of course." Vivian realized she was still wearing the golden spectacles, and she hastily slid them off. She'd already tangled them in her curls once by sliding them up onto her head like she'd done with sunglasses. Alfred had been forced to render assistance in extracting the delicate spectacles from her hair. Though she'd been impressed by the dexterity of his mist-hands, it was an experience she didn't want to repeat anytime soon.

"The mortal Quinn says that the Seer has had a vision, and they request your assistance in its interpretation," Forin relayed.

"They request *my* assistance?" Vivian repeated.

"Yes, Lady Paladin," replied the Glasidhe patiently. "And furthermore, they request that you send a reply. They will gladly meet you here or somewhere else, but Quinn thinks that perhaps here would be best as this is where your resources reside." Forin glanced up at the countless books lining the circular walls.

Vivian swallowed down the tremor of excitement that wriggled in her throat. This was the first time that someone had come to *her* asking for help. She took a deep breath and said with careful calm, "They are welcome to come here. I'm doing research for the expedition and I'll gladly try to help with whatever it is they need."

"I will take them the reply, my lady," said Forin with a bow. He zoomed toward the door. The sleeves of Alfred's robes flapped behind him as he rushed to keep up with the quick Glasidhe. Vivian stifled her chuckle; somehow, she didn't want Alfred to think that she didn't appreciate all that he did for her, and he might be hurt by her amusement. For a centuries-old enchantment, he could be very sensitive sometimes.

After Alfred shut the door behind Forin, she walked over to the long table where stacks of books awaited her. On a smaller table a few paces away, she'd carefully chosen a few books that she thought would be useful for the journey: a small rune-book so old that it took the spectacles laborious moments to translate each page; a primer of healing that had a helpful cross section on which herbs affected mortals and Sidhe differently, though she'd have to find a modern reference when she returned to Louisiana because she didn't recognize most of the names of the herbs from the mortal world, sketched in painstakingly minute detail; and a similar book that seemed to be a companion to the healing primer, this time on poisonous creatures both magical and mortal. That one gave her shivers when she read it, mostly because there were some seriously scary monsters that she couldn't have dreamed up despite her active imagination.

"Some of them no longer exist in this world or the mortal world," Tyr had said when she'd asked him about a few of the more terrifying creatures. "Some of them only exist when they are brought into being by a Dark power."

"So, they *could* exist," Vivian had clarified, staring at a page that depicted what looked like animated corpses in varying states of decay. There was even a raven with half its skull showing that the author had drawn in great detail.

"They could," said Tyr, "but as long as you are with me, you needn't fear them."

Vivian had bitten her tongue rather than let her sharp retort loose – something to the effect of asking Tyr why he hadn't slain the *garrelnost* single-handedly, if he was such a great warrior…which was patently ridiculous, because he'd been unconscious on the floor of her bedroom when they'd fought the *garrelnost* on that back road in Louisiana. But she still felt a little prickly every time he asserted, even obliquely, that she needed his protection.

Alfred sailed past her with a tray expertly balanced on his mist-hands. She watched as he fastidiously arranged the copper kettle and mismatched china tea service on one of the larger tables closer to the fire. He whirled away, disappearing around one of the freestanding bookcases that Vivian suspected concealed some sort of hidden door into his room of supplies, because he returned in short order with several plates of assorted biscuits and, to Vivian's surprise, a little tray of donuts. She opened her mouth to ask but then shut it again, having quickly learned to trust Alfred's judgment. After all, he had centuries of experience as a host. She'd watched Evie serve customers at Adele's with kind efficiency and observed Mike suavely handling the more difficult and fickle night crowd; she'd worked a few summers behind the counter, but she'd never been particularly good at sensing when a customer – a *guest*, as Evie called them, as though Adele's were actually a home – needed a bit of extra attention or help in choosing their order. Evie had mastered the upsell in her years in the business, but Vivian had always blushed when she'd tried to get people to spend more.

A worm of homesickness wriggled in her stomach at the thought of Evie and Mike. She sat down in one of the hard chairs at the big table with a sigh. She hoped that they didn't worry about her. She hoped that the emails she'd set up to send automatically at intervals convinced them enough. She'd even left a roster of generic voice recordings with Ross – things that she'd leave as voicemails if she were actually calling them from an epic around-the-world, go-find-yourself kind of adventure. Her roommate had dubiously agreed to leave the recordings as voicemails for Evie, who always let the shop phone ring through to the message if it was during business hours.

For a moment, she put her head in her hands. Sometimes it was easy to forget the world she'd left behind…*too* easy. But it would have been harder to deny the possibility of stepping into this adventure in Faeortalam. That was a truth she knew down to her bones, just like she knew she could never go back to pretending that she didn't know about the Exiled and *taebramh*, just as she could never forget the feeling of her first rune flaring to life, just as she could never deny the fascination she felt at every aspect of the Fae world and the excitement that coursed through her at the thought of delving into all the books left to her here in this magnificent library. She swallowed and pushed back sudden tears. It was silly to be homesick when this was so much more than she'd ever dreamed. Maybe she could ask Quinn how he handled it…or Liam, for that matter, even though she knew that he was something other than just mortal now. They'd both left the mortal world behind, and they were fine, weren't they?

As though in answer to her thoughts, a knock sounded on the door, this one crisp and businesslike. She hastily swiped the heel of her hand over her eyes as Alfred glided over. He motioned to his arms as though putting on sleeves – Quinn's tattoos, she understood; and then, after a pause, he brought one diaphanous hand to an approximation of where his eyes would be, if he had them, pantomiming looking into the distance – Liam's Sight. She smiled. "Quinn and Liam are both welcome."

Alfred bowed and then flew over to open the door. Belatedly, Vivian realized that Liam and Quinn had never encountered the enchanted servant. She hurriedly followed him, thinking of worst-case scenarios in which a startled Quinn stabbed a knife into Alfred or Liam reacted by using his *taebramh* against him. She knew that both of the men had steadier nerves than that, but that strange protectiveness surfaced again. Alfred belonged to the Tower, and the Tower belonged to her. He was her responsibility, just as protection of all the books and magnificent objects on the shelves were her responsibility as well.

Quinn raised an eyebrow at Alfred, watching him warily for a moment, and then he nodded. "Nice. Didn't know the place came with a butler."

"His name is Alfred," said Vivian as Quinn stepped into the Tower, followed closely by Liam. Alfred shut the door behind them.

"You're just about as much of a nerd as I am," said Quinn approvingly, his eyes sparkling green in the light.

"Yep, card-carrying nerd," she replied absently, watching Liam. "Are you okay?" she asked the Seer. She could see the similarity to Tess in the planes of his cheekbones and the green of his eyes, though his hair was a bit darker than the Bearer's.

"He had a rough vision about an hour ago," Quinn said.

Alfred motioned them toward the chairs he'd grouped comfortably around the table by the fire. Vivian didn't miss the way that Quinn glanced at Liam every few steps, as though he wanted to ensure that the other man didn't pass out.

"Should I send for Sage or someone else?" Vivian asked in concern.

Liam shook his head with a tight smile. "I'll be fine." Some of the tension left his face when he finally sat down in one of the armchairs.

"Donuts!" said Quinn with an unmistakable note of appreciation in his voice. He addressed Alfred. "You're definitely now my favorite non-living magical entity. I mean, I only know a few other ones, but still…major bonus points for the donuts."

Alfred tucked his hands into the sleeves of his robe, bowed and glided away with a very self-satisfied air. Quinn grabbed a plate, piled two donuts onto it, and took the middle armchair, leaving Vivian to settle into the last one.

"Would you like some…" Vivian sniffed the steam from the copper kettle. "Coffee?"

"Like…*real* coffee, not *khal*? Not that *khal* is bad, but…man, I'm gonna visit more often." Quinn nodded as he surveyed the massive library.

Vivian poured them all coffee, slightly surprised that Alfred didn't swoop down on her and insist on pouring it himself…but perhaps the rules required the servant not to intrude on conversations held between the Paladins and their guests. She tucked that thought away. Sometimes if she asked Alfred directly about the rules, he could answer her with a simple nod or shake of his head.

Liam's hand shook visibly as he raised his cup of coffee to his lips. Quinn caught her look of unease and pressed his lips together, warning her not to ask…or at least, she amended silently, not to ask *right now*. Another question to file away.

"So," she said, settling back into her armchair with her cup of coffee, "what can I do for you?"

"I had a vision," Liam said, staring into the fire.

"I gathered as much from your message," she replied. "I don't mean to be rude," she said quickly at his sharp glance, "I just need to…use time efficiently. There's a lot to do before the expedition departs."

"It'll feel like you're not ready, no matter what," said Quinn around a mouthful of donut. He swallowed and elaborated, "Always feels like that, no matter what flavor of mission. If you feel like you're completely ready, you're overconfident."

"I'll keep that in mind," Vivian said.

"I had a vision that was different from anything I've Seen before." Liam's voice sounded stronger after a few sips of coffee. Vivian made a mental note: Coffee was a good option after a vision or possibly other out-of-body mystical experience. She didn't know how Alfred had managed to obtain it, but she didn't really care. Liam turned his green eyes toward her. "Have you read anything yet about a people in Faeortalam who sail the seas on great ships?"

"No," said Vivian slowly, "but I've seen people who don't rightly belong to Seelie or Unseelie or *ulfdrengr*. They were something else entirely."

"You have the Sight?" Liam asked, a sharp edge to his voice.

"No." She shook her head. "I should have explained that better. My fault." Holding up the silver key on its leather cord around her neck, she continued, "When I first walked through the great doors of the cathedral, I felt compelled to touch them. The last Paladins before me had left a vision of sorts for me, contained within the doors and activated by my touch."

Quinn gave a low whistle. "That's new. There've been a lot of people moving in and out of those doors."

"I don't know how it all worked," she confessed, "but I saw *this –* "she waved a hand, encompassing the great tower and its countless treasures – "and I also saw a few other things. One of them was a sort of council. There were people sitting at that table that looked like they came from the ocean – they had glittering scales on some parts of their bodies, and their skin and hair were colors that I've never seen before in real life. Blue and green, mostly."

"Have you spoken to anyone else about this vision?" Liam asked, his focus intensifying.

"I…may have mentioned it to Tyr, but I didn't really know what it meant, so…no." Vivian felt color rising to her cheeks. It sounded silly now that she hadn't reached out to others to try to decipher the vision that the last Paladins had left her.

"My vision was of a ship with blue sails," Liam said. His brow wrinkled and his eyes went distant as he recalled the details. "I didn't get a very good look, my Sight was a bit blurred since it was so far away. I Saw the Captain of the ship. He looked Sidhe, though not like any Seelie or Unseelie that I've seen. Like a mix between the two, almost." He drew a breath, as though the next words pained him. "He was whipping a younger man tied to the mast."

Vivian winced. "Old-school sailors, then."

"Or pirates," contributed Quinn. He reached for another donut, offering one to Liam. "Sugar may do you some good."

To Vivian's slight surprise, Liam accepted the donut and devoured it in three bites. "How do you know that they're in Faeortalam?"

"Because my Sight doesn't go between worlds," said Liam, shaking his head. "I'm pretty sure about that. I didn't See things in Faeortalam when I was back in the mortal world, not even when Tess went missing and I was trying my best to direct my abilities to find her."

"Can you do that? Direct your abilities, I mean," Vivian asked curiously.

"I thought I was making headway, but then…" Liam grimaced and motioned to his side. He turned his head and stared into the fire. When it became apparent that he wasn't going to explain that enigmatic statement, Vivian shifted her attention to Quinn, raising an eyebrow in silent question.

"Andraste stabbed him during the battle of the Dark Keep," explained Quinn, "but she was really the Dark Archer, then, under Malravenar's control. And then Arcana, who was a living vessel for the Morrigan, the First Queen, offered to heal him, swap his death for hers. Oh, and she was inhabiting the body of Vell's younger sister, who had been taken from the North in the Reaping and made to torture other *ulfdrengr*." He elbowed Liam. "Did I get all that right?"

"The main points," said Liam.

"I...think I got that," Vivian said as she ran through it again in her mind. "What does that have to do with your Sight?"

Quinn looked at Liam. "Is it okay if I tell her?"

Liam shifted in his chair and then finally sighed. "As long as she understands that it's not common knowledge, and I'd prefer it stay that way."

"I'm sitting right here. I can hear you," Vivian pointed out.

They both looked at her, and then Liam went back to staring into the fire.

"Fair," said Quinn. "Well, there's a fragment of Arcana – the First Queen – still rattling around inside Liam. Supernatural shrapnel, if you will. And it's messing with his Sight."

"I see." A dozen other questions crowded Vivian's mind, but she pushed them all away. Now was not the time to indulge her fascination and curiosity with all new things that she encountered in Faeortalam. Now was the time to focus, and try her best to sort through anything that might be helpful. "So what do your visions usually mean?"

"I wasn't done," said Liam. "There was a kind of second part to the vision, which also makes it unusual. It was a long look at something. Usually I just get a flash of a scene or a premonition, but this time it was like I got two pieces of the puzzle."

"And what was the second part?" she prompted. That would've been good to know before they detoured into the history of why exactly Liam's Sight was out of whack.

"A smaller boat, with only one sail, putting ashore among ruins. I Saw a girl, maybe sixteen or seventeen if their ages work the same as ours. In places, her skin looked...terrible. Like boils and burns combined."

"Some sort of plague?" Vivian guessed.

"I don't know. There were two others with her."

"Any other details you can remember?" she pressed.

"The girl's hair was starting to turn white, and I think one of the others that was with her was the man who'd been whipped."

"Okay," Vivian said slowly. "Why exactly did you come to me with this?"

Liam shrugged. "It was a feeling. Sometimes the Sight nudges me toward someone. I wanted to talk to you."

"I'm just the faithful friend making sure he doesn't fall on his face looking for you," said Quinn, but the glint in his eyes reminded Vivian of Duke, who'd been anything but a bystander during their struggle against the bone sorcerer and Corsica.

"Somehow I doubt that you're *just* anything," she muttered. Quinn actually smiled at that. Vivian took a sip of her coffee and sat back in her chair. "Let me think for a minute."

Fortunately, the silver arm by the fireplace chose that moment to flex its fingers and reach for a log. Quinn instinctively reached for the hilt of a dagger at the top of his boot, while Liam merely watched the arm in interest as it selected a log and curled its silver digits around it, placing it directly into the flames.

As the two men watched the enchanted fire-tending tool, Vivian used the time to try to make sense of what Liam had told her and what she already knew. She hadn't read anything about a people that sailed the sea on great ships in the histories of Faeortalam, but those histories focused mostly on the Sidhe Courts. She'd been able to find a history of the Glasidhe and even a few scrolls that she surmised were from the *ulfdrengr*, or at least copied from original source material by some long-ago scholar, but she hadn't found anything about mariners. She thought about the vision that the last Paladins had given her, trying to remember the details of the beings with the blue-tinted skin and glittering scales on their brows. How did they relate to Liam's vision? He hadn't mentioned seeing anyone like them, only the man being whipped and the girl with the boils on her skin. But try as she might to put all the different pieces together, she couldn't understand how they connected.

Then she remembered one of the last Paladin's words, spoken in that whirl of blue and silver light.

"*And when you journey afar, look to the sea,*" she murmured. "*They will return.*"

Liam tore his gaze away from the silver arm, now poking about the embers of the fire with its forefinger. "What did you just say?"

"It was what one of the last Paladins told me," she said slowly, "in the message they left me." She drew in a breath, strange excitement washing over her. "'When you journey afar, look to the sea. They will return.' Those were his words."

"Curiouser and curiouser," quipped Quinn.

"That still doesn't answer the question of who *they* are," said Liam.

"But it's a start," said Vivian with a smile. She tilted her head to one side. "There's a port on the coast of the Seelie lands, isn't there?" She unfolded her legs and stood, setting her cup on the table. Alfred immediately whirled over to her. "Could you please fetch one of the older maps, Alfred? I'm thinking around the time of the last Bearer before Tess, when the Great Gate was closed."

"Queensport," said Liam, pushing himself up from his seat and following her as she walked toward a table that wasn't completely covered in books. "That's the name of it. But…the strange thing is, I've never heard of it being used as an *actual* port."

"Why would there be a port for no ships?" Quinn said, frowning.

"From what I read, it was used to transport people and goods up and down the Seelie coast, but they never ventured out of sight of land," explained Vivian, quickly stacking books and making a space for the map. Alfred helpfully held his side of it as she unrolled it. Quinn weighted down the corners with books. Vivian surveyed the map, centuries old but only slightly yellowed with age thanks to the preservation runes circling the edge of the parchment. "There." She put her finger on Queensport, well to the east and south. "That's weeks of journeying across land, if not more."

Quinn eyed the distance. "Half that time if it's Valkyrie making the trip."

"I think we need to take a moment to think about why my Sight and the last Paladins turned our attention toward these people, before we start thinking about *another* expedition," said Liam.

Vivian glanced at him, hearing the agitation in his voice. She noted that Quinn was watching Liam surreptitiously too, and she wondered just how much the shard of Arcana really influenced Liam. "I agree," she said. "What do you think?"

Liam stared down at the map and spread his hands on the table. Finally he said, "I think it's a warning."

The pendant at Vivian's throat heated sharply. She hissed and grabbed at the leather cord, pulling it away from her skin.

Liam stared at it. "That's Tess's pendant. She's worn that every single day I've seen her in this world."

"She gave it to me," said Vivian, hating the note of defensiveness in her voice. What, did he think that she was ballsy enough to *steal* something this personal from the Bearer of the Iron Sword? Just the idea seemed ridiculous. She supposed she could take it as a compliment, but her hackles rose all the same. "After the battle in the throne room…when we were watching the pyres burn."

Quinn nudged Liam. "Not up to you who Tess decides to divvy out her magic jewelry to."

Liam rolled his eyes at Quinn's sarcasm, but he relaxed. "What's it telling you?"

"It reacted when you said it was a warning," Vivian said, still holding the pendant away from her skin. She still felt its pulsing heat, hot enough to burn. "You'd think it would have some sort of safety switch," she muttered, mostly to herself.

"Reacted…in agreement?" Liam asked.

"I don't know, it just got really hot. You tell me whether that's agreement or not." Vivian looked down at the map. "Maybe we should ask someone who's been around the Seelie Court a lot longer than any of us about Queensport." She arched an eyebrow. "I'm assuming I'm allowed to take this and run with it?"

"Keep the circle close," said Liam, "but I'd like to find out what this means."

Vivian nodded. "I'll talk to Niall about it. I'll have to tell him that part of it is a vision from you, but that wouldn't be hard to figure out."

"Not many with the Sight around," agreed Liam, shrugging one shoulder. "Let me know if you find anything in these books."

"It's not going to be my focus," said Vivian. "I still have to be ready for the expedition."

"You're never gonna feel ready," repeated Quinn.

Vivian resisted the urge to cross her arms over her chest and glare at Quinn, because she knew that she'd come off like a petulant teenager, and she definitely didn't need that. She was already the youngest mortal here amidst the centuries-old Fae. She settled for raising an eyebrow. "Got it. Thanks for the advice." Then she nodded to Liam. "I'll let you know if I find anything. Are you…do you think you'll tell Vell? The High Queen, I mean."

"Yes." Liam nodded. "Perhaps she'll pay you a visit as well."

The thought of the fierce High Queen with her golden eyes and huge black wolf visiting *here* in the Paladin's Tower alternately made Vivian excited and sick with dread. "She's…welcome anytime."

"I'll pass that on." Liam smiled, looking very much like Tess. "Thank you for taking the time to listen. If I came across as…" He paused, searching for the right word.

"Rude? Gruff? Blunt?" supplied Quinn in rapid-fire succession.

The Bearer's brother sighed. "Pick your poison. If I came across as less than polite, I apologize. My Sight makes me…" He paused again.

"A pain in the butt," said Quinn firmly.

Vivian raised her eyebrows, waiting for Liam to erupt at the tattooed man. But instead, he just chuckled and shook his head. "Let's get out of her hair."

She turned and leaned against the table, watching the two men cross the tower.

"Wait, wait, I want another one," said Quinn, running over to the little table by the fireplace. Alfred got there first, snatching the tray of donuts away from Quinn's reaching hand…in order to put them into a neat little bag for him. The enchanted servant held out the bag of donuts to Quinn. "I think he likes me," said Quinn with a grin. Alfred pretended as though he hadn't heard the tattooed man, gliding over to open the door with stiff courtesy.

"See you later," called Vivian, her voice echoing through the Tower. Quinn waved over his shoulder as he exited.

She turned back to the map on the table, silence settling around her like a comforting blanket. Only the snap and crackle of the logs in the fireplace disturbed the quiet. After a moment, she moved the books at the corner of the map and rolled it neatly, thinking that she and Niall would have a lot to discuss at their next lesson.

Chapter 19

The whistle signaling land cut through Mal's sleep. She jerked awake, blinking, mind grasping at the pieces of her new reality and struggling to put them all together. The rough canvas of their makeshift tent came into focus above her, lit by the pale gray light of early dawn. Her body ached from sleeping on the hard planks of the deck rather than her hammock. She closed her eyes briefly as the last piece slid into place and it all came rushing back.

The *Dragonwing* had already been heading toward Haven before mast. Mal tried to tell herself that it was because they needed to resupply, but she couldn't shake the suspicion that the Captain had intended to put *someone* ashore, banished. Had he suspected that Hex would pound on his cabin door, making demands of the man who might as well be a god on this ship at sea?

Jem had tended Hex for nearly three days straight after he'd cut him loose from the mast. Hex had almost died several times. Mal pushed away those memories – even just the hint of them made her stomach curdle with a deep, sickening fear. Jem had somehow procured most of what he needed to save Hex's life, producing strange vials and packets of herbs from his satchel, slathering salves on Hex's back and binding ampoules of strong-smelling liquids against his forearm. Mal helped when she could, shivering and pushing away the memory of the cat o' nine tails biting into her skin. In a hasty moment spared from Hex, Jem checked her back and quickly applied a salve, saying that she might have scars but she was mostly healed.

Mal hated the spark of awe that flashed through Jem's eyes when he looked at her after examining her miraculously healed flesh, just as she hated that some of the thirds and even a few seconds pressed their fingers to the deck near them, where her dried blood still shimmered bronze despite efforts to scrub it away.

They were still fighting the fever that stubbornly held Hex in its grip, but he'd improved enough, if they could call it that, that Jem had finally caught a few hours of exhausted sleep, letting Mal watch over him. She'd sat close to Hex, closer than she'd dare if he were awake, feeling the fever burn off him and resting her hand on the deck near his mouth to keep track of his breathing. She worried about him, and when her mind had gnawed that thought down to the bone, she worried about Jem and their fates as banished Seafarers. No other ship would take them on. The Captain of the *Dragonwing* had as good as branded them on their foreheads.

After she'd thought about that for a few hours, she contemplated the mystery that she'd somehow become. She revisited Calinth and Serena. She picked at her bubbling patches of skin, searching for glittering scales beneath, only succeeding in making herself bleed and earning an irritated reprimand from Jem. She could tell he was stretched thin keeping Hex alive, and she felt guilty for causing any more trouble than she already had, so she kept her musings and questions to herself.

During the second night, she'd had enough of watching Hex shiver, and she snuck down into their berthing, hastily unstringing her hammock and Jem's, bundling them back up on deck and rigging their little tent with the canvas. She'd pricked herself a few times sewing it together with some coarse thread and a long needle.

"Never been as good as you with a needle," she'd said to Jem, sucking her thumb.

"Just as well it's me stitching him up and not you, then," he'd replied, looking up briefly from his examination of Hex's back.

In the end, she'd managed the tent. It was the least she could do, all things considered. It helped trap their warmth and keep the sun off during the day. On the fourth day after mast, it rained, and while a few drips made it through the canvas, they were much better off than being out in the open.

The other thirds brought them supplies, though not when any of the firsts were on deck, and most of the time at night. They'd leave food and other small things on the other side of the mast, and Mal would go gather up their offerings. Somehow she felt that they were doing it for Hex, not her, but she didn't voice those thoughts. She'd been proven wrong before her mast. There were those in the crew that cared about her...but would they still care about her now, after she'd been revealed to be some unknown creature, flesh healing as quickly as the Captain's lash flayed it? The sight of her dried blood gleaming on the deck made her feel almost as sick as the sight of Hex's raw, lacerated back.

"Stop thinking that you're a monster or whatever ridiculous thought you have in your head right now," Jem had told her in the red light of the last evening's sunset. He'd grabbed a few hours of sleep while Mal had sat close to Hex again, hand in front of his mouth to feel his breath.

"What?" she'd said, pretending to be surprised.

"You're a terrible liar and a worse actress, Mal," he'd told her tiredly. "I can see it. You're wondering *what* you are. It's written on your face every time you look at the deck."

"Wouldn't you wonder?" she'd muttered defensively.

"Of course," Jem said in his easy way, stretching. "But just so you know, I don't care *what* you are. You're Mal, and that's quite enough for me."

Now, staring up at the tent of their canvas, Mal wondered if it would really be enough. Sometimes she wished she had Jem's quiet confidence. He always knew what to do. She shifted and then pushed herself to her elbows, wincing as the movement awakened every ache in her sore body.

"Morning," said Jem from his post by Hex.

"Morning," she returned hoarsely, running one hand through her disheveled hair. She hadn't trimmed her hair as she usually did since the storm, and it was long enough now to tie back in a little tuft at the base of her neck. "How is he?" She yawned, her jaw cracking.

Jem didn't answer her and she sighed. He'd explained to her tersely that first night that Hex needed to make it through the first two days, and then after that he needed to wake up. The longer he lingered in that grayness between life and death, between returning to them and slipping away, the worse the odds that he would never open his eyes again.

"You've kept him alive, Jem," she said. "That's more than anyone except maybe Bonesaw could've done."

Jem didn't reply. Mal clenched her jaw, wishing there were something she could do to make him look less…defeated.

"We'll have to move him today or tomorrow," he said, his slim figure bowed with exhaustion. "That might kill him."

"It won't," Mal said fiercely, even as that insidious fear clutched at her guts.

Hex coughed. They both froze. He groaned, shut his teeth on the noise, and shifted. Jem quickly put restraining hands on him. Mal could only see one of his eyes, laid as he was on his stomach so Jem could tend to his back, but her heart leapt as she saw the gleam of his open eye within the pouch of bruised and swollen flesh, still discolored from the beating.

Hex blinked and swallowed painfully. His whisper was so quiet that she leaned closer to hear it. "At least Mal…is on my side."

Mal felt herself grinning like an idiot through the stupid tears that suddenly flooded her eyes. "Of course I'm on your side, you daft, cracked fool."

"Water," Jem said, nodding to the flask. They'd collected some rainwater, and the other thirds had managed to slip them at least two cups a day. Mal felt constantly thirsty, but they'd had water rations before and she'd gotten through that. Now she grabbed the flask and one of their cups, also liberated from the berthing when she retrieved their hammocks. She soaked a twisted bit of clean cloth in the water and slipped it into the corner of Hex's mouth.

The light of the new day washed the canvas over them in gold. Mal painstakingly soaked the cloth a dozen more times, and Jem nodded approvingly when she showed that Hex had managed to drink a quarter cup of water. It wasn't enough, they both knew that, but it was a start.

"If we move you to your side, it'll be easier to drink," said Jem, but the tightness in his voice let Mal know that he didn't look forward to shifting Hex. She tried to keep her face blank.

"Yes," whispered Hex.

Mal helped Jem roll Hex to his side – he was still larger than both of them put together, and *heavy*. She felt a brief flash of wonder that she'd managed to tow him to the surface of the ocean during the storm. Jem muttered curses as he tapped Hex's shoulder – one of the only parts of him within reach that wasn't bruised or broken – to try to keep him from passing out. Hex made a small sound of pain, and Mal felt like someone had punched her in the stomach.

"Your cursing has gotten more inventive," Mal said to Jem in an attempt to distract them all, and then her breath caught in her throat. Hex's face looked…terrible. Blood had pooled on the side he'd laid on, outlining his cheek and eye socket with frighteningly dark bruising. It was clear his nose had been broken – it looked a bit crooked, though Mal couldn't be sure – and both of his lips had been split.

He opened his eye again. The other was swollen shut. "That… bad?"

Mal swallowed. "You look like you got in a tavern brawl with half the crew of the *Dreadfire*," she said, naming one of their rival ships.

"Only…half?" Hex returned.

She grinned at his attempt at humor. Just seeing him awake made her feel strangely giddy. "What, does it feel like you took on the *whole* crew?"

Hex made a wheezing sound that she thought started as a chuckle and then trailed off into a painful gasp.

"Easy," said Jem, rummaging in his satchel. He handed Mal a paper packet. "Another quarter cup of water. Mix all of it in."

Mal obediently poured the requested amount of water from the flask and mixed the greenish powder into it. She sniffed it and grimaced.

"Well, now he's just going to *expect* it to taste foul," muttered Jem under his breath. He helped Hex raise his head slightly as Mal brought the cup to his lips. "Slowly," he said, a note of warning in his voice.

Hex took a sip of the concoction and grunted. "It *does*…taste foul."

"It'll help with the pain," said Jem, his voice gentler than Mal expected.

After Hex finished drinking the mixture in small swallows, he closed his eye for a few moments. Mal thought he'd slipped back into unconsciousness, or maybe just gone to sleep. Then he asked, "How long?"

She licked her lips. "This is the morning of the fourth day. The lookout just sighted Haven."

"Here, bend your leg like this," instructed Jem as he arranged Hex's body so he was more stable on his side. The ship swayed beneath them.

"We're going to be put ashore," she continued, some compulsion urging her to be honest with Hex. Hiding things from him wouldn't change anything. He'd find out soon enough.

"Banished." He winced as though just saying the word caused him pain.

"Banished," agreed Mal grimly. She leaned forward, looking intently at Hex's disfigured face. "But we'll be together, the three of us, and we'll figure it out."

"We always do," said Jem in a voice that brooked no argument.

Hex's swollen lips twitched as though he wanted to smile. "I know."

And with that, he slid into real sleep, breathing deeply. Jem busied himself checking his supplies – he'd left Hex's wounds bare save for a light dressing of linen soaked in an antiseptic, but Mal listened to him talking to himself about preparing Hex to go ashore. She leaned back against the mast and watched Hex sleeping, a strange fullness in her chest.

"Mal."

The authoritative voice lashed through the small confines of their tent. Mal recognized the voice and felt a barb of pain lodge somewhere near her heart as she realized that Kalinda had not addressed her as a third, because she was no longer a third. She was an outcast. Nonetheless, she glanced at Jem and then scrambled out from under the tent, blinking owlishly as her eyes adjusted to the bright light.

Kalinda's sharp gaze raked over her, and Mal suddenly felt very rumpled and dirty – which she was, after four days trying to keep Hex alive beneath their little rigged shelter on the deck of the ship. At least she'd changed out of her torn shirt, she thought.

"You and the other two will be put ashore in eight hours when we make port at Haven," said the wind-whistler. She held out a scrap of vellum, scraped so thin it was almost transparent after so many uses. It was folded over and sealed with the sigil of the Captain. Mal stared at it and fought the urge to knock it from Kalinda's hand as her hatred of the man who'd ruined their lives and nearly killed Hex rushed up, overwhelming her.

"Take it," ordered Kalinda sternly. "You will be afforded a month's rations and a few other supplies when you take this to Black's warehouse."

Mal took the little square, her skin crawling as she thought that the Captain must have touched the vellum when he'd sealed it…unless he had one of the firsts to do it for him. She settled on that idea. It made her feel less sick to her stomach.

Kalinda's eyes flicked over her shoulder to the little rigged tent, fastened to the rings that Mal and Hex had gripped during their mast and held down at the other end by an empty barrel that they'd managed to appropriate. "He is alive?" she asked, her lips barely moving.

"No thanks to any of you," Mal growled.

Kalinda didn't reply, but she gave an almost imperceptible nod and Mal though she saw the first *smiling* as she turned away. She crawled back into the tent, fuming. "We give our entire lives to the *Dragonwing* and we get a month's rations." She threw the sealed bit of vellum down on the deck. Jem promptly rescued it and stowed it safely away in his satchel.

"He could have keelhauled or hung us," he replied with a shrug.

"You and I both know that's not true."

"Isn't it?" Jem raised his eyebrows. "You broke the law of the kraken, and for all we know, Hex could have started a mutiny. At the very least, he challenged the Captain in a very public way."

"It wasn't out on deck," Mal countered.

"Yes it was," Jem replied mildly. "He shouted at him during mast, remember? And at least a few firsts probably saw him pounding on the Captain's stateroom door."

"At least a few firsts helped give him that beating," said Mal, a snarl still rippling in her voice.

"Also true," said Jem with his immutable, calm logic. "But we're not going to turn down a month of rations for each of us just on principal."

"I still want to rip it up," she muttered, throwing herself down onto the deck and crossing her arms over her chest. He gazed at her and she found her anger draining away. Jem was their anchor. He helped settle her fiery spirit in the moments when she needed to see the bigger picture. She sighed and leaned her head back against the mast. "What are we going to do?"

"Survive," Jem replied promptly.

"And how exactly do you propose we do that? We're Seafarers without a ship." A yawning hole opened in her chest as she said the words. She swallowed hard, pushing away the brief thought that it might have been better to die during mast or drown in the storm.

"Stop that." Jem's eyes flared with an anger she rarely saw from him, and she straightened, shifting.

"Stop…what?"

"Thinking that you'd be better off dead. Because if *you* think that, how do you think that's going to affect Hex?" he demanded in a low voice.

"He's not the only one who's being punished," she retorted, even though she knew she sounded like a fourth arguing with one of the older sailors.

"You're right. You were punished for breaking the law of the kraken and saving Hex's life. And I'm being punished for saving both of you." Jem stared at her until she looked away. "So let's not compare who deserves what. Let's think about taking it one day at a time."

She took a deep breath. Her ribs still felt bruised and her back was sore, but her lashes were nearly healed. Jem couldn't explain it. He didn't even think she'd have scars. The footsteps of the other thirds pattered around them. She knew without looking that they were leaping into the rigging, trimming the sails as they neared the channel into Haven's bluewater port. Her heart squeezed. She'd never fly up the rigging again, never watch the sea from a perch high up on the mainmast, the ship swaying beneath her. Then she swallowed and nodded. "You're right."

"Of course I am," Jem muttered as he set out rolls of bandages. "We'll let him sleep for a few hours, and I'll bandage him right as we're approaching the pier."

"There wasn't any raid," Mal said, mostly to herself. "No one's going to be much itching to get off the ship to spend any rings."

"The seconds always have rings," said Jem. "I've always thought it strange, though. The firsts seem to actually *like* staying on the ship, even when we're in port."

Mal managed half a smile. "If I didn't have anyone with a boot up my rear all the time, I might like staying on the ship too."

"Only boot up a first's rear is the Captain's," said Jem, raising his eyebrows.

Mal grimaced. "Let's not talk about him. I just calmed down."

"You're never calm."

She glared at him. " You're not helping."

"I always help."

"If you say so," she grumbled, settling herself into a more comfortable position against the mast.

"I do."

Mal watched Jem run through the supplies in his satchel as she thought about what she could do before they put into port. Even if the thirds and a few of the seconds might look the other way, she couldn't get to the spots that she'd hidden her rings. She scowled at her own lack of foresight – but then again, she hadn't thought that they'd be *banished*. Her worst-case scenario had been death. She'd worn the purse at her belt to mast, though it only contained a few copper rings and the silver that Telen had given her after saving his life, along with her length of spider-silk, a needle and thread, and a little carved comb. She felt a little better when she remembered she had the silver ring. That could buy them at least a fortnight in a small room at one of the taverns…if the Captain didn't put out a ban on doing business with them.

"Think he'll black-mark us?" she asked Jem quietly.

"He would've already, if he wanted to." Jem shrugged.

"That means, though, that when the Captain dies…we can be taken on as crew again."

"If anyone will take us. And you know that could be half a century from now or more."

She sighed. "I know. It feels like a little bit of hope, though."

"Then hold onto it, if you want. Just don't forget that we need to take it day by day. You can't be frozen in time until the Captain dies and we're free of his curse."

"It's not a *literal* curse," she pointed out.

"He'll put out a ban. But maybe he doesn't want to black-mark his own son."

"He didn't have any problem almost killing him." Mal let her hatred of the Captain roil up again, wallowing in it like a pig settling into a deep mud puddle.

"Almost." Jem's lips turned up in a small smile of satisfaction.

Mal glanced down at Hex's face, slack in sleep, still bruised and battered but looking more like himself than since before she'd dove off the platform after him in the storm. She imagined the black-mark branded on his forehead and winced. She'd never thought the black-mark barbaric before; she'd just accepted that and the other brutal punishments that existed in their world as a part of their way of life. The ocean was a vast, unforgiving mistress, the raids brutal and violent, the many dangers in the deep lurking beneath the hull of their ship, waiting to strike in a moment of opportunity; and thus their Captain had to be armed with the tools to discipline his crew, because they couldn't afford discord, not with everything else trying to kill them. Now the thought of keelhauling or witnessing another lashing with the cat o' nine tails made her stomach clench.

Perhaps she wasn't born to be a Seafarer after all. She held one hand up to a strip of light that filtered through the seam in their tent where she'd sewn the two hammocks together. Her skin looked worse than before, now turning strangely purple at the edges of the scaly patches. Jem had lanced some of the largest boils in a wholly unpleasant experience she had no desire to repeat, but she poked idly at one of the pustules anyway.

"If you keep picking at them, they'll scar," said Jem without looking up from his inventory.

"I'm not going to scar from the lash, so why would I scar form these?" she retorted. The bright pain of the boil popping gave her a strange satisfaction…until, as the boil wilted, the edge of something hard and glittering pushed through her skin. She clenched her teeth together and caught the splinter between thumb and forefinger, hissing as she pulled it from the inflamed skin.

Except it wasn't a splinter. It was a scale the color of a ruby, roughly the size of the nail on her smallest finger. She cleaned it on the edge of her shirt, glancing at Jem. He was still picking over his supplies. She cupped her hand and stared at the scale for a long moment, and then she quickly slid it into the pouch at her belt. Her hands shook slightly. She told herself that she didn't want to tell Jem because he had enough to worry about, what with them going ashore and Hex still in a bad way from the Captain's lash.

But her heart tripped as she tried to understand what the scale meant. Would she die on land if she didn't return to the sea? What kind of creature *was* she, really? Was she half-Seafarer, or wholly a monster? Did *anyone* actually know the truth about her, or had her story been lost in whatever events had swept her onto the *Dragonwing*, prompting Hex's mother to take her as her own?

She took a deep breath and then cleared her throat. "I should probably cover these." She motioned to the ugly patches of skin visible on her forearms. "Don't want anyone to think I'm carrying a plague."

Jem tossed her a roll of bandages. "We could probably get you some gloves."

"Don't want to waste rings," she muttered. She'd appropriated one of Hex's daggers, though it felt large and heavy in her hand, and she used it to cut a length of cloth. She wrapped both her forearms rather clumsily but at least it didn't look like she was carrying some foreign disease when she lobbed the remainder of the roll back to Jem.

The ship rolled beneath them and the wind shifted. The sounds of the crew manning their stations to bring the *Dragonwing* into port only underlined Mal's feeling of loneliness. She was a monster, and she was an outcast.

"Whatever you're thinking," said Jem, "just remember that you've got us. Me and Hex."

She almost asked him right then whether he'd still count her as a friend if he knew she wasn't Seafarer, if he knew she wasn't Sidhe or Nuremian, Seelie or Unseelie or any of the other long-ago ancestors of their kind. She brushed a thumb against her forearm where that scale had emerged from her skin, swallowed hard, and nodded. "I know. And you've got me."

Jem sat back on his heels. "These next days will be hard. But we'll figure it out."

She smiled, even though it felt like her face had gone numb. "We'll figure it out together."

"Together," Jem repeated in satisfaction.

The lookout high above them sounded the whistles signaling they were about to heave to, setting course for the channel into Haven. Mal slid Hex's dagger back into the top of her boot. She leaned back against the mast and closed her eyes, trying to imprint the feel of the ship moving beneath them through the waves into her memory, because once they were ashore on Haven, it was possible that she would never set foot on a ship again.

Chapter 20

"**I** offer myself as a sparring partner, if the Queen wishes," Ramel said conversationally, glancing at Guinna over the rim of his cup. "It looks as though her skills have greatly benefited from her tenure as the Dark Archer."

"Is that *vinaess*?" she asked, more sharply than she'd intended. She chose to ignore his improper remark about the Queen despite the spark of indignation it kindled. Despite his knightly comportment in the training yards, it seemed like Ramel still hungered for a fight whenever one could be had.

"Just water," he replied, holding it out for her inspection. Short of tasting it herself, she had no way of knowing if it was anything other than water – it certainly *looked* like water. The way Ramel swirled it in the cup, though, raised her suspicion. He took another sip. "I haven't been seized by my ear and lectured like that since I was a page. I thought it best to comply with your demands."

"Finnead did his share of lecturing when you were his squire, if I remember correctly," Guinna said. She glanced around Ramel's compartment. "And I didn't seize your ear or demand anything. I was only trying to remind you of your…responsibilities."

"Satisfied with the improvement in my housekeeping?" He

arched an eyebrow drolly and leaned back in his chair, crossing his legs at the ankles and looking every inch the insouciant, lovable rogue that she remembered. But there was still something she couldn't quite describe that set off warning bells in her head.

Guinna narrowed her eyes. "I don't *enjoy* being suspicious of you, Ramel. But I've seen firsthand how good you are at convincing yourself that everyone else needs saving except you."

"I don't need *saving*," he responded immediately, hazel eyes flashing.

"Because you were too busy drowning yourself in *vinaess* and distracting yourself with any Vyldgard woman who would have you?" Guinna retorted. She felt the conversation slipping out of her control.

"Don't speak about the Vyldgard women as though they're beneath you just because they know how to enjoy themselves," Ramel said, his voice hardening though he didn't move from his relaxed position. "We could die tomorrow, so what's the use in not living today?"

"If that were how everyone acted, there would be no thought to the future," she replied with measured calm. "But I didn't come here to argue with you about the morals of the Vyldgard women."

"No, it seems you came to lecture me again on my own," said Ramel.

"We're both making this difficult." Guinna fought the urge to sigh. Instead she raised her chin fractionally and caught his gaze. "Can we please start again? I really did come here to talk to you…to ask your advice, actually."

"And the expedition leaves in two days, so your time is running short." Ramel placed his cup on the table, crossing his arms over his chest.

Guinna glimpsed the dark red edge of a scar revealed by the unlaced collar of his shirt as he moved. She wondered if any of his old scars were still visible – the pale silver lines drawn across his chest by the claws of a *garrelnost* during those fateful days after the kidnapping of the Princess. Niall had spoken to her and Sayre about Ramel's injuries after they'd returned from the mortal world. Ramel was, after all, still a part of their Court, though his bond with the Unseelie Queen had been broken. "Do your injuries still pain you?"

Ramel pressed his mouth into a thin line. "That doesn't sound like asking for advice, Guinna."

This time she did let herself sigh. "All right then, since you're so determined to keep us speaking of business. Have you considered your position within the Court?"

"In what sense?"

Guinna looked pointedly at the other chair on the opposite site of the table.

"Oh, of course, sit." Ramel gestured, but he didn't stand as she walked over to take the seat. Guinna noted that fact. Even in his darkest days after the Princess's kidnapping and Finnead's capture, he'd still adhered to the courtesies expected between Knights and ladies. But then again, that was centuries ago. He'd been a new Knight just given his Sword by Queen Mab, and she hadn't been one of the Queen's Three. She settled into the chair, smoothing her skirts over her knees with the palms of her hands.

"In the sense that you were once one of Queen Mab's Three," said Guinna. "You are one of the Knights of greatest skill left within the Court. Many from our youth died in the war against Malravenar…"

"Or were killed by the Mad Queen," finished Ramel darkly. He looked into his cup and Guinna's suspicion intensified that it was something other than water, some clear liquor she'd never had herself. His deep, desperate swallow of the stuff only deepened her wariness. "You're here because Queen Andraste wishes to make an example of me."

Guinna straightened. "Pardon?" Even now, her well-bred manners, suitable for a companion to the young heir to the throne, shepherded her words down carefully manicured paths.

Ramel smiled mirthlessly. "I was one of the Mad Queen's Three, thus I must pay the price for allowing her rule."

Cold realization curled through Guinna. "Ramel, that is the *opposite* of why I came to you."

"Oh, the opposite? What would be the opposite of a traitor's death?" Ramel swirled the liquid in his cup, wearing a mocking expression of thoughtfulness. "A hero's celebration?"

"You are the one naming yourself traitor," Guinna said. "That word never passed my lips."

"Until just now," pointed out Ramel.

"You helped the Queen in the practice yards. I thought you were…improving," Guinna said. She swept her gaze over Ramel again. True, he had changed out of his rumpled, stained clothes into suitable garments, and his red-glinting hair was only its normal sort of unruly rather than the unkempt mess she'd seen when she'd given him his lecture. But the dark circles beneath his eyes remained, and there was something in his gaze that sent a chill down her spine.

Under her examination, Ramel gestured to himself with a flourish. "An improvement, is it not?"

"Yes," said Guinna slowly, "but…"

"But what? Do I still not meet your standards?" A hint of the same terrible anger she'd seen when Trillian had brought her to Ramel nearly a fortnight past surfaced in his voice.

Guinna tried to think of a way to keep him on an even keel. "Ramel, I didn't mean to imply that you needed to prove anything to me. I was concerned about you." She almost added *I still am*, but the words stuck in her throat.

"And thank you for that *concern*," he said with a sneer. It sounded unnatural.

"Has the Bearer been by to visit?" Guinna asked.

"I thought you were here to ask my advice, not conduct an interrogation."

"It's clear to me that you aren't in a mood to give advice."

"Well," he said, finishing the rest of the contents of his cup, "seeing as how you haven't asked anything other than these probing mother-hen questions, I don't see how you can make that determination."

"I was going to ask you whether you had any idea why Andraste has not chosen her third," Guinna said quietly.

Though he tried to look nonchalant, Ramel waited for her to continue.

"When she was crowned…when Mab was killed…why did she only choose two? And why was it Sayre and I?" Guinna shook her head. "I've been trying to understand. Sayre is a Guard and I'm not a Knight or a Guard. It doesn't make sense."

"Why not?" Ramel shrugged.

"Because Queen Titania's Three are renowned warriors, and Queen Vell's Three are fast becoming legends in their own right," explained Guinna. She spread her hands over the gray silk of her gown.

"The Queen chose you for a reason," Ramel said finally, his voice closer to her memory of him before the Mad Queen had so cruelly abused him. "And there must be a reason that she has not chosen her third."

"What do you think that reason is?"

Ramel sighed and ran a hand through his hair. "Damned if I know." He shrugged again. "Maybe because my sword was made into a Dark sword."

"Neither Sayre nor I have blood-blessed blades," Guinna pointed out.

"Have you destroyed it?" Ramel stood abruptly, pacing the length of his small compartment.

"The Dark sword? No. The Queen locked it away in a place with many wards on it."

"Don't think it escapes my attention that you didn't tell me where exactly she's hidden it," Ramel said, pointing a finger at her. His eyes flashed.

Guinna kept her face smooth of surprise at the sudden accusation. "She charged us with helping her protect it."

"*Protect* it, as though it is a precious thing," Ramel growled. He thumped a closed fist on his chest. "My life force was what created that blade."

"Then how are you alive?" Guinna asked carefully. Perhaps if she could make him see the fallacies in his own logic…

"I told you before," he said in agitation, "*she* killed me and then brought me back. Ask Farin. She saw it."

Guinna's eyes widened as Ramel so casually named a witness. Had it actually happened, then? "I will, if I have the occasion to speak with her."

"And as for why the Queen has not chosen a third…perhaps she is waiting for someone." Ramel stopped his pacing abruptly. "Perhaps she is waiting for…Rye." He spoke her name with a reverence that startled Guinna. One moment he was snarling with rage and the next he uttered the name of their long-lost companion with such tenderness.

"Rye would certainly provide the Queen with the skills with weapons that I lack," she said in cautious agreement. She decided not to voice what she'd discussed with Sayre: the possibility that Rye, if she was indeed alive, had been driven into madness as Andraste had been. The High Queen had destroyed the Lethe Stone, so there would be no help from that quarter.

"Or perhaps she is waiting for Finnead," Ramel mused.

"Finnead is one of the High Queen's Three," Guinna replied. The thought of Finnead returning to the Unseelie Court both jarred her and ignited a strange spark of longing within her chest. She wondered if that had slipped through her bond with Andraste, or she was simply wishing to return to the bright days of their youth, when Finnead had gone by just Finn, Ramel his squire, Rye teaching Guinna how to handle a blade, all unaware of the terrible tide of darkness and sorrow looming over them, ready to crash down and wrap them in its cold depths.

"He has changed Courts before," said Ramel.

"But that was during the Bearer's journey," Guinna pointed out. "He drowned and broke the bond."

"And the Vyldgard break the bonds of the Courts every time they baptize a new warrior. I don't see much difference." Ramel shrugged.

Guinna circled back to her original question. "Those are both good points, and I shall think on them. But that leaves me to ask again, what do *you* want, Ramel?"

She had come armed with the argument that he would be a respected advisor to the new Queen, who knew him from their youth and would value his experience. She had come ready to convince him to take his rightful place in their Court after he'd finished this expedition to lay Rye's memory to rest. But she couldn't bring herself to say the words, because though he'd put his chambers in order and dressed neatly, even coming to the practice yards and sparring, speaking courteously to the Queen, she still saw through it all. Her carefully planned conversation turned to dust as she realized that Ramel was putting on this show of changing his ways, climbing back out from the depths of his despair, in order to go on the expedition. That was all.

"I didn't get through to you after all, did I?" she murmured.

Ramel laughed. She recoiled at the sound, so different than his usual mirth. The depth of despair in his voice opened a pit in her stomach, prompting her to stand. He raked both hands through his hair as she approached with light steps.

"Ramel," she said.

He looked at her wild-eyed. Even all those years ago in the forest after they'd endured being hunted by *garrelnost* and he'd been wounded, she hadn't seen him look so lost. Perhaps it was because their youth shielded them from feeling too much. Perhaps it had been that they'd survived, and their hope had buoyed them. The consequences of that fateful night in the clearing when Andraste, Finnead and Rye were captured hadn't unfurled all at once; the effects had rippled through the Court, gaining strength as the years went on, warping the very foundation of their lives.

She moved to touch him, but he shied away. It nearly made her give her own mirthless laugh – the irony that he avoided her touch when he sought comfort from the beautiful women of the Vyldgard. But she let her hands fall to her sides and said instead, "Promise me that you won't get yourself killed."

He blinked and took a few breaths. An echo of his wry smile twisted his lips. "I won't, at least not until after we find Rye."

"If she's – if you *don't* find her, what will you do?" The question passed Guinna's lips even as she winced at its bluntness. But sometimes diplomacy didn't work. Sometimes asking directly was the only way to get a straight answer out of someone.

Ramel looked away. "If I answer that truthfully, you'll speak to Queen Andraste or the High Queen and try to bar me from the expedition."

Guinna opened her mouth and then closed it again. Finally she said, "I said it before and I'll say it again, Ramel. I care about you. You saved my life, all those years ago in the forest." She reached out and touched his sleeve. He went still, like a deer that scented a wolf. "Let me help you now."

She saw him swallow. A muscle worked in his jaw. Then he pulled away from her light touch and said, "I think you would've managed to kill that *garrelnost* yourself anyway, so don't give me too much credit."

"Finnead will be with you," she said.

"He'll be on the expedition," Ramel replied tightly, his eyes darkening at his former Knight-master's name. "That doesn't mean he's going to be *with* me."

So Ramel's anger extended to Finnead, who'd reported Rye dead just as he'd told the Queen that Andraste had been dead…which, she supposed, had technically been true. They hadn't exactly counted on the bone sorcerer's resurrection skills. There had been so much that they hadn't understood about the darkness, despite their beautiful Queen's power and the radiance of their Court in its Golden Age. There had been so much taken from them because of that youthful yet willing ignorance. "Do you ever think it's sad," she said slowly, "that we don't realize the best parts of our lives are the best until they're over?"

Ramel turned and met her gaze. He sighed. "All the time."

And then he brushed past her to pour himself more of whatever liquor was in the pitcher on his table. Guinna fought the urge to seize the pitcher and smash it on the floor. Instead, she said, "I hope you find her, Ramel."

He didn't answer her, already drinking deeply from his cup.

She quietly walked toward the red curtain that marked the door to the passageway, his silence louder than any words he could have said as she left. The golden sunlight of the afternoon did nothing to lift her mood as she walked quickly down the paths of the White City toward the Unseelie stronghold.

That, at least, had improved somewhat in the past few days. Galvanized by her time in the practice yards and her newly liberated sense of self, Queen Andraste had conjured significant improvements to their living quarters. Her power chased away the drafts and the damp, and it was even beginning to remind Guinna of Darkhill, though no threads of *taebramh* ran through these walls. The hidden presence that Guinna had sometimes felt at Darkhill – less so in recent years, but that she remembered from her younger days and again when Tess had first come to the Unseelie Court – seemed to slumber here, hidden deep beneath the surface, driven into hiding by the breaking of the Great Gate and the occupation of Malravenar's creatures. Guinna wondered if the presence of the High Queen would awaken the White City again as she walked through the passageways, the *taebramh* torches flickering into life just ahead of her.

She found Sayre in his chambers. Though she could have reached out and determined his location through their bond, she decided that she wanted to speak to him first. The Queen had probably felt some of her disappointment in Ramel, but she wouldn't know specifics unless one of them reached out. Guinna carefully kept her awareness focused on the passageway around her as she knocked at Sayre's door. Sayre opened it himself, dressed in a plain white shirt and trousers, barefoot.

"You know you can do that with *taebramh*," she said conversationally as she stepped into his rooms. He favored darker colors, but the chamber still felt warmer than most at Darkhill, infused with a certain relaxed comfort that Guinna recognized as one of Sayre's inherent qualities. She felt some of her tension drain away as he gladly ushered her into the room, shutting the door behind her.

"I'm a Guard," Sayre replied with an easy grin. "We don't much hold to using *taebramh* for frivolous things like opening doors."

Guinna smiled. It was hard to remain in a bad mood around the younger man. "I suppose I'm very frivolous, then."

"All in the eye of the beholder," Sayre replied. He motioned her toward his table, set in a corner beneath an old-fashioned *taebramh* lamp that hung suspended from the ceiling.

"This is new," Guinna said, examining the lamp in fascination.

"We found a storeroom that hadn't been ransacked during the Dark time," Sayre replied. "Apparently these lamps are modeled after something in Doendhtalam – the Paladin called them *oil* lamps. In any case, she's getting to be quite good at fixing little things like this, figuring out how they work and setting them to rights."

Guinna nodded. "She's curious. That's a good thing, I think. I don't remember any of the Paladins – I think I was too young, and I certainly never talked to them myself."

"I wasn't even born," Sayre said cheerfully.

Fixing him with a look of mockingly severe disapproval, Guinna said, "I doubt it was necessary to remind me of that."

"It was completely necessary," countered Sayre as he took the seat across from her. "Have you been to the Paladin's Tower, by the way? I think you would like it."

"You know I haven't," she replied.

"We would have nothing to talk about if I just kept track of everything you did through our bond," Sayre pointed out. "Which, by the way, went completely silent when you went to speak with Ramel."

"And that's why I'm here to talk to you about it."

"Then it didn't go well," Sayre said. He picked up one of the dozen or so books stacked haphazardly on his table.

"That would be accurate," sighed Guinna.

"I thought it was a long shot, but I don't know him like you do," said Sayre. "Do you think he's going to cause trouble on the expedition?"

Guinna remained silent for a moment, smoothing her skirts and gathering her thoughts. "That's not for me to say. I know he wants to find Rye. That might be the only thing keeping him from completely breaking."

"So nearly killing himself with *vinaess* and white shroud isn't *completely* breaking?" Sayre said skeptically.

"No," she replied. "I think that if the expedition isn't successful, he might take his own life."

"We should tell Knight Finnead," Sayre said immediately, all impishness gone from his face.

"Ramel isn't exactly on speaking terms with Knight Finnead."

"Does that matter? Should we speak to the Queen about it – should he even be going on the expedition?"

"As I said, I think the possibility that Rye may be…found…is his only focus," Guinna replied. "There's no good answer here."

"No, there *is* a good answer here – intervening! We can't just let a Knight of the Unseelie Court take his own life."

"I never said we would *let* him," she said, heat surfacing in her voice. "He didn't actually *say* that, but that is what I fear."

"Even if Ramel isn't on speaking terms with Finnead, Knight Finnead wouldn't want to see harm come to him." Sayre stood, decided against pacing and instead restlessly stacked the books on his table into neat piles by size and color. "We can't just do nothing."

"But if we do something," Guinna said, "we could be wrong. We could push him farther down this path."

"If we intervene and we are wrong, Ramel is still alive. If we *don't* intervene and we are wrong, Ramel will be dead, just like so many others – but it will be by his own hand." Sayre flattened his hands on the table and looked gravely at Guinna. "I cannot speak for you, but I would be hard-pressed to forgive myself if that happened."

"How do you think *I* would feel?" Guinna said thickly. She swallowed. "You're right. I had not thought of it that way." She nodded. "We should speak to Finnead, and then perhaps the Paladin too."

"The Paladin is young," said Sayre.

"You're young, too, and I don't question your ability to make a difference," replied Guinna, arching an eyebrow. "If the Bearer were going on the expedition, I would ask her. But she's not, and the Paladin knows Ramel from their time together in Doendhtalam."

"True," murmured Sayre thoughtfully, barely seeming to have heard her half-serious jab at his age. He settled into his chair again, but this time with an attentive posture. "We shall have to speak to Andraste if we are speaking to Knight Finnead and the Paladin."

"Naturally," agreed Guinna.

"I haven't heard any mention of another council before the expedition departs."

"I don't think the Queens deem it necessary," she said. "It isn't an expedition of huge implications, if you know what I mean."

"Pretend I don't," Sayre said, leaning forward in interest.

"Well," Guinna explained, "it's not as though this is the Bearer's journey across Faeortalam to free Queen Titania at Brightvale, or the journey of the Courts across the Deadlands to face Malravenar in the Dark Keep."

"I don't think that makes it any less important to those going," Sayre said. He looked at her silently for a moment, seeming to gather himself. "I'm surprised, actually, that you're not going."

Guinna took a deep breath. "I'm surprised it took you this long to say that."

"It isn't meant as a criticism," Sayre said quickly. "I just – from what I understand, you were with Andraste and Finnead and Rye when..."

"When they were attacked and taken prisoner," Guinna finished for him. She nodded. "I was. My sister Rose was also taken, though I thought she was killed in the clearing. Finnead told me later that she died at the hands of the Dark sorcerer who abducted them."

"Does he still have those memories?"

"I do not know," Guinna answered truthfully. "You and I can both guess at what the Lethe Stone took from Finnead's head to restore the Princess."

"I am sorry for the loss of your sister," Sayre said in a quiet voice, his brows drawing together in empathy.

"It was a long time ago," Guinna replied almost gently. Odd, she thought, that she was comforting Sayre over her own loss, but she only felt a fond remembrance and affection for Rose now, as though her sister had embarked upon a journey and never returned from distant lands. The pain still existed – it would always exist – but she had learned long ago to wrestle the fathomless agony of grief into its defined space. She imagined that space as a small, lacquered black box, gleaming softly in her mind's eye. The box was beautiful in its own way, and it helped to imagine it wrapped in silver chains to contain the raging emotions within it.

Guinna straightened as a thought occurred to her.

"We can speak of something else," Sayre said, thinking that her sudden motion had been due to the pain of her memories.

"No," she said, shaking her head. "It isn't that. I just – I was not fair to Ramel, just now. I did not truly think about what I would feel if someone told me that my sister was possibly alive."

"That is not...a possibility?" Sayre ventured. "Since Knight Finnead was the one to pronounce both Queen Andraste and Lady Rye as dead, there has been some speculation..."

"No," Guinna said firmly, shaking her head again. "I will not entertain it. Queen Andraste is alive because of the bone sorcerer's Dark necromancy. Rye may be alive because Finn escaped as she sacrificed herself. He did not see her dead with his own eyes, but he assumed it."

"Oh." Sayre worked out the implications with his agile mind and said nothing more.

Then they both felt the call of the Queen, almost courteous in their heads but insistent nonetheless.

"She'll probably want to spar," said Sayre, standing from the table and collecting his sword-belt from its hook on the wall by his wardrobe.

Guinna sighed but didn't allow herself to groan. She didn't possess the endurance of the Guard or the passion of the Queen when it came to blade work, but she couldn't deny that she found certain satisfaction in sending arrows unerringly into the archery targets at the training yards.

"That'll include you today too," Sayre said conversationally.

At that, Guinna *did* groan as she remembered Andraste's remark at the end of their practice session yesterday. The Queen had said that Guinna ought to be comfortable enough to spar with her on the morrow, and the Queen's suggestion was more of a command, even to one of her Three.

"I'll have to go change," she said, glancing down at her skirts.

"Perhaps you should just wear breeches under your skirts from now on, and then you could just strip down at the practice yards," Sayre said brightly.

"Oh, that's a brilliant idea," said Guinna with a chuckle, her tone making it clear that she thought exactly the opposite.

"Or Thea would probably let you slip into the back room at the forge," Sayre continued as though she'd enthusiastically agreed.

"I'm going to go change in my chambers," she said firmly. "It'll be just a moment, so if you could please tell the Queen, I'd be much obliged."

Sayre grinned as she slipped back into her habitual courteous speech. "Of course."

"Let me know where the Queen wishes us to meet," she said, already heading for the door. For whatever reason, she and Sayre communicated easily, almost with words though not quite, more with images through their bond.

"Aye," said Sayre, finishing arranging his sword at his hip. "I wouldn't keep the Queen waiting long. It feels as though she's truly looking forward to this training session."

"Better than refusing to come out of her chambers and worrying herself sick," replied Guinna, even as she became acutely aware that they were discussing their Queen as though she were younger than them both and temperamental – which, in a certain way, was true.

"Very good point," Sayre said as he pulled on his boots.

Guinna reached the door and slipped out of his chambers, stretching her legs into a long, quick stride and hiking her skirts up from about her ankles. She would not run in a dress – she was not *that* uncivilized – but it also wouldn't do to keep the Queen waiting. She resolved to bring up Ramel at the conclusion of their sparring session, when Andraste would be basking in the afterglow of working with weapons as she hadn't been able in her younger years. Hopefully the Queen would agree with their course of action – Guinna didn't want to consider the alternative. She reached the door of her chambers, opened it with a flick of her wrist and a flash of *taebramh*, and turned her thoughts to what clothes she would wear for the afternoon's activities.

Chapter 21

"The wolves are going to leave," said Liam as they traversed the passages of the cathedral, headed toward the healing ward and then to the practice yard.

Quinn felt like their days had settled into a rhythm: They met outside at first light for a run through the city and then a few rounds of calisthenics – pushups, squats, lunges – on the wide plaza in front of the great staircase. Then they ate breakfast, usually in Liam's chambers, and parted for a few hours to their own activities before their afternoon practice session at the training yards. Quinn had decided to pick up his volunteering at the healing ward again. Niamh, after all, was no longer bedridden, and her mother Maeve seemed to bear him no ill will. The older Sidhe woman had seemed to look upon Niamh and Quinn's relationship with certain forbearance, as though she merely had to wait for her daughter's infatuation with the mortal to pass. In a way, she'd been right, Quinn thought with only a hint of bitterness, but they never discussed it openly. Even the Vyldgard had too much courtesy for that.

"If the wolves leave," he said, picking up the conversation, "does that mean the *ulfdrengr* will go too?"

"I think so." Liam nodded.

"Your Sight hasn't told you how many pups Rialla is going to have?" Quinn asked with a grin. It had become a common pastime among the Vyldgard, especially the women, to bring little offerings of choice meat to the silver-and-black wolf where she'd made a den out of a little-used room in what Quinn thought had once been a temple on the outskirts of the City. He'd overheard silver-haired Chael remark dryly that Rialla would have to be careful or she would be too fat to head North into the forest when the time came, but no one could mistake the affection in Chael's voice.

"You're not the first to ask me that," said Liam in an aggrieved tone. "Certain people seem to think that my Sight spits out answers on command."

"If that were true, you would've won the Powerball ten times and bet on who won the World Series every year," replied Quinn.

"Instead I just get these fantastic headaches and crazy dreams," said Liam darkly.

"First of all, I think the headaches are from Arcana. Ditto with the dreams." Quinn couldn't keep the note of concern out of his voice. His work in the healing ward had also allowed him to unobtrusively observe the combinations of herbs that the healers used to induce dreamless sleep. White shroud was dangerous for prolonged periods of time, so he hadn't tried that yet, but he'd convinced Liam to let him try a few other remedies with limited success.

"Well, whatever they are, they suck," Liam muttered.

"Yeah, well, we'll figure it out," Quinn replied, trying his best to sound certain. "Just have to find the right combo of meds, right?"

"Don't make that one from last night again," his friend continued. "It tasted like Duke's dirty socks smelled."

"I can't apologize for something I can't control," Quinn said, though he made a mental note to ask Maeve or Sage or one of the other healers if adding ingredients to mask the taste of a remedy rendered it ineffective. He thought it would probably depend on the ingredients. "Are Vell, Luca and Chael going with the wolves when they leave?"

"I think so, though Vell won't give me a straight answer." Liam glanced around them as they emerged into the common area at the front of the cathedral, the great doors open before them. Golden light streamed across the white stone floor. A few places still showed cracks from the harsh use by Malravenar's creatures or perhaps the shocks of Mab's airborne weapons, but Quinn found that he hoped the cracked stones weren't repaired. Sometimes it was good to keep small reminders of difficult battles. He steered them toward the healing ward.

Sage sat at the front desk. Maeve had been sufficiently impressed with his skill to allow him to take shifts with her now that the flow of charges into their care had slackened with no war to feed it. There were a dozen Unseelie still in their care, even now, and it seemed that many of them might never open their eyes again, their spirits broken after the torture that Mab inflicted upon them. The Seelie healer glanced up, carefully marked his place in the book open before him, and stood with a smile.

"Good afternoon, gentlemen," he said with typical Seelie courtesy.

"How's Tristan?" Quinn asked without preamble. After the explosion in the training yard, he'd visited Tristan often, sometimes seeing Ariel by his bedside as well, along with Robin and some of the other younger Vyldgard and Seelie.

"He may awaken soon," Sage said, nodding. He moved from behind the desk into the healing ward, walking over to the long table against the wall that held the ready supplies of their healing implements and herbs. Quinn followed a step behind him, glancing down the rows of beds and the healers on duty moving among them.

"That's good news," he said, watching Sage tuck packets marked with different colors into a satchel. He noticed belatedly that Liam hadn't followed them and took a step back toward the front of the ward and the desk...but then he reminded himself that Liam was a grown man, one who'd fought in wars in both the mortal and Fae worlds, and if he didn't want to walk into a healing ward, well, that was his deal.

"Yes," replied Sage. He finished packing the satchel and marked down the supplies on the ledger at the table before handing it to Quinn. "Have you decided whether you want to apprentice?"

Quinn cleared his throat. Maeve had offered him an apprentice-ship with the healers, a no-joke position that would be difficult to back out of once he started. "I'm still thinking about it, honestly." He shrugged. "I like working here and I know the basics. I don't know if that's my path in this world."

"There's no offense taken if you turn it down, you know," Sage said, raising a pale eyebrow.

Quinn looped the strap of the satchel over his head. "Thanks for saying that out loud."

Sage chuckled as they walked unhurriedly back toward the en-trance of the ward. "Did you think we would shun you if you chose not to apprentice?"

"I didn't know whether anyone would take it personally," Quinn replied honestly. He'd been thinking about it and meaning to ask Liam, but trying to figure out the headaches and help where he could there had taken up most of their time outside the practice yard. He'd even gone back to the Paladin's Tower to talk to Vivian, even though he felt vaguely disloyal, like he was betraying Liam's secrets…but was it really a secret anymore?

"It would be different if you offered us true insult," said Sage, bringing Quinn's attention back to the current conversation. "But simply deciding that, as you say, apprenticing with us isn't your path – that certainly isn't the threshold for any ill will."

"I'll still be able to come and learn, won't I?" Quinn said, stuffing down the sudden sense of alarm. He hadn't realized how much he'd come to enjoy his work in the healing ward. At first he'd forced himself to do it to rid himself of the memories of Niamh that still paralyzed him, but now he truly valued the opportunity to do something worthwhile – though he reminded himself that sparring with Liam was certainly worthwhile. Even though they didn't have an enemy to fight at the moment, they needed to stay ready.

Sage nodded as they passed the threshold. "The more who know the rudimentary skills of our craft, the more who can help us in truly dire situations. The Bearer helped us after the dragon hunt and on the battlefield, and I am glad there are those following her example."

"Tess sets a good one," Quinn said in agreement as they approached Liam. The other man looked up at his sister's name. "Sage was just saying that Tess was a big help in the healing wards during the war, and they aren't going to shun me if I choose not to apprentice."

Liam smiled, though it was a bit strained. "Tess has always had a habit of doing all she can for others."

Quinn punched him lightly in the arm. "Wonder where she gets it from."

"Not me, lately," Liam muttered in an undertone.

Raising a hand in farewell to Sage, who took his place behind the desk and went back to his book, Quinn said, "Stop feeling sorry for yourself. You know it doesn't do anyone any good." He surreptitiously glanced at Liam as they passed through the great doors and down the front steps of the cathedral. "You sleep well last night?"

"I don't ever sleep well anymore," Liam said.

"You're gonna think I'm prying, and I am a little, but I just need to understand the whole picture. Doesn't Vell notice that you're not sleeping?"

"She's been spending a lot of time on the outskirts of the City with the wolves," Liam replied evasively.

"That didn't answer my question." Quinn didn't even need to think about their route at this point; his feet knew their own way to the practice yards. It left him free to focus on the conversation.

"We're still…together," said Liam finally, "but I try not to sleep when I'm near her."

"Why?"

"Why do you think?" the other man said, his voice sharpening with frustration.

Quinn let the dust settle as he thought, and then he said, "You don't want to say anything during those nightmares. You don't want to hurt her by bringing up her sister again."

Liam's silence was confirmation enough. They were saved from further exploration of the uncomfortable topic by two Glasidhe who zipped overhead, came to a halt in midair and then backtracked, zooming directly for their heads. Quinn tried not to flinch and mostly succeeded. One of the Glasidhe whirred past his ear and alighted on his shoulder, one small hand grabbing his ear for balance.

"Mortal Quinn!" piped Farin. "It is good to see you, and I hope you do not mind our intrusion into your conversation."

"We don't mind at all," Liam said before Quinn could reply. Farin's twin Forin stood sedately on his shoulder, while Farin fluttered her wings and patted Quinn's ear every so often to emphasize her words.

"I hear you have been to the Paladin's Tower! Forin thinks it is very interesting, all those books, though I like weapons better," chattered the diminutive yet fierce warrior.

"It's possible there is an armory attached to the Tower," contributed Forin. "Perhaps the young Paladin has not found it just yet."

"We taught her how to handle a blade, you know," Farin reminded them.

"I do remember," Quinn said with a nod.

"We are going on the expedition, and so we will have the opportunity to teach her more, if she wishes," said Farin, her excitement irrepressible.

"I'm sure she could not wish for better instructors," said Liam.

"You flatter us," said Forin with a graceful bow. "We have had the honor of instructing your sister as well, Seer."

"And I believe she's still more skilled with me than a blade," replied Liam with a smile, though Quinn noticed the humor didn't reach his tired eyes.

Farin hummed in consideration. She gripped Quinn's ear with both hands and leaned forward on his shoulder so that she could address Liam directly. "If you used your Sight, you would be equal to Tess, I think, though the Caedbranr might have an answer."

"I have no wish to use my Sight in the sparring ring," Liam said, keeping his tone light. "In a real fight, I'll take whatever advantage I can get, but I feel like it's cheating during training."

"Tess does not use the Caedbranr in the training yard," Forin said in grave agreement.

"Only when the wall collapsed from the Mad Queen's bombs!" contributed Farin.

Quinn brushed his chest where the still-red scar traveled from his shoulder to his solar plexus. He remembered the chaos and confusion after the explosion. He'd been one of the first to recover, and he thought that was probably because he'd encountered sudden detonations during his combat tours in the desert. It still sucked, no doubt, but once you'd been through it once, you could at least recognize the reaction and fight through it. It was easier to get to your feet, but the memories still haunted just the same as the first time.

"Sage said that Tristan might awaken soon," he said.

"The others that the Lady Bearer rescued all who survived," said Forin. "According to our cousin Wisp, it is because they were touched by her power."

"Wisp very much likes to embroider tales," retorted Farin with a snort.

"Are you saying you do not think the Bearer could have done so?"

Quinn raised his eyebrows. He hadn't heard the twins disagree in a while. Apparently the shock of Forin's near-death experience and their capture by the bone sorcerer had worn off, thrusting them back into their complementary roles.

"No," rejoined Farin, her wings quivering and tickling Quinn's neck. "After all, she healed Calliea!"

"That she did," agreed Quinn. The headlong rush back to the pavilion after their failed raid made his stomach tighten again. He'd thought that Calliea was going to bleed out, despite their best efforts at doctoring her terrible wound. Today was apparently a great day to dredge up recollections of all the near-misses he'd encountered in the not-so-distant past.

"What other news have you heard lately?" Liam asked, plainly redirecting the conversation away from the twins' disagreement. "I know that the Glasidhe hear much more than we do."

"Because we are small and often overlooked," replied Farin. Quinn could tell by her voice that she was grinning her sharp-toothed grin.

"Never overlooked by anyone worth their salt," said Liam.

Farin fluttered her wings in pleasure at the compliment, and Quinn made a mental note to turn on the charm when talking to the Glasidhe from that point on.

"Well, of course there is the talk of the High Queen taking some of the Vyldgard into the mountains for the birth of Rialla's pups," said Farin with the air of someone starting on a long list. "But I think you probably hear enough of that, do you not, being her lover?" A hint of wickedness laced her words.

"I do hear of it," Liam replied, merely raising an eyebrow and glancing at Farin.

"You're a little troublemaker," Quinn said, turning his head slightly to direct his words to Farin. "Tell us something we don't already know."

Farin took a moment to think. "There is talk of other Exiles who have crossed through into Faeortalam."

"Now who is embroidering tales?" said Forin in disapproval.

"I am not embroidering anything," Farin replied with a dignified air. "I am merely repeating what has already been said."

"It is a silly rumor." Forin flicked his wings dismissively.

"Where did this rumor originate?" asked Liam.

Quinn heard the tightly controlled interest in his friend's voice. Exiles, he thought, would be mostly Unseelie, though he'd learned that a few Seelie had rebelled as well. What would they do if they found their way back into the Fae world?

"Oh, here and there," replied Farin, leaping off Quinn's shoulder to pirouette in midair and turn dizzying circles overhead.

"It is nothing to take seriously," Forin said. "There are guards on the Gate, here and in the mortal world."

Quinn thought of Tyr. "But don't the Exiled know things that have been forgotten sometimes?"

"You are suggesting they somehow managed to slip past the guards?" Forin asked thoughtfully.

"Perhaps through disguise?" Quinn suggested. He shrugged. "I don't know all the tricks you have up your sleeve."

"Why would they not have come through before, then?" Forin tried to follow his theory. "In some time other than this one?"

"Maybe they didn't know where the Gates were," Liam said.

"The Gates were moved and well concealed in the days before the war," said Farin in agreement, diving down to land neatly on Quinn's shoulder again.

"Opening another Gate might have tipped them off to its location," said Liam.

"Did anyone *ask* Tyr?" Quinn said. "Did anyone think to ask him whether there were other Exiled still alive, other than him and Corsica?"

"Maybe he talked about it with Vivian," said Liam, "but he hasn't been particularly friendly with anyone else."

"He is adrift," said Farin with a hint of sadness.

"If there were other Exiled who came through the Gate," said Liam slowly, "what do you think they would do here in this world?"

No one spoke for a few long moments. Finally, Forin said in a voice so low it was almost inaudible, "We should not even speak of such things."

"They would seek revenge," whispered Farin.

"Tyr isn't seeking revenge," Quinn said.

"He killed Mab. That was his revenge," Liam replied.

"Then who else would the rest of the Exiled want to kill for revenge?" Quinn swallowed against the sudden bitterness in his mouth. The conversation had turned so quickly from meaningless small talk to this discussion of possible assassinations.

"Perhaps their leader," said Forin.

"Perhaps still the Queens," Farin said in a small voice.

They walked in silence again.

"If anyone has any proof of this, I need to know immediately," Liam said to the Glasidhe. His tone brooked no argument and there was no question that he was giving them the task as one of the High Queen's Three.

"Aye," said Forin, leaping from his shoulder. He gave Liam a sharp salute and flew away. Farin still stood on Quinn's shoulder for a moment more. Quinn watched her out of the corner of his eye; she wrung her small hands, looking uncertain, and then she clenched her fists by her sides, drew back her shoulders and launched herself into the air.

"I did not mean to tell tales," she said earnestly, her aura sparking a plaintive shade of lavender.

"Rumors always start somewhere, even if it's someone with too much free time and bad intentions," said Liam. "I'd be grateful if you would help your brother get to the bottom of it."

Farin bowed as well and then arrowed away.

"How much truth do you think is in it?" Quinn asked as the rounded the last corner and the entrance to the practice yards came into view.

"Maybe none at all," said Liam with half a shrug. "But Farin thought it was interesting enough to repeat. That means at the least we might have to do damage control and stamp out the rumor as best we can. Reinforce security on the Gate, maybe. It means people are worried about the other Exiled."

"Should we talk to Tyr?"

"I don't think we should do anything right now," Liam said. "Not until the Glasidhe have dug a little deeper."

"They're fast," Quinn said with a nod.

"It wouldn't surprise me if they had the answer before we're done with this practice session."

They entered the training yard, the familiar sounds rising around them: the clash of blades, the slide and leap of boots on the hard-packed earth, the low conversation of those watching or taking a breath mixed with the occasional sounds of triumph or effort from those in the rings. Liam nodded to one of the sparring rings as they passed. Quinn glanced in interest at its occupants: a slender yet well-endowed young woman with the dark hair and pale skin of the Unseelie, crossing swords with another Unseelie. The hilt of the young woman's sword flashed with gemstones, and Quinn's sneaking suspicion was confirmed as he caught a glimpse of the young woman's face and glimpsed the distinctive scars left by the bone sorcerer. So, the Unseelie Queen sparred in the training yards among the other Knights and Guards of the Seelie Court and the fighters of the Vyldgard.

Quinn scanned the rest of the yard. Thea sparred with golden-haired Calliea in a ring near the forge; he raised a hand in greeting as they passed, and though the women didn't pause in their match, they both grinned. Merrick raised a hand in answer from the edge of the ring.

"Getting in some last practice before we depart," he said by way of greeting.

"I never got a copy of the final roster for the expedition," said Quinn with a grin, "so I'm kinda in the dark." He raised his eyebrows at Liam. "Even though I have some inside connections."

"Oh, it's a small enough group," said Merrick, watching Calliea whirl and twist with nimble speed. "Thea and I are going, though Calliea will be staying here since Finnead is coming as well."

"The Vyldretning couldn't be expected to allow two of her Three to go," said Liam.

"Since when has the Vyldretning held to what any of us *expected*?" Merrick replied with an easy grin. He gripped Liam's forearm in welcome. "But you are right, and the rest of the Vyldgard needs to be prepared for the journey North."

"You and Thea," said Quinn, "and Vivian's going, so I guess that means Tyr as well."

"Rye is his twin," said Merrick. "The Queen would be hard put to order him to stay behind."

"Does he even heed a Queen anymore?" Liam said.

"From the Seelie," continued Merrick, "there's Niall. The Valkyrie are sending Moira and Trillian."

"So will Calliea be the commander in Trillian's stead while she is gone?" Liam asked.

Quinn tried to focus on the fast, skillful match playing out in the ring rather than listen to talk of the Valkyrie, and he was only partially successful.

"They mostly answer only to themselves," said Merrick. "Though they'll be adding to their ranks soon too, did you hear?"

"Selaph's foal," said Liam with a nod.

Quinn clenched his jaw at the mention of Niamh's mount. He'd spent a lot of time with the white *faehal* in the days after the battle. The other Valkyrie had ensured she was tended well, of course, but he'd liked the idea that the graceful winged *faehal* cared whether Niamh lived or died almost as much as he did.

Calliea grinned in triumph as she slid her blade through Thea's guard, resting the tip delicately against the other woman's throat. Thea bared her teeth in something between an answering grin and a grimace at her defeat. Calliea stepped back and neatly sheathed her blade.

"Would one of you like the next round?" she asked, barely seeming out of breath.

"You'd take me apart," said Quinn bluntly.

"But you'd enjoy it," she replied, an impish cast to her heart-shaped face. Merrick chuckled fondly.

"Isn't it unfair for someone so beautiful to be so deadly?" he said to no one in particular, stepping forward and sweeping an arm around Calliea's waist. He kissed her thoroughly; Thea whistled and Calliea grinned against Merrick's lips.

"Apparently they've made up," Liam said in an undertone.

"Come on then, if you don't want to spar the Laedrek at least come and try your skills against me," said Thea, raising her sword in invitation to Quinn.

"A warm-up round," he conceded, unsheathing his blade and running a few passes through the air, evaluating the feel of his body. He was only a little sore today, and he'd slept well the night before. The morning session had been light, so he felt like he stood a decent chance at holding his own for a bit.

Merrick and Calliea stepped out of the ring, still pressed against each other, the Valkyrie's tawny skin flushed pink over her cheekbones. Quinn heard Liam murmur to them in low conversation as he stepped across the line inscribed in the hard-packed dirt.

"I'll go easy on you," Thea said, though her devilish smile didn't reassure him.

"Never asked you to go easy, just said I needed a warm-up," Quinn replied, and he launched into one of the series of strokes that Liam had recently taught him.

Thea proved to be a good teacher, pressing him and then backing away again, calling out a mistake here and there and demonstrating why it was important to emphasize the follow-through on that particular stroke or so crucial to take *exactly* three steps in the footwork of that pattern. Quinn found himself relaxing even as he pushed himself harder, sweat prickling beneath his shirt, the sunlight warm on his back as they danced about the ring.

Then something whistled through the air over their heads, and before they could even call an end to their session, a scream rose above the ordinary sounds of the practice yard. Thea pointed her blade at the ground, eyes widening, and then there were more whistles and someone tackled him to the ground. After checking that he'd managed not to impale himself with his sword, Quinn twisted in the grip of whoever had decided that they were both better off on the ground – Liam.

"Arrows," he said, rolling off Quinn.

"Shields!" roared Thea in a voice that echoed through the yard, running fearlessly toward the shields stacked against the wall of her forge. More whistles, and as though in slow motion Quinn saw a black arrow slicing toward Thea. He scrambled to get to his feet, even though he knew he couldn't cover the distance in time, and then with a hiss Calliea's golden whip arced out and knocked the arrow from its path. It landed instead in the dirt, its sharp tip buried in earth nearly as hard as cement.

"No, no, no," a woman's voice said, over and over. Quinn vaguely recognized it. He grabbed the strap of his healing satchel and scanned the yard. Over by the ring where the Unseelie Queen had been sparring, someone lay on the ground. Thea tossed a shield to Calliea, and he ran with them over toward the downed fighter.

"Get the Queen to safety," said a gray-faced young Unseelie, the one on the ground. The small Unseelie woman kneeling by him was the one who'd spoken, her face white and her eyes wide. A scarlet-fletched arrow protruded from the man's side, and another pierced his thigh.

"Queen Andraste," said Calliea, "come with me, my lady."

The Queen stood staring down at the young man, the scars standing out lividly against her pale face.

"My lady," he coughed, his gray eyes widening, "*go!*"

Three more arrows rained down on them. One punched into Calliea's shield, Thea deflected another, and Quinn instinctively threw himself toward the unmoving young woman. In that moment, he didn't think of her as the Unseelie Queen. Pain seared across his shoulder as he encircled her with his arms and threw them both to the ground, trying to shield her from the roughness of landing on the hard packed dirt. A quick check told him that the arrow hadn't actually embedded itself in his flesh, just scored him with a cut. He quickly rolled away from the Queen, not allowing him to think what he'd just done – he'd just *tackled* one of the most powerful beings in the Fae world.

"My lady!" urged Calliea, crouching in front of the Unseelie Queen with her shield held at an angle. Thea protected the downed Unseelie man.

"We should get him to your forge," Quinn said quickly to Thea, who nodded but didn't look away from scanning the sky for more missiles. The ground suddenly felt cold and a strange ripple passed through the air. "What's his name?" he asked the small woman urgently.

"Sayre," she said, tearing her gaze from him to where the Unseelie Queen slowly stood behind Calliea's shield. Frost ringed the Queen's feet. "I need to go to the Queen," she said, touching Sayre's cheek in what Quinn thought was apology.

"Go," he managed.

"This is gonna hurt, man, but we don't want you out here," said Quinn. He heard Liam in the background, giving orders for groups of three and four Sidhe to search the buildings and the rooftops on either side of the training yard. Quinn looped one of Sayre's arms over his shoulder – carrying him fireman style wasn't a good idea with those arrows, and this wasn't going to be much better.

"Ready?" Thea said shortly.

"Now," said Quinn, hauling Sayre up and half-carrying, half-dragging him in an awkward but quick run toward Thea's forge.

Thea protected them with the shield until they were all through the doorway, and then she dropped it, hastily clearing a worktable and helping Quinn lay Sayre upon it.

"Hey man, stay with me," Quinn said, rubbing a knuckle against Sayre's sternum. The younger man made a sound of pain. "I know it hurts, but you gotta stay awake."

A freezing blast of air screamed through the forge like a wintry storm imbued with a life of its own. Thea leapt to close the door and stoke the embers of the fire.

"Why isn't anyone else in here?" Quinn asked as he tore open the flap of his healing satchel – the satchel that Sage had just stocked not even an hour before.

"Runes on the threshold," Thea said shortly. She glanced out the one small window of the forge and gave a low whistle.

"What?" he said shortly as he tightened a tourniquet around Sayre's thigh.

"Queen Andraste is going full winter," Thea said, coming over to help him. She laid an ear on Sayre's chest and listened to him breathing. "The one in his side didn't hit a lung."

"Good," Quinn managed. "She's going full winter on *what*?"

"On who, more like," said Thea. "There's a good lad, keep your eyes open."

Sayre shivered, his eyes glossy with pain. "She will find them." His blue lips curved in a smile. "She will make them pay dearly."

Quinn swore as Sayre's words cost him too much effort and his eyes rolled back in his head.

A tapping on the window drew Thea away from the table; when she opened the window, Farin tumbled over the sill. The little Glasidhe gave a cry when she saw Sayre lying still and bloodstained. "I will get a healer!" she shrilled, and dove out the window again.

"Lucky we have half of one," Thea said, smiling grimly at Quinn.

"It only counts if he doesn't die," he replied. The worst of the bleeding staunched for the moment, he took a breath and considered their options. "I'm going to leave removing these to Maeve and Sage."

Thea didn't question him. She glanced at the window. Frost curled on the panes of glass. "Gods help whomever decided to try to kill the Queen."

Quinn looked up at her.

"They missed their target, and for that they will wish they were dead," the smith said as wind whipped snow against the window-pane. She turned to stoke the fire, and Quinn turned back to Sayre, hoping his training would be enough to save the life of one of the Unseelie Queen's Three.

Chapter 22

Vivian glanced up from her work at the knock on the door of the Tower. She'd started exploring the various doors that led off the Tower – though she suspected that the rooms were enchanted and kept moving, she found a small but well-appointed bedroom behind a door painted her favorite shade of robin's-egg blue. Though she was leaving on the expedition, she'd decided to move into the Tower, and so her visitors had increased daily. The knowledge of the Tower's existence and the path to the door was no secret now, at least among the upper echelons of the Courts and the Queens themselves.

"Were you expecting someone?" asked Tyr, glancing at her from across the table from where he was reading an arcane text that looked like it was written in a rune-language without the benefit of any translation spectacles.

"No," Vivian said, "but I've had a lot of visitors over the past couple of days." She marked her place in her book, a rather dry history that Tyr nonetheless said was important for her to read, and stood from the table. She stretched, grateful for the interruption. Maybe after whoever it was left she could convince Tyr to spend at least *part* of their lesson on something new. He'd insisted that they should take advantage of the library before they departed on the expedition. Vivian privately thought that maybe Tyr couldn't focus well enough to teach her with the possibility of his sister's survival at the forefront of his mind.

Alfred appeared from behind one of the bookcases, dusting rag in hand. He gestured to the door.

"It's all right, Alfred, I've got it," Vivian said, stifling a yawn. "But maybe some coffee?"

She still didn't know how the Tower servant managed to procure coffee, but she didn't question it.

"And *khal*," she added, glancing at Tyr. He'd already bent his silvery head over the ancient book again.

Alfred bowed and swept off with a flourish. Vivian smiled. She'd come to be fond of the rune-created servant. It was almost like having a cat in the library, but a very useful cat almost painfully anxious to please. As she walked toward the door, she thought that perhaps Alfred would like some sort of decoration or embellishment to add to his robe as a sign of her gratitude for his service. She didn't think she could change the robe itself, not unless she managed to recreate the runes stitched into it, and she'd never forgive herself if something went wrong and Alfred vanished altogether.

One of the lights by the door flickered oddly. She made a mental note to check it after greeting whatever guest was at the door. Three more knocks sounded, louder than last time.

"I'm coming!" Vivian called. She made another mental note to ask Alfred if there was some object up among the shelves that would tell her who stood outside the door. That would be eminently handy with all her visitors. She reached the door and opened it, stepping back in shock.

Ross stood on the other side of the door, her fist still raised from knocking. They stared at each other for a moment. Ross grinned.

"I...what are you doing here?" Vivian said dumbly. Something about Ross's grin seemed strange to her – feral, almost.

"I came to visit," said Ross, and though her voice *technically* sounded like Ross, there was something about that too.

"Where's Duke?" Vivian asked. "Did you come through the portal? Did someone send you a message?"

"Aren't you going to invite me in?" Ross asked.

"Vivian?" Tyr called, standing from the table.

"This is strange," Vivian said, frowning. The pendant at her throat heated as her skin prickled in warning.

Ross slid a booted toe across the threshold of the door, and her grin widened. "Stupid young thing," she hissed, and then she leapt through the door, the air tightening as the Tower stripped the woman of her disguise. Ross's dark hair flashed silver, her dark skin rippled with layers of thick white scars, and her body stretched until she landed on her feet, cat-like, a tall and slender Sidhe woman.

Vivian pivoted, intending to run for her sword and tool belt, hung on the wall near one of the smaller tables. Before she took two steps, an invisible force slammed into her, lifting her from her feet and sending her crashing down onto the ground. She lay stunned for a moment, the breath knocked out of her, and then she coughed and struggled to her knees, the sounds of a fight wavering in her ears. Blinking away stars, she dragged in a breath and began constructing a shield rune in her mind, but then Alfred was there, holding her belt and her sword out to her insistently.

The woman had surprised Tyr, upending the table and pinning him beneath it. He bared his teeth and pushed its weight upward with herculean effort, but his agonizingly slow progress wasn't going to be fast enough. The silver-haired woman advanced on him with a prowling gait that reminded Vivian of Corsica; her mouth went dry with sudden fear and her stomach clenched, but she told herself firmly that Corsica was dead.

"Help Tyr," she ordered Alfred as she grabbed her rune-stick and hastily began drawing a shield-rune on the back of one hand. Alfred zoomed away. The Exiled woman didn't seem concerned about any kind of threat from Vivian, stalking toward Tyr almost lazily. Vivian finished the shield rune and started on another rune on her other hand, concentrating on remembering the proportions and curve of each line exactly right. Her hands shook slightly.

With a final heave, Tyr freed his legs from the table and staggered upright; the woman sprang in a graceful, too-quick-to-follow handspring, vaulting off the edge of the table. Something flashed in her hand and Tyr staggered as a dagger appeared beneath his collarbone. Vivian's heart dropped into her stomach, but she forced herself to finish the rune on her hand: She was no use to him if she couldn't stop the Exiled woman from killing him.

The woman landed with feline elegance in a crouch, one hand touching the floor. Vivian finished the rune, called up her *taebramh*, ready to activate them, and pelted across the floor toward them. Alfred swerved around a book case, a kettle in his nebulous hands, and the Exiled woman shrieked as he threw the hot water onto her. She recovered quickly, hissing and snatching at the edge of Alfred's robe, but then Tyr tackled her, bodily lifting her, both of them tumbling to the floor in a tangle of limbs. Vivian glanced at Alfred quickly in concern, but he looked unhurt, examining the tear at the edge of his robe with an offended air and watching Tyr fight the woman with detached curiosity.

A sound from Tyr drew her attention back to them: The Exiled woman had gained the upper hand, straddling Tyr and viciously pulling the dagger from his shoulder. "I will kill you slowly," she purred, grinning that feral grin again as she licked the bloody blade.

In answer, Tyr moved as quick as a striking snake, grabbing the hand that held the dagger and arching up from the floor, throwing her from her perch atop him and driving his other fist into her stomach with brutal force as he broke her grip. The woman grunted but managed to draw up one leg as Tyr bore her to the ground, planting her boot on his chest and sending him staggering backward long enough that she regained her feet. The bloody dagger gleamed in her hand, and another appeared in her other hand. Vivian blinked: a long, slender dagger almost long enough to be a sword had appeared in Tyr's hand. They circled each other with slow predatory steps, their eyes intent upon each other. She paused, uncertain: would she just get in the way?

Alfred descended to block her path, stretching his arms out to keep Vivian from pushing past him. He was actually infuriatingly nimble for an enchanted being made of a rune-robe and silver mist, and his form was very solid when he firmly prodded Vivian back a few steps.

"I have a shield rune," she protested, showing him her hand even though she didn't know if he even recognized runes.

"Stay there, Vivian," Tyr ordered.

She watched over Alfred's robed arm, feeling helpless as the Exiled woman leapt at Tyr, her movements acrobatic and agile. They went down again in a blur of fast-moving limbs, and when the woman sprang away, blood trickled down Tyr's arm.

"You never were quite the best at fighting, Tyr," the woman said tauntingly, both her blades stained dark and gleaming.

"No need to be the best," Tyr returned with half a grin.

"Oh, come now, you can come up with a wittier retort than that," she said, twirling her daggers and again reminding Vivian of Corsica. "I remember when you convinced us all to cast our lots with you, Silvertongue. I remember the sweetness of your words and the poison of your certainty."

Vivian tried to feint around Alfred, but he intercepted her and even gave her a little push.

"Let me past," she growled. He'd never disobeyed one of her orders before, but there was a first time for everything. He crossed his arms over the chest of his robe and managed to somehow convey that he was unmoved.

The woman flashed into a dizzying series of acrobatics, handsprings and cartwheels and a magnificent leap as she turned somersaults through the air. Vivian watched her wide-eyed. The woman whirled past Tyr and though he brought his dagger up and stabbed at the center of the silver and black blur, he didn't inflict any major wound, and a slice appeared on his thigh, blooming blood over the scar where Corsica had stabbed him. Vivian's breath caught in her throat and she tried to push past Alfred again, but he caught her around the chest in a strange sort of bear hug, immovable even though she struggled.

"I can't watch her kill him," she said desperately. Then Tyr's voice sounded in her head as he used the silent communication that he'd effectively abandoned since they'd crossed through the Gate into Faeortalam.

Trust me, he said. *Neither of us will kill her. She is far more valuable alive.*

She wants to kill you! replied Vivian.

She will not, Tyr replied simply, though she felt a shiver of pain through their connection.

Let me help, she said, pleading now, as the woman readied for another attack.

No, he said firmly, and then he drew away from their silent bond. "Paladin!"

The voice made the very floor beneath her feet tremble, not with its volume, but its authority. Vivian instinctively threw a spark of *taebramh* at the door, bidding it to open, and no sooner had it swung inward than a great black wolf bounded through, landing before the overturned table, its golden eyes quickly fixing on the silver-haired woman. Tyr feinted at the woman and she lunged toward him, daggers extended; the black wolf covered the distance in one great leap, its forepaws landing on the woman's back and driving her to the ground. A low growl rumbled from its throat and Vivian glimpsed one glistening white tooth as long as her fingers as the wolf curled its lip in a snarl. Astoundingly, the Exiled woman tried to struggle.

"If you resist Beryk, he will make you so you cannot resist," said the High Queen, striding into the Tower. She raised one dark eyebrow. "And if you injure him, I will kill you."

A golden-haired woman with a whip coiled at her belt followed a pace behind the Vyldretning. She unclipped the coil and snapped it against the floor almost idly, her eyes glimmering. Alfred took one look at their guests and zoomed away, probably to fetch the coffee and *khal* that he had been preparing before the attack, Vivian thought. That left her view of the tableau unobstructed: the black wolf Beryk pinning down the Exiled woman, his growl so low that it was difficult to hear; Vell, dressed as though she were going to the practice yards, walking toward them with a hard expression; and the woman following her curving her whip through the air with practiced flicks of her wrist.

Tyr inclined his head to the High Queen; Vivian tried not to stare in surprise. It was the first time she'd seen Tyr display any kind of respect toward the leaders of the Fae world.

"Queen Andraste captured another at the training yards," said the High Queen, gazing down at the prostrate Exiled woman who had ceased struggling but still gripped her daggers with white-knuckled hands. "Drop them."

The woman gave her own snarl in response. Vell lifted an eyebrow and tilted her head. The golden-haired woman glanced at her, face alight with anticipation. The Vyldretning shrugged. "Have it your way, Exile." She nodded to the woman holding the whip. "Calliea, if you please."

Beryk leapt away from the woman, quick as a shadow despite his size, and the golden whip flashed out once, twice. The Exiled woman's daggers sailed through the air and hit the stone floor with a clang. Calliea flicked her wrist again and her weapon coiled around the woman's arms.

Satisfied that Calliea had the situation in hand, Vell turned toward Vivian, her eyes quickly assessing her. "Are you hurt?"

"No, my lady," said Vivian.

Vell waved a hand. "None of that now. I'm the High Queen, yes; we all know that. You are a Paladin. I don't ask you to bow to me."

"I…what should I call you then?" she asked.

"Vell is fine," replied the other woman with a grin. She looked at Tyr. "Better sit down before you fall down."

Vivian broke free of the fascination and awe that had frozen her in the presence of the High Queen and the black wolf. With a surreptitious glance, she glimpsed Beryk trotting through the myriad of bookcases, gazing with intelligent interest and sniffing a book here and there. Tyr sat down heavily in one of the chairs that had somehow remained upright by the overturned table. Vivian hurried over to him, thinking that he looked paler than usual.

"Her name is Evangeline," he said to the High Queen, nodding at the glowering silver-haired woman.

"Traitorous coward," hissed Evangeline, her narrow face sharp with fury.

"Quiet, or I'll gag you as well," said Calliea mildly as she finished binding the woman's hands behind her back.

"Should I call for a healer?" Vivian asked as she neared Tyr. Blood smeared his arm and underscored one cheekbone, and the entire side of his shirt was soaked from the wound under his collarbone.

"One should be arriving shortly," said Vell, "though I'm happy to offer my services if you wish."

Vivian blinked at the unexpected offer. Not only had the High Queen saved Tyr's life and probably hers as well, now she offered to get her hands dirty – she was already rolling up her sleeves past her elbows, in fact. Vivian decided she most definitely liked Vell.

Alfred hurtled past with a tray of coffee and *khal*, the mugs rattling but not a drop spilled despite his high speed. Vell watched the Tower servant in mingled interest and mild amusement as he set down the serving tray on a smaller table and with one movement righted the heavy table behind them, careful not to crush any of the books knocked to the floor. With a nod of satisfaction, Alfred retrieved the tray and set it on the table, gesturing to it courteously and inclining his head to the High Queen.

"Thank you," Vell said, though she made no move to pour any *khal.*

"Alfred, could you fetch one of the healing kits, please? It's all right if it's the one I had packed for the expedition," said Vivian. Alfred bowed to her and whisked away. "I've been training with Sage and the other healers for at least two hours a day," Vivian explained to Vell, "but I'm sure you have more experience than I do."

She half-expected Tyr to protest but he was worryingly silent as they pulled aside the edges of his shirt, and she didn't like the bluish cast to his lips. Vell produced a dagger and cut away the remnants of the shirt in short order, using some of the cloth that wasn't already sodden with blood as a makeshift bandage, pressing it against the wound on Tyr's shoulder. Vivian ran her fingers lightly over his back and found no exit wound. Vell gestured and she took over applying pressure. Alfred returned and set her satchel of healing supplies on the table, and then applied himself to pouring three cups of *khal* and a cup of coffee.

"Evangeline was one of your rebels?" Vell asked as she bound the cut on Tyr's thigh. "It's not deep enough to be deadly," she said to Vivian reassuringly.

"That's...good," Vivian managed in reply. She sent a tendril of awareness toward Tyr, through their bond, and to her surprise he let her in.

"Yes," Tyr answered Vell. His voice was low and tight with pain. "Evangeline was a rebel."

"And she seeks her revenge on you because the rebellion failed?"

Tyr winced as Vell prodded at the cut on his upper arm that still sluggishly bled, painting stripes down his pale skin. "Yes."

Vell made a noncommittal sound, and then they worked quietly for a few moments. Calliea had decided to gag Evangeline after all, the Exiled woman's voice muffled but still clearly full of anger and spite. Alfred fixed Vivian's coffee exactly how she liked it – one sugar, a dash of milk – and then folded his hands into his robes, hovering with an anxious air now that the fight was over. Tyr's eyes slid half-shut, and Vivian tried to think of something that would hold his attention.

"You and Rye trained with the *ulfdrengr*," she said. She glanced at Vell.

Tyr nodded. "We traveled back to Court with King Rothgar and his *volta* Queen."

Vell smiled. "You speak of my grandfather and grandmother." She tilted her head, seemingly in thought, and the smile faded from her face.

"Did you know them?" Tyr asked quietly, sweat starting to stand out on his brow.

Vell glanced at Vivian, as though deciding whether to share such intimate details about her life with Vivian listening.

"I can…help Calliea," Vivian said, though she didn't want to leave Tyr's side, and it was clear at a glance that the Valkyrie had their prisoner well restrained.

"Nonsense," said Vell briskly, drawing back her shoulders. "We'll speak of this at another time, Tyr, when you aren't bleeding profusely onto this lovely carpet."

Tyr chuckled. The sound seemed foreign to Vivian. Could he still drink blood? Would that help him heal? She nudged him through their link. *Would blood help?*

He shook his head slightly. *I no longer need blood.*

Did someone help you break that…need? She really wanted to ask if one of the Queens had assisted him, and she immediately scolded herself. He'd very nearly just died from Evangeline's attack and she wanted to indulge in petty jealousy.

Tyr looked at her with a strange consideration in his eye. Finally, he asked, *Why do you feel envy?*

You're avoiding the question, she responded.

As are you, he replied, and then he briefly closed his eyes.

"Shouldn't the healer be here already?" Vivian asked with an edge of worry in her voice.

"Your Tower is in a far-fetched part of the cathedral, and even with his destination fixed firmly in mind, it may be a few minutes before anyone else arrives," Vell said. She finished bandaging the cut on Tyr's arm and wiped the blood from her hands on the front of her black breeches.

"Or there may have been other attacks, and other wounded," said Calliea. She nudged Evangeline with one foot. "Are there others?"

The Exiled woman glared hatefully up at them, showing them her teeth in a silent snarl.

"Evangeline often traveled with Arianna," Tyr said.

Evangeline growled at him and tried to lunge; Calliea hauled her back by the scruff of her shirt with an amused expression.

"And sometimes Dryden," he added.

"Stop that," Calliea told Evangeline calmly, shaking her by the neck a little as she strained against her bonds and made sounds of anger through her gag.

"How did they get here?" Vivian asked. Now that the rush of the fight was over, she felt very tired. Alfred offered her the cup of coffee and she gratefully accepted. He nodded in satisfaction as she sipped.

"That's the question of the hour," said the High Queen, padding toward the bound Exile with sinuous grace. It wasn't hard to see the echo of her great, deadly wolf in her motions. "Although I wonder if they would rather die than give up their secrets."

Vell palmed her dagger and slid the point beneath Evangeline's chin, raising her head. Vivian watched in fascination as stillness descended over both women, the Vyldretning searching the Exile's pale, scarred face with intent eyes as the would-be assassin stared up at her defiantly. Evangeline's scars rippled every inch of her skin, thicker and more pronounced than Tyr's. Vivian wondered if that meant she'd had a more difficult time adapting to the mortal world, or if she was less skilled with runes and *taebramh* than Tyr.

Beryk appeared from behind the bookshelves, flowing liquidly as a shadow across the floor. A low growl almost beyond the reach of Vivian's ears vibrated from the black wolf. He circled the High Queen and the Exile. Calliea still held the woman by the back of her shirt, and the Valkyrie gripped her whip in loose coils in her other hand. Finally, Evangeline looked down, though her head was still held carefully still. Vell sheathed her dagger.

"She'll talk," she said in a quiet, confident voice.

"Where would you like me to take her?" Calliea asked.

"Perhaps the old granary by the training yards," said Vell. "That will have to serve as our dungeon for now. We've had very little need of anything of that sort, you see, until you came along." The High Queen directed her last comment to Evangeline, who'd gone from defiant to dull-eyed and staring.

"I'm sure the Unseelie would oblige," Calliea said brightly, hauling Evangeline up and marching her toward the door. "I hear their dungeons are particularly cold and frosty. And seeing as you were once Unseelie, you'd probably feel right at home!" She glanced at Vivian. "All right, Paladin?"

Vivian blinked, caught off guard at the Valkyrie's direct inquiry, and then nodded. She cleared her throat. "Yes, thank you."

"No thanks needed, especially when there's a bit of a brawl involved," Calliea said with a grin. Alfred sailed after her, a cup of *khal* held inquiringly in his nebulous hand; she paused in frogmarching Evangeline toward the door to politely accept the cup, sip it experimentally, and then down the whole cup in one impressive draft. She handed it back to Alfred with a nod of thanks, and the Tower servant happily disappeared with the used cup.

"Quite an elegant and curious enchantment," Vell said thoughtfully, watching Alfred. "He came with the Tower?"

"I certainly don't have the skill to make him myself," replied Vivian.

"But Tyr does," said Vell, that note of certainty in her voice again.

"He came with the Tower," Tyr said, his voice strong though his eyes were still closed.

"Well," Vell said, "even in the North we heard old tales of the Paladin, just as we heard tales of the Bearer. It seems as though we remember more than the Courts sometimes."

"Blood oaths have a way of erasing things from memory," murmured Tyr.

"True," Vell agreed gravely. Beryk leaned against her side and she stroked his great head briefly. Calliea and the unfortunate Evangeline had exited the Tower, and Vivian felt suddenly awkward before the High Queen with the immediate danger subdued and out of sight. Alfred bowed to the High Queen and offered her the remaining cup of *khal* hopefully. He bowed again after Vell accepted it.

"More bowing than I usually tolerate, but I suppose it's his nature and he can't help it," she commented as she sipped the *khal*. "He *does* make a good cup of *khal*."

"What should we do now?" Vivian asked. It seemed like an obvious question, but she didn't know the procedures for an unexpected rebel invasion in the White City.

Vell took another sip of *khal*. "Put wards on your Tower – or stronger wards, I suppose, since they *did* strip Evangeline of her disguise." She sipped again. "And beyond that, stay here with Tyr. It's one of the safer places in the City."

Vivian nodded. "There's a book of wards that I've been studying. Alfred, could you...?" She didn't need to finish her request; Alfred was already halfway to the shelf that housed the specific rune-book.

"Very elegant," murmured Vell again, and then she finished her *khal*, setting the empty cup back on its place on the tray. She looked at Tyr, and then at Vivian. "I must go and see what other mischief these Exiled have wrought."

'Mischief' seemed too trivial a word to Vivian – Evangeline had clearly intended to kill Tyr. But she nodded. "Thank you, and you are welcome in the Tower any time."

"Be careful how many blanket invitations of that sort you issue," said Vell lightly. "Words have power, Vivian."

"I'll remember that," Vivian said.

Without a formal farewell, the High Queen strode across the Tower and through the door, pulling it shut with a clear, definite sound.

Tyr shuddered and slid down a little in his chair.

"Putting on a good face for the High Queen?" Vivian asked as she folded a bandage for his shoulder.

"She is not so easily fooled," Tyr said, his eyes glassy and half-shut.

"You should go to the healing ward." She winced as she peeled away the wad of cloth that had once been his shirt. "This looks like it needs stitches."

"Then stitch it," he said shortly.

Vivian looked at him sharply, then drew back her shoulders and started pulling out the necessary supplies from her satchel. She tried to thread the needle three times because her hands were shaking, but she took another bracing swallow of coffee and managed it.

Half an hour later, she snipped the excess thread close to the last knot. Tyr hadn't made a sound other than a sharp intake of breath every so often. Sometimes she thought that he forgot he'd regained his voice. She quickly mixed a salve that she'd learned just two days ago from Sage himself. After applying it and bandaging his shoulder, she sat back in satisfaction. She didn't know why the healer hadn't arrived – perhaps Vell had told them that the Paladin had the situation under control. A little curl of pride bloomed in her chest at the thought.

Alfred had taken away the tray with the *khal* and coffee, but now he returned with a different, smaller tray. The two heavy earthenware mugs reminded Vivian of the oversize coffee mug she kept below the counter at Adele's. She pushed away the twinge of homesickness. Alfred set the tray on the table and pulled what Vivian had first thought was a kind of waiter's napkin from his arm – it turned out to be a clean shirt for Tyr, black and sewn in a style that struck Vivian as somewhat archaic, even though she'd only been in Faeortalam for a few weeks.

Tyr slowly pulled it over his head and then nodded to Alfred in thanks. The Tower servant pressed one of the mugs into Tyr's hands and then set about cleaning up around them, poking at the bloodstains on the rug and gathering up the rags of Tyr's old shirt.

"Would you like to go back to your rooms?" Vivian asked. She didn't know exactly where Tyr slept, in all honesty – he hadn't deigned to tell her, one of the many details about their new lives that she didn't know.

"I think…I'll sit in front of the fire," said Tyr. He took a sip from his mug and then stood, very nearly spilling it; Vivian didn't know how to help without hovering, so she just watched him make his way unsteadily to one of the overstuffed armchairs by the fireplace, which had crackled into life. The silver arm curled its fingers and rearranged one of the logs before resuming its station.

Vivian gathered up the book that Tyr had been reading and the rune-book that Alfred had fetched from its shelf. She took her own mug and sat in the armchair opposite Tyr. He looked lost in thought, pale but not abnormally so, the silver threads of his scars highlighted by the firelight. Vivian set her mug on a little table beside her chair and opened her book. She'd found three good wards to set when Alfred swept past her. She looked up just as Alfred rescued the half-full mug capsizing in Tyr's hands: he'd fallen asleep, head leaning against the wing of the chair's back.

Vivian glanced at her own tea suspiciously, but she didn't feel anything beyond the tiredness that the excitement of the fight with Evangeline had wrought. As she stood and pulled her rune-stick from her belt, Alfred returned with a blanket, tucking it fastidiously over Tyr's legs.

"Mother hen," Vivian said affectionately as she passed. As she set her rune-stick to the lintel of the door to the Tower, her mind slid into the soothing, blank focus of crafting runes that would best hold her *taebramh,* and she was able to set aside all her questions about the Exiled woman Evangeline, at least for the moment.

Chapter 23

"How is he?" Jem slid through the door of their room over the stables at the Blind Dragon, a rather grandiosely named little tavern that rented a few rooms and called itself an inn as well. He tucked the key on its length of twine back under his shirt and made sure to draw the bolt behind him.

"Same as when you left," said Mal, glancing at Hex. "Still sleeping."

The journey from the *Dragonwing* to the Blind Dragon had been nearly as harrowing as Mal had imagined, Hex gray with pain as they supported him down the brow, the back of his shirt soon speckled with flecks of blood. Mal had cursed roundly under her breath but Jem had once again borne them all through it with his solid, unshakeable calm, insisting they stop every ten minutes or so for a rest as they helped Hex stagger through the streets toward their destination. He'd sent Mal ahead to ask after rooms and pricing at the various establishments in the port. They'd chosen the Blind Dragon because while it wasn't the absolute cheapest, it was tucked away in a quieter corner of the town away from the bustling wharves, and it wasn't frequented by the sailors of the dragon ships as a general rule. Their room smelled like hay, but it was warm and dry, larger than they'd expected and clean.

Mal's silver ring had bought them more than she'd hoped: a full month's lodging and meals as well at the common table. She thought she saw a flash of pity in the innkeeper's rheumy eyes as he nodded at her desperate bid, but she firmly ignored it and shook hands despite the indignation simmering in her chest. They were outcasts now, and if people pitied them, perhaps that was for the best. If it helped them survive, she'd swallow down her pride every morning along with the breakfast that her ring had bought them.

Now Jem slung the sack off his back, less full than Mal expected. "Black wouldn't exchange the month's supplies for anything else. He said that we'd need food eventually."

"Not for another month," said Mal under her breath.

"He did cut us a good deal on these, and some healing supplies," Jem continued, as though he hadn't heard her belligerent mutter. He pulled a stack of neatly folded clothes out of the sack: half a dozen plain shirts, two of them obviously larger to fit Hex and the other four for her and Jem; three pairs of black breeches and three pairs of trousers made of a heavier cloth; and, to Mal's horror, a long dress.

"Mrs. Black added this when she overheard," Jem said.

"What, you just go prancing about trumpeting that I'm a girl?" Mal gingerly picked up the dress, holding it at arm's length between two fingers as though it was something that would suddenly twist and bite her.

"Apparently the story of the three thirds turned out by the *Dragonwing*'s Captain has been making the rounds at the taverns," Jem replied. He cleared his throat, his voice wavering oddly as he continued. "And she gave me these as well, said that you should come down to the shop by the warehouse if you have any questions or would like to buy some new." He passed Mal a smaller drawstring sack, pressing his lips into a thin line, and she realized he was trying not to laugh.

She untied the drawstring and recoiled as though the bag contained live snakes: an assortment of women's undergarments was folded neatly within, and there was even something that Mal thought looked suspiciously like a waist-cincher that many of the women in Haven and Horizon who fancied themselves true ladies wore beneath their dresses. She tossed the bag away from her in disgust. "What good's all this?" she demanded. "A dress won't make Hex better or change the fact that we're banished."

Jem coughed, concealing the last of his mirth, and then sobered at her question. He gathered the tossed bag and deposited it neatly beside the rest of their things. "I couldn't offend Mrs. Black by turning down her gifts, and it might make Black himself more likely to cut us good deals in the future if…"

"If what?" Mal growled, crossing her arms over her chest. The movement made her forearms itch abominably, but it would ruin her glower if she scratched like a dog with fleas.

"If perhaps you wore the dress next time we went to the warehouse," suggested Jem with no hint of humor now.

"Bollocks," said Mal immediately, scowling as fiercely as she could with her bandaged arms driving her mad. "You just want to see me humiliated."

"Mal," said Jem with a hint of reproach. "You really think that?"

She took a deep breath and rubbed at one of her arms. "No," she mumbled finally. "I just…don't want to."

"I have a feeling we're all going to have to do things that we don't much want to in the coming days," Jem replied tiredly.

Mal sighed and sat down in one of the worn chairs. The two chairs and the rough-hewn table along with a wash-basin were the only other furniture in their room, other than the bed with its similarly rough-hewn frame, rope webbing stretched between the beams and a surprisingly comfortable mattress atop it. There had been no question that Hex got the bed, despite his half-formed protests. Sleeping on the hard wooden floor certainly felt different than their hammocks, but their days on deck after mast in the little rigged tent had prepared them and it didn't much bother her anymore. "I'm sorry. I shouldn't snipe at you. It's not your fault we're in this mess."

Jem managed a smile. "This mess is our lives now, so we might as well make the best of it. And yes, it would make things easier if you kept your tongue-lashings reserved for those who deserve it."

Mal returned his smile. "And who's that, do you think?"

He shrugged. "I'm sure you'll know when the time is right." Then he turned his attention to unpacking his newly acquired healing supplies.

She went over to the basin in the corner and washed her face, hoping it would soothe her restlessness. After a moment, she unwrapped the bandages around her left forearm, thinking that maybe washing the patches of skin would help with the itch, and her mouth went dry. The inside of her forearm was nearly covered in scales, some as small as the one she'd pulled from her skin a few days before and others larger than the nail on her thumb. The skin around the scales looked bluish, and when she rubbed a finger against it, the touch sent a shiver through her, as though she prodded at the still-sensitive flesh beneath a scab.

Mal glanced over her shoulder, keeping her arm out of sight, a sick feeling twisting in her stomach. There was no arguing now that she wasn't Seafarer, no possible way to explain away the scales. Why hadn't Calinth and Serena taken her with them? she wondered miserably. Was she some mixed-blood that they disdained? Would any other changes come upon her suddenly, and how would she know what to do? She shivered again, remembering the feeling of Serena's long-fingered hands around her throat, tightening and then snapping whatever it was back into place at the base of her skull.

She had to tell Jem, though the nausea in her stomach roiled at the thought. What if he thought she was a monster? She took a deep breath, trying to tell herself that it was the three of them against the world, no ship to their name, stripped of their future – but the whispering voice in her head pointed out that it would be easier for

Jem to make a way in that world without her, with only Hex to care for. After all, her decision to dive into the storm had touched off all this, the match to the powder, and no matter that she had saved Hex's life. She was a monster, and Jem would see it.

She gritted her teeth and turned, gathering up her courage; but then Hex groaned and Jem moved quickly to press the back of his hand against the prostrate man's forehead. "Fever," he said grimly.

Mal shut her mouth and turned back to the washbasin, quickly rewrapping her bandages. "What can we do?"

"There's an herb called feverwort that would be best," Jem said, already moving toward his healing satchel and laying out ingredients on the table. "But it comes at dear cost."

"You mean we can't afford it," Mal said, her stomach sinking as she glanced at Hex.

"Not right now, we can't, not with all our rings combined." He blew out a breath and raised an eyebrow at her. "I forgot to tell you. I fetched yours before mast, right after you told me where they were."

Mal blinked. "You did?" she repeated stupidly.

"Couldn't just leave them for anyone else," he said. "I had the feeling one of you would be banished, and that meant all of us."

Jem's pronouncement made it sound so simple – one of them meant all of them. She almost told him right then and there about the scales, about Calinth and Serena, about all of it, but Hex groaned again and they both turned their attention to him.

"What can I do?" Mal asked.

"See if one of the serving girls will let you take a kettle of hot water," said Jem, grinding dried leaves in his well-used pestle and mortar.

"Will that help?" She gestured to the crushed leaves, now a greenish powder.

"Hopefully, if he can keep it down," said Jem, his voice clipped now. "I wouldn't ordinarily use this, it's hard on the stomach and can have some nasty side effects, but we don't have much of a choice."

"Because we can't afford feverwort," Mal said. Jem's silence was enough of a reply for her. She drew back her shoulders, tucked the trailing edges of her shirt into her trousers as neatly as she could, and passed a hand over her hair, which was tied back in its neat little tail at the nape of her neck. "Key?" She held out her hand to Jem, and with one hand he slipped the loop of twine over his head and deposited the tarnished key into her palm. She drew back the bolt, opened the door and locked it behind her, the tumblers clanking in protest as they fell into place.

Tucking the key under her shirt as Jem had done, she ran light-footed down the narrow stairs that led down from their room into a hallway, just as narrow, a few doors opening into the more expensive rooms that didn't smell like horses and pigs. The stairs leading down into the common room, which was attached to the tavern proper, were wide enough for two people to pass abreast at least, though Mal had yet to encounter anyone at all on the stairs during their stay.

One of the serving-girls, Meg, straightened from cleaning out the ashes of the common room's fireplace. "Somethin' amiss?"

"Hex has a fever," Mal answered truthfully, "and we need hot water."

Meg tucked back a tendril of her straw-colored hair behind her ear, leaving a smudge of ash on the side of her face. "He's the one who got whipped?"

Mal nodded. "Yes." She decided it wouldn't hurt to try to capitalize on the flash of interest in the girl's eyes. "Our Captain was uncommon cruel, but Hex took it bravely."

The serving girl sucked on her teeth and made a sound of sympathy. "Never understood it, meself."

Mal didn't know whether the girl meant Seafarers in general, the system of punishment aboard ships, or their Captain specifically, so she didn't say anything. Meg didn't seem to expect further explanation, though, wiping her hands on her apron as she walked toward the tavern. "Jus' let me go tell Higgs and I'll draw a kettle right up.

Not sayin' he won't approve, mind, I jus' have to tell him, lets him know I'm honest and all."

Mal bit back a retort – it was a kettle of hot water, not anything extravagant, and after all Higgs knew exactly where they lived in the room over the stable. But Meg bustled back after a few moments, holding out a scrap of vellum in her hand. "Came for you," she said simply, shaking the sealed missive impatiently when Mal recoiled instinctively, thinking of the Captain. After Mal finally took the folded message, she disappeared through the door to the kitchens, a wisp of steam and waft of cooking meat for the common table's dinner escaping before the door swung shut.

Mal looked down at the message in her hand. Who would send a message to *her*? They'd learned to read when they were fourths, necessary to a Seafarer to read charts and do basic figures and take stock of supplies if that was what they were asked to do as they were assigned different duties. Jem had even purchased a few slim hide-bound books at great cost, one of Nuremian poetry and another on different methods of healing.

With a sigh, she slid a finger beneath the wax seal – it was marked with a ring and a few curling lines, reminding Mal of smoke or perhaps wind. The scrap of paper held two brief sentences, written small to conserve the precious vellum, the letters neat and precise:

Mirror Cove, tonight an hour past dusk. Burn this.

There was no signature. Mal frowned and refolded it, tucking it into her belt pouch as Meg reappeared, holding a whistling kettle by the loop used to hang it on the hook over the fire, a rag protecting her hand. "Careful," she cautioned as she transferred it to Mal's grip. "You'll come down for dinner?"

"Ah – I think so," said Mal.

"You should eat more," Meg advised with a motherly air, eyeing Mal's boyish form beneath her shirt and trousers. It took more than a girl wearing trousers to scandalize the serving maids who worked the taverns of Haven, even one as nondescript and sleepy as the Blind Dragon, but now they'd taken to giving Mal little bits of unsolicited advice. They acted like she ought to collect their tidbits of wisdom like a magpie gathering worthless bits of shine, Mal thought a bit ungraciously, though she forced her face into what she hoped was a pleasant expression – or at least not an openly hostile one – and nodded. Meg seemed happy enough with the response, turning back to the fireplace briskly.

Mal carried the hot kettle carefully up to their rooms, walking slow and steady on the stairs like she was creeping out on one of the high yardarms, toeing the ratlines. She was pretty sure that her skin would still burn if she poured hot water onto it, and anyway there was no saltwater unless she wanted to run the half hour to the sea. Turning the key and opening the door one-handed was tricky, but she managed it, her palm beginning to sweat from the heat rising from the kettle.

"Pour it into this cup here," Jem directed with only a brief glance in her direction. She didn't even draw the bolt, hurrying to comply. Even in the time she'd been downstairs – it couldn't have been more than a quarter hour – Hex seemed worse, his breath rasping wetly in his chest and his shoulders damp with sweat. They didn't have a fireplace in their room – she was almost sure that none of the rooms for rent had one.

Jem let the tea cool for a few moments and then managed to get Hex to sip at it. The swelling around his eyes had at least gone down a bit, and the bruises were fading to green and yellow at the edges. Mal watched and felt useless after she'd safely stowed the kettle on a folded rag and bolted the door.

"It's going to get worse before it gets better," Jem said, and Mal wasn't sure whether he was talking to himself, Hex, all three of them or no one at all. She bit her lip.

"Can I do anything?" She thought she already knew the answer, but asked anyway.

"I'll need you to eat and get some rest," Jem said. "I'll stay up with him tonight, but I won't be any use by morning."

Mal sat in one of the chairs by the table and watched Jem work. He applied a salve to the lashes that had torn open again during the long stagger from the piers. Hex's dark hair clung to his forehead in curls as he sweated, panting and flinching every so often, his eyes twitching behind closed lids.

"He's probably started fever-dreaming," Jem said, wiping his hands on a clean cloth and picking a few other packets out of his satchel. "It won't be pleasant."

"I know," Mal replied, a little more sharply than she'd intended. "We saw Rill go mad with fever before he died, remember?"

Rill had gotten caught between the rails when they'd swooped down on a prize through one of the seams. It'd been when they'd just made thirds, just allowed to come on the boarding party if a second thought they were small and fast enough and good with a blade. Mal had heard the wet snapping as the rail of their prize collided with the hull of the larger *Dragonwing*, crushing Rill's leg into a bloody pulp. He'd managed to claw his way onto the deck and even stabbed one of the crew who'd decided to fight in the back of the leg. But he'd died a fortnight later, his voice gone from screaming and the pitiful stump of his leg green and black with rot. She'd felt guilty for weeks afterward, because she'd taunted Rill that she would be aboard the prize faster than he, and she was sure he wouldn't have tried to make the jump so quickly if not for following her closely to prove her wrong.

Mal swallowed down the bile that rose in her throat at her vivid recollection. That wouldn't happen to Hex. He was stronger than Rill had ever been, and besides, he hadn't had a limb sawed off. Her attempts to reassure herself didn't really work, and she drew her legs up onto the edge of the chair, curling her knees to her chest in an attempt to relieve the sick knot in her stomach. The time passed in a strange slow crawl, though it felt like she'd just sat down and blinked when she heard the bell for dinner at the common table.

"Go eat," Jem said, busy again with another tea. He looked pale and drawn around the mouth. Hex murmured something in a broken voice, and Mal fled the room, promising to bring Jem a plate. She took the stairs two at a time, breathing hard; the air in their room had begun to remind her of the sickly smell that lingered about Bonesaw's door and always preceded a death.

"Everythin' all right?" Higgs, the rheumy-eyed owner of the tavern, ate at the common table with any paying customers. Though the Blind Dragon didn't often host rowdy nights of bar brawls, they did have a reputation of a quieter sort: a hot, filling meal could be had at the table for one copper coin, and if the exchange rate was good for the ship's rings at the time a few of any crew might stop in for something that wasn't salted or fish.

Mal slid into a seat a respectful distance away on the long bench. "Our friend tore some of his wounds open again and he's a bit uncomfortable, is all." She didn't want to tell him that Hex had a fever – some people didn't care if it was plainly taken from a wound, they'd turn you out in a trice on your ear, fearful for their own lives.

"Ah, the big lad who took the lashing," said Higgs. He picked up his tankard and drank some ale with a thoughtful air. "Nell will heat some bricks for you."

Mal swallowed. Heated bricks were very nice overall, especially since nights on Haven could get cool with the breeze off the water; but she didn't like the fact that Higgs guessed so near the mark with his offer. Since they didn't have a fireplace, heated bricks could help them sweat the fever out of Hex.

"And," added Higgs in a low voice, almost gentle, "if he needs to sleep by the kitchen fire for a night or two..." He shrugged and lifted his tankard again, his long white whiskers trembling as he swallowed.

Nell, one of the younger serving maids that Mal thought could perhaps be Higgs' granddaughter, brought out a bowl filled to the brim with hearty stew and a thick crust of day-old bread. She set these in front of Mal and then returned a moment later with a tankard of small ale. Mal's stomach rumbled at the savory steam and she burned her tongue a little, not letting it cool, but it tasted almost as good as the meal that the seconds had put together for her before mast.

Halfway through the bowl, she set her crust of bread down, stricken: how could she be enjoying a meal so thoroughly when Hex lay senseless with fever? Then the more practical side of her reasoned that it wouldn't do anyone any good if she starved herself, and she finished the bowl, though she didn't feel quite up for the second helping that Nell eagerly fetched. Instead, she drank the rest of her ale and took the second bowl up to their room with a promise to bring it back down to the kitchens after Jem had finished.

Jem scarfed down the stew sitting by Hex's bedside, very little of his attention diverted by the food.

"You're lucky that cooled on the way up," Mal commented.

Jem didn't reply, his eyes fixed on Hex. The uncomfortable, sick knot grew again in Mal's stomach. The Blind Dragon served dinner right as the sun set; if she left now, she could make it to Mirror Cove without running.

"Going to go for a walk to clear my head," she said to Jem, sliding her borrowed dagger from Hex into the top of her boot, the hilt visible against her trousers.

That, at least, caught his attention. "Since when have you gone for walks to clear your head?"

"Since I can't climb the rigging up into the crow's nest," she replied.

He knew better than to tell her out loud to be careful, but she saw it in his eyes and she nodded. Again, words crawled up her throat like bile, threatening to spill over her lips – she'd always told Jem everything, or *near* everything, and it was mostly habit, or at least that's what she told herself as she firmly pressed her lips together. Instead she said, "Higgs said at dinner that Nell would heat some bricks for Hex."

"Did you ask?" Jem said.

"No. And I don't think he wants any rings, if that's what you mean." She shifted in front of the door. "I don't know why he's being so kind. It makes me…nervous."

"Because you're used to our way of life," said Jem with a hint of weariness. "On the sea, you never give something for nothing."

"That's not how it is," she said in agreement.

"People think different on land."

"Well, I *knew* that." They just hadn't had to rely on anyone's kindness when they were part of the *Dragonwing*'s fierce crew.

"Knowing it and experiencing it are two different things. Like you said, we don't have a ship to go back to."

The loss cut again into Mal's chest like a blade, the pain just as fresh as when she'd heard those fateful words at mast. She held out her hand for Jem's bowl and he gave it to her.

"You could start going by your full name, if you want," he said.

The notion of having three syllables without a white shirt made Mal shudder at the wrongness of it. She hadn't been able to bring herself to change out of her gray shirt, either – she'd expected the Captain to forbid them from wearing gray, or to take their shirts, but somehow the fact that their proud symbol of their rank seemed below his notice or caring stung more.

"I'll return this to the kitchens," she said instead. She cursed herself for a coward as she trotted lightly down the stairs again. After leaving the bowl on the table, nesting it neatly into another dirty trencher, she slipped out the front door of the Blind Dragon, passing the handful of customers drinking ale at the tables, no one giving her a second glance.

Mirror Cove had earned its name from the breakwater too distant to see at the mouth of the cove that smoothed the waves from the sea before the water came to lap against the white sands. On days with no wind, the cove reflected the clouds above with perfect symmetry, and at night it looked as though the horizon disappeared, the constellations picked out in pinpricks of silver light on the silken water. There weren't any other crews in port at the moment, but nonetheless Mal hid in the shadow of a particularly tall sand tree, its trunk hiding her from full view of the cove proper.

The waters of the cove looked lavender, the sky still holding the last rays of the day's light. Mal crouched down, brushing her fingers against the hilt of Hex's dagger for reassurance. She scanned the white sands of the cove, silvery now in the fading light, and after a few moments a slender figure walked unconcernedly down the beach, stopping every now and again to gaze out at the pretty, still water. Mal waited until the figure drew closer, and then she straightened in the shadow of the sand tree as recognition swept through her.

Kalinda did not wear the white shirt of a first; she wore instead breeches of a shocking bright blue and a bottle-green shirt, a scarlet sash about her waist and her wind-whistler's bandolier across her chest. She carried a well-worn leather satchel, its narrow strap slung opposite her bandolier. Mal didn't see any weapons, but she knew full well that the first could whistle up a wind to snap her bones just as easy as drawing a sword.

A prickle of suspicion raised the hairs on the back of her neck: more than once, she'd wondered if Kalinda were the Captain's lover. Would he send her to finish what he'd wanted to start at mast? Then just as quickly she flushed with shame, remembering Kalinda's hands quickly tucking the edges of her cut shirt into her breeches to preserve her modesty, and the calm intent in Kalinda's voice when she doused Mal in that last bucket of seawater against his orders. If anything, she'd used her position with the Captain to toe the line, doing things that perhaps would have earned other sailors a reprimand.

Kalinda walked down the beach and then paused barely a stone's throw from the sand tree, deliberately turning her back and looking out across the water as if in thought.

"Hog's balls," muttered Mal. She pulled back her shoulders and strode forward. Kalinda didn't break her contemplative pose until

Mal stopped next to her and held up the little folded piece of parchment. "You write this?"

"You were supposed to burn that," Kalinda replied.

"I'll take that as a yes."

"It has a wind-whistler seal, girl. Use your head." The authority in Kalinda's voice crackled like the air just before a storm.

Mal crossed her arms over her chest. "Not like I've gotten many messages from wind-whistlers before," she muttered belligerently.

After a moment, Kalinda chuckled briefly and shook her head. "Good to see that being banished hasn't broken your spirit."

"Not yet at least," replied Mal. She turned to face the other woman. When they were standing on even ground, she was taller than Kalinda by over half a head. Somehow the height difference between them hadn't stood out so starkly on the ship.

"Hex still alive?" Kalinda asked. The light of the rising moon gleamed on her dark skin.

"He took a fever just within the past hours," Mal said. Hope rose within her. Maybe Kalinda would be willing to loan them the rings for feverwort – it would still be an astronomical sum, even to a first, but she seemed to care about Hex's welfare…

"Don't look at me with those eyes," Kalinda said with a sigh. "I can't give you rings. I shouldn't even be giving you this." She looped the strap of the satchel over her head and held it out to Mal, shaking it a little when Mal glanced at it dubiously. "It's not going to bite."

"What is it?" Mal said slowly. The satchel felt strangely heavy as she took hold of the straps. She weighed it in one hand, feeling something large and curved pressed against the side of the bag, the leather made supple after years of use.

"Hex's mother found you," Kalinda said abruptly. Her face was unreadable. "You looked uncommon blue as a babe. She said it was because you were left out, a foundling. Kellorin – the Captain – he loved her, and he let her keep you more for her sake than yours."

Mal swallowed hard and barely dared to breathe, standing very still as though she'd frighten away the new, precious story of her origin like a skittish cat.

"We were friends, back in the day. Close. Almost like you three." Kalinda nodded, her dark eyes fixed on a point beyond Mal's shoulder. "We had letters left in each other's keeping, spelled so that they would only open if the writer died."

Mal restrained her low whistle: that was an impressive bit of magery, and no mistake. Most of them knew enough to conjure a *taebramh* light, but that was all. Some didn't even have enough for that, and there was no shame in it. They fought with blades, not runes or spells. Anyone with a lick of talent went straight to wind-whistling, but that needed a lot more than just *taebramh*.

"That satchel was stored in Nimara's stash," continued Kalinda. And then she fell silent and crossed her arms.

"What's…in it?" Mal asked.

"No idea," said Kalinda promptly. "Though I suspect some of Nimara's better skrells are in there – she certainly didn't give them to me," she amended, naming the peculiar little pipes that wind-whistlers used for most of their work. "She thought perhaps that Hex would have some talent."

"Hex, a wind whistler?" Mal almost laughed at the absurdity of it.

"Most are women, but that doesn't mean men can't pick it up if they try," Kalinda replied calmly. "And Nimara was better than me. She just happened to get herself killed."

Mal stared at the satchel in her hand. "Sounds like this belongs to Hex, not me."

"She was very specific. It was for both of you. She loved you like her own, you know, even though you were a strange child."

Mal blinked. "You have a lot of opinions for someone who never said more than two words to me before I jumped into the storm."

Kalinda looked out over the water. "Thought it was best that way." She didn't look at Mal, but she waited. Mal found her hands acting almost of their own accord, her fingers finding the loop of waxed string and cool, round brass that held the satchel closed. It took her a moment to work the string over the metal, and she sank down onto her knees in the soft sand to better be able to slide the contents out of the satchel without fear of dropping them. Her mind felt curiously blank, though her hands trembled a little.

Light bloomed over them. Mal squinted up at the *taebramh* light hovering over her. Kalinda watched with undisguised interest, her eyes fixed on the open satchel. Mal thought that she'd be curious too if Jem or Hex left her something now and she couldn't open it for a dozen years. She dipped her hand inside the satchel, finding that hard, rounded object, cool to the touch even through its light cloth wrapping and with a vaguely brittle feel. The object was a little larger than both her cupped hands, and it glimmered in the *taebramh* light as she pulled away a corner of the wrapping. The top of the object, the inside of the curve, was a pale creamy color, swirled here and there with a bit of blue. The other side of the object gleamed darkly – at first Mal thought it was black, but as she turned it in the light she realized it was a very dark red, flecked with bits of gold. The swirls of blue on the interior of the shell – for that was what it was, a shell, or part of one – corresponded with curls of ruby on the exterior.

It was the most beautiful thing that Mal had ever seen, and she held her breath as she turned it over in her hands, pulling it free of the rest of the cloth. Her fingertips tingled strangely. Did the egg have some magical property? She heard Kalinda's intake of breath, suddenly very close; and she tried not to jump as she looked up to find Kalinda crouched opposite her, eyes riveted to the piece of shell. Mal resisted the strange jealous urge to move further away from Kalinda, clutching the piece of egg. Instead, with effort, she said, "What kind?"

What kind of creature hatched from such an egg? A thrill ran through her as she thought that perhaps this was part of a dragon-egg, though the practical part of her mind retorted that it would be very small for a dragon-egg. She'd only ever listened to the tales of mythical beasts with half an ear; practicing climbing the rigging or memorizing the constellations for navigation had always seemed a better use of time to her. Now she wished she had listened closer.

Kalinda sat back on her heels, her awestruck expression fading into thoughtfulness. "Merrow, I think."

"Merrow?" Mal repeated, losing her breath as realization crashed into her. What a fool she'd been, what a ninny-headed, cotton-eared sparrow! Most Seafarers discounted the tales of Merrow folk as pretty stories to entertain the lads during those boring stretches between raids. There were always one or two old salts, though, who claimed to have seen a Merrow-maid or heard their song during treacherous passages, luring the ship toward the rocks.

"I saw one, once," Kalinda said with the same strange abruptness as the beginning of the conversation. She looked at Mal strangely. "Right after Nimara brought you onboard, actually."

Mal didn't know whether she was going to retch or laugh. All the pieces fell into place: the ruby scale still rattling in her belt pouch, her ability to breathe underwater, Calinth and Serena appearing as the kraken approached to make her its meal. She wrapped the egg in a daze – *her* egg, a voice in her head corrected. *Her* egg.

"I should go." Kalinda stood and brushed the sand from her blue breeches.

"I...thank you." Mal set the egg carefully on top of the satchel and stood. She wished briefly she hadn't spent the silver ring, because that and more was what she owed the first for giving her this strange key that made so many other things fall into place. Before she could think too much, she scrabbled in her belt pouch until she found the scale she'd pulled from her skin. Feeling a bit silly, she held it out in her palm to Kalinda. It glittered like a ruby in the *taebramh* light.

With a twist of her fingers, Kalinda extinguished the light, but Mal glimpsed the flash of surprise that darkened quickly into avarice. They raided for treasure, after all, and firsts took their share of the prize no less than any of the crew.

"Thank you," repeated Mal, still holding out the scale.

Kalinda took it delicately from her palm between two fingers. She held it up to the moonlight and then carefully transferred it into one of the small pouches on her bandolier. She turned as if to leave, and then said over her shoulder, "The zephyrs have told me there was a dragon, in the Old Lands."

Mal opened her mouth to say that there hadn't been a dragon in centuries – the scavenged bones of Bratchith the Blue had formed the hull of the *Dreadfire*, the youngest of the dragon ships. Bratchith the Blue at least had the courtesy to wing out to sea before plunging into waves and dying.

"Zephyrs don't lie," Kalinda said, seeing the disbelief on Mal's face. She glanced down at the half-wrapped egg, straightened and nodded to Mal. "Keep those two boys alive, Mallora."

She turned and walked away down the silver strand of the cove, no waves to wash away her footprints, leaving Mal staring after her with the night breeze sighing in her ear.

Chapter 24

"Perhaps you should get some rest, my lady," Eamon said to the Queen. The healer had only lately risen from his own sickbed after torture at the hands of Mab when he refused to do her bidding any longer, but he had helped the Seelie healer Sage save Sayre's life. He had been sure enough of Sayre's improvement the following evening to allow him to be moved carefully to the Queen's own chambers. The main chamber had been busy with the comings and goings of Glasidhe messengers to the other Courts and novice healers bringing supplies to Eamon. Sayre lay on a low pallet by the fire, now resting as comfortably as they could manage to make him.

Guinna watched Andraste carefully. The Queen hadn't said much since the attack, never leaving Sayre's side, her face pale but composed. She gave no sign that she'd even heard Eamon.

"I think Eamon is right, my queen," Guinna said with gentle firmness. She'd caught a few hours of sleep the night before, reasoning that *one* out of them all had to keep their wits about them, but even that had been fitful rest curled in one of the armchairs by the fire. She hadn't wanted to leave Sayre and the Queen. "You should rest."

Andraste raised her blue eyes to Eamon. "You will rouse me immediately if anything should change."

Eamon bowed his head in acceptance. "Of course."

The Queen stood. She still wore the shirt and breeches that she had donned before their fateful trip to the practice yards, blood staining the hem of her shirt and dirt caked on her breeches. Guinna stood as well, her legs protesting stiffly. She followed the Queen into her bedchamber. "Perhaps a bath, my lady?"

Andraste sighed and all the regal rigidity left her body. She put a hand against the closed door, shoulders bowed. "Please stop calling me that, Guinna. I feel like I'm suffocating." She rubbed one hand across her face, leaving a trail of grime. "And you aren't my lady-in-waiting, you have to understand that."

"I'm not," Guinna agreed, already moving toward the bathing-pool sunk into one corner of the chamber. She hadn't seen any of the other chambers outfitted thus and had to conclude that it was a particular modification that Andraste had crafted herself. "But as one of your Three, I still need to ensure that you're taking care of yourself."

"And who will make sure that *you* are taken care of?" Andraste said with a weary smile.

"Oh, I'm sure that someone will," Guinna replied as she set the bathing-pool to filling with gently steaming water. She pushed away the image of Merrick that arose in her mind's-eye. Before the attack had started, she'd glimpsed him kissing the Valkyrie commander with undisguised passion. The sight had only confirmed her sinking suspicion. Any kindling of romance between them would only cause them both pain – and perhaps create conflict between their two Courts. Besides, it had been a silly thought, something to which she could cling after being swept adrift by the storm of Mab's madness. Now she had Andraste and Sayre – and her entire Court, the ragged survivors of the Mad Queen's rage.

A flurry of movement in her peripheral vision alerted Guinna that Andraste had indeed decided to take a bath; the Queen tossed her filthy shirt and breeches in a pile on the floor. "Those probably need to be burned."

Guinna focused on adding sweet-smelling oil to the water in the bathing-pool. She kept her eyes courteously averted as Andraste slid into the bath, the water instantly darkening as grungy rings radiated from the Queen's slender form. Though her own body ached for a hot bath and sleep, she walked over to the wardrobe and selected a long, soft sleeping-shirt, bringing it over to the little table by the bath.

"I've been thinking," Andraste said, the edges of her voice ragged with tiredness now but her face more animated than Guinna had seen since Sayre's wounding. "Do you think we could reason with these Exiles?"

"In what way?" Guinna asked, folding her legs and sitting by the table.

Andraste dipped beneath the water and combed her fingers through her wet hair. "In the way one usually reasons with someone, with words. In the end I would want a treaty from them."

"A treaty?" Guinna tried not to stare. "Andraste, they just tried to kill you."

"Only because they seek revenge on my sister," replied Andraste. She scrubbed a patch of particularly stubborn dirt on her left elbow. "Maybe if I explained that I'm not her, they won't want revenge anymore."

"Or they've been driven mad by their time in the mortal world without the proper protections."

"It's a possibility," Andraste allowed. "But I should have been driven mad by my time as Malravenar's assassin, yet here I am."

"The High Queen used the Lethe stone to restore you."

"She did." The Queen nodded in agreement. "All the same, I was offered a chance at redemption. I see no reason why I should not offer them the same."

Guinna remembered the howl of the frigid wind that had screamed through the practice yards, Andraste's face white with fury.

The wind had thrown the Exiled archer none too gently onto the frozen ground before her. Two Unseelie Guards had bound his hands, though Guinna had thought that the Queen meant to kill the attacker right then and there. Her slender figure had seemed much taller and whiter amidst the swirl of snow, but then the howling wind had suddenly died, and the Queen ordered the men in a low voice to take the white-haired man to the dungeons.

"Just because I am the heir to the throne my sister held for centuries does not mean I should do everything as she did," Andraste said. The gravity of her statement was somewhat ruined by a pile of iridescent soap bubbles that detached from a little pile and floated into her dark hair, sticking there like a cluster of transparent pearls.

Guinna suppressed a shiver. "No. It does not."

Andraste smoothed her wet hair and then rinsed her face, her fingers traveling lightly over the scars on her cheeks. "He didn't give me any other scars," she said quietly. "Finnead he spared because he found him beautiful. He carved my face because he said it would always remind me that I belonged to him...that my soul was black and ugly because of my deeds."

"We could find something to cover them, some cosmetic or rune," offered Guinna.

Andraste smiled. "No. I will keep them." She leaned back in the water, her dark hair spread like a nimbus about her head. "I will use them as a different kind of reminder."

As the young Queen rinsed her hair and began to braid it, Guinna ventured, "What else do you want to change?"

Andraste made a thoughtful sound. "Not all of it should rightfully be called change, I suppose. Some of it is restoring the Court to something like what it was when we were young."

"Before you were kidnapped."

"Before I was taken prisoner." She nodded. Her eyes darkened for a moment, but then she straightened and reached for the drying cloth folded at the rim of the bathing pool. She climbed out and wrapped herself in the cloth, her wet skin gleaming alabaster. "Mab allowed women to try for their swords, so that is one change I don't have to make. I think there should be greater friendship between all the Courts, so I have to think on what allowed our natural rivalry to deepen into such bitterness."

"I think perhaps some of that has been healed by fighting side by side during the war," Guinna said.

"Fighting and dying," Andraste agreed darkly.

They sat in silence for a few moments, watching the runes at the edges of the bathing-pool do their work, the grayish water spiraling into them and disappearing.

"You should wash too," Andraste said.

Guinna glanced at her. Sitting like this, cross-legged and speaking as friends, she could almost believe that the past centuries hadn't happened – that they were still young and innocent, Finn still a squire and Ramel his page, Rye just returned from the North with her fascinating heathen ideas. Then she felt the twinge of pain through her bond with Sayre – it strengthened when he neared consciousness. She paused as it lingered, wondering if he was going to wake up, but then it faded into a dull ache again as he slid back into sleep.

"I think he'll wake up tomorrow," said Andraste. The Queen yawned, an oddly vulnerable sight. She drew her legs up to her chest and rested her chin on her knees. "Go on then. You can borrow a sleeping shirt."

Guinna pushed herself to her feet and slid out of her clothes, feeling her cheeks color at her nakedness. She had none of the intrepid shamelessness of the Vyldgard women, her Court sensibilities still firmly in place despite her wearing of breeches and shirts. The warm water, just shy of too hot, wrapped around her body soothingly. She felt her tense muscles loosen as she quickly washed her face and hair.

As Guinna wrapped herself in the drying cloth, Andraste said in a low voice, "Do you think Rye is alive?"

Guinna took a deep breath. She'd been expecting this question, but all her logical, well-reasoned replies deserted her. She swallowed hard. "I hope so."

"It isn't impossible," the Queen said.

"We do not know all the curses and spells used by the bone sorcerer and the Enemy," said Guinna.

"Gryttrond and Malravenar," Andraste said firmly. "Naming a thing diminishes its terrible power."

Guinna wasn't sure she completely agreed, but she held her tongue. Exhaustion pressed down on her as she climbed out of the bath. Andraste had already fetched another sleeping shirt for her, which she pulled over her head unceremoniously. She braided her hair, just as Andraste had. Most of the women their age in the Court had the same habit.

"If Rye is alive," she said, feeling almost reckless, "will you make her the third one of our Three?"

Andraste drew in a deep breath. She shook her head. "No," she said sadly. "That would not be fair to her. If she is alive, she will have the choice. She wanted nothing more than to return to the *ulfdrengr*, and the Vyldgard is the closest that remains."

"So then who will be our third?" Guinna pressed.

"That is one of the things I am thinking of changing," murmured the Queen.

A strange, blind panic clutched at Guinna at Andraste's words, and she gasped at the force of the unexpected reaction, as strong as a physical blow. Andraste looked at her and her eyes widened.

"Oh, no!" she said quickly. "I would never – you two will be with me always, or until you wish to be parted from me – I did not mean…" She trailed off as she gathered Guinna into her arms and embraced her fiercely.

"I will never wish to be parted from you," Guinna mumbled into the Queen's shoulder, feeling both like a silly child being comforted after a bad dream and like some prized, useful creature, perhaps a warhorse or a hunting hound. The two sensations wrestled in her chest, and Guinna finally decided to feel simply like a cherished friend, a trusted confidante.

"But you both should know," said Andraste, her voice trembling slightly, "that you have the choice. And I would not punish you."

Guinna drew back. "You truly do mean to be different than the other Queens."

"Not so different from Queen Vell, I don't think," returned Andraste. She yawned again. "Enough serious talk." She motioned to her bed. There was more than enough room for both of them once they'd slid beneath the silken sheets, and besides, Guinna remembered all the women sleeping close together for comfort on their journey to the White City. This felt no different. With a flick of her wrist, Andraste extinguished the lights, and they both settled with a sigh into the waiting arms of sleep.

Guinna awoke what seemed like five minutes later to a knocking at the door. She swallowed and scrunched her nose – her dry mouth and stiff muscles told a story of at least a few hours' sleep.

"I think Eamon or one of his apprentices will be telling us that Sayre is waking up," said Andraste from over by her wardrobe. She tossed soft gray breeches and a blue shirt onto the bed. "Those should fit you, though the shirt will be a little long."

"Just as well," yawned Guinna. She took a moment to stretch, noting all the small aches of her sore body. Perhaps her centuries were beginning to tell. She wondered idly when mortals started feeling aches and pains – they barely lived a century, if they were lucky, though most that traveled into Faeortalam lived longer than usual for their kind.

Andraste had already dressed in black breeches and a dove-gray shirt. Guinna realized that the clothing once thought scandalous for women in their Court was fast becoming the Queen's everyday attire. She reminded herself that she'd nearly died running from Mab's hounds partly because she'd been running in skirts, which wasn't nearly as easy as moving in breeches.

She dressed quickly, feeling for her bond with Sayre. She'd learned the rhythms of his thoughts, felt distantly like vibrations along a length of spider silk; when he was asleep, the vibrations fell into the long, slow rhythm of deep breathing. Sometimes the sensation made her a bit sleepy herself, if she was awake and he was deeply dreaming. She wondered if the other Three in the other Courts experienced their bond in the same manner. Would it be impolite to ask? Perhaps the Seer would be willing to discuss it; he hadn't been raised with the stiff, formal courtesy of the Courts. She wondered, too, if they felt their own Queens, or if the connection was mostly one-way and with each other, as it felt like for them.

"He's not awake yet," she told the Queen, pulling the shirt over her head and sighing as it came down to her knees. "But I think perhaps he will be soon." She felt little plucks at the connection, like the stirring of a restless sleeper.

"Here. With a belt, it will look a bit like a dress. You'll start a new fashion," Andraste said, rummaging in her wardrobe and fishing out a woven silver belt picked with sapphires that matched the blue of Guinna's borrowed shirt.

Guinna knew better than to tell the Queen that the belt was much too fine for her to wear, and she did have to admit that the affect was quite pleasing. She pulled on her boots, brushing some dust from them.

"I'm going to have a council," Andraste said into the silence as she finished braiding her hair.

"A council with the other queens?" Guinna asked, sliding her fingers through her own hair.

"No." Andraste shook her head. "As the third one of my Three – I haven't quite figured out how it will work, exactly – I'm going to have a council, chosen by the people of the Court as their representatives to me."

Guinna narrowed her eyes. "Have you been talking to the Bearer and the Seer?"

The Queen glanced at her. "Yes." She shrugged. "We think we are so superior to the mortals, and yet it has been mortals who have saved our world from destruction." She raised an eyebrow. "Why shouldn't we look to them for some ideas now and again?"

"It's an admirable idea," said Guinna slowly, eyeing the Queen and trying to think of the best way not to offend her.

The Queen saved her the trouble. "But you do not approve."

Guinna swallowed. "It is just that – how *many* will be on the council? If they are all a part of your Three, will they be…connected, as we are?" The thought of a dozen strangers intruding into their sacred bond prompted a feeling of nausea and vague vertigo.

"Oh, my dear, *no,*" Andraste said, her eyes wide. "I would never do that to you and Sayre."

"Perhaps…perhaps there is a third that you could choose, elected by the Court?" Guinna offered weakly.

"That in itself will not be enough, I don't think," the Queen replied. She glanced at the door. "It must not have been very urgent."

Guinna checked her bond again as she finished braiding her hair. "Sayre is stirring but still not fully awake." She took a deep breath. "Not enough for *what*, my lady?"

Andraste frowned slightly, cocking her head to the side.

"Choosing the third by a vote. You said it wasn't enough. It isn't enough for *what*?" Guinna clarified.

The Queen pressed her lips together for a long moment. Finally, she said, "To heal the divisions made by my sister." She raised her eyes to Guinna and then looked away. "Right after the High Queen brought me back into my right mind, I thought that perhaps I would be able to refuse the crown somehow. I thought that maybe it was time that our Court ruled themselves."

An icy chill slipped down Guinna's spine. "Why would you think such a thing?"

Andraste smiled sadly. "Tyr led the rebellion after Rye was gone precisely because Mab refused him the freedom of choice. That wound still festers with Dryden and Evangeline, and perhaps even Tyr." At Guinna's look of incomprehension, the Queen quickly launched into an explanation. "Oh, Evangeline is another Exile who attacked the Paladin's Tower. Really, she was attacking Tyr. He survived, mostly because the Vyldretning and her wolf went straight to the Tower along with the Valkyrie commander. They knew somehow that he was vulnerable when the messengers brought them the news of the attacks. Perhaps they were more concerned about the Paladin than Tyr, but they saved his life all the same." The Queen settled back into her thread of thought. "And then the war against Malravenar claimed many lives. If Mab had taken the threat of the Enemy seriously much sooner, perhaps it would not have come to that. *That* wound still festers. Then, my sister went mad and tortured half our Court, killing those who dared speak against her, and it was only her death that stopped it."

"That wound still festers," Guinna finished quietly. Her bones ached with the truth of the Queen's words. They were broken and sundered, all of them marked by scars upon their skin or in their minds, seared by memories they could never forget, battered by the vagaries of war and the terrible wrath of a capricious, cruel monarch.

"Those, and a thousand other smaller cuts that I cannot even name," Andraste said heavily. She raised her chin and met Guinna's eyes. "I need to show our people that I am not my sister. I need to show them that I will listen to them, that they are not merely pawns to me." Her mouth thinned. "It doesn't help that I spent the last few centuries hunting them."

"Do you remember any of it?" Guinna ventured. Though the Queen's words unsettled her, she nevertheless felt a spark of hope. *This* was the Andraste she remembered from the days of their youth: impassioned, searching for answers, willing to take risks.

"Sometimes," Andraste replied darkly, and fell silent.

"We are here to help bear that burden," Guinna said into the quiet. She tugged at the hem of the gray shirt, bereft of skirts to smooth. "If you wish it, that is, my lady."

"You and Sayre are already burdened beyond what I would ever want a friend to bear," the Queen said.

"I am glad to hear you think of us as friends," Guinna said carefully, "but you must also remember, my Queen, that we are here to serve you and our Court as best we can. If helping you to bear the burden of these memories is part of our duty, then we will bear it gladly."

Andraste's face softened. For a moment, save the scars, she looked as young as when she had sat by her sister's side at the high dais in Darkhill, those merry nights of radiance long past. Guinna felt a pain in her chest, like a splinter sliding through her ribs. At first she thought it was the nostalgia, the grief for what they had lost, made sharp again by Andraste's restoration. But then the pain intensified sharply, and she gasped. Another starburst of pain pulsed in her leg. She realized belatedly that the sensation thrummed through her connection with Sayre, her body aching in response. Did the Queen feel it as well? Andraste seemed too calm to have felt the sudden phantom sensations.

"Sayre is awake," Guinna said. It was hard to gather enough breath for the words: the stabbing pain in her side made it hard to breathe. Why was she feeling this now, not when it had happened? She thought back to the training yard and to her surprise her memory supplied her with the feeling of numb impact, like someone had struck her on the side and in the leg, but there hadn't been any pain. Maybe that had been what Sayre had felt in the moment. She'd never been wounded that badly; the closest she'd ever come was being knocked off her *faehal* by the *garrelnost* in the forest, and a few minor scrapes from riding out in the final battle against Malravenar's forces.

For one not trained to hold a sword from her youth, she had been remarkably lucky in the war.

The Queen walked toward the door of her bedchamber, Guinna following. She had to force herself not to limp: her leg worked perfectly fine, but her mind kept telling her to favor it. Stars above, how did the other Threes of the Seelie and the Vyldgard function in battle? Granted, they had centuries more practice, but they'd been new to being one of the Three at some point.

The fire in the main chamber crackled gaily, the room much warmer than the cool bedchamber. Eamon glanced up as they entered, nodding to the Queen and then resuming his work grinding herbs in his mortar and pestle. Andraste knelt by Sayre's side without hesitation. Guinna clenched her jaw and tried not to give in to the nearly overwhelming impulse to collapse in a chair and clutch her leg and side. Sayre's eyes glittered in the firelight. He tried to move when Andraste knelt, but she shook her head and laid a gentle hand on his shoulder.

"No need for that," she said, her soft voice still carrying authority. Her white hand moved from his shoulder to cover one of his hands. "I am glad to see you awake, Sayre."

Sayre's lips curled slightly in a dry smile, as though he wanted to comment on the very lackluster nature of his alertness. Guinna walked softly behind the Queen, allowing herself to put a hand on the table and lean on it next to Eamon.

"He is in pain," Guinna said in a low, urgent voice to the healer.

Eamon didn't spare her a glance as he measured a careful silver spoonful of the fine grayish powder into a copper cup. "This will take the edge off it," he replied quietly, his voice not unkind.

"May I help?" Andraste asked, looking up as Eamon approached with the cup in hand. The healer showed no surprise at her request, handing her the cup.

"He needs to drink all of it," he told the Queen. Andraste nodded and busied herself with propping Sayre up so that he could drink, a slow and laborious process. Guinna winced as agony flashed through her side. She wondered if she could distance herself from their connection by ignoring it somehow, but the very thought felt disloyal.

"You're feeling it too, yes?" Eamon asked, his eyes flicking to her leg and then her face.

She realized she was indeed favoring the leg with her posture, not putting any weight at all on it; and the healer was clearly versed in the concept of the bond between the Three. She nodded. He handed her a little packet.

"Chew one leaf every few hours. You'll feel when it wears off. It will help relax your mind. It might even help him as well." He nodded at Sayre, who was sweating and gray-faced as he drank the last of the concoction in the copper cup, the Queen quietly encouraging him.

"He'll feel it too?" Guinna said suspiciously, glancing at the square of paper in her palm.

Eamon angled them both away from Sayre and the Queen, leaning close to Guinna. "He has little control over anything right now. His body is struggling just to survive. I believe the worst has passed, barring infection," he amended, "but his bond with you is basically just reflex right now, transmitting everything he is feeling. And you feeling his pain is only feeding it, if you understand my meaning."

"I'm doing my best to follow," Guinna admitted. "How do you know this?"

"Not all wounds are visible," Eamon replied enigmatically.

Guinna almost told him that he hadn't answered her question, that he hadn't explained how he'd developed this knowledge of the connection between the Three, but Sayre settled back with a sigh, Andraste holding up the empty copper cup for Eamon's inspection. The healer turned away. Guinna opened the little packet. The leaves – fresh, not dried, which suggested that Eamon had obtained them *after* Sayre had been wounded – tasted faintly of mint, her tongue and cheek tingling vaguely. It was odd but not unpleasant, and the pain of Sayre's wounds receded almost instantly. Sayre sighed.

Guinna walked over to his side quickly, suddenly afraid that she'd somehow hurt him, but some of the tension eased out of his face, and he nodded at her sleepily. That slight motion set her at ease. She tucked the leaf into her cheek and nodded in return.

Andraste leaned forward and kissed Sayre on the forehead, a tender gesture that took Guinna by surprise – and Eamon too, though the healer recovered quickly. Sayre had already drifted into sleep, but Guinna thought she might tell him when he next woke that he'd garnered a kiss from their Queen. She smiled at the thought.

The Queen stood and said to Eamon, "Please convey my thanks to all the healers who have helped in the past hours."

"I will, my lady," Eamon said, bowing from the waist. "And if I may, I must say that the smith Thea and the mortal Quinn also deserve recognition for their quick action. Without their help, I am not certain that Sayre would have survived."

"They will also receive tokens of my gratitude," Andraste replied with a graceful smile.

For the second time, Eamon's surprise fractured his calm demeanor for just an instant. "My lady, I require no payment for my services. It is my duty and my honor to serve you."

"I did not say it was payment," said the Queen, still smiling. "From time to time, I believe it is my right to bestow small gestures to those who have performed admirably in my service."

Eamon said nothing more, merely bowing again, deeper this time.

"Guinna, if you would accompany me? I wish to send a few messages that will require Glasidhe messengers."

"Of course, my lady," Guinna said, following the Queen again to the door.

In the passageway, Andraste sighed, her regal mask falling away. She glanced at Guinna. "I'd like to hear your thoughts on what Eamon and his healers would appreciate, as well as Thea and Quinn."

She tilted her head, the lights of the passageway gleaming on her dark, silken braid. "Quinn protected me. He did not move as though he were injured, but did you hear of anything?"

"I've been with you, my lady, so I haven't had the chance to inquire," Guinna said honestly, "but I will ask. I think the Vyldgard would know."

The Queen nodded. "Thank you. Now, we must see if we can gather enough Glasidhe to send out a summons to the entire Court." She drew her shoulders back, her queenly mien falling back into place. "It is time we move forward. I will tell them about the council, and we will depart for Darkhill at the next full moon."

Guinna quickly calculated in her head. The last full moon had been merely a few days ago, so that gave Sayre and their other wounded almost a full month to recover before the journey. She hoped it would be enough time.

"It is time for us to honor our past by drawing our Court toward a new age of prosperity," Andraste said with the air of practicing the phrase, tasting it on her tongue and nodding at its sound.

Guinna smiled. Again hope rose in her chest at the young Queen's words. "I could not agree more, my lady."

Chapter 25

Quinn rolled his shoulder and eyed the doorframe thoughtfully. He glanced over at Liam and silently walked over to the door. Itching stitches were the absolute worst. He rolled his back against the angle of the doorframe, sighing at the mingled relief and pain.

"You look like a cat scratching its back," commented Liam, raising one eyebrow.

"Dude, they *itch*, and I can't reach them," Quinn replied, repositioning himself slightly to reach the last few inches of the cut. Thea had fairly dragged him to the healing ward when she'd discovered his injury, despite his protests. She was *strong*.

"You could just ignore the itch like a normal human being," Liam replied.

"You and I both know that I'm not normal," he retorted. "Adapt and overcome, man."

The door opened behind him and he nearly fell through the frame, catching himself just in time. Finnead walked into the room, glancing at Quinn bemusedly. Quinn narrowed his eyes at Liam's smirk: he was pretty sure that Liam would've felt Finnead's close proximity. The lack of warning wasn't *quite* the same as a blatant setup, but he still shook his head at Liam.

"We're leaving in the morning," Finnead said – a bit unnecessarily, because they all knew the countdown to the expedition's departure. It felt like there was a giant clock ticking away inside their collective consciousness. Quinn wasn't exactly sure how he felt it, but he did.

Liam nodded. "How are you feeling?"

Finnead tilted his head. "I believe I should be the one asking you that question."

Liam looked sharply at Quinn. Quinn pushed away from the door and crossed his arms over his chest. "Why are you giving me the evil eye?"

"He didn't tell me anything," Finnead said, glancing between the two of them. "But even if he had, he would only be fulfilling his duties as a friend." He motioned to the two of them. "Come, let's sit down and discuss this."

Trust the too-pretty, pointy-eared Mr. Perfect to come in and commandeer the room like it was his, Quinn thought grumpily, but he walked over to the table anyway, taking a seat beside Liam and opposite Finnead. Even if he and Liam poked at each other sometimes, he wanted it to be abundantly clear whose side he was on. Even though Finnead seemed a lot less brooding-tragic-hero since Vell had lifted his memories with the Lethe stone, Quinn still didn't really like him. He hadn't forgotten the heartfelt conversation with Tess during the ride across the Deadlands.

"I hear you saved the Unseelie Queen during the Exiled attack," Finnead said to Quinn, his perfect face expressionless as a marble carving.

"I thought you weren't here to pay me compliments," Quinn replied, just enough levity in his voice to bring it to the right side of too harsh.

Finnead smiled, unruffled. "It isn't a compliment when it is merely an observation of fact."

Quinn narrowed his eyes. He felt like there was something going on behind the scenes that he didn't know about, something he couldn't quite grasp happening behind the curtain. "I wouldn't say I *saved* the Unseelie Queen," he said grudgingly. "I just knocked her down when she froze up. Not *literally* froze, that came later, but she was just standing there, and I couldn't let her get shot."

Finnead said nothing, just staring at him with those ridiculously blue eyes. Quinn fought the urge to snort – because really, it was *unfair*. The Sidhe as a whole possessed supernatural beauty appropriate to their status as Fae, but Finnead just seemed to have been given an extra dose of fairy dust or whatever it was that made them all so attractive. In all honesty, Quinn couldn't really blame Tess for falling head over heels. He bristled a little more at the idea of Liam's little sister – thus, *his* little sister – contending with the cold arrogance of this incarnation of perfection.

"Are you here to talk to Liam about his problems or not?" he said finally, the silence making him notice his uncomfortable stitches even more. At least if they were talking he had a distraction.

Liam sighed. Finnead leaned back in his chair, glancing between the two of them again, as though he were measuring something. Finally, the dark-haired Knight nodded.

"I feel it sometimes," Finnead said. "Especially if I am awake and you are sleeping."

Liam put his elbows on the table and leaned forward. "How much can you see?" he asked heavily.

"Enough," Finnead replied.

"That's not much of an answer," said Quinn. "If you're gonna ask Liam to put everything on the table, I think it's only fair you do the same."

Again, Finnead gazed at him silently for a moment. Then he said, "You are correct. It's only…fair." He looked across the table at Liam. "At first it was only feeling, vague impressions that I felt during your nightmares. But within the past few days, I've been able to catch glimpses. I've seen some of the things that she forces you to relive."

"And you were just gonna let him struggle on alone?" Quinn said. Anger coursed through him. "I know you guys can be cold, but I didn't expect you to be completely heartless."

"Quinn," said Liam, tired reprimand in his voice.

"Especially after all he's done for you," Quinn pressed. "Listening to your whole sad story and even writing it down to try to help you remember when it was all said and done. But you know what? You *volunteered* to let Vell take your memories, so stop trying to use that as an excuse to act better than us."

"*Quinn*," Liam said sharply.

Quinn settled back in his seat. If he angled his back right, he could scratch the line of stitches with the back of his chair. He crossed his arms over his chest again. "Just sayin', you didn't *choose* to have this weirdo in your head shoving memories at you."

"It's a valid point," Finnead said, his eyes glittering like shards of sapphire.

Quinn looked at him in surprise. "It is?"

"Of course." Finnead took a breath. "This isn't the first time that my behavior before the use of the Lethe stone has been called into question."

"I'm not…wait, what?" Quinn frowned.

"I'd hazard a guess that your dislike of me stems from my…interactions…with Tess," Finnead continued calmly. "You knew her in Doendhtalam and consider her to be your own sister, do you not?"

"Yeah," he said. He decided to wait this one out, see where pointy-eared Mr. Perfect took it.

"So it stands to reason that your immediate hostility centers around my actions regarding her."

"I wouldn't say I was *hostile*," Quinn muttered.

Finnead only smiled. "All I can say is that I do remember most of the last century, the last years especially, and I have to say that I am just as angry at myself over that as you are." He looked away. "I would wager I am angrier, actually."

"Okay," Quinn said slowly. "This still has nothing to do with why you originally wanted to talk to us."

"Oh, it all weaves together at some point," replied Finnead. "But yes. Let's get back to you, Liam." He nodded to the other man.

Liam ran one hand through his hair. "I don't know what you expect me to say. I haven't figured out anything that works."

"Vell is getting worried."

He nodded. "Yes."

"You've been pulling away from her."

Two spots of color burned high on Liam's cheeks. "Yes." He interlaced his fingers on the table and stared down at his hands as though they were a mystery to be solved. "I don't want her to hear anything that I say, or see anything…"

"It's from the perspective of her sister," Finnead said in sudden recognition. Understanding dawned in his eyes. "The memories. The dreams. I didn't know *who* it was…but it is her sister."

Liam nodded miserably. "Vell's sister willingly gave Arcana her body because she didn't want to be forced to torture her own people anymore. Arcana must have absorbed some of her memories and experiences…or maybe she lived with her for a bit, before Vell's sister died. I don't know. It could have been symbiotic for a while." He shrugged. "Either way, pretty much every night is a horror show now. My own private front-row seat to the destruction of the *ulfdrengr.*" He rubbed his eyes with the heel of one hand. "Is Calliea seeing everything too?"

"You could just ask her," murmured Finnead.

Quinn glared at him.

"But I think she would have said something," the Knight continued. "Her bond with us is newer, so there is the possibility that she is not as deeply attuned to either of us." He paused. "The question that remains is what you intend to do about it."

Liam growled low in his throat and leaned back in his chair. "If I knew what to do about it, I would've already done it."

"That wasn't the question. The question is what you *intend* to do."

"I don't know!" The words burst from Liam with sudden vehemence. "Try not to die? Try not to hurt Vell? Try not to become a liability? How about all of that!"

"Try to find a solution?" Finnead asked, his voice a quiet, steady counterpoint to Liam's eruption. "You are one of the High Queen's Three. You need to…"

"Don't tell me what I need to do!" roared Liam, surging to his feet. Quinn jumped up too, ready to intercede…though he wouldn't say no to seeing Liam land a couple of punches first.

"You are one of the High Queen's Three," Finnead repeated, rising from his seat gracefully. "You need to solve this problem, with the Queen's help or without it."

"He's right," Quinn said.

Liam stared at Finnead with his fists clenched by his sides for a tense moment, and then the anger drained from him. He sat back down heavily, covering his face with one shaking hand. "And how exactly do you think I should solve it? Do you think I haven't been *trying*?"

"I think perhaps you've been trying the possibilities that don't require you to reveal anything to anyone," Finnead said. "Asking the healers for some white shroud isn't going to do anything about the fragment of a goddess in your head."

"I'm afraid there is no solution," Liam said, in a voice so soft that Quinn barely heard him.

"Hey, don't you say that," Quinn said instantly.

"I agree with Quinn," Finnead said, his delicately arched brow underlining the gentle humor in his words.

"Then what do you suggest?" Liam's sudden shift from enraged to weary worried Quinn more than the shadows under his friend's eyes and the way he'd been finding excuses not to keep up with training over the past few days.

"You really want to hear what I have to say?" Finnead asked.

"You clearly came to give me counsel before you leave," Liam replied.

"I came to have a conversation," Finnead said. "There are many ways it could have gone."

"Well, it's going the way you want it, so I'd take it and run," Quinn contributed, raising his own eyebrow. How Liam put up with this stuffed shirt on a daily basis, he didn't quite understand. Then again, every unit had *that guy* that was just a little too big for his britches and thought he was better than everyone else. They all had to deal with it in different ways.

"I think you should go talk to Vell," Finnead said. "Tonight. Tell her everything. She probably already knows more than you suspect."

"That's a given," muttered Liam.

"So be less concerned about hurting her," pressed Finnead. "Stop shying away from the difficulty. Whatever you both are to each other, you are also one of her Three. It's our responsibility to tell her the truth, always, even when it hurts."

To Quinn's surprise, Liam nodded slowly. "You're right."

A brief glint of satisfaction surfaced in Finnead's eyes before disappearing. "And Quinn and I will go see the Paladin."

"We will? News to me," Quinn said dryly.

Finnead addressed him directly. "Do you want to help him or not?"

"You're *seriously* asking me that question?"

"Yes, because you clearly have not been able to effectively address this problem. If you're unwilling to accept any advice from me just because of my past, then you are less of a man than I thought."

"Finn," Liam said with that same weary reprimand, "that's a little harsh."

Finnead shrugged and smiled his infuriating little smile.

"Fine, man, I'm always up for a road trip." Quinn spread his hands. "Let's go see Vivian."

Finnead looked expectantly at Liam.

"I'll go speak to Vell now," Liam said. He seemed unhappy but also vaguely relieved at the prospect.

"Nothing to it but to do it, then," said Quinn. He pushed aside his irritation: he loved Liam enough that he could work past the fact that it was Finnead who'd been the one to set this plan into motion. Frustration followed hard on irritation's heels. He'd been trying to get Liam to ask for help for weeks, and they'd even gone to talk to Vivian about the vision of the kid with the plague.

"I took the liberty of sending a messenger," Finnead said as they walked toward the door of Liam's room. "It would have been rude to show up completely unannounced."

Quinn was about to point out that Finnead had done exactly that, but he swallowed his words. No use in arguing just for the sake of argument. He didn't want to turn into that guy who always had something negative to say, so he let Finnead take the lead as they transited through the passageways, little glowing globes flickering into light just ahead of them and dimming behind them.

"So, what exactly do you think Vivian can do?" he asked finally.

"It's not really about what she can *do*," Finnead replied. "She's leaving tomorrow with the expedition. It's more about the resources she can offer, even when she's gone."

"Oh." Quinn could have smacked himself. Why hadn't he thought of asking Vivian before this? She was only living in the biggest library he'd seen in Faeortalam – and even though he hadn't seen Darkhill or wherever the Seelie lived, he'd bet that Vivian's library would give any collection of books a run for its money. "Wonder what Alfred will think if she says we can borrow books while she's gone."

"Alfred?" Finnead asked. "Who's Alfred?"

"Well, it's not a *who*, really, more of a *what*, but I think maybe he *does* have feelings, or at least very strong opinions. Better to just let you see him in person," Quinn finished.

Finnead frowned.

"He's like a servant," Quinn tried to explain. "I guess there's runes or something woven into the fabric, he wears this robe and flies around fetching books and just being helpful in general."

The other man made a thoughtful sound. "It sounds very convenient."

"Very," agreed Quinn. "He's part of the deal, I guess, with the Tower. Vivian inherited him, you could say."

"So he is a very *old* enchantment," said Finnead with more interest. "He was created by the last Paladins?"

"Don't know who else could have made him." Quinn shrugged. The motion set off a prickle down his back, like a spider making its leisurely way down his line of stitches, all eight legs tickling against his skin. He resisted the urge to stop and scratch against one of the light sconces like a bear against a tree. If he'd been walking alone, he would've done it, but not in front of stick-up-his-butt Pretty Boy.

"You *really* don't like me," said Finnead with a hint of a chuckle.

"Oh, sorry, did I think that out loud?" Quinn knew he didn't sound sorry in the least. His expression must have given him away. Note to self: Work on poker face again.

"You know," Finnead said, stopping and looking at him, "I have nothing against you, even though it's clear that you despise me."

"I think *despise* is a strong word."

"This is not an excuse or an explanation," the Knight continued. "But perhaps it will help you to understand. The Lethe stone took many memories from me, and I put myself forward for that task. Liam tells me I did it for love of Princess Andraste, but it's rather a neat trick that I can't even remember that love now." He shrugged and smiled a little to show Quinn that talking about it didn't upset him. "What does keep me up at night sometimes is remembering the more recent past. I think about how I treated certain people who were only trying to help me. I pushed away those who cared about me, because my past haunted me." He shrugged again. "Now I don't remember much of that past."

"Do you remember Rye?" Quinn asked.

"Yes." Finnead nodded. "I do remember most of our time in captivity, though some things have been blurred out of the kindness of time and the natural instinct of the mind to protect itself from such horrible things."

"Rose-colored glasses," agreed Quinn grudgingly, "although I don't know if there was anything rosy about your time in that cave. Liam told me," he added, in case it was confusing for Finnead that he knew the basics of his story.

"I expected so. And…there was, actually. Something rosy, or close to it. Rye." Finnead smiled fondly, his eyes distant with memory. "Her strength sustained us both. It was after her sacrifice that Queen Mab reconsidered her edict that women could not train as Knights or Guards. It took a century or so, until well after she trusted me again, but…" Finnead shook himself free of the threads of his recollection. "So yes. I remember Rye." He smiled, this time sadly. "Best of warriors and best of women."

"She sounds pretty solid," Quinn said. He wasn't sure whether it would be rude to prod Finnead along toward the Tower…and he found that he actually cared a little bit about offending him. Stupid empathy.

"She was. Is," Finnead corrected himself, sounding surprised. "Anyway…what I meant to say, Quinn, was that…I hope eventually I will be able to make amends to everyone I've wronged. I can see now that I let the guilt and shame of my past freeze my emotions."

They started walking again.

"Well, it's great you're in a sharing mood," Quinn said finally, "but I'm just gonna be up front with you, I'm probably not going to be your biggest fan for a long time."

"I understand," Finnead replied. "As long as you realize that I intend to do everything in my power to correct the mistakes of my past. *Recent* past," he amended, "seeing as how everything beyond about two and a half centuries ago gets a bit muddied."

"*Recent* past," Quinn repeated with a snort. "I really know I'm in another world when someone's talking about two hundred fifty years ago being recent."

Finnead chuckled as they reached the door of the Tower. He held up his hand and a spark bloomed in his palm, drifting through the air to melt into the center of the door.

"Guess it's too much to ask for people just to knock," muttered Quinn. He wanted to shove his hands into his pockets, but he remembered belatedly that he had no pockets to shove them into. His faithful camo pants were reserved for actual ops now, since they'd already been patched multiple times before he was dropped into the middle of a Fae war.

The door swung inward silently.

"I'm a bit busy at the moment," called Vivian without looking up from examining a table laid out with various books, instruments, clothes and supplies, all stacked and arranged with meticulous care. "But what can I do for you two?"

Alfred swooped down beside Vivian, adding a slim volume to one of the stacks of books. He tilted his nebulous head and arranged the book so that it was precisely stacked.

"Alfred is behind all this organization," the redhead said with a confessional grin. "You should have seen my room at home." She made a face. "At the house in Louisiana."

"We leave tomorrow morning," said Finnead, raising one eyebrow.

"I know, Finn," Vivian sighed, "but I wanted to go over the packout one last time. I know *you've* probably been packed for *days* but this is my first expedition in…well, *ever*, and I want to make sure I don't forget anything…oh, thank you, Alfred." She took the little black case that Alfred offered her, sliding a compass-like instrument out into her palm. Quinn tried not to let it irritate him that Vivian had used a nickname with the Knight with such an air of familiarity. He reminded himself that Vivian only knew the Finnead newly freed from the demons of his past.

Alfred paused, hovering in front of the table. He bowed his silver-mist head to Quinn deeply, and dipped a nod to Finnead before zooming away. It was the first time, Quinn thought, that he'd been greeted before the Sidhe. He supposed it stood to reason here in the Paladin's Tower. It had been the stronghold of powerful mortals in the Fae world for centuries.

"Is that another scrying-glass?" Finnead said in undisguised interest, striding forward.

"Yes. I had a hunch there might be one somewhere up in the shelves. Alfred has been searching for it in spare moments for a few days now." Vivian held it up for his inspection.

The light glimmered on delicate golden runes etched into the bottle-green casing of the scrying-glass. To Quinn's eye, it looked a little more archaic than the one he'd glimpsed Merrick using – not in a less-useful-archaic kind of way, just a different-from-the-current-model kind of way.

"Merrick said that I can see if I have any talent scrying," Vivian said happily.

"You're just piling on the subjects, huh?" Quinn said.

She frowned slightly at him. "How's that a bad thing? I have to learn as much as I can, and I might as well make use of our time while we're traveling."

"Didn't say it was a bad thing," he said in a friendly tone.

Vivian tossed some red curls over her shoulder as she slid the green scrying-glass back into its case and placed it alongside some other cases of varying sizes and colors. "All right, well, you guys came here for a reason, didn't you?"

Finnead smiled. "Yes. We came to talk about Liam."

"The Seer and one of the High Queen's Three," Vivian said, sounding as though she were repeating something from a textbook. "*Another* one of the High Queen's Three," she amended with a nod to Finnead.

"You know the story of the battle at the Dark Keep?"

"The basic outlines, yes, but if it's something specific, you'd better fill me in. Should we sit? I think Alfred is getting coffee and *khal*." She motioned to one of the clusters of wing-backed chairs by the cold hearth. "I can start a fire, if you'd like."

"We're good," Quinn said.

"That won't be necessary," Finnead assured her at the same time.

Vivian looked between the two of them and shrugged. "Okay."

They followed her over to the chairs. She sat down in a chair upholstered in a velvety fabric that might once have been red but had faded over time to the point where it looked almost golden, and it clashed horribly with her vibrant red hair. Quinn sat in the dark blue chair to her left and Finnead took the seat on her right.

The Paladin folded one leg underneath her and clasped her hands around her knee. "So. Tell me what I need to know."

"Liam was stabbed at the end of the battle," Quinn said. He pushed down the tight, sick feeling that always accompanied memories of one of his brothers being injured or killed. "By Andraste, actually, but that was when she was still being controlled by Malravenar."

"They called her the Dark Archer, didn't they?" Vivian murmured, her eyes alight with the sort of interest that appeared in people who loved learning for learning's sake. Quinn had only ever felt that passion with weapons and ways to kill bad people who did terrible things, but he recognized the feeling.

"Yes," Finnead replied calmly.

"She was trying to break the seal on the Great Gate – mostly succeeded, because that was when Duke and Luca and Merrick got pulled through into the mortal world – and Liam tried to stop her. Anyway, he was dying. Tess made a bargain with Arcana to save his life," Quinn explained.

"Arcana was a part of the First Queen." Finnead picked up the thread of the story, and Quinn let him – he wasn't great about explaining the hocus-pocus of the Fae mythology.

"The First Queen, also named the Morrigan," said Vivian, almost sounding as though she were talking to herself.

"You *have* been studying," Finnead said with a smile.

"I have good teachers," Vivian said. For some reason, two spots of color appeared on her cheekbones.

"The Morrigan – or the part of her that was left on this plane of existence – inhabited the body of the girl who'd been the High Queen's younger sister in life. She was taken during the harrowing of the North, and during her captivity she was forced to do terrible things by the Enemy." Finnead paused, maybe remembering his own time in captivity. "She tortured and killed her own people, other *ulfdrengr*. She took Chael's eye. She may have helped bind a cursed dagger to Luca's hand." Finnead shrugged elegantly. "We do not quite know. In any case, Arcana offered Tess a bargain. She would take Liam's place in death."

"What was the price for the bargain?" Vivian asked keenly.

"There wasn't much time to negotiate," said Quinn, remembering Liam going gray and still on the stone floor. "She just said that she didn't want to exist here anymore, and she'd kept Malravenar from taking over, so it was time for her to punch the clock."

"Tess agreed to the bargain, and Arcana healed Liam, but we discovered later that he still carries a shard of the First inside him."

"Inside him?" Vivian wrinkled her nose.

Quinn tapped his temple. "Somewhere in his noggin. At least that's what he feels it as. At first it wasn't bad. It supercharged his Sight in a way that we thought could maybe be an okay thing, but lately it's had other effects."

"Such as...?" She raised her eyebrows.

"Nightmares which are actually memories from Arcana before she was Arcana," Finnead said quietly. "Seizures and visions that grip with dangerous intensity. Increasing loss of control over his abilities."

Alfred interrupted the serious tone, setting a silver tray on the circular table between all the chairs. Quinn squinted at the table: He was pretty sure that hadn't been there a minute ago, but he didn't think too hard about it. He'd given up on trusting his own eyes half the time with small details like that. What *did* catch his eye were the donuts on the tray. He grinned and saluted Alfred with one. "Seriously, dude, you're the best."

Alfred bowed deeply, tucking his hands into his robe before gliding serenely away.

"He tucks his hands into his robe like that when he's particularly pleased about something," Vivian said fondly. "He'll be preening over that compliment for days."

"Deserves it," Quinn said around a mouthful of donut. He had to stop his eyes from rolling back into his head in pure pleasure. It wouldn't have surprised him if he'd found out that Alfred had a secret Gate into the mortal world next to a fantastic donut shop. There were so many shops that tried to make donuts fussy and complicated. No one appreciated the delicate art of a perfectly fried, balanced cake donut anymore. He chased the bite of donut with a sip of coffee and leaned back in his chair, deciding that it had been worth putting up with Finnead just for this.

Vivian thoughtfully sipped her coffee. "So, you're looking for a solution to Liam's problem. You need to extract the splinter of the Morrigan before it permanently messes him up."

"That's one way of putting it," Quinn said.

"And the same method that was used on Malravenar can't be used on the Morrigan?"

Finnead shook his head. "The binding and breaking of Malravenar was for the capture of his spirit after the destruction of his physical body."

"We'd rather not destroy Liam's physical body," Quinn said dryly.

She hummed and balanced her coffee cup precariously on her knee. Quinn resisted the urge to rescue it; maybe if she spilled coffee on the upholstery she could change the horrible color of that chair.

Then Vivian threw her arms into the air excitedly and Alfred appeared out of nowhere to scoop up the coffee cup.

"Lacuna!" Vivian said.

"Gesundheit," Quinn replied.

Alfred set the rescued coffee cup back on the silver tray with an indignant quiver of the silver mist that comprised his face. If he'd been a butler, Quinn was pretty sure he would have been sniffing in disapproval.

"No," Vivian said, waving a hand at Quinn, "*lacuna*! That's what you need for Liam." She grinned and looked at Finnead. "It's an object – or it could be a person, it doesn't *have* to be inanimate – that can hold other things, mostly powerful things like souls or parts of deities, things like that, without any damage to itself. *Lacuna* means 'the space between,' or that's the rough translation." She chewed on her lower lip. "Alfred, could you find that text, please, I can't remember whether it's by Cerelle or Amidalus, but it has a pretty comprehensive description of a lacuna…"

"You want 'A History of Lost Objects,' by Cerelle," said a new voice. Tyr glided into view, walking in that panther-like way that seemed common to many of the Sidhe. "Amidalus wrote 'A History of Lost People,' but the titles are easy to confuse."

"They're not easy to confuse," retorted Vivian. "I just couldn't *remember* which one."

Something in the way Vivian glanced at Tyr made Quinn's spidey-senses tingle, but he reminded himself firmly that Vivian was an adult, and he hadn't exactly made a great first impression with her anyway. He couldn't hover over everyone else wringing his hands just because he'd gotten his heart broken by a beautiful Sidhe.

"Tyr," said Finnead, nodding to the silver-haired man.

"Knight Finnead," Tyr said with a hint of exaggerated courtesy. He turned his attention back to Vivian. "Why are you speaking of lacunas?"

"Because it might help the Seer," Vivian replied, picking up her coffee cup again and leaning back in her chair.

Tyr's silvery eyes, unsettling in a bit of the same way as Vell's golden gaze, settled on Quinn. He forced himself not to look away.

"I'm not quite sure how to help, though," Vivian continued. "We're all leaving tomorrow on the expedition…"

"Quinn is not," said Tyr. "And he is mortal."

Vivian tilted her head. "That's true." She nodded at Quinn. "You could get past the new wards without any *taebramh*, actually. If I gave you permission."

"I have no idea what that means," he replied honestly.

"Ah, thanks, Alfred," Vivian said, taking the small, thick book that the Tower servant handed her. She set her coffee cup on her knee again and Alfred snatched it up, waving a hand at her in a clearly scolding way. Quinn fought the urge to chuckle as Vivian cracked open the little tome without even a glance at Alfred, oblivious to his second rescue of her imperiled coffee. She apparently found the page she'd been looking for and handed the book to Finnead.

"Do you think you'll need to do more research?" she asked Quinn.

"Probably," he said. "Honestly, I don't know how long finding this solution is gonna take. All I know is that I have to try my best to help Liam."

"This would certainly be an elegant solution," Finnead said, "but it would take more time than we have before our departure."

"I know," Vivian said, nodding. She slid a leather cord necklace over her head, deftly untying the knot and sliding off a silver key. She held it in her hand for a long moment, then closed her fingers over it and held it out to Quinn.

"For me?" he said in surprise.

"No, for the other brown, tattooed guy," she replied sarcastically, a smile taking the edge off her words. She shook her hand. "Take it before I get cold feet."

Quinn held out his hand and she dropped the key into his palm, warm from her touch.

"Don't lose it. It should open the door of the Tower for you."

Quinn blinked as the enormity of the gift settled over him. "Seriously?"

"Seriously," Vivian replied with a smile.

"I guess I redeemed myself after that first impression," he said.

She chuckled. "I don't know whether I'd quite say *that*, but you're the only other pure mortal here right now, if you don't count the Bearer and her brother. Apparently they're not entirely mortal anymore." She shifted in her chair. "Alfred should be able to help you if you need anything. You won't be able to bring anyone else in, I put some new wards on the doors after Evangeline got in." She glanced at Tyr.

"Heard about that," said Quinn, nodding. "Glad you're both okay."

"You'll be fine to depart tomorrow?" Finnead asked Tyr.

"I've traveled with worse," the silver-haired man said with a shrug.

It was almost funny how men insisted on trying to prove they were tough, even here in another world, Quinn thought. He was as guilty of it as any of them. Liam, too. Maybe that was why it was easier to recognize.

Vivian cleared her throat as she finished retying the knot of her leather necklace and slipped it over her head again. "Well, this has been *lovely*, gentlemen, and I'm happy I was able to help, but I really have to finish packing and I should go see Nyx as well, make sure she's set for the morning…"

With that firm yet courteous dismissal, Quinn stood, still holding the silver key. He'd have to find a length of cord for it. Maybe the magnitude of Vivian's casual gift would sink in later, after they'd figured out what to do about Liam.

Lacuna.

He tested the word again in his mind, trying to think of anything that he'd heard about in the Fae world that would fit the description.

No dice. Finnead was saying something to Tyr and Vivian, and then Vivian slurped down the rest of her coffee, wiped her mouth on the back of her hand and strode with determined steps back over to the table. Tyr and Finnead talked in low voices for another moment, and then Tyr followed Vivian, moving silently as a shadow.

"Here," Finnead said, handing the little book to Quinn. "This is of better use in your hands than mine."

As the door to the Paladin's Tower shut behind them, Quinn caught himself thinking that maybe he'd misjudged Finnead. He weighed the book that might contain the biggest clue to helping Liam, his other hand closed around the key to the Paladin's Tower. Maybe Finnead deserved a second shot, after all.

Chapter 26

T he silvery predawn light washed them all in muted tones of gray and pale white and charcoal as the expedition prepared for departure a small distance away from the paddocks behind the cathedral. Vivian ran one hand down Nyx's warm, smooth neck, checking the girth strap of her saddle and the security of her saddlebags and camp roll for what must have been the hundredth time. Her mount blew out a warm breath and turned her head to look at Vivian as though to ask when she'd be done with all her nervous silliness.

"Sorry," Vivian murmured to the beautiful *faehal*. She'd gone through a horse-obsessed phase as a kid, and sometimes it came rushing back when she realized that this gorgeous creature had chosen to work with her.

There was no two ways about it, the *faehal* chose their riders and possessed uncanny intelligence. Moira had explained as much to her before she'd even gotten into the saddle, but her first few days of riding lessons demonstrated Nyx's cleverness. The mare always seemed to know when Vivian felt off balance, shifting her path slightly to nudge Vivian back to center, slowing if she was ever really in danger of falling until she regained her seat. Vivian swore that

Nyx listened to Moira's instructions as well, because when they added a wooden blade to simulate fighting from horseback, Nyx always managed to make Vivian look at least half decent. She felt like she didn't have to divide her attention between giving direction to her mount and fighting.

"But the war is over, so the chances of encountering anything on the expedition are low, aren't they?" she'd asked Moira as she splashed water on her face during a break in one of their lessons.

"Oh, I'm sure there are still some trolls wandering around," Moira had replied cheerfully. "The patrols have done a good job at cleaning up the forests around the White City, and some creatures really don't have an interest in hunting us now that they're not in thrall anymore. But there's always the chance."

Moira's grin had made Vivian think that the Valkyrie scout *wanted* to fight something on the trail.

"Need a leg up?" Tyr said in a low voice, leading his own roan *faehal* to stand beside Nyx.

"Are you sure you should be offering?" Vivian replied, raising an eyebrow at him. It had only been three days since the Exiles had attacked the White City.

"I would not offer if I were not capable," Tyr said with precise courtesy, his gray eyes glimmering in the twilight.

He'd slept in the armchair by the fire all that night. Vivian had fallen asleep in her own armchair, to be awoken by Alfred who prodded her off to her room with silent assurances that he'd fetch her if Tyr took a turn for the worse. She'd opened her eyes to golden sunlight streaming into her room through the mullioned windows, and Alfred had hurriedly motioned for her to be quiet when she banged her way into the library, rubbing her eyes and wrinkling her nose. Tyr had still been asleep in the armchair, the fire glowing and warm. Apparently, his insistence that Alfred keep Vivian out of the fight had raised him in Alfred's estimation, because the Tower servant, when he wasn't fetching a book or performing any of the normal tasks he usually did for Vivian, hovered by Tyr, poking at the silver arm when he thought the fire needed tending and fetching another blanket.

Now, in the silvery light of morning, Vivian realized that the time she and Tyr had spent alone, studying ancient texts and practicing runes, wouldn't be the same while they were traveling with the expedition., so she nodded and let him create a stirrup with his hands to boost her into the saddle, even though she was fairly certain that the movement hurt both his shoulder and his leg.

From her vantage point atop Nyx, Vivian took a deep breath and surveyed the rest of the travelers. Two Valkyrie were coming with them: Moira, much to Vivian's delight, and another tall, muscled woman with an eye patch named Trillian. Their winged *faehal* stood a little apart from the rest of the mounts, drowsing with their heads tucked under one wing. She picked out the pale gleam of Niall's hair and the reddish glint of Ramel's, both of them making their final adjustments to the packs on their mounts.

Tyr swung up onto his own saddle, a grimace flashing over his face like a cloud passing over the moon. The high, bright chatter of their Glasidhe scouts cut through the muted sounds of their mounts blowing out breath and the creak of the leather of their packs and saddles. It seemed as though no one other than the Glasidhe wanted to break the silence of the morning, even though it was the day of departure for the expedition that had been planned for nearly a month.

"Somehow, I thought there would be more fanfare," Vivian murmured to Tyr.

He raised a pale eyebrow. "Pomp and circumstance is often just a mask to cover the truth."

Vivian thought on that for a moment and then nodded. "I can see what you mean." She shrugged. "Still, I thought maybe some people would come to see us off."

"Lady Paladin," said a smooth, pleasant voice. Vivian didn't miss that Tyr stiffened somewhat in his saddle.

She turned to the speaker. "Good morning, Finn," she greeted the Knight. At first, he'd intimidated her in the way that all the beautiful, unreadable Sidhe had intimidated her, but she'd grown to like him. He seemed younger than most of the other Knights, even Ramel. In the planning meetings for the expedition, he'd always made it a point to ask Vivian for her thoughts, even though all of them had much more experience in this sort of thing than she did.

Finn looked over her setup. "You have a good, balanced pack," he said in quiet approval, "and your sword is within reach." He nodded. "Good. Do you feel comfortable with a bow while mounted?"

"I wouldn't say *comfortable*," Vivian said, "but I've practiced some with Moira."

"Good. There will certainly be opportunity to train in the mornings before we break camp, and perhaps in the evenings as well, once you are used to being on the road," he said, not unkindly.

"I'm always willing to learn," she replied.

He smiled, nodded to Tyr and then nudged his great black mount into motion, riding toward the head of the group.

"Ready to go, Paladin?" asked Merrick as he rode past, his *faehal's* hooves striking the ground with dull thuds.

"Of course," she replied with a grin. She felt like the group going on the expedition embraced her presence. While most of the Sidhe had welcomed her as a Paladin, she'd begun to notice the dark glances and unpleasant whispers that sometimes followed her at the training yards. Most of them seemed to originate from the dark-haired Unseelie. The Seelie didn't seem to be temperamentally suited to subtlety, even in their dislike, and she'd only had one unpleasant encounter with a Seelie woman who seemed to be strangely jealous of Vivian, though she couldn't quite understand why.

Her time in the Tower gave her the opportunity to think about such things in the quiet moments when she took a break from reading an ancient text or practicing a new rune, and she could understand why the Sidhe maybe wouldn't be over the moon about her. Their survival in the war against Malravenar had hinged on the grit and determination of one mortal woman: The Bearer of the Iron Sword. She could understand how a proud, powerful, ancient people would be a little dismayed at the thought of their entire existence depending on an untried girl who'd followed her best friend into the Fae world out of stubborn loyalty.

Goosebumps raised the hairs on Vivian's arms every time she thought about the fact that it *could have been her.* She thought about the tale of Tess's journeys in Faeortalam – there were several ballads already, and apparently a few of the Scholars were working on a history of the war. She wasn't sure she'd have been up to the challenge. The pendant at her throat heated at that thought, and she pressed its reassuring warmth against her skin with the palm of one hand.

A few did come out to see them off: Calliea, her whip at her belt, who kissed Merrick fiercely in unashamed view of everyone before talking to her Valkyrie and then kissing him again; the other two of the Seelie Three, speaking to Niall in low voices and embracing him in a brotherly way before taking their leave; and Guinna, who strode toward Ramel with determined intent. She patted the shoulder of his *faehal* as she spoke to him, her pretty face stern. Vivian watched: She'd been honing her observation skills, when she didn't think it would be rude if she were caught taking in the conversation. Guinna seemed to be giving Ramel some sort of lecture. It was hard for Vivian to read the Unseelie Knight, but he nodded graciously enough. Guinna stopped to talk to Finn as well, her posture more relaxed.

"Their history is intertwined, those three," said Tyr quietly beside her.

Vivian jumped guiltily and then settled back into her saddle, telling herself that she had nothing to feel guilty about. "Your history is intertwined with them too, isn't it?"

"Yes," said Tyr. "But not quite as closely. Finnead chose Ramel as his squire when he became a Knight, and Ramel rescued Guinna after they both escaped the attack that took Andraste and Finnead prisoner."

"Rye was captured as well," said Vivian, well aware that she was venturing onto shaky ground. After Ramel's insistence that Rye may still be held prisoner by some spell of the bone sorcerer, and Finnead's admission that he hadn't actually *seen* Rye die (much like Andraste, who was still alive as well), Tyr hadn't spoken much about his twin. Vivian hadn't pushed very hard. She reasoned that Tyr deserved a bit of privacy, and he would talk to her about Rye when he was ready. But now, waiting to depart on the mission to resolve Rye's fate, she wondered if he would *ever* be ready.

"Yes," Tyr replied. She couldn't read his face in the half-light.

"How are you feeling about the expedition?" She asked the question quietly out of habit, although she knew the keen hearing of the other Sidhe meant that they could probably hear her anyway.

Does it matter how I feel? Tyr answered her silently.

Vivian found herself grateful for the shadows as she felt a blush rise to her cheeks. She would have asked the question wordlessly as well, if she'd thought that Tyr didn't object to the idea of their silent communication. He'd used it so little during their time in Faeortalam that now she just assumed he didn't want to use the more intimate method of speaking. But she drew back her shoulders and gathered her words carefully, sliding them down the gossamer string between their minds with smooth alacrity. *It matters to* me *how you feel, or I wouldn't have asked. I don't have any brothers or sisters, so I don't know what it is that you are feeling. Many things have happened since we came to Faeortalam.*

Tyr's mount shifted as the Valkyrie walked over to their winged steeds, strapping themselves into the harnesses that they wore during flight. Nyx tossed her head and stamped impatiently as the winged *faehal* half-spread their wings and pranced while their riders mounted. Vivian leaned forward and stroked her smooth, cool neck, feeling the muscles of her Fae steed ripple.

I have not given myself permission to hope, Tyr said finally. She glanced at him and he was turned away from her, watching the Valkyrie. Trillian gave her mount its head and with a snort of delight, the *faehal* surged into a gallop, its hooves parting the light mist washing over the ground and its wings sweeping downward in a great arc as it leapt into the air, gaining altitude with each powerful beat. Moira gave a cheeky little salute in their general direction before leaning forward and urging her own mount into the air.

You feel as though hoping is tempting fate? Vivian asked, watching the Valkyrie fly overhead in graceful circles.

It is not fate that worries me, Tyr replied cryptically.

Vivian tried to puzzle through his answer and then gave up. *What worries you, then?*

I mourned Rye once, he said. *I do not know if I have the strength to lose her again.*

She took a deep breath of the cool morning air as understanding washed through her.

The odds of finding her alive in body and whole in mind after all these centuries are not in our favor, he continued grimly. *If I had thought even for a moment that she was in need of my help, that she was still alive and held captive by the Enemy, I would have fought to return to her.*

But you didn't know, Vivian pointed out. *You couldn't have known. No one did. So, if you're about to start blaming yourself and letting the guilt eat you alive like Ramel, I'd prefer you just cut to the chase and tell me now.*

Tyr looked at her in surprise. *Why?*

She narrowed her eyes at him. *If you don't understand by now that I care about you, you aren't as intelligent as everyone gives you credit for.*

Tyr shook his head. *There are far more suitable objects for your affection.*

She snorted. *Objects for my affection? I like how you just* assume *that I'm speaking about a physical attraction. I know that a lot of our relationship in the mortal world was out of necessity on your part, but I had a choice, and I chose to help you, to give you blood, to watch over you as you healed when Corsica almost killed you, so don't think you can just brush aside whatever I feel as some childish infatuation, especially when I didn't specify that I was talking about* that *kind of caring.*

When she finished her silent tirade, Tyr just looked at her, his face unreadable. She knew for a fact that it was light enough for him to see the color burning in her cheeks. His silence and her own heightened emotions conspired against her. To her horror, she felt tears tightening behind her eyes. That was exactly the last thing she wanted – to cry in front of Tyr and validate his assessment that she was just a silly girl. She firmly checked that their invisible connection was closed, and at that moment the small company began to move. She gratefully let Nyx slide into a canter; her beautiful little mare kicked her heels up and frolicked with just enough restraint to remain respectable and not look like a filly again, but it was plain that even the *faehal* knew they were setting out on an adventure across the entire land of Faeortalam.

The company had planned the route in precise detail over large maps that covered entire tables. Vivian had felt like she'd contributed to the mission in a concrete way after finding the old tome that detailed different methods of repairing scrying glasses. With his broken scrying glass repaired at last, Merrick had been able to scout along their route, much to Vivian's fascination and the satisfaction of Finnead and Niall, the de facto leaders of the company. Finnead and Merrick had discussed the destruction of the bridge over the river Darinwel in voices that were almost fond, like soldiers recounting a firefight that had been terrifying in the moment but once everyone had survived transformed into a good tale to tell around the fire. Their Glasidhe scouts – the twins Forin and Farin, and their cousins Flora and Wisp – had assured Finnead in grave tones that they would be able to bear the weight of a length of rope across the gorge, and the Vyldgard Knight had accepted their offer with equal gravity, but the final plan called for Trillian and Moira to carry the loose end of the rope bridge across the river. They would have to craft the boards once they reached the Darinwel, but Merrick and Finnead assured them that there would be ample materials available.

From the Darinwel, the party would continue heading eastward toward Unseelie territory. The party traveling with the Princess had not crossed the Darinwel all those years ago before they were ambushed, so they'd agreed that the most likely place for the cave in which Finnead and Rye had been held would be on the Unseelie side of the river. There had been some conversation too quick and serious for Vivian to follow about scrying for Rye – Ramel had affirmed that he had a few things of hers still, and if those did not work, Merrick thought with a fair degree of certainty that they might be able to use Tyr's blood, since he was, after all, her twin.

Tyr had said in a low voice that his blood might not be acceptable for any kind of incantation, but the other men had seemed to regard his comment as something not to be taken entirely seriously.

Now their small company rode through the streets of the White City in the gentle morning light, no fanfare accompanying their departure. Vivian gazed up at the great white buildings on either side of them and the statues that seemed to change expression each time she saw them looking down upon their departure. To her eyes this morning, the statues gazed down benevolently, small smiles upon their carved lips, a softness in their faces as they watched the expedition ride through the streets toward the gates of the city.

During their training, Nyx had patiently allowed Vivian to put a light bridle upon her, seeming to understand that her new rider was much less experienced and needed the additional method of communicating – because even at the beginning, Vivian understood that any thought of *control* over Nyx was just an illusion. It was very much like a conversation between her and the gleaming black *faehal*. Now she held the reins lightly in one hand and tried to absorb everything she could about the morning: the feel of the light breeze upon her face, the shadows of the Valkyrie slipping silken over the white of the path, the morning light turning golden as the sun rose fully over the eastern horizon, the echo of their sounds of passage through the quiet city.

In the distance, she heard the muted sounds of the training yard, the clash of blades and the occasional call from sparring partners. She wondered if any of them knew the expedition was leaving at this very moment, or if any of them cared. She wondered if Alfred would feel lonely – she'd explained to him that she was going on a journey for at least a few months, and he'd nodded as though he understood, but she didn't know if that was simply his eagerness to please. Somehow the thought of the Tower servant becoming increasingly despondent ate at her more than any thought of those she'd left behind in the mortal world. The realization cut through her like a knife.

Did that make her a terrible person, worrying more about Alfred than about Ross or Evie? She let the thought settle in her mind for a moment, trying not to let it resurrect the tears still lurking behind her eyes. No, she decided, it didn't make her terrible or anything else. She'd made the decision to travel into the Fae world just the same as if she'd made the decision to leave everything behind and travel to India to study yoga with a guru or backpack across Europe or train to climb Mount Everest, all things that people did. Granted, they weren't in another *world*, but they might as well be. It was her life, and her decision. She hadn't been cruel, and she hadn't worried anyone unnecessarily by trying to explain. Alfred, though, felt different. His purpose was to take care of her and the Tower, and it pricked her conscience to think of him all alone, dusting the shelves all day with more and more sad lethargy as he thought he'd been abandoned again. She'd tried to find the rune to put Alfred back into that dormant state, but he'd shaken his head indignantly at her when she'd finally asked him for help in finding the exact book.

Quinn and the High Queen had permission to visit the Tower, she thought as they turned another corner and the street suddenly widened into a grand thoroughfare. Hopefully that would be enough to keep Alfred occupied until she got back.

The pink wash of dawn clarified into soft blue as they rode toward a great archway that had clearly once contained gates. Vivian wondered if the High Queen planned to replace the gates, or simply leave the White City open to any who wished to enter. The blocks of stone used to build the archway each stood higher than Vivian atop Nyx, and she stared up in awe as they passed under the massive arch. The air shivered around them, feeling like dozens of small cool hands pressing onto her skin for an instant, and then the sensation faded just as quickly. *I should have known the Queens would not leave the White City unprotected,* Vivian thought, rubbing her arms to dispel the lingering strangeness of the unexpected spell.

Two great statues, three or four times as large as an actual person, stood like sentries directly outside the gate. One was clearly a woman and one a man, dressed in a kind of armor that looked similar and yet different from what Vivian had seen the Sidhe wear. It was like seeing a painting from a few hundred years ago, she decided, the differences of time both subtle and glaring. She picked out the different helmets: these swept back to a point behind the wearer's head, and engravings of feathers along each side gave the impression of wings. She twisted in her saddle to keep the statues in sight, trying to pick out more differences: the entire leg was armored, and both the man and woman wore something like a chain mail skirt. The woman held a curved sword that looked similar to a scimitar, and the man held a long, thick spear taller than he was.

"You are always trying to learn," said Niall. She didn't know whether Nyx had caught up to his mount or if he'd maneuvered to ride beside her, she'd been so absorbed in looking at the statues.

"There are a lot of things to learn, and I'm starting from scratch," she replied with a smile.

The Seelie Knight and her teacher motioned to her clothes. "You've developed an interesting style."

She brushed aside her initial defensive instinct. Niall had never been unkind to her, even when she'd accused him of teaching her simply because he'd lost his own *taebramh* from the effort of saving Forin's life. Instead, she surveyed herself. She'd chosen to pack a mixture of the clothes she'd brought in her backpack and some of what Alfred had helpfully procured for her during their preparations. Today she wore black rock climbing pants, which she particularly liked because of the small, convenient zippered pockets; the belt that she'd outfitted with customized pouches and holders for her rune-sticks and a few other essentials; a plain blue long-sleeved shirt in the Sidhe style, and a dark cloak that had kept the morning chill from seeping into her skin. "I'm an interesting person," she replied with a smile. "Plus, I'm a Paladin, so I figure that comes with certain liberties, like dressing oddly."

"I did not say it was *odd*," Niall clarified, his pale eyes sparkling with humor. "I simply said it was *interesting*."

Vivian chuckled. She'd noticed during their lessons that Niall possessed a certain innate sense of fashion that he hadn't been able to indulge during his journey into her world. He wasn't a peacock by any means, but he did know how to dress to his advantage. Every item of his wardrobe was tailored and immaculately matched by color palettes. All of it flattered him without seeming flamboyant, and Vivian had found herself looking forward to their lessons just to see what he would wear. From a purely aesthetic perspective, she enjoyed seeing the display of Seelie beauty.

"Your wardrobe has impressed me," she confessed to Niall with a grin. They'd moved back into an easy friendship, though every once and a while she remembered the tension between them back when they'd first been setting limits with each other. Sometimes she winced at the memories of those early days; the beauty of the Sidhe men had certainly turned her head. Merrick, Ramel and Niall all had their own charms, though she'd quickly determined that Merrick wasn't available for any sort of fun. That was before she'd properly understood the opportunity in front of her. All she'd wanted to do in the beginning was bask in the reflection of their beauty, these enigmatic beings from another world that she barely dared to believe in.

And then it had all changed when Tyr had pronounced her a Paladin, and Niall had agreed with him. She was no stranger to responsibility – sometimes the idea that the dozen or so employees at Adele's depended on her for their livelihood squeezed her chest with anxiety. When she was eighteen, she'd tearfully confessed to Evie that her worst fear was letting everyone down by making some catastrophic mistake with the business.

Now the stakes weren't people's paychecks – it was people's lives, including her own. This time around, she'd managed not to sink into the morass of worry that had sucked her under when she'd stepped into a bigger role at the coffee shop. Now, as the walls of the White City retreated toward the horizon behind them, she wondered if she'd be able to maintain that composure for the entire journey.

"How has my wardrobe been impressive?" Niall drew her attention back to the present moment with his amused question.

"Well, you just have this sense of what looks *good* on you," Vivian replied.

"I've had a few centuries or so of practice," Niall replied drily. "And Queen Titania expects us to represent her well."

"Did you have to adjust the colors you wore after your hair and eyes were washed out?" she asked with genuine interest.

Niall chuckled and tilted his head. "Now that you ask, I think all three of us did. It was part of regaining our balance and our sense of self."

"It must have been a relief when you woke up," she mused, thinking now about the time that Niall had spent in a catatonic state, sustaining the Seelie Queen through her metaphysical imprisonment by Malravenar.

"It was strange," he replied thoughtfully.

"Tell me?" she asked, hearing the hope in her own voice. Tyr was so tight-lipped about his history in the Fae world, and now it seemed as though Niall was willing to talk to her.

"It's a long story," he said.

She glanced at the loose column of riders before them, some of them paired and talking quietly as she and Niall were, others riding silently. Ramel kept his mount distinctly apart from everyone, his face like a beautiful mask. Vivian looked back at Niall and said, "We have time."

He nodded, thought for a moment, and then began.

Chapter 27

"How is he?"

The words left Mal's mouth before she had even fully stepped into the room. The weight of the satchel containing the strange, beautiful gifts from Hex's dead mother pressed against her hip.

Jem looked at her and shook his head silently. The rasp of Hex's breathing broke the silence, as loud to Mal's ear as the crack of the cat o' nine tails that had inflicted the wounds that were now killing him. She swallowed hard and her suddenly shaking hand rattled the key as she pulled it out of the lock. Shutting the door as quietly as she could, she drew the bolt and took a deep breath, grasping at some sort of composure.

But when she turned around and got her first good look at Hex, she crumbled.

"Gods above," she whispered, even though she didn't believe in any gods and she'd certainly never made a habit of praying to any of them.

Hex looked like he was dying...and he was, she realized. He was dying. The knowledge curdled in her stomach, drawing everything into a sickening ball of hurt and grief that expanded into her chest and closed off her throat.

Jem had apparently stopped trying to sweat out the fever. The room was warm but not stifling like when she'd left. Hex wasn't sweating anymore, anyway. He lay gray and still except for those terrible rattling breaths, the bruising on his face still awful green and blue, fading to yellow along his jaw. His lips were cracked and bloodless, his dark hair stiff with dried sweat. She *smelled* the sickness in the air as she walked toward the bed, the scent sour and hot.

"Would feverwort save him?" she asked, reaching out hesitantly and touching Hex's hand. He felt hotter than the sands of Mirror Cove at noon on a summer day.

"Mal," Jem said wearily, shaking his head again. He looked…defeated.

"Would feverwort save him?" she asked again, this time demanding, her voice hissing across the space between them. Jem never looked defeated. Jem was always the one anchoring them with his mixture of practicality and steady optimism, his buoyant hope tempered by the lessons he'd learned onboard the *Dragonwing*. Mal felt a seed of anger plant itself in her chest.

Jem heaved a sigh. "Maybe…only if administered in the next few hours." He clenched his jaw and to her horror, Mal saw tears in the corners of his eyes. "He won't last the night, Mal."

"No," she said automatically. She shook her head, breathing heavily. The anger took roots and bloomed rapidly. "No. He's not going to die." She looped the strap of the satchel over her head. Jem didn't even ask what it was as she placed it carefully on the little table and marched in determination over to the supplies laid out neatly on the floor.

She'd only ever seen other women wear skirts and other silly frippery, but she laid out all the parts on the floor and examined them with a critical eye as she stripped out of her trousers and shirt. She knew how to tie twelve different kinds of knots, could climb up to the topmast rigging faster than anyone on the ship, and had fought a kraken. She could figure out how to wear these blasted skirts.

The linen bloomers were simple enough, if a little ridiculous, but the corset gave her trouble. She couldn't pull the laces tight enough and then slide it back around. Finally, she turned to Jem in exasperation, holding the contraption over her chest and trudging over to him, offering the laces to him. When nothing happened, she looked over her shoulder at him.

"Come on then, we don't have any time to waste. Hex doesn't have any time to waste," she corrected herself grimly.

A strange pity surfaced in Jem's eyes for just an instant, but then he pulled at the laces and after a few uncharacteristically clumsy attempts got them tied tightly enough that Mal nodded and strode back over to the rest of the getup. The underskirt thankfully only had a few petticoats, and the bodice actually fit her pretty well. Merchant Black's kindly wife hadn't included any other shoes, so Mal pulled on her boots. They'd be hidden by the skirt, anyway, and she was able to slide one dagger into a boot top sheath. The other dagger she laid on top of the wrapped curve of the egg in the satchel. There wasn't anywhere else to hide a blade in this stupid costume; thankfully the satchel was similar to the kind that many of the women carried for their sundry purchases and whatever other items ladies were supposed to carry around with them. Mal was sure that didn't include daggers, but she didn't give a rat's ass at this point.

"I'll be back in a few hours," she said to Jem. The corset felt stiff and the skirts clung to her legs as she walked over to the bed again. She stared down at Hex and after a moment of hesitation bent down and kissed his temple, the least bruised bit of skin visible. He shuddered and sighed. She swallowed and stepped back. "I'll be back fast as I can," she said in a lower voice, not sure if he could hear her.

"Mal," said Jem, "you should stay here."

She locked eyes with him and raised her chin belligerently. "Keep him alive, Jem."

"Mal," he said again, but she was already moving toward the door, drawing back the bolt savagely and closing it behind her before he could say anything else.

"Oh, didn't recognize you, Mal!" called out Nell with innocent cheer as Mal emerged from the staircase and walked quickly across the common room. "Here, wait, oh, your skirt is crooked and you can see your laces! Don't you have a kerchief?"

Mal eyed the door but stopped, turning back to the serving maid. "Can you fix me quick? Please," she added belatedly.

"Course I would've helped you get dressed, if I'd known," Nell said conversationally, setting down her cleaning cloth and fussing over Mal's skirts. She chattered as she worked, her touch surprisingly firm as she tugged the skirt straight and tucked in the laces of the corset. "We don't have many women who stay here, you know, and I would have loved to help – how's your friend doing, eh, is he feeling better? This color looks right charming on you. Now, you should really have a kerchief, that bodice is a bit too low to be rightly comfortable, en't it? Wait here, I'll be back in a trice."

Nell pattered away into the kitchens. Mal looked down at her newly straightened skirts and tried to understand why the bottle-green color of the skirts would have anything to do with how the dress looked on her. She thought that maybe it had to do with the contrast between the dark color and her pale skin.

"Here," said Nell breathlessly, waving a square of white linen at her. Mal stared at her blankly: What was she supposed to do with that little bit of cloth? Nell sighed good-naturedly and expertly folded the linen and draped it around Mal's neck, tucking the edges into the bodice of her dress to create a sort of collar. "There you are. Oh, is no one going with you? It's dark out now..."

"Thank you, Nell," Mal said firmly, turning toward the door. She checked the closure on the front of the satchel and then stepped into the heavy shadows outside the cheery light of the Blind Dragon.

The only light in the streets came from the moon overhead and the greasy flames of the tallow lamps outside the taverns and a few shops that stayed open past dark. Mal wished she'd brought a cloak, but then she savagely pushed all the doubts in her mind aside. Hex needed her. She gripped the strap of her satchel and walked quickly toward the merchant district, striding boldly down the middle of the street like a girl who walked alone every night. She scanned the shadows as she went, but she saw only a few sailors staggering out of a tavern, roaring with drunken laughter. She didn't look at them long enough to see if it was any of the crew of the *Dragonwing*.

Finally, she turned onto the main street of the merchant district. Here, the roads were paved with flat stones, and a few lamps burned clear and bright beside the gilded signs that proclaimed the names of the wealthier merchants who set up their shops on the best street in Haven. Mal found the bright blue sign with gold lettering, traced it with her eyes, and squared her shoulders.

The front of Boteler's shop boasted two mullioned windows and two oil lamps whose cheery light pooled golden in front of the immaculately painted white door. Mal suddenly became very aware of the dirt beneath her fingernails as she reached toward the unblemished white of the door, but it opened before she grasped the handle. The shop assistant, a young man elegantly attired in black breeches and a blue silk shirt, motioned her inside, a small smile on his lips. The embellished pistol at his hip didn't escape Mal's notice.

Mal took a deep breath and stepped inside. She didn't allow her eyes to wander, because she knew if she did, she'd stop and stare at all the wonders on the shelves of this shop. Boteler was well known to take pride in his rare and valuable collection of treasures from this world and the many others plundered by the Seafarers. She'd picked up snatches of conversation about the shop from the firsts, who sometimes took their haul here if they had something they thought was particularly valuable. Mostly Boteler dealt with the captains of the dragon ships – he was uninterested in the usual sacks of gold coins or jewels netted from a typical prize ship. It took something truly unusual to catch his eye, and if there was ever anything truly unusual among the hoard of treasure, it naturally went to the captain of the ship that took the prize.

The shop stretched longer than it looked from the outside, or perhaps it was just a trick of the gleaming dark floors, crafted from a wood with a luster like a black pearl. There was a *fireplace* to her left – who'd ever heard of such a thing, a hearth in a trader's shop? – with two red leather chairs and an artful little table arranged by the flames. The light of the fire glinted on a cut crystal decanter filled with amber liquid and a dark bottle filled with wine as dark as blood. A great desk with clawed feet loomed at the far end of the shop, and behind it a man with silver hair tied into an elegant tail at the nape of his neck turned the pages of a book with his long fingers.

Mal set her course for the desk and the silver-haired man. But then, without a sound, somehow the shop assistant was beside her, touching her arm with good-mannered delicacy.

"Do you have an appointment, miss?" he asked in a wonderfully smooth voice.

"No," Mal said. Her voice sounded like a rude squawk after his cultured words. She cleared her throat, feeling like a grubby little intruder into this sophisticated shop. But then, she reasoned, they dealt with ship captains, and captains were still Seafarers. "I'm afraid I don't have an appointment," she said, managing a silkier tone, "but I've come across something that I believe is rare and valuable, and I would like to sell it."

Something like amusement brightened the assistant's eyes. "And what is it that you have found?"

She raised her chin. "I would like to speak to Mr. Bodelet, please."

"If you do not have an appointment, then I'm afraid that will be impossible," replied the assistant courteously.

"It's important that I speak to him," she said, digging in her heels even as the beginning of panic clawed at her throat. Hex's life hung in the balance.

"I am afraid it is impossible," repeated the young man, looking down at her with cool blue eyes.

She took a step forward, determined to reach the desk, and his hand encircled her arm with a bruising grip.

"Now, Alexander," said a voice as rich as the dark sheen of the floorboards. "When you say 'impossible,' you really mean 'improbable,' and I am willing to make an exception for a lovely young woman."

For some reason, a chill skittered down Mal's back at the man's words, but Alexander released her arm and motioned her toward the chairs by the fire as though he hadn't just been ready to drag her from the shop. The man with the silver hair unfolded himself from behind the desk and walked toward them. He was much taller than Mal had thought, and though his face was lined, he hadn't let himself go to seed. His trim figure exuded a power that Mal usually didn't see in those who didn't sail on the dragon ships.

"What is your name, my dear girl?" Boteler said, inclining his head gracefully toward the red leather chairs.

"Mallora," she replied, though speaking all three syllables made her feel a bit sick. Just another reminder of all that she'd lost.

"Mallora," he repeated in his rich voice. He wore a red vest with gold buttons over a shirt as immaculately white as the door of his shop, and his black breeches were tucked into calf-high black boots polished to a high shine. "That is an unusual name for a Seafarer as young as you look to be."

She must have shown her surprise on her face even though she tried hard not to react, because he chuckled as he sat down and plucked the top from the glass decanter, pouring two glasses of spirits with practiced ease.

"My dear girl," he said, "I have owned this shop for nearly fifty years. I can see what people are the moment they step through that door."

"What they were," she said, regaining her voice.

He raised his eyebrows in question, taking a swallow of his drink.

"I'm no longer a Seafarer," she said. Her voice only trembled a little.

"Please, sit." He gestured to the other chair. "Share a drink."

His suggestion sounded more like a command, and though she didn't like the idea of drinking liquor – she needed all her wits about her – she also couldn't afford to offend him, so she sat, tucking her satchel against her side, and curled her fingers around the cool cut glass of the tumbler. The amber liquid tasted smoky and burned her throat, but she managed not to cough. Warmth immediately bloomed in her belly.

"Scotch," Bodelet said, holding his glass up to the light and swirling the liquid in the bottom of it. "Quite the drink, and quite difficult to procure."

Mal wondered sickeningly if he expected her to *pay* for the scotch she'd just swallowed. The panic closed around her throat a little tighter. Hex, she reminded herself. She was here for Hex.

Bodelet finished the rest of his glass of scotch as he gazed into the flames. He poured himself another, sat back in his chair and then said, "So what have you brought that you think I will have such interest in, Mallora?"

Suddenly she was seized with the conviction that she shouldn't have brought the *entire* shell to the shop, but there was nothing for it now. She unfastened the flap of the satchel and drew the curve of the cloth-covered egg into her lap. Out of the corner of her eye, she saw Bodelet lean forward just slightly, his shrewd eyes sharpening. "I wish to sell a piece of this Merrow shell," she said, tugging aside the covering just enough to reveal the dark red of the shell's exterior. The firelight caught the gold flecks, making them glow like smoldering sparks. The inside of the egg gleamed pale white, a streak of blue swirled through the pearly color.

"My dear girl," said Bodelet in a very quiet voice, "where did you get this?"

"I found it washed up on the beach," she said with such confidence that she almost believed it herself.

Bodelet made a sound that could have been agreement. He downed the rest of his scotch in one swallow. "And you wish to sell a piece of it?"

"Just a piece," Mal said firmly, even though she had the sudden dreadful thought that perhaps she wouldn't be able to break the shell – it *was* unnaturally heavy and thick, unlike any other shell that she'd seen.

"And what do you ask for a piece?" Bodelet said in a velvet voice. His eyes had never left the shell.

Mal had thought about the price of feverwort, and the money they would need for their room and board while Hex recovered. She glanced at Bodelet, who was still transfixed by the shell, and doubled the outrageous sum that she'd settled on during her walk to the shop. "Two hundred pieces of gold for a piece as large as my palm." Her breath left her as the words hung in the air.

"Two hundred pieces of gold, and one length each of rubies, pearls and emeralds for half that," Bodelet said immediately.

She stared at him, stunned. Was he jesting? She'd never dreamed of such a sum, not even when they'd spun tales of taking prizes rich beyond imagining as fourths.

"Child," he said, looking suddenly much older, "if I am not honest in this dealing, I will die a terrible death. I have dealt with powerful objects long enough to know this much." He looked at her in consideration. "What is it that you truly need? Why are you selling this?"

"Feverwort," she said, dazed into honesty.

"The lad from the *Dragonwing*," he murmured, settling back into his chair and steepling his fingers. He looked at her in consideration. "If you are willing to wait half an hour, I will procure that for you as well. You already have a healer?"

"One of the others who sailed with us," she said, nodding.

He shook his head. "Never mind. I have a better thought. I will send Demelda. Which inn?"

"I…why are you doing this?" she asked, frowning. Her instincts came roaring back. No one did anything for free, and this seemed too good to be true.

Bodelet reached toward her; she covered the egg and almost pushed it back into the satchel, but instead his long fingers brushed her forearm. He touched the place where, beneath the sleeve of her dress and the bandages, her white skin turned to scales. She fought the urge to run out of the shop. How had he known? And why did it make a difference?

I can see what people are the moment they step through that door.

His words echoed in her head, but he said nothing, sitting back in his chair. She sat carefully still. After a moment, he called Alexander over and gave him instructions in a low voice. Mal didn't miss the suspicious look that Alexander slid over his shoulder at her when Bodelet turned back to his decanter of scotch. The older man waited to speak until the shop assistant had disappeared into the back room.

"Let us drink to your health and your long life, *muirgen*," he said.

Mal repeated the word to herself until she knew it was branded in her mind, and resolved to ask Jem what it meant even as she touched her glass to Bodelet's with a gentle clink. She took another swallow of scotch and then set the glass down.

"Now," said Bodelet, "what tavern are you staying at?"

"I believe our healer will be just fine, as long as he has the feverwort," Mal said. She shifted uncomfortably.

"Nonsense," the silver-haired man replied. "Demelda has been healing for nearly as long as I've run this shop. Do you want your friend to survive or not?" He asked the question as though he were merely commenting on the weather.

Mal swallowed hard. "The Blind Dragon," she said finally.

Bodelet stood and walked over to his desk, producing a small white card from one drawer. He dipped a white feather quill in ink and scratched at the card for a moment. Alexander emerged from the back room carrying a small black velvet bag. Bodelet folded the card and sealed it with wax, then exchanged it for the drawstring bag. Alexander bowed to Bodelet and strode to the door of the shop. He rang a bell and a boy appeared out of the shadows, hand already outstretched for the message.

Mal watched in silent fascination and a little awe. She hadn't ever seen this side of Haven or Horizon – all thirds could afford was a tankard of ale and a hot meal, and a room off the ship if two or three of them pitched in after taking a good prize or saving their haul for a while. In this shop, in front of the pleasantly warm fire, it seemed like Bodelet had merely to think of something and it would be accomplished with silent, smooth precision.

"Demelda should be at the room within the hour with the fever-wort," Bodelet said.

"Thank you," she managed.

He placed the velvet bag on the table between the decanter of scotch and the bottle of wine. It clinked gently.

"Do you have tools to take the piece?" she asked, lifting up the shell.

Bodelet chuckled. "Child, it will yield to *your* hands, not mine."

She pulled back the cloth and placed her hand over the edge of the shell, thinking about the size of the piece that she wanted. A strange little shiver ran through her as she applied gentle pressure. The shell breaking sounded like a bone snapping, but the piece came off cleanly, gleaming like a gemstone in her palm.

Bodelet unfolded a square of white cloth and gently picked up the piece of shell, carefully folding the edges of the cloth over itself and tucking it into a pocket inside his vest. It was all a bit anticlimactic, Mal thought – until she picked up the black drawstring bag. It seemed obscenely heavy. She rested it in the curve of the shell and tugged the strings loose. The glimmer of gold and gemstones made her dizzy. She quickly tied the bag shut and shoved it into the bottom of her satchel, her fingers brushing the leather case that she knew contained the wind-whistling pipes of Hex's mother. The shell she placed back in the satchel with more care, and she made sure that her dagger still lay along the top, easily accessible.

"Thank you," she said to Bodelet. "This…wasn't what I expected."

"It was not what I expected of this night either," the silver-haired man replied, "but we must take what comes to us in this world without questioning it too much." He stood. "You must be eager to return."

Mal stood as well, brushing at her skirt. The satchel pressed, newly heavy, against her hip, the weight of it pulling down on her shoulder. "I am."

"I would be happy to have Alexander escort you back to your inn," Bodelet said.

"I'll be fine," she said. Somehow the idea of the shop assistant following her back to the Blind Dragon didn't reassure her as Bodelet had to think it did, but he didn't argue.

"It has been a pleasure, Mallora," he said elegantly.

She wasn't sure what to say, so she just smiled. Alexander opened the door for her, his face unreadable, and she stepped out into the night.

She walked in the center of the street as before, careful not to look rushed or afraid. The well-lit, prosperous street faded behind her, but the moon shone brightly overhead. All the same, she almost didn't see the two men detach from the shadows until they were almost upon her. She dropped to one knee, hissing a curse as her hand tangled in her skirt and lost her precious time as she went for her dagger. Her heart leapt into her throat – had they followed her from the shop? If they robbed her, she didn't know what else they would do. At least the healer would be on the way to help Hex anyway. She managed to close her fingers around her dagger as one of the men wrapped his hand in her hair, dragging her painfully to her feet.

"Pretty thing like you walking the streets at night," hissed one man into her ear.

"Nothing good happens after dark, darling," drawled the other.

Mal stabbed the one gripping her hair, feeling her dagger glance off a rib as she shoved it deeply into his side and dragged it as far as she could reach. He exhaled in surprise and staggered back. She aimed a kick at the other man, but he dodged and punched her, his knuckles hitting her cheekbone with a sickening crack. She felt his other hand claw at the bodice of her dress and she let him back her against the grimy brick wall of a nearby shop – if he wanted to really *hurt* her, he'd have kept hitting her. If they wanted to rob her, they would've gone for the satchel. They were clearly after something else. She shoved aside the queasy feeling in her stomach as his hand groped and prodded her flesh, her hands busy with the flap of her satchel.

"Pert little thing," the man breathed into her ear. "I'll teach you some manners."

"How's this for manners?" she growled, and she shoved her second blade into his belly. He choked. She slid the dagger through him with a long dragging motion, pulling the edge through his major organs, coldly calculating that she'd done enough to kill him even as a savage anger rose up in her. Anger had no place in a fight like this—emotion got people killed more often than not. He fell against her and she shoved him away. He staggered, blood bubbling from the gaping wound, the flaps of his torn shirt hanging like rags. Her dagger dripped black in the moonlight as the man slid down the brick wall, leaving a lurid smear of blood.

She watched him from a few paces away. His eyes glittered in the moonlight and his mouth opened and closed like a fish on the hook. She could have just stopped him—could have sliced the muscle at his thigh or the back of his leg to make sure he couldn't run after her…but then he would have been able to caterwaul to the constables, such as they were in the port. That would lead to questions, more questions than Mal wanted. And besides, she thought, still waiting and watching, he would've cornered some other girl that didn't have a dagger. The man wheezed once more and then slumped to the side.

With steady hands, Mal retrieved the other dagger from the first man, who'd already died. She held her breath against the stench of his evacuated bowels – everyone shit themselves when they died, she'd learned that as a sparrow – as she wiped the blades on his shirt to clean them as best she could. The man against the wall moaned something unintelligible and pleading. She replaced the dagger in her boot and kept the other in her hand, half-hidden in the folds of her skirt as she strode quickly down the center of the street again, the sightless eye of the moon staring down at her from the black night sky.

Chapter 28

"We had a time of it, summoning everyone," Guinna said. "It took every Glasidhe messenger we could find to carry the Queen's summons."

"I should have been there," Sayre said, his eyes darkening.

"You took the arrows meant for our Queen," she replied in a low voice. "No one questions that you would have been there if you could."

"I should have been *carried* there," he retorted, but his face drew tight with pain as he simply shifted on his bed.

"Stop being ridiculous," she admonished him, sitting on the edge of the pallet. "You heard most of it through me anyway."

"It's not the same," he said grumpily.

Guinna took a deep breath and resisted the urge to comb Sayre's dark hair back from his forehead. He probably wouldn't appreciate the motherly gesture. "You need to take the time to rest and heal," she told him gently. "*Andraste* needs you to take the time to rest and heal."

"I understand," he said, closing his eyes. "It doesn't mean that I *like* it." He took a few deep breaths and the lines smoothed from between his eyebrows. When he opened his eyes, he said, "I'm sorry, Guinna. You don't deserve to be spoken to in such a manner."

She took his hand and pressed it between her own. "Sayre, our lives have changed so much since Andraste came to the throne. I'm grateful I have you here with me, and I understand that this must be frustrating for you." She smiled. "It's not the first time I've dealt with Knights and Guards who think that resting and healing is an insult to their manhood."

Sayre smiled a little at that. "I don't think it's an insult to my manhood," he objected. "I have no qualms about *that*."

Guinna lifted an eyebrow. "Oh, you don't, do you?"

He chuckled and then winced, his good arm reflexively reaching toward his wounded side. "I just feel…distinctly useless."

She glanced at the books piled by the side of his bed. "Is that what inspired the sudden interest in research?"

"You are training with weapons," said Sayre, "so I thought that I could venture into some books."

Guinna eyed the titles of the books. "Are you looking for anything in particular?"

"I thought there might be something…about how the Three were originally created," he explained.

Eamon hadn't yet given them permission to move Sayre to his own chamber yet – there had been a particularly worrying episode in which the wound in Sayre's thigh had started bleeding again unexpectedly. Guinna remembered her horror when she saw the pool of blood soaking the pallet and the gray pallor of Sayre's face, Eamon and one of the other healers working feverishly over him.

"It's interesting, isn't it," she said, "how little we know about our own origins."

"Most of those who would be able to tell us in our own Court are dead," he replied reasonably.

Guinna tilted her head. "In *our* Court, yes. But not in the Seelie Court."

"Queen Titania has ruled since the beginning," Sayre agreed.

They both sat with this thought for a while. Would Andraste be willing to speak to the Seelie Queen about the genesis of her bond with her Three? Had the First proclaimed it, or had the Queens invented it independently? It suddenly seemed unlikely to Guinna that Titania or Mab would have willingly bound themselves to three warriors without some edict from the Morrigan during their baptism. "So many questions and not enough answers," Guinna sighed. Not for the first time, she felt *old*. Her centuries weighed on her in a way that she'd never noticed in the past. Perhaps this was how those in power at the Court gained that grave gaze.

"There are answers," Sayre said. "We just aren't looking for them in the right places." He shifted again and winced. "What do you think about some tea? We've got a bit of time before Eamon comes by on his rounds." He looked at Guinna. "Tell me about what the Queen said."

"You heard it yourself," she said in half-hearted protest as she stood and checked that the copper kettle contained enough water for tea. She hung it on its hook over the fire and stoked the flames, prodding the logs with the silver poker until little showers of sparks kissed the bottom of the kettle.

"I heard it through you, which isn't the same," Sayre retorted.

"You could ask her yourself."

"Or you could just tell me."

Guinna chuckled. At least she had Sayre's light-hearted youth to remind her of her younger days.

"And stop thinking about how old you are," he added, a puckish glint in his eye. "I can always tell."

"Maybe because we share an invisible magical bond," murmured Guinna as though she were talking to herself. Then she took a breath and settled again onto the edge of his bed. "We gathered everyone in the Hall of Lights."

They had named the largest chamber in the erstwhile seat of the Unseelie Court the Hall of Lights after the hundreds of small silver *taebramh* lights suspended in delicate glass globes from the arched ceiling. It had been a more recent manifestation of the Queen's burgeoning power, and the name had quickly spread through the Court in the days after the small, beautiful constellations appeared.

"We are less in number than I thought, if everyone could fit in the Hall of Lights," murmured Sayre.

"I'm sure it wasn't *everyone*. We sent out Knights and Guards with the Vyldgard and Seelie patrols on the edges of the City, and there were those on watch and at their other duties," Guinna said, but it felt too much like she was trying to explain something that couldn't be explained. She remembered the tight feeling in her stomach as she'd stood one step lower than the Queen on the dais at the far end of the Hall. The Scholars had kept records of births and deaths, but there had been no births for years...perhaps even centuries, now that she thought of it. Not since the rebellion. Guinna blinked. It felt as though she were realizing that for the first time, but they *must* have taken note when the training masters had no more young ones to teach, when the squires had no more pages to choose, when the Guilds had no apprentices to rise through their ranks...

She cleared her throat.

"Andraste looked magnificent – as she always does, but I think she looked particularly regal, even though she wasn't wearing a gown."

"She wore breeches and a shirt, didn't she," said Sayre fondly.

"Magnificent breeches and a shirt, and a vest besides, but yes," replied Guinna. "Black breeches, a blue shirt, and a silver vest that looked a bit like armor, if armor were crafted from silk and pearls. She wore her sword at her hip as well."

"A warrior queen," murmured Sayre.

"Some did not seem to love that idea," Guinna said honestly. She could at least tell *him* her true thoughts. The Queen did not need to hear everything.

"Can we blame them?" Sayre said. "The last years have not been easy, and they were lived by the sword."

"But Andraste is different," Guinna said fiercely.

Sayre smiled. "You don't need to convince me. It's *them* we need to make understand that she isn't Mab."

"And she isn't the Dark Archer," she added.

He nodded, letting her words settle into silence.

"She held up a hand, and the quiet that just descended over everyone…that, at least, shows that they still respect the crown."

"Or they fear it," he murmured.

"That is also a possibility. Regardless, the silence was…breathtaking. It was like a physical force. And Andraste spoke into it so calmly." Guinna found herself reliving the memory, trying to get the words exactly right. "She gazed out at the Court and said, 'We are the Court of the Night and the Winter, but we are not heartless and cold.'"

Sayre smiled. He let his eyes slide half closed as he listened, motioning for her to continue. Guinna felt her gaze go distant, staring into the fire, transported back to the Queen's echoing words in the Hall of Lights.

"And then she said, 'I am your Queen, but I am also one of you. The reign of the last queen, my sister Mab, ended with years of war against Malravenar and then the darkness of her madness. I spent those years in thrall to the Enemy, and I have caused much suffering as well.'"

Sayre made a quiet noise that could have been dissent or agreement; Guinna continued, the words drawn from her inexorably, as though she had no choice, wrapped in the memory of the Queen's speech to the Court.

"There were a few murmurs at that. I wished I had my sword with me, or that you were there."

"I felt that," murmured Sayre.

She nodded. "But the Queen stood until the murmurs quieted again, and then she went on. She said, 'We cannot move forward if we are bound by the suffering of the past. We cannot heal the divisions within our Court and within our world if we allow hatred to overwhelm our hearts. We cannot go on as we were, and we must make a choice, now, together.'"

She heard Sayre's indrawn breath as though from a distance.

"I think the whole Court held their breath then. The power in her words…it was *different* than Mab. Mab demanded obedience, and Andraste was *asking*. Then she said, 'I have only two of my Three, and I wish to make a council, chosen by all the members of my Court to represent you to me. This council will be the third of my Three, chosen by ballot every Solstice.' No one said anything, and Andraste just…she clasped her hands in front of her and nodded, like it was done. And then she said, 'We start this new journey together. In this spirit, I hereby pardon any who have acted against the throne in rebellion or resistance, in my sister's reign or mine. I will not require any blood oath to ensure any obedience. Those who are Unseelie by birth will now remain Unseelie by choice, and thus it shall be until the end of my days.'"

Guinna swayed slightly as the sensation of her body rushed back, the memory fading.

"I still cannot quite believe that she pardoned them all," said Sayre quietly.

"By pardoning them, she is also pardoning us," Guinna pointed out. "I resisted Mab. I deserted the Court. You rebelled against Mab and helped the Valkyrie commander free Andraste."

"The Exiles," Sayre said. His hand drifted toward his side. "She is pardoning them as well?"

"Yes," said Guinna.

"I do not know whether I will be able to forgive them for trying to kill the Queen," he said wearily.

"You anchor us with your heart, Sayre," Guinna said. "Perhaps think of it this way: You are forgiving them for almost killing *you*."

He huffed a breath that would have been a chuckle if he hadn't suppressed it. "You know me too well."

"No such thing," she retorted affectionately. The whistle of the kettle threaded thinly through the room, and she stood, retrieving the kettle efficiently and pouring the steaming water into the two earthenware mugs. Their healers and cooks had started experimenting with a concept brought back from the mortal world: rather than brewing an entire pot of tea, they took pinches of tea and sewed them into small pouches. Tea bags, they called them. Guinna had to admit their convenience.

Sayre slowly and painfully pushed himself into a sitting position. He grimaced as Guinna checked the bandage on his thigh with a critical eye, handing him his mug of tea. "I'm fine," he muttered.

"You're fine until you're bleeding to death again," she retorted.

They sipped at their tea for a few moments in companionable silence. Guinna made it a point to spend a few hours each day with Sayre. The closeness seemed to help him – whether it was from their bond through the Queen or just because they enjoyed each other's company, she didn't know. It didn't matter.

"So," he said finally, "is the Queen going to release Dryden and Evangeline?"

The Vyldgard, much to Guinna's surprise, had turned over the Exile Evangeline after her capture by the Vyldretning in the Paladin's Tower.

"I believe that is her intention," said Guinna with a nod. "But I also believe that she will speak to you about it first."

Sayre raised an eyebrow in question as he sipped his tea again.

"Because Dryden almost killed you," she explained. "And Evangeline wounded Tyr."

"Not badly enough to prevent him from going on the expedition," Sayre said.

Guinna wasn't sure if she'd imagined the note of jealousy in Sayre's voice. If he was jealous, it was probably because Tyr wasn't confined to a bed to heal. "I still have to think of proper gifts for Eamon, Quinn and Thea," she said.

"You're changing the subject," said Sayre.

"I am," she agreed serenely.

"Fine," he sighed. "Do you have any ideas at all?"

"Eamon is a healer, so I thought perhaps a rare book or something of that sort. A healing kit seems too obvious," she confessed.

"Because it *is* too obvious," Sayre agreed.

She laughed. "Well, offer a better suggestion, then!"

"Give me a moment," Sayre said, drinking more tea. Then he raised his head in sudden inspiration. "What about a blood-blessed blade? One of those specifically made for healing."

"Mab ordered all of them destroyed," said Guinna thoughtfully. "That would truly be a magnificent gift."

"Even if Mab hadn't ordered all of them destroyed, would they still retain their power after her death?" Sayre mused.

"You should offer that idea to the Queen tonight," she said.

Sayre brushed her words away. "It doesn't matter if it's you or me who says it, just as long as it is brought to her." He tapped a finger on his mug. "For Thea…perhaps something for her forge."

"Everflame," Guinna said suddenly. "Why didn't I think of that before?"

"Because you weren't talking to me before." Sayre lifted his mug in a toast to her idea. "Everflame would be quite the royal gift to a smith. She wouldn't have to use forge runes to light the fire every morning."

"Do you think we need to talk to the Valkyrie commander or the Seer before offering the gift since Thea is one of the Vyldgard?"

"I find it hard to believe that the Vyldretning would object to one of the Wild Court accepting such a gift," Sayre replied. "She allows them many liberties."

"Liberties that may soon be echoed in our own Court," Guinna reminded him.

"I didn't say it was a *bad* thing," he retorted.

"So…a blood-blessed blade and everflame. The two of us are particularly good at thinking of gift ideas," Guinna said teasingly. "What about Quinn?"

"He is mortal," said Sayre thoughtfully, "but that hasn't prevented him from proving his worth as a warrior."

"What about a shadowcloak?" she said.

"I would think perhaps a shield of some description," replied Sayre. "And besides, shadowcloaks are…"

"Children's toys?" smiled Guinna. "Yes, the kind that we used to weave…but imagine one made by the hand of a Queen! Quinn looks different than any of us, so he could use it when he wanted to move about unnoticed."

"And are we sure that's a power he would use wisely?" Sayre asked dryly.

"I'm sure we could convince him that the Queen will know if he uses it irresponsibly."

"Guinna," said Sayre in a tone of mock chastisement. "Are you suggesting that we *lie* to Quinn about the nature of his gift?"

"It's not exactly a *lie*, more of a…creative management strategy," she replied. The phrase sounded familiar, but she couldn't remember where she'd heard it.

"You've been spending entirely too much time with the mortals," Sayre said, narrowing his eyes. "That sounds like something Tess or Liam would say." He took a long sip of tea and then grinned. "Either way, I like your thinking. Subtle, yet powerful."

"Not *literally* powerful," Guinna pointed out.

"A blood-blessed blade for the healer, everflame for the smith, and a shadowcloak for the mortal," said Sayre musingly. "It does have a ring to it. Not a literal ring," he added quickly. "That shouldn't be on the list. Giving magical rings as gifts really doesn't work out well most of the time."

Guinna frowned. "What in the world are you talking about?"

"Oh, it's not from our world, it's a story from Doendhtalam," Sayre explained eagerly, reaching for a particularly thick tome beside his bed. "The Paladin was kind enough to lend me her copy of the legend."

"Tolkien," Guinna read off the cover. "I've never heard of this Scholar."

"He's not a Scholar, really, more of a bard from what I understand," Sayre said.

"Well, I'll take your word for it," she said, placing the thick book back onto the top of the precarious stack.

"If you're ever confined to your bed for days on end, you should consider reading it," he said seriously.

"I shall rely on you to make the recommendation again," she said.

He sighed, holding his mug with both hands. "I think I need to sleep," he pronounced with an air of irritation.

"The more you sleep now, the quicker you'll heal," Guinna said, reaching out to take his mug.

"Don't you go lecturing me too," he muttered. "At least this way I'll be asleep when Eamon stops by."

"You should be flattered that our head healer is paying such personal attention to you."

"It isn't flattery when you're one of the Queen's Three," muttered Sayre as he carefully rearranged his pillows in his preferred configuration. "And I'd rather not need a healer at all."

"Soon you won't," Guinna told him encouragingly. Still holding the two mugs, she leaned forward and kissed him on the cheek. "Sleep well."

He rolled to his good side and sighed, his eyes closing. She stood and watched until he settled into the easy, slow breathing of sleep.

"A blood-blessed blade, everflame and a shadowcloak," she repeated to herself quietly as she set their mugs on the little table by the fire. She wondered if the gifts would be acceptable to the Queen. At the very least, it gave them a starting point. She glanced at Sayre again and then sat down in one of the chairs by the little table, some wordless worry about leaving him alone taking hold of her.

She refreshed her mug with more hot water from the kettle and sipped at the tepid tea in contemplation. The Queen's announcement of pardon and the council had certainly stirred some within the Court. Andraste had made it a point to sit in the Hall of Lights for a few hours every day, in the morning or afternoon, to speak to those who wanted to express their thoughts on the changes. Guinna had offered to sit with her, but Andraste had shaken her head.

"I know you are fulfilling your duties as one of my Three," the Queen had said. "But this is part of what has to change. I do not want to be isolated from the Court. I don't want to be a figurehead, unreachable and untouchable, only sending emissaries. See that Sayre doesn't wake up alone."

"For you to be untouchable would not be a bad thing," Guinna had said, the silent implication clear. The Queen's new ideas would come to nothing if she were assassinated by Exiles seeking revenge or disgruntled members of her own Court.

"I will be vigilant," Andraste had said firmly, "but I will not lock myself away. I need to understand our people."

Our people. Guinna drank her tea and put the question to herself: Did she truly feel bonds of affection for *all* of the Court? Her mind drew her back unwillingly to the dark days of Mab's reign. Suspicion and fear had run rampant among the Court. Men and women disappeared without a trace nearly every day, with no explanation given by the Queen or those who served her; and the few who had been brave enough to resist and demand answers joined those who vanished. Guinna felt her insides shriveling in hot, familiar shame. She had not been one of those to stand up against the Mad Queen.

But all those who stood up against her are bones and dust, said the small, logical voice that had kept her alive in those dark days. *You survived. You did what had to be done.*

She had never had to hurt anyone, so she had convinced herself that she hadn't harmed anything by her careful, calculated apathy. But now, as one of the new Queen's Three, she recognized the peculiar twisting in her gut as guilt.

Guilt that most had suffered so much, and she bore no scars from the Mad Queen's reign.

Guilt that the bravest among them had been tortured and killed, and she had been rewarded for her cowardice.

Guilt that she had not done more, that she had not spoken out, that she had compressed herself into a small, fearful space, watching as Ramel and Donovan slowly lost their souls bound in service to Mab, counseling Bren not to speak so loudly against the brutal regime. Bren's voice suddenly echoed in her head.

Our victory over Malravenar doesn't make us heroes, Guinna. It doesn't absolve the Queen of her wrongs. It doesn't do anything at all other than preserve the kingdom that Mab rules.

Bren and her messages, Bren and her fierce defiance. She had been a Scholar, but she had been more courageous than them all.

Guinna sighed. If they'd guessed, those centuries ago, who other than Finnead would have become one of the Queen's Three, no one would have mentioned her name. What had she done to deserve her place here?

"Enough," she muttered to herself, sitting up straight and drawing back her shoulders. She did the Queen no good by dwelling on the past. No matter what guilt clawed at her heart, she could not change anything that happened, no more than she could make the sun rise in the west and set in the east.

This was her life. This was her duty, and she would do right by the Queen and by Sayre. She would do right by the entire Court, because she had been among those who failed them during the Mad Queen's reign.

There are many more to blame than just you, if you insist on placing such blame, said that small, practical voice in the corner of her mind.

"More than enough to go around, then," she murmured, finishing her second mug of tea.

She jumped and nearly dropped her mug at the pounding on the

Queen's chamber door. Sayre stirred as she leapt up and ran to the door, wrenching it open.

"This is a sickroom," she hissed, but the wild eyes of the messenger – a Guard whose name she couldn't remember – struck unnamed panic into her chest. She stepped outside and shut the door behind her. "What is it?"

"One of the Mad Queen's Three," the Guard said, "he took a blade to his own wrists…"

"Ramel left with the expedition," Guinna interrupted him. "They sent back word?"

"Not Ramel, my lady," he said, shaking his head. "Donovan."

Guinna stared at him in a moment of suspended shock, and then she started running toward the healing ward as though Mab's hounds were at her heels.

Chapter 29

"**I** still can't believe Vivian gave you the key to the Tower," Liam said from the side of the practice ring.

"What, you don't think I'm responsible enough? Or are you just annoyed that you didn't make the cut?" Quinn grinned. The weight of the silver key on its length of leather around his neck felt like a natural part of him now. He hadn't used it yet, but it had only been a few days.

"It's the *Paladin's* Tower," Liam said. "You don't exactly fit the definition."

"Well, neither do you," replied Quinn, even though he knew it was a lame response. If the whole team had been there, he was pretty sure Duke would have ribbed him pretty hard for that.

"Nothing says I can't be a Paladin," Liam said, brushing his hair out of his eyes. He refused to spar now, instead just running through drills on his own. Quinn knew that wasn't a good sign, but it was better than Liam not showing up for training at all.

"Dude, you're one of the High Queen's Three," he pointed out. "Pretty sure that takes you off the ballot for any other jobs that are even remotely cool."

"I told Vell last night that she should disavow me," Liam said quietly, looking down at the hard-packed dirt.

"What?" Quinn said blankly. "I have no idea what that means but I'm guessing it's something to do with pushing everyone away and isolating yourself." He shifted his grip on his sword and stared at Liam, waiting for his answer.

"She should disavow me," he repeated stubbornly. "I'm a liability at this point. I don't know how much longer I'll be able to hold out against Arcana. The Morrigan. Whatever she is now."

"And Vell hasn't been able to come up with anything?" Quinn asked. It seemed weird to him that the High Queen didn't know how to solve the problem – but then again, he reminded himself, she wasn't omnipotent or omniscient. Vell was scary-powerful, but she was still fallible. She couldn't solve all their problems with a snap of her fingers.

"Seer!" shrilled a Glasidhe messenger, her aura sparking as she dove toward them. "The Lady Bearer asks if you can spare the time to join her."

"Is everything all right?" Liam said, immediately sheathing his sword. Quinn followed suit, both of them watching the small winged Fae.

"I do not know," she said with an air of honesty, "but the Lady Bearer was upset when she sent me to bring you the message."

"Her room?" Liam asked, already striding across the practice yards. He stumbled and stopped for a moment, swaying with one of the bouts of dizziness that had become frighteningly common over the past few days. Quinn caught up with him and grabbed his arm, steadying him.

"Yes!" chirped the Glasidhe. She bowed to them. "If you will excuse me, I have other messages to deliver!"

"That was abrupt," Quinn commented as the messenger zoomed away.

"They're couriers," said Liam, sounding breathless. "Their job is to be fast."

"Come on, let's get you to Tess," Quinn said.

"I'm fine," Liam protested, but his knees buckled as he tried to shake off Quinn's grip.

"Dude, you're just making it harder on yourself," muttered Quinn, hauling him up again.

"See? Liability," Liam said in disgust.

"Stubborn, more like it," he replied.

Liam frowned. "Whatever's happened, it's not anything that Vell or Calliea are tracking."

"That's a good thing, right? No more nasty sneak attacks or anything." Quinn resisted the urge to scratch at his scar. The itching had mostly gone away since his stitches had been taken out a few days ago, but sometimes it was like his body remembered the persistent annoyance a little too well.

"Vell and Calliea don't track all the bad things that happen in the White City," Liam replied darkly, his voice a little stronger.

"Okay, then, let's get you to the cathedral, you little ray of sunshine," Quinn said, even as he wondered what had happened to prompt Tess to ask for her brother. Had something happened to the expedition? Was there some sort of problem with Luca or the wolves? Maybe Tess had found something about a solution for Liam…although he found it hard to believe that she would have summoned them over that.

After a few minutes, Liam was able to walk on his own, and they picked up the pace to a quick stride. Quinn glanced at Liam every few steps.

"Stop looking at me like I'm going to keel over at any moment," Liam growled.

"But you might keel over at any moment," Quinn pointed out.

Liam sighed. "How did I end up with you as my shadow?"

"Because I'm the only team guy left and I'm kind of used to following you around anyway." Quinn shrugged. "Plus, I don't really have anything better to do since Niamh dumped me."

"Well, that's a ringing endorsement," Liam muttered.

Jocelyn A. Fox

"Could be worse," Quinn said. "You could be stuck with Duke. Or Jess's old grumpy ass."

"Jess is a lot quieter than you."

"But also a lot grumpier. And did I mention older?"

Liam gave a dry chuckle as they turned down the path that they knew like the back of their hand by this point. He paused to catch his breath before tackling the flight of stairs leading to the great doors of the cathedral. More Sidhe than usual stood in small clusters outside the healing ward. Liam didn't spare them a second glance, concerned again with slowing his breathing.

Quinn kept an eye on Liam but perked his ears, listening to some of the snatches of conversation.

"One of the Valkyrie flying a patrol found him," said a Vyldgard woman with bright blue feathers in her dark hair. "Brought him here as fast as her mount could fly."

The Seelie man standing next to her shook his head, his expression grave.

"...one of the Mad Queen's Three," said another man in a low voice. "It's said that he was one of her executioners."

"Guilt and shame," murmured the woman closest to him.

"Are you coming or not?" Liam said, already three steps ahead of him.

Quinn caught up without much trouble, the wheels in his mind already turning. "Hey," he said as they turned down the passageway toward Tess's room – or he assumed it was the passageway, since most of them looked alike to him and he was just trusting Liam to lead them in the right direction.

Liam raised an eyebrow and glanced at him. "Yeah?"

"Have you heard of Sidhe committing suicide?"

"Not any recently, but Calliea tried, before she was sent to the Saemhradall," Liam replied.

"Ok, did not expect that bit of information," Quinn said, "but...it happens, then?"

– 450 –

"One of the Unseelie Three talked to Finn about it, before the expedition left," Liam said. "She was worried about Ramel."

"Well," said Quinn, "I think Ramel wasn't the only one that people should have been worried about."

Liam frowned at him, but they reached Tess's door – or rather, tapestry. Quinn wrinkled his nose. He didn't know if he'd ever get used to walking through things that looked solid, but after Liam disappeared he held his breath and stepped through it. By the time he blinked and reoriented himself, Tess had already thrown herself at Liam. Her brother staggered slightly but recovered, wrapping his arms around her in a brotherly hug.

Quinn's heart sank as he glimpsed the tears on Tess's cheeks. Someone had died, and it was someone Tess had known from her time at the Unseelie Court. He tried to put the pieces together, but he was missing some key information, so he stood by the door and waited until Tess finally drew back from Liam. She wiped at her tears with the knuckle of one hand. Her war-markings pulsed brightly emerald through the sleeve of her white shirt.

"I talked to Ramel before he left," said Tess in a choked voice. "But I never even thought about asking Donovan."

Donovan. Quinn's stomach contracted uncomfortably as he realized that was the guy whose face he had rearranged with the stool in the healing ward.

"You couldn't have known." Liam put a comforting hand on Tess's shoulder.

"I *should* have known," she fired back, her eyes flaring with anger. "I should have known, Liam, because who *wouldn't* have trouble after everything that they went through?"

"You talked to him in the old throne room," Liam said. "When you went to help with the bones."

Tess hugged herself and rubbed her arms unhappily. "I did talk to him then," she admitted grudgingly. "He seemed...he seemed *happy* that Mab was dead. He didn't say anything at all about…about…" She swallowed hard and looked down, tears clinging to her lashes.

"About killing himself," Quinn finished quietly.

"I don't understand." Tess shook her head. Shards of emerald light raced jaggedly down her war-markings like lightning. "I don't *understand.*"

"This is a tough one," Liam said, nodding.

Quinn caught the tiredness in his friend's eyes. They both knew too many guys who'd lost the battle with their demons after war.

"It doesn't ever get easier, no matter how many times," he said.

"How could he do this?" Tess demanded, her brows contracting into a fierce scowl. "Why did he think it was *okay* to just…to just *leave all of us*?" Her mouth twisted as a sob shook her. "I don't understand."

"It's like banging your head against a wall," Liam agreed. "You're never gonna understand, Bug. It was a choice he made."

"I wish he were here so that I could punch him in the face," Tess said vehemently. "What makes it okay for him to decide that he just wanted out, no matter how much he hurt everyone else?"

"It's not okay," Quinn said. "And like Liam said, we can't understand it. He decided that the pain was too much, whatever it was, and he punched out."

Tess growled a string of colorful curses, the words waterlogged with tears. Quinn glanced at Liam and mouthed: *Luca?*

"Luca's out with Chael," Tess said, grabbing a handkerchief from the table and blowing her nose. "He should be back soon. I just needed…I needed someone to talk to about it because I just can't…I don't…" She trailed off, tears streaming down her blotchy face. She stared at the ashes of the fire in the hearth and clenched her jaw, her body shaking with grief.

A low hum filled the room. Quinn glanced over at the table, the nexus of the sound, and saw the scabbard of the Iron Sword slung over the back of one chair. The emerald in its pommel glowed softly, and the sound emanating from it inexplicably calmed him. Tess hiccupped and wiped her face again.

"Do you have one of those nifty tables in here?" Quinn asked. "I feel like we could all use a drink."

"Liam actually just convinced me to give it a try," Tess said nasally, grimacing at the sound of her voice. She waved at a small table set off to the side that looked nearly identical to the one that stood in Liam's room.

Quinn walked over and told it clearly, "Wine. Or whatever that stuff is that you guys drink here."

"*Vinaess,*" said Tess.

The runes around the edge of the table glimmered, and a silver pitcher appeared on the table, sliding through a strangely thickened patch of air. It was like watching something take shape through the heat waves rising from asphalt in summer, Quinn decided. He took the pitcher and appropriated three clean mugs.

"Mugs of *vinaess,*" muttered Tess, but she took hers and downed half of it in a few hearty swallows.

"Hey, take a breath," Liam said. "Let's sit down and talk."

Quinn refrained from telling him that he looked like he was going to fall down, so sitting down was pretty much his only option at this point.

"I don't want to *talk,*" muttered Tess, staring moodily into her mug. "I want to...I don't know what I want to do, but I don't want to *talk.*"

"Well, we can do whatever it is you want when you figure it out," Quinn said, pulling out the chair with the Sword slung over its back. She slid into it with a sigh, propping her elbows on the table. Quinn sat across from Liam. He took a swig of *vinaess,* wincing at its sweetness. "Not my favorite," he admitted as he put the mug down. "Never was much of a wine guy."

"You want some *ulfdrengr* liquor? It's like whiskey," Tess said matter-of-factly.

Liam caught his eye and shook his head minutely.

"I saw that," Tess muttered into her mug, finishing the rest of her *vinaess.*

"I'm guessing the Unseelie Queen and her Three – or well, the two that she has – they know?" Quinn asked after Tess refilled her mug.

"Everyone knows," she replied darkly.

"Okay, hey, maybe slow down a little," Liam said, reaching for Tess's mug after she downed half of the second serving. She pulled it out of his reach.

"I am an *adult,*" she enunciated with grave sincerity, glaring at him.

"You're also my little sister."

"I wouldn't call her *little,*" Quinn advised. He shrugged when Liam gave him a disbelieving look. "I'm just saying, she's the Bearer of the Iron Sword and all that. Definitely not 'little.'"

"Don't act like you've never drank away your sorrows," Tess added, upending her mug decisively.

Okay, maybe this was going to get a little out of hand, Quinn thought as he watched her pour a third serving. He took another swallow of the stuff and tried to estimate its alcohol content. Maybe being the Bearer meant she could handle more.

Tess stared down into her mug and her face crumpled as she started sobbing again.

Or…maybe not.

"*In vino, veritas,*" Quinn said to himself as he sipped.

They both sat quietly as Tess cried herself out. Finally, she drew a shuddering breath and took a bracing swallow of *vinaess.*

"Donovan was one of the group," she said, staring into the distance. "Bren brought me to the feast that Mab put on to celebrate Finnead's return. Ronan and Emery had an argument…Ronan was a Knight and Emery a Guard…and Donovan, he played the peacekeeper, reminding them that they were all brothers." She drew in a shuddering breath and then her eyes widened. "Oh, I didn't remember," she said, her tear-roughened voice weighted with sadness. "Bren and Donovan…I think they were together. They didn't talk about it much, but I remember Bren saying she was worried for Donovan, back when I was still in Darkhill. Before I found the Sword."

"And Bren was executed by Mab," Liam said quietly.

They looked at each other with varying expressions of horror as the same thought occurred to them all at once.

They say he was her executioner.

"I feel sick," Tess said miserably, covering her face with her hands.

"We don't know that it happened that way," Quinn said.

"There's a lot we don't know about the Mad Queen's Court." Liam sat back in his chair.

"Doesn't that make it worse?" Tess demanded. She grabbed her mug angrily. "I want to know *why.*"

"Dude, let the anger flow through you," Quinn said. "Honestly. You're not gonna find the solution. You're not gonna suddenly understand why Donovan killed himself."

"Bren," said Tess bleakly.

"There are a lot of people that lost someone," he replied.

"But if he had to kill her…" Tess convulsed with a shudder that ran through her entire body and drank a long draught of *vinaess* as though the strong Fae wine could chase away all the sorrow and anger running through her.

"We don't know that," Liam said firmly. "Don't let your imagination run wild. It'll just make it worse."

Tess stared broodingly into nothing for a few moments. Quinn settled into the silence. He'd learned that especially in the tough times, you had to be comfortable with saying nothing, because a lot of times there was nothing to say that would help.

"I should've talked to him," she said softly.

"Sometimes people don't give any sign at all," Liam said.

Tess sighed.

"Don't think this is your fault," Quinn said. "In the end, it was his decision. Be mad at him, be sad that he's gone, remember the good times and talk about him with his other friends. But don't blame yourself."

"It's hard," she said in a choked voice. "I'm used to…fixing things." One of her hands brushed the scabbard of the Sword. "I'm used to fighting an enemy I can see. I know what to do then. This…" She shook her head. "This terrifies me because I don't know how to fight it."

"Love your friends as hard as you can," he said. "That's all you can do. That's all any of us can do."

Liam pressed his mouth into a line and nodded.

"I'm sorry for sending a messenger to you and then falling apart," Tess said, tears filling her eyes again.

"Don't apologize for that," Liam said immediately. "Don't ever apologize for reaching out."

"You're allowed to fall apart every once in a while," Quinn added. "We all are. And this is a pretty big deal."

"I don't know what to do with all these feelings," she said, a hint of disgust in her voice. "It's like…I'm angry…I'm *furious* with Donovan…and I'm so sad that my chest hurts…I hadn't seen him a lot since I left Darkhill, and then he was one of Mab's Three, but we did talk after the throne room…" She swallowed hard. "This sounds terrible, but I guess I didn't expect to feel so sad about it."

"You're allowed to feel it however you feel it," Quinn said. "And maybe you're feeling it harder because he killed himself. It's tough. He was a warrior, he made it through the battle with Malravenar and he survived Mab, and then he checked out. He chose to leave. It sucks." He took a swallow of *vinaess*. "Heck, last time I saw him I smashed a stool into his face."

"I thought you were going to start another war that day," Liam said in a confessional tone.

"I was ready to battle," he agreed. "The dude was being a prick. I mean, looking back on it now, he probably couldn't help it, but I didn't really know that at the time."

"He did almost kill Calliea on the raid, too," Tess said. "God, I was so angry at him after that."

"You did that glowy, pour-your-life-force-away healing thing on Calliea," Quinn said, nodding.

"I would've done it for Donovan, too, but it was too late," she said, her words wavering.

"You were there when they brought him in?" Liam asked.

Tess nodded. Tears slipped down her cheeks again. Her eyes were beginning to swell from all the crying. "Niamh and Calliea were flying an easy patrol, and Niamh spotted him. Calliea brought him in." She shook her head. "I could tell when I got there that he was gone."

Quinn tried to suppress the little flare of concern that ignited in his chest at the mention of Niamh. He reminded himself that she was a big girl, and she had her own friends and her mother if she was having trouble with the after-effects of finding Donovan. But he still sighed, "Man, that sucks."

"All of this sucks," she agreed. "Out of the whole group that night…Emery died at the Dark Keep. Bren died on Mab's orders. I haven't seen Ronan, so maybe he made it through, but I don't know. Guinna is one of Andraste's Three, Finn gave up his memories so he's a completely different person, and I'm the Bearer of the Iron Sword." She shook her head. "If you had told me all that on that night, I wouldn't have believed you. I would've thought it all sounded too crazy."

"That's how life works sometimes," Quinn said. He leaned back in his chair and stretched. "I mean, if you'd tried to tell me a year ago that I'd be sucked through a portal into a magic world filled with Valkyrie where dragons and who knows what else exist, I would've said you were off your meds." He shrugged. "But here I am."

"That is how life works sometimes," Tess said, nodding in weary agreement. She pressed the heels of her hands into her eyes. "I'm going to look terrible at the pyre tonight."

"You have a good reason," Liam pointed out.

"Doesn't mean I *like* it," she retorted.

"Will Luca be back for the pyre?"

"I don't know," she admitted. "They're scouting out locations for Rialla's den and seeing if they can make contact with any of the packs nearest the City. They'd all moved farther north when Malravenar's creatures were here, but Luca said that they think a few might have moved back into their old territory."

"So there would be Rialla's pups and then pups from other packs?" Quinn asked. He felt a little relieved that they'd been able to change the subject. Tess needed to cry it out, but she didn't need to completely implode because she got stuck in the same feedback loop of grief.

"From what Luca explained, it doesn't *have* to be pups, although that's what the *ulfdrengr* tradition has always been," Tess said. She pulled aside the collar of her shirt and turned her neck toward Quinn.

"I have no idea what you're trying to show me," he said bluntly.

She half smiled. "I don't know if you can still see them, but there are silver teeth marks there from the White Wolf. He's one of the *ulfdrengr* gods."

Quinn leaned forward and barely made out a series of pale dots on Tess's neck, nearly indistinguishable from her skin. "And what do those teeth marks mean?"

She shrugged. "Beats me. Maybe it has something to do with being able to help bond pairs. I think it's to help rebuild the *ulfdrengr* somehow."

"You don't think it means you're going to get your own wolf?" Quinn asked.

The Sword let out a deep, booming peal that rattled his teeth. He blinked and looked at it with new appreciation.

"Well," he said, "I guess that answers that question."

Tess touched the hilt of the Sword fondly. "I don't think it's kosher to be both the Bearer and an *ulfdrengr*."

"Might be a conflict of interest," he agreed gravely.

Tess pushed away her mug of *vinaess*. "Do you want something to eat? I drank too much on an empty stomach."

"You don't say," Liam said under his breath.

"I'll have whatever you're having," Quinn replied.

"Don't feel like you *have* to stay," she said quickly. "I mean…I'd appreciate the company, but if you have other things to do…"

"Nothing better than a few drinks and good company," Quinn said firmly, lifting his mug first to her and then to Liam. He took a swallow of the sweet drink and watched Tess as she made her way, a bit unsteadily, over to the rune-inscribed table to conjure up some food.

"Thanks," Liam said, nodding to Quinn.

"You two are my family," Quinn said. "Nowhere I'd rather be than here."

And despite the turmoil of the afternoon, he realized that what he'd said was entirely true as he sat back in his chair. The weight of the silver key suddenly pressed against his chest. Maybe Tess could help him with some research, help take her mind off the tragedy of Donovan's suicide. He sipped his wine thoughtfully, mulling it over until Tess triumphantly deposited a tray overflowing with bread, meat and cheese onto the table.

"Good choice," he said approvingly, and though it didn't seem that she could fully smile yet, she at least wasn't crying at the moment. He helped himself to a portion of food. Some problems stayed the same, no matter what world you were in, even if there was magic and other fantastic things. Not everyone chose to save themselves, and he was used to being there to help pick up the pieces.

He finished arranging his sandwich and said to Tess, "So, what've you been working on in the training yard lately?"

She swallowed her bite of food and obligingly launched into an explanation of the archery skills she was refining. Liam listened attentively but didn't eat. Quinn felt like he was expanding, filling the cracks in everyone, holding everything together…and that was okay. He'd do it for as long as he could, for as many people as he could, because that was what friends did for each other.

He tucked away his thoughts for later and turned his attention back to Tess, hoping that he'd be able to help her understand that Donovan's death really wasn't her fault. There was enough guilt to go around in this place – something else that hadn't changed when he'd been sucked through that rip in the fabric between the worlds.

He sat back, sipped at his *vinaess*, and listened.

Chapter 30

"You know," Vivian said to Niall, "I went camping exactly once before this, and I hated it. Granted, I was seven, and it rained for all three days...but I haven't spent the night in a tent since."

"And how does this trip compare?" Niall rode beside her with easy grace; his mount didn't even wear a bridle. Vivian watched him and tried to copy his subtle movements.

"Well," she said, gazing out at the expanse of what had once been the Deadlands, "it's not raining."

Niall chuckled. "You expected more excitement?"

Vivian smiled. "Something like that. I knew in my head that it wasn't going to happen – more excitement, I mean – but I couldn't help *wanting* it."

The first three days of the expedition had been uneventful save for the small moments that Vivian found herself savoring unexpectedly: watching the last remnants of a fiery sunset as they made camp; looking back to the west and glimpsing the glimmering white walls of the City just barely over the horizon; gazing up overhead as she waited for sleep and counting the blazing stars; waking up in the gray, cool silence before dawn and listening to the small sounds of the day stirring around her.

"This is what many don't expect when they set out on a mission," Niall said. "There are many days where nothing happens, and you can either loathe them or make good use of them."

"I plan to make good use of them," she replied with a nod.

She glanced over her shoulder and her eyes found Tyr riding silently beside Ramel. Tyr had returned to his long silences after Evangeline's attack, and she'd barely heard Ramel speak at all in the three days since they'd set out from the City. She'd made a point of unrolling her sleeping mat near Tyr every night, watching him surreptitiously to reassure herself that his injuries were healing. She glanced at Niall. The bright sunlight polished his pale hair, tied back neatly at the nape of his neck, and when he met her eyes, she thought she could see the blue that had once been their color, very faintly near the darkness of his pupils.

"Why did you want to come on the expedition?" she asked, raising an eyebrow.

He smiled. "Because my Queen asked it of me."

"Not because you still think you have to protect me?" Vivian pressed.

"You are still a very young Paladin," he replied calmly, "and not all dangers take the form of ravening beasts."

She squinted at him. "If you want to say something, can you just say it? I don't like hinting and tiptoeing."

"Hinting and tiptoeing," he repeated, amusement coloring his voice. He shrugged his broad shoulders. She couldn't help but notice that he'd put on muscle since returning to Faeortalam, regaining what he'd lost during the harrowing days after the bone sorcerer's escape and his own convalescence after losing his *taebramh*. It made sense, really. He was back in his element – back in his *world*.

"Since you insist," he said with a nod, "though you have to understand that part of the reason I didn't want to broach the subject directly is that we will be traveling together for the foreseeable future."

"I won't be awkward about it if you won't," she retorted.

Nyx snorted and tossed her head as if to agree with that proclamation. Vivian grinned and patted the mare's neck.

"I still believe that Tyr is dangerous," Niall said in a low voice.

Vivian resisted the urge to look over her shoulder at the Sidhe in question. She swallowed and reminded herself that she'd just promised not to be awkward, so she said, "Why do you think that?" Her voice came out only slightly strangled.

Niall didn't answer for a few long minutes. A breeze sighed around them, cool and grassy. The Deadlands looked more like rolling plains to Vivian's eye now. She had to trust in the others' descriptions of a dusty wasteland where nothing living grew.

"I'm afraid that you will think me self-serving," Niall finally said.

Vivian shrugged. "You won't know until you tell me. And even if I do think you're self-serving, you're a good teacher and I'll still want to study with you."

"How practical," he replied, his pale eyes bright with amusement.

"I try," she said, smiling. The breeze plucked a stray curl out of her braid and she tucked it behind one ear.

"I think Tyr is dangerous because he is unpredictable," Niall said. "And he attracts remnants of his past, none of which have been desirable."

Vivian considered Niall's words, checking to make sure that her bond with Tyr was firmly closed. It had been closed since they'd left, but the last thing she needed was for Tyr to catch even the hint of her thoughts. "He can be unpredictable," she agreed quietly. "But not any more than anyone else, I don't think."

Niall's pale eyebrows drew together. "I disagree. He has no loyalty to any Court. He hasn't declared himself."

Vivian shifted in her saddle as she thought of Tyr's orders to Alfred in the middle of Evangeline's attack. Nyx felt her movement and pranced sideways. Niall waited patiently until she corrected their trajectory.

"A man without loyalty is the most unpredictable," he said with a finality that told Vivian of the firmness of his belief.

"Maybe his loyalty just isn't the traditional vow to a Court," she replied.

"What makes you think so?"

She took a deep breath, tucking the rogue spiral of hair behind her ear again. "During the attack in the Tower, he ordered Alfred to protect me. I was going to try to...to jump in, I guess, because it looked like Evangeline was winning." Her cheeks grew hot and she felt a vague shame at admitting that she'd doubted Tyr's ability to handle the Exiled woman.

"Are you blushing because you think you are reaching too far, thinking that you could have helped him?" Niall asked mildly. "If that is the case, I would remind you that you handled Corsica quite well on your own."

"I don't like implying that Tyr couldn't have handled it," she muttered. "Handled *her.*"

"Affection shouldn't cloud honesty," Niall said.

"That strikes me as a very Unseelie thing to say," Vivian countered.

"Perhaps we have been spending enough time in our sister Court's company to absorb some of their more utilitarian concepts," he replied.

The shadows of the Valkyrie slid over the rolling hills beside them. Vivian looked up and shaded her eyes, watching Trillian and Moira maneuver their magnificent mounts through a pattern of diving drills.

"You believe that Tyr holds loyalty to someone?" Niall prompted, though he was watching the two Valkyrie as well now. Trillian let her blue roan have her head, tucking her body tight against the mare's neck, and the winged *faehal* arrowed down toward the ground in a corkscrewing dive that made Vivian dizzy just from watching. She caught her breath involuntarily at the speed at which they hurtled toward the ground, now just a shimmering streak of dark blue and gray, Trillian's hair a gold ribbon streaming close to her mount's great folded wings. The pair spun and gained more speed, falling so fast that Vivian thought irrationally that something must be wrong, because why would they *want* to plunge so recklessly toward the unforgiving earth?

And then, with precise and perfect grace, the winged *faehal* rolled upright and snapped her wings out to their full extent, translating their momentum into a breathtakingly fast glide, no higher above the ground than Vivian's head, their shadows contracting beneath them to a dense, dark blot. Trillian let out a whoop and stood up in her harness, drawing her sword and then throwing herself to one side, her sharp blade cutting the tops from the tall grasses.

Vivian let out the breath she hadn't quite known she'd been holding. The winged mare pumped her wings and Trillian righted herself, her grin evident even at a distance as she sheathed her weapon and leaned forward to speak to her mount.

"Beautiful," Vivian murmured, watching them climb into the sky.

"But not without risk," Niall commented.

She wrinkled her nose. "You're really not letting me out of answering, huh?"

"You said you were willing to speak about it," Niall said.

Vivian pressed her lips together. "Well, you've got me there." She sighed. "Look, I just think that saying Tyr doesn't have any loyalty at all is maybe painting him with a broad brush. Being too general," she clarified at Niall's look of inquiry. She forgot sometimes that it took him a moment or two to understand common idioms. "What I was saying before…he wanted Alfred to protect me, to keep me from trying to fight Evangeline. I think that's a type of loyalty."

"So you believe he has loyalty to *you*," Niall murmured.

"You were already implying it," she said.

"I was, but I am glad that you recognize it as well."

"What, you just wanted me to *confirm* it?" She raised her eyebrows. As recent as a few weeks ago, Niall's manipulation might have lit a spark of anger. But now she recognized that the Sidhe were simply *different* than humans. She couldn't expect to interact with them exactly as she would talk with someone from her own world. They felt things differently and they had a different perspective, Niall included.

"Yes," he said, unruffled. "Your self-awareness has improved since the beginning of your training."

She narrowed her eyes. "I'd prefer if you didn't play mind games with me in order to prove a point."

Niall chuckled. "They are not 'mind games,' as you call them, Vivian." He looked at her with a smile lingering on his lips. "You must understand that everything is training: every conversation, every interaction, every waking moment. If you truly want to become one of the great Paladins, you must understand that."

She blinked as a strange sense of vertigo took hold of her. "That means that I'd never be able to have a real friendship. Every time I talk to someone, every word I say and interaction that I have...that's...that's too much." She shook her head.

"It is a very difficult concept to grasp," Niall said, almost gently. "I would say that you are not entirely correct. The first days will be difficult as you adjust to evaluating everything. But then it will be second nature."

"You're saying that this is what *you* do?"

He nodded. "It is part of my responsibilities as one of Titania's Three. We have to understand everything that is going on around us to the best of our ability. In part, we are the eyes and ears of the Queen. We help her to understand the Court, because it is ever-changing."

Vivian let Niall's words settle into her mind. Was what he was telling her really any different than what she'd already done naturally her entire life? It was just looking at things with an eye to collecting useful information, noticing details and cataloguing them for future use, appraising conversations and understanding the motivations of those around her. She nodded as the sense of vertigo receded. "I think I understand."

"Not everything will come to you at once," Niall said. "Don't mistake me for telling you that you should expect to perfect your skills quickly."

She grinned. "I haven't forgotten that I almost roasted myself like a campfire marshmallow in my own backyard not too long ago."

"That is a memory I could do without," Niall said dryly.

"It could have been worse," Vivian reminded him brightly. Her fingers found the section of hair that had been singed in the incident – she'd activated a fire rune with a bit too much gusto, nearly incinerating herself in the blaze. Tyr's quick reflexes had saved them both from injury, though not from Niall's fury. At least they weren't at each other's throats anymore, Vivian thought, glancing back at Tyr. Her eyes met his with a jarring connection, fizzing through her like the effects of physical touch. He held her gaze for a long moment. She swallowed and turned back around in her saddle as Nyx snorted.

Their days began to settle into a pattern, though to Vivian every day brought those moments of unexpected novelty and beauty. She felt as though she'd sliced herself open and her heart was exposed to this new world, drinking in as much as she could. In the quiet moments before sleep or when she rode alone and gazed out at the rolling grasslands, she felt keen, piercing flashes of homesickness, yearning for the familiarity of her little house and her haphazard but fulfilling life back in the mortal world. She learned to ride the crests of those waves until the searing emotion subsided, giving way again to the wonder and fascination at the Fae world.

In the mornings, all the riders awoke just as the sun crept over the horizon. After packing their sleeping mats and eating a cold breakfast, they all dispersed into knots of two and three with their swords and other weapons. For the first week, Vivian focused solely on sparring with her sword. Moira kept her role as a reliable and encouraging sparring partner; Vivian enjoyed watching the two Valkyrie test their skills against one another. They had both once been Seelie but were now Vyldgard, their golden coloring belying their origins. When they skirmished, they moved so fast that Vivian sometimes couldn't distinguish between the two of them, the silver flash of their blades punctuating the whirlwind.

Finnead and the navigator, Merrick, started out most mornings as partners, though Finnead clearly outmatched Merrick, despite the slimmer man's speed. After two mornings, Niall made their duo a trio, and his willingness to spar with Finnead provided the most magnificent spectacles of the morning practice sessions. Moira and Trillian moved with mind-bending speed and feline grace, but the two men fought with a ferocity and power that sometimes left Vivian holding her breath, sure that one of them would wound the other. Perhaps because they were both bound to Queens, Finnead and Niall never forced each other to yield or appeared discourteous toward each other. They always clasped forearms in a brotherly way after every intense session of pitting their skills against one another.

Even their Glasidhe scouts participated in the practice sessions every morning, zipping through the air and calling out encouragement to the fighters below or engaging in their own matches. Their auras glowed too brightly for Vivian to see exactly what they were doing most of the time, but she got the impression that they took their training just as seriously as the Sidhe Knights. Forin and Farin occasionally watched one of her matches against Moira and offered helpful advice. Farin showed her a few drills to build the strength in her arms and make each strike of her blade more powerful, because, as she told Vivian seriously, "You are always going to be the smallest fighter, just like us!"

The other two Glasidhe, Flora and Wisp, watched more than they talked for the first few days, especially when it came to Vivian. She felt that they were taking her measure, and it made her vaguely anxious when she thought about it, but finally on the afternoon of the fifth day, Wisp hovered in front of her and bowed courteously.

"May I ride with you, Lady Paladin?" he asked in his bright, clear voice.

"I would greatly enjoy the company," she answered seriously. He didn't land on her shoulder, as was Farin's habit, but alighted on Nyx's head. She flicked an ear at him; he patted the curve of her ear with one small hand, and she apparently decided that she'd suffer the indignity of being used as a Glasidhe perch. Wisp settled himself cross-legged on the glossy black of Nyx's forelock.

"How are you finding your new duties, Lady Paladin?" he piped, dimming his aura just enough that she made out his puckish, heart-shaped face and the feather tucked jauntily behind one ear.

"I'm finding them very interesting," she said honestly. "There's a lot for me to learn."

"There was much for the Lady Bearer to learn as well," he replied, nodding sagely. "She saved the world, in the end."

Vivian smiled. "I don't think I'm going to do anything as important as defeating Malravenar."

"You never know what the future will bring," the Glasidhe messenger said seriously. "We never thought that the Three Trees would be lost, but one night we awoke to the flames burning."

"Would you tell me about the Three Trees?" Vivian asked. "I'd like to know more. I read in one of the books in the library that the Glasidhe do not consider themselves a separate Court, like the Seelie and Unseelie, but you have your own Queen?"

"Lady Lumina," Wisp said, his wings fluttering as his aura sparked. "And no, we do not quite consider ourselves a Court apart. We are our own people, in the sense that we are not bound in loyalty to Night or Day – or the Wild Court, now." He paused thoughtfully.

Vivian found Wisp to be an entertaining and knowledgeable traveling companion. His elfin humor reminded her of Farin, though he was markedly less bloodthirsty than his fierce cousin, while his willingness to share the history of his people made her think more of Niall. He spent the rest of that afternoon describing in detail the many wonders of the Three Trees: the intricate dwellings built to the scale and comfort of the Glasidhe; the aviary where their fiercest warriors trained goshawks to carry them into battle; the carefully tended gardens composed specifically to attract the most beautifully colored butterflies. Vivian listened, letting Wisp's words paint a portrait of his lost home in her mind's eye even as she still gazed out at the rolling hills of the plains around the White City.

"And then it burned," Wisp finally said, his voice sad but matter-of-fact. "Some of us fled to Darkhill. The Lady Bearer gave us refuge, even though she didn't yet have the Sword. *We* knew she was to be the Bearer before she knew it herself," he added with a hint of smug pride. "I thought about it when I first spoke to her. She read the missive from the Queen of Night, you know," he said. "Not many mortals at all would be able to do that, unless they had Fae blood or came from the line of the Bearer."

Vivian felt her cheeks heat as the Glasidhe messenger looked at her contemplatively, tilting his small head.

"You would have been able to read it," he said with a nod. Nyx snorted, as though to comment that of *course* her rider would have been able to read whatever mysterious letter they were discussing.

She smiled, even as she thought about what her life would have been like if Wisp had found her instead of Tess. But that was all smoke and dreams, impossible. She drew back her shoulders. She wasn't the Bearer, but she was a Paladin. That was still more than anything she'd ever dared to hope. This whole world was more than anything she'd ever dared to really believe in.

Every day, they rode until the sun touched the western horizon, washing the sky with brilliant colors. Vivian was never really sure who ultimately approved the camp site each night – she thought it was Finnead or Niall, but she never saw either of them actually give the signal to stop. It seemed to be a collective decision, so she just allowed Nyx to follow the lead of the other mounts. That had proven to be a good strategy during the day as well, though sometimes Nyx tossed her head when two or three of the other mounts raced by at breakneck speeds, their riders crouched low over their necks. But to the mare's credit, she hadn't joined any of the impromptu contests of speed, though Vivian felt vaguely guilty that she wasn't confident enough in the saddle to wholeheartedly embrace the spontaneous races.

In any case, the Valkyrie landed in the dusk and they all unsaddled their mounts, leaving the *faehal* to their own devices during the night. They made camp in a loose circle around the fire. On the third day, Vivian had gotten up the courage to use one of the little boards inscribed with the runes for fire that she'd spent a day creating in the Tower. Dry wood wasn't exactly plentiful on the plains, and the rune-created fire consumed less fuel than one struck from flint and tinder. After that night, the others waited for Vivian to light the fire when they made camp. Finn teasingly began calling her "the Firemaster."

"Fire*mistress*," he corrected himself, arching an eyebrow and giving her a little bow from the saddle.

"Firemaster has more of a ring to it," Vivian replied with a grin. "I won't accuse you of being sexist unless you take it *too* easy on me during practice sessions."

"Does Niall know you're asking me to spar with you?" Finn smiled.

"If I thought I needed to tell anyone I'm asking you, it would be Moira, since she's been teaching me for a while now. I don't need Niall's permission to arrange my own training," Vivian replied.

"Indeed, you don't," Finn said easily, deftly turning the conversation to other topics.

The others assured Vivian that there would be deer when they reached the forests. As it was, the Valkyrie hunted from the wing and the Glasidhe twins helped as well – they didn't scare away game, small as they were; so most nights they had rabbit or one of the dun-feathered birds that reminded Vivian somewhat of a turkey to roast over their fire. They filled their water skins from the small streams that meandered every so often through the hills – apparently, they had been created on the journey of the Courts through the Deadlands, fresh water called forth by the Vyldretning every day for the massive army.

"That's…impressive," Vivian said when Finn told her of the water's origin.

"It was very impressive to observe," he agreed. "Queen Vell has an ease with her *taebramh* that I've seldom seen, even in the earlier days of the Unseelie Court."

"What was it like, to go from Unseelie to Vyldgard?" she asked keenly. Nyx flicked an ear back as though she disapproved of the question.

"You are the first one to ask me outright," Finn said. He rode silently for a few moments. "It was not exactly a conscious choice, in the end. I did make the choice to journey with Tess from the Royal Forest in Unseelie territory to Brightvale, the seat of the Seelie Court."

"Tess wanted to seal an alliance with Queen Titania," Vivian supplied.

"Yes, although we found out that Titania was in need of the Bearer's help first," Finn said. "Her Walker-form had been captured by Malravenar. Her body still sat on the throne in Brightvale, but…"

"But she wasn't there." She nodded. "I've heard some of this from Niall."

"In any case, to return to your question, Merrick discovered we were being tracked by a man and wolf. Luca attacked us, and Vell spared his life though he asked her to kill him. Tess removed the cursed dagger from his hand and his spirit. Then we learned that the wolf with him was not his own – it was Rialla, which left us the choice to rescue Chael and Kianryk...or press on with our own quest."

"That's not much of a choice," remarked Vivian, "and I'm not surprised that Tess chose to rescue them."

"It came at a cost," said Finn, his blue eyes grave. "Kavoryk, one of the fiercest warriors I have fought beside, gave his life so that we could escape from the creatures of the Enemy. And then Tess, Luca and I were trapped on the bridge across the Darinwel."

"The bridge was destroyed," Vivian murmured, transfixed by the story despite Finn's sparse description.

"We fell into the Darinwel," Finn said. A furrow appeared between his brows. "I was mostly unconscious when we fell, so I don't remember. I drowned. Tess struck a blood deal with the sirens of the river and brought me back." He took a breath.

"Brought you back...how?"

"Tess is a Walker of some talent, though she chooses not to venture into the ether at all anymore," Finn said. "She Walked to the Gray Cliffs, the world between death and life. I had shown her the way, actually. She was poisoned not long after she became Bearer, and I brought her back."

"How exactly does that work?" Vivian asked, her voice so quiet she almost whispered. The idea of wielding power so great that one could bring someone back from the realm of death made her dizzy. Her stomach lurched as she realized that the dizziness was *want* – because what else would prove so definitely that she possessed the rightful power of a Paladin? Pulling someone back from death, restoring them to life, giving them back the gift of all their days stretching before them – what else could be so gilded with awe and gratitude?

She realized too late the sharpness of Finn's gaze, and she tried to school her face into polite curiosity, but she'd never been good at hiding her emotions.

"I don't remember much beyond a century ago," Finn told her, "but I *do* remember how to read people, Vivian." He shook his head. "Venturing to the Gray Cliffs is dangerous, and it exacts a price. It may not be apparent in the moment, or even years afterward, but bringing the spirit back from the brink of death takes a toll."

"Just like killing someone in battle?" Vivian said, trying to make him see that she was just interested in this as an academic matter, as something intriguing she hadn't yet explored in her studies.

"Not at all like killing someone in battle," he replied cryptically. "In any case, when I drowned, Mab severed the link between us. If she'd kept drawing power from me, I could have dragged her into death."

"So then, you were released from the Unseelie at the Darinwel," said Vivian, "but you weren't made one of the High Queen's Three until her baptism at Brightvale."

"A baptism that none of us knew was to occur," Finn said, nodding.

"For a while you didn't have a Court," she said.

"For a while," he agreed.

"But you did *choose* to be one of the Vyldretning's Three?"

He looked thoughtful. The sun glimmered in a blue and purple sheen across his hair. Once again, Vivian thought of how cosmically unfair it was for the Sidhe to possess such unrivaled, unconscious beauty. She patted her curls, wrestled into a thick, unruly braid.

"I suppose there was choice," Finn said finally. "In the moment when the Crown of Bones baptized Vell, there was a choice. I accepted its power. I wanted to feel whole again."

"That makes sense," Vivian said. "You were one of Mab's Three for what, nearly a century? That was what you knew."

"It was more than what I knew," Finn said. "It was what I was meant to be. From the moment I was old enough to understand what it was to be a Knight, I knew I had been born to hold a sword. And then, after my captivity, I wanted nothing more than to avenge those who had been killed...and that meant wielding as much power as possible."

"Revenge is a powerful motivation," said Vivian. Her eyes found the copper glint of Ramel's hair, riding ahead of them in the column. Ramel steadfastly ignored all attempts to make him feel a part of the group, rebuffing any attempt at conversation and riding alone. He hadn't joined in any of their sparring sessions, and the few times that Vivian had passed close to him, she'd been almost certain that she could smell some sort of liquor permeating the air around him.

Finn followed her gaze. "This is not revenge for Ramel," he said.

"I wasn't talking about Ramel," Vivian said, "although the person I *am* talking about certainly sent Ramel spinning out of control." She glanced at Finn. "You brought both of them into this world, right?"

He raised an eyebrow in inquiry. "Both of whom?"

"Tess and Molly."

He nodded. "Yes. Queen Mab sent a summons to Molly. She ignored the summons, and I was sent to collect her."

"To collect her," Vivian repeated in an undertone. "Did she have a choice?"

Finn stiffened, just enough for her to notice. She was getting better at reading the subtle body language of the Sidhe.

"We were fighting a war," he finally said.

"So that means that taking away her choice was all right?"

"That is not what I said."

Vivian felt vaguely guilty about pressing Finn so hard on something that seemed to make him genuinely uncomfortable, but she felt the familiar urge to *understand*. She needed to understand this world and its people if she was to help protect it. "I apologize. I shouldn't have put words in your mouth." She paused. "Can you please explain your perspective?"

Finn frowned. "My perspective...?"

"On bringing Molly and Tess into the Fae world. No one knew that Tess was going to be the Bearer, so I'm assuming that she refused to let you take Molly without her. That seems like something she'd do."

"She killed a *garrelnost* at great cost to herself," said Finn. "The beast followed me. I am still very strong in the mortal world, but there are times when I am…vulnerable."

"So you were in her debt," Vivian murmured. She'd heard bits and pieces of the story from her various acquaintances and teachers in the White City, but there was nothing like getting it from one of the participants.

"Yes, and I…" Finn stopped and looked at Vivian with narrowed eyes. "We've strayed far from your original question." A bit of a smile touched his full lips.

"I'm willing to listen as long as you're willing to talk," she replied, giving him her own half smile.

He chuckled. "You have a way with words."

"I've been told that's my strong suit."

Finn shook his head. "I wouldn't underestimate your other skills. I can tell that you're devoted to your studies. Runes fell out of fashion centuries ago, but you're single-handedly bringing them back."

"I wouldn't say single-handedly," she demurred. "There's Thea with her forge-runes, and I'm pretty sure that Tyr has forgotten more runes than I'll ever know." Ramel's copper hair caught her eye again. She pressed her lips together. "Have you tried to talk to him?"

"I've been keeping an eye on him."

"That's not what I asked."

Finn chuckled. "You are merciless." He took a deep breath, his face unreadable to Vivian's eyes. "I was told by a friend before we departed that Ramel might not take kindly to any overtures of friendship from me."

"I think he needs all the friends he can get," Vivian said quietly. As she watched, Ramel unhooked a flask from his belt and took a long swig.

"All the friends in the world cannot turn him from a path if he is determined," Finn replied.

"So that means you don't try?" she demanded.

"You sound like Tess," Finn said. He looked at her. "I'll think on it."

She nodded, feeling distinctly like she'd pushed enough boundaries with enigmatic Vyldgard Knights for one day. Clearing her throat, she said, "So. What's the next landmark we're aiming for?"

"We're heading for Dragonshead," he said. "We just named it, actually, because that's where we killed Malravenar's dragon."

"A dragon," repeated Vivian.

Finn grinned. "It was far and away the best hunt I've ever ridden, even if I did almost get crushed by the beast."

"Now *that* is a story you sound like you *want* to tell," Vivian said.

Finn glanced up at the sun. "I should be able to tell it with enough time for you to still have your afternoon lesson with Niall before we set camp for the evening."

"Fantastic, everyone is keeping track of my school schedule now," Vivian said dryly, but she couldn't keep her droll face for long. Despite herself, she grinned as Finn started to tell the story of the dragon hunt. The cool breeze washed over them, smelling of the grassy plains of Faeortalam, and Vivian thought, not for the first time, about her unbelievable good fortune in stepping through the Gate into this beautiful world.

About the Author

Jocelyn A. Fox is the bestselling author of the epic fantasy series *The Fae War Chronicles,* which include *The Iron Sword, The Crown of Bones, The Dark Throne, The Lethe Stone,* and *The Mad Queen.* The series also includes a full-length prequel novel, *Midnight's Knight. The Dragon Ship* is her seventh novel. She believes that storytelling can change the world, superheroes do exist in real life, dogs are the best kind of people, and there is no such thing as "too much coffee."

You can find her at *www.jocelynafox.com,* or on the following platforms:

Facebook:
www.facebook.com/author.jocelyn.a.fox

Twitter:
www.twitter.com/jafox2010

Instagram:
@jocelynafox

Amazon Page:
www.amazon.com/Jocelyn-A.-Fox/e/B0051DX7G0

Made in the USA
Las Vegas, NV
26 October 2023